*More Ultramarines from Black Library*

BLADES OF DAMOCLES
A Space Marine Battles novel
*Phil Kelly*

THE PLAGUES OF ORATH
A Space Marine Battles novel
*Steve Lyons, Cavan Scott & Graeme Lyon*

DAMNOS
A Space Marine Battles novel
*Nick Kyme*

DAMOCLES
A Space Marine Battles novel
*Phil Kelly, Guy Haley, Ben Counter & Josh Reynolds*

ULTRAMARINES
A Legends of the Dark Millennium anthology
*Various authors*

THE CHRONICLES OF URIEL VENTRIS
A six-volume series of novels beginning with NIGHTBRINGER
*Graham McNeill*

FLESH TEARERS
A novel featuring the Flesh Tearers
*Andy Smillie*

WAR OF THE FANG
Includes the novel *Battle of the Fang* and the novella 'The Hunt for Magnus',
featuring the Space Wolves
*Chris Wraight*

THE WORLD ENGINE
A novel featuring the Astral Knights
*Ben Counter*

SONS OF WRATH
A novella featuring the Flesh Tearers
*Andy Smillie*

BLOOD AND FIRE
A novella featuring the Black Templars
*Aaron Dembski-Bowden*

VEIL OF DARKNESS
An audio drama featuring the Ultramarines
*Nick Kyme*

# CALGAR'S SIEGE

PAUL KEARNEY

*For my brothers, Sean and James*

**A BLACK LIBRARY PUBLICATION**

Published in Great Britain in 2016 by
Black Library,
Games Workshop Ltd.,
Nottingham, NG7 2WS, UK.

10 9 8 7 6 5 4 3 2 1

Produced by Games Workshop in Nottingham.
Cover illustration by Mikhail Savier.
Internal illustrations by Dave Gallagher, Paul Dainton,
John Michelbach, Kevin Chin.



A CIP record for this book is available from the British Library.

UK ISBN 13: 978 1 78496 476 4
Product code: 60040181213



Printed and bound in China

It is the 41st millennium. For more than a hundred centuries the Emperor has sat immobile on the Golden Throne of Earth. He is the master of mankind by the will of the gods, and master of a million worlds by the might of his inexhaustible armies. He is a rotting carcass writhing invisibly with power from the Dark Age of Technology. He is the Carrion Lord of the Imperium for whom a thousand souls are sacrificed every day, so that he may never truly die.

Yet even in his deathless state, the Emperor continues his eternal vigilance. Mighty battlefleets cross the daemon-infested miasma of the warp, the only route between distant stars, their way lit by the Astronomican, the psychic manifestation of the Emperor's will. Vast armies give battle in his name on uncounted worlds. Greatest amongst his soldiers are the Adeptus Astartes, the Space Marines, bio-engineered super-warriors. Their comrades in arms are legion: the Astra Militarum and countless planetary defence forces, the ever-vigilant Inquisition and the tech-priests of the Adeptus Mechanicus to name only a few. But for all their multitudes, they are barely enough to hold off the ever-present threat from aliens, heretics, mutants – and worse.

To be a man in such times is to be one amongst untold billions. It is to live in the cruellest and most bloody regime imaginable. These are the tales of those times. Forget the power of technology and science, for so much has been forgotten, never to be re-learned. Forget the promise of progress and understanding, for in the grim dark future there is only war. There is no peace amongst the stars, only an eternity of carnage and slaughter, and the laughter of thirsting gods.

# PROLOGUE

It is more than fifty years since we hurled the tyranid swarm from Ultramar, and still we bear the marks of that great conflict, like wounds not yet healed that run through the very marrow of the Chapter. My beloved First Company is a mere relic of what it was before Hive Fleet Behemoth spewed its filth upon Macragge. It will be decades, centuries perhaps, before it is whole again.

Fifty years. They go past so quickly now. There have been other wars since, but none to match the squalid hell that we knew upon our own home world. There I, too, would have died, upon Cold Steel Ridge – were it not for the sacrifice of my honour guard.

I pray for those lost heroes every day as the sun rises, for I am here and they are not. They made that choice, and I am eternally in their debt because of it.

The glorious dead. They go to the Emperor's Peace, and if they are blessed then their gene-seed is retrieved, and something of their flesh rises to fight again. And so it goes, and has done for thousands of years. This is how our universe works. We are bound in service for all eternity. We serve mankind.

*Suscipiat Imperator sacrificium nostrum.*

May our sacrifice be worthy of the Emperor.

Mortal weariness does not often rise within me, not in the flesh and bone that my divine father graced me with. But there is at times a weariness that creeps into my mind, like the last shade of the dusk before the fall of night. I know not from whence it comes, unless it be some insidious lurking taint of the immaterium, Throne forbid.

I expunge it, eradicate it, burn it from my mind. In prayer, in battle, my faith in my Redeemer liveth. The Throne of the eternal Emperor sustains me.

I have spoken to no one else of this, not my most trusted battle-brethren, not even the silent shadows in the corners of the Fortress of Hera. I hold it within me, a crack, a fault line that must be borne like a hidden wound.

I can bear it, for all life is like a wound, and the bearing of it sets our character, and sears our soul into something greater, anneals it into a vaster whole.

Pain. I embrace pain. It is the universe's way of telling you that you are alive.

# I
# THE FRONTIER

*Si vis pacem, para bellum*
*'If you want peace, prepare for war'*

– ancient Terran axiom

# ONE

THE BLACK DREAM that was the unending warble of the war drums went on and on, as fierce and insistent as the beating of an ork heart. It stilled the jungle noises, and thrummed up into the star-spattered sky. The ork host danced and cavorted and bayed at the moons above the many fires of the encampment, thousands of enormous primates baring their fangs and grappling and killing and lacerating one another's flesh in an outpouring of sheer bestial energy.

The prisoners were turning on the spits, their screaming long done. Brug sat on his throne-stone and rested his knuckles on the ground, his knees as high as his ears, his head like some savagely sculpted mountain rock that an avalanche has smashed into jagged relief. His eyes gleamed red. Watchful, full of angry malice and an intelligence that none of his tribe could match.

His time had come. He could feel it humming in his blood.

Around him the three warbosses of the host stood glowering, impatient, full of the aimless rage of the ork, and yet cowed into silence by their lord's mere presence. These were creatures out of a primeval nightmare, brought into being for one purpose only, as single-minded as a wildfire. It took an enormous will to bend such beasts to a single purpose, to bring them together and make them cooperate.

Brug had that will. He brought such fear into his fellow orks that they were willing to obey rather than rebel. They were incapable of affection or loyalty, but they knew respect. As long as Brug could kill the strongest of them, as long as his plans worked, and there was fighting and loot and blood to be had, then they would follow him, as the stones roll in the grip of the flood.

'We gots to have more than this,' Brug said, the words spat out from between mismatched fangs. 'We needs more than this. Our big-ships is ready and full and round our heads right now.' He looked up, the massive skull turning on a neck as thick as a bull's.

'This world is eaten through. There ain't nothing left here for us but bones and rock. We needs to go and find a new place, and other tribes to mangle. Otherways, these boys will turn on one another, and we'll piss away all that was done here. All that I done here.' He looked at the three warbosses, hulking shadows with red-lit eyes.

A deep '*Huuurgh*' of assent came out of them.

'Let 'em have fun for a little more, but anyone starts a big fight, you take their heads and remind 'em that they belong to me.'

He paused, the red glare of his gaze turning slowly to catch the warbosses one by one. They looked away. To meet his eyes was to challenge, and they were not ready for that. Brug had slain all challengers to his rule, and there had been many. There was no longer an ork left on the planet that could come close to matching him for guile or for sheer brute strength, and they knew it.

As did he. Something like humour flashed across his face, a savage sneer.

'You all belongs to me. I gives the orders, and you obeys. That way, we is mighty. If it wasn't for Brug yous would all be little warchiefs still, running in the jungle and raiding farms by night. Now we have us a whole world in our fists. I did that, Brug Greenstorm. I brought the clans together. I set yous at the cities, and was first over the walls of the big capital, the high place of the pink flesh. Don't you never forget it.'

The fires blazed, the night was bright with them. On the horizon behind Brug there was a mighty red glow: a burning Imperial city. It was still being sacked by the orks. Brug had brought out his bodyguard and his warbosses from within the broken walls after they had run riot for three days, leaving the rest of the army to eat and loot and pick over the survivors for slaves.

He was always most comfortable out here, in the jungle. He hated the stone and plascrete cities of the pink flesh with a vengeance. Even their manufactoria he wrecked and despoiled and destroyed, rather than keep running. He wanted nothing from the enemies of the orks but sport and spoils. And a name. He wanted that most of all. Brug Greenstorm, he would be remembered as. He would write that name across whole worlds in the blood of their inhabitants.

'You is to start after the middle of the night, and get the clans all gathered up together. Come sunrise, we'll call us down the shuttle-ships and start to load up the boys for the big wagons, up in the Great Dark. There is a skinful of other worlds out there just waiting for us, ripe as red meat.'

'Where is they?' one of the other orks ventured.

With a roar, Brug sprang up, leaping off his throne-stone. He came down like a green flailing tree on the ork who had spoken, and swept one great arm across the creature's face. His claws ripped out an eye, tore the meat from the bone, and sent the powerful warboss flying backwards, a thousand pounds of flesh and bone toppling into the grass.

'No one asks Brug questions. You obey me, see? Or I will eat you, maggot.'

He stood over the fallen warboss. The other two backed away, clashing their teeth and opening their hands in submission. The injured ork on the ground spat out blood.

'Yes, chief.'

'Next time, I chews on your tongue, Krobag, and serves you up as snotling meat.'

'I hear you, boss.' The injured ork cowered, but was unable to dim the furious hatred that blazed out of its remaining eye.

'I is the high boss of this here army. I will make us a Waaagh! the likes of which none of the pink-flesh scum of this here sector of the Dark has ever known. I will find yous foes to kill and stomp which is worthy of the fight. Do yous hear me, you filth?'

'We hears,' they all said, snarling on the words.

'We is the ork. We is the fear in the Great Dark, the red light in the night. They will hear our drums out there in them stars, and they will know we is coming for them.'

Brug opened his massive arms wide. 'And we will chew it all up, kill it all, taste every gobbet. Nothing is stronger than us. There ain't nothing can make us stop.'

He gurgled out a laugh that was part speech, part meaningless, hungry bellow.

'We was made for this, boys. And *ain't it sweet.*'

# TWO

LORD LUCIUS FENNICK looked down upon Zalathras from a balcony off to one side of the grand chamber he liked to call his map room.

A teeming sea of low-rise buildings rolled out halfway to the horizon, tawny under the sun, and from it reared up the looming spikes of two hive-spires, both still under construction. Jagged mountains erected not by nature, but by the hand of man. The smoke haze hung blue in the still, humid air about them.

Zalathras. How many millions toiled in those high spires, or down in that tawny sea? More than at the last census, by far. Now that the space port was finished, they came almost daily – in creaking shuttles from Iax and Espandor, and in dribbles even from the agri worlds – Quintarn, Tarentus, Masali – places long tamed and civilised.

To this world – green, steaming Zalidar, this barely polished gem of a planet on the Eastern Fringe, beyond Ultramar, almost beyond the bounds of the Imperium itself. A place that had been nothing more than a wilderness a generation before, but was now on the brink of full Imperial compliance.

Most of the backbone of the workforce was from the Zalidari System itself – they came because they were restless, or discontented, or they sought a wider horizon, a new challenge. Well, they got it here.

Others were indentured workers brought in by the thousand to fulfil labour quotas – the grist that was ground in the mill of the burgeoning Zalidari industries.

Four million inhabitants at the last census, ten years ago. There must be double that now in Zalathras alone, Fennick thought, savouring the number in his mind.

We are on the brink of great things on Zalidar. One day we might even rival Iax for production. If only we can keep up the pace!

The building crews worked in shifts round the clock. His people needed housing; the shanty towns that they had once hacked out of the jungle were a mere memory. Now, Zalathras was a city, a true city with high walls and paved streets and thrumming manufactoria. At long last, the labour disputes were ended; brought to a close by the iron fist of the Zalidari militia, which now patrolled orderly districts of true citizens. One day soon, it would be the Adeptus Arbites who did so, and the militia would give way to the Imperial Guard.

We are so close, Fennick thought. If Ultramar's resources were not stretched so thin, we would have been brought into compliance by now.

So dense was the population that the walls could barely encompass it. So they had begun to build upwards more and more, rather than let the city sprawl beyond the defences. The hive-spires grew day by day, so that the tallest of them lost their lofty heads in cloud when the rains came. The Imperium was rising up here in all its glory.

This is civilisation, Fennick thought. This is how worlds are made. One day, we will be a pillar of Ultramar, and if the Emperor wills it, I will make a pilgrimage to Macragge itself, and I will look upon great Guilliman in his shrine, and see the wound that bleeds eternally through the shimmer of the holy stasis field that sustains him. I will look upon the face of a primarch. That, I have promised myself.

'Throne be praised,' a voice said behind him. 'The Kalgatt Spire looks near finished. I have not seen the view from this high in an age. Zalathras looms above the Tagus like a titan rising from the sea. Standing this high, it almost seems we have tamed this damned world.'

'If only that were so, Boros,' Fennick said. He turned and smiled. He was a long, lean man with the grace and poise of someone much younger than his fifty years. His black beard was oiled to a point, and his eyes were as grey as a sea from a colder world.

'You know as well as anyone that over most of the planet, the Tagus still holds sway. Our logging teams have cleared a quarter of one continent, no more. There are places near the poles where man has not yet set foot – not even that damned mountebank, Morcault – and mountains yet unclimbed in the hinterland of Zalathras itself.'

'All in good time, my lord,' the man called Boros said gruffly. He was a brown man, brown of hair, brown of skin, heavily tanned and stocky as an owl. The scars on his face were all the more livid for his colouring, white lines that striped his cheek from eye to chin. He wore a leather battle-harness, old-fashioned armour crafted to protect against blade and claw, but for all that there was a laspistol holstered at his hip, and a colonel's stars on his shoulders.

'Soon we must think more on the outlying towns, it's true,' he said. 'The roads are still all but impassable in the rainy season. They must be paved, all the way out to the coast. And the Dromion Bridge is insufficient for the traffic that now crosses it.'

Fennick waved a hand. 'You tell me nothing that I and the Council do not know, Boros. We were discussing it all morning. But eventually I made Vanaheim and Rosquin see sense. We must increase the supply of building material substantially, especially now that we have the two hives under construction.'

'Then the plascrete manufactoria are to be enlarged at last?'

'We voted on it this afternoon. Timber has served us well hitherto and Throne knows there is no shortage of it on this world, but if things are to endure in this climate, then we must build in more durable material. I have commissioned an expedition to the foothills of the Zalidari Range. We must open more quarries and blaze a trail through there for the big loaders. The Ballansyr works are almost exhausted. Even Vanaheim had to admit that.'

Boros grunted, slapping a hand on the butt of his pistol. 'Good. His reluctance to admit his limitations has curbed all sorts of projects. And his near monopoly of construction–'

Fennick held up a hand wearily. 'I know, Boros. But there was a time when his company was the only place I could go to for any large enterprise. The walls, for instance.'

Boros frowned. 'I am glad of our walls, my lord, but there are young officers even among my own command who deem them something of a luxury for a city as desperate for good stone as this one.'

'Strange words from my guard commander, Boros.'

Boros shrugged. 'The walls may have meant something once, but the beasts of the jungle have been thrown back many miles. It is the outlying farms that face them now, not this metropolis. The defences of Zalathras were ruinously expensive to build – they tied up our resources for the better part of twelve years. I wonder sometimes if our energies might not have been better spent elsewhere. Decent roads, for instance.'

'There are always enemies to be defended against, not all of which are on this world, Boros.'

'You do not have to tell me that,' Boros said, touching the scars that marred his brown face. 'But a third hive-spire, my lord? Is it really necessary? Perhaps we should save the resources and let the people throw up more towns outside the walls. After all, the planet is large enough for us all without cooping up millions within them.'

'Here, they can be more easily controlled, Boros – that is the brutal truth of it,' Fennick said, and his cold eyes flashed. 'The manufactoria are all concentrated here, in Zalathras. Employment is here, order is here. The day will soon come when Zalathras shall be called upon to make its own contribution to the war effort of the Imperium – in materiel, in men… When that day comes, I do not intend that we shall be found wanting.'

'The surrounding system is quiet now,' Boros said stubbornly. 'That is to say–' He hesitated, and then looked down. 'This is Ultramar, my lord, or near as damn it. The Adeptus Astartes guard this sector of the Fringe, not some Imperial militia.' He smiled crookedly, and tapped his hand upon his own armoured chest. 'Though there is something to be said for an honest militia.'

'Ultramar,' Fennick said in a low voice. 'Yes, I suppose it is. But we are on the far fringes of that great realm, Boros, an outlying world which I am sure barely registers on the consciousness of the high lord who sits on Macragge.'

He looked down at the teeming city below, and the man-made hills that rose up from it, wreathed in the smoke of combustion and construction. Half a century before, it had been virgin jungle. Now it was this raw, seething metropolis. It never failed to amaze him, what men could do to a planet, given time and the will to succeed.

'What I would give, Boros, to bring Zalidar to Macragge's attention. To remind them that we exist. To see them here, even.'

'The Ultramarines?' Boros, too, lowered his voice, in something close to reverence. 'Be careful what you wish for, Lucius. Not for nothing are they known as the Angels of Death.'

'They are the guardians of mankind,' Fennick said crisply.

'When they retook Thrax they did not hesitate to issue the Exterminatus,' Boros said stubbornly. 'To erase the Chaos taint they scorched the planet down to the stone.'

'I know,' Fennick said quietly. 'I was there too, my friend.'

But Boros was not done. 'They are pitiless, the Adeptus Astartes. Let them watch over us by all means, but the day we see their kind set foot on our world there will be sorrow to follow. That is the way of things.'

'We are building a whole new world for them here,' Fennick persisted. 'I would that they saw it for themselves, just once.'

'I doubt they even know we exist.'

'Oh, they know, Boros. We send shuttleloads of Zalidari goods to Macragge every few months, as is our duty as an Imperial world. We cannot compete with the long-established planets, like Quintarn or Tarentus, or beautiful Iax – but we make our contribution, all the same. Eight thousand tons of iron ore went out only last week, and tomorrow a grain shuttle will follow them. I trust that some of our foodstuffs have even ended up on the table of Marneus Calgar himself.'

'Perhaps,' Boros snorted. 'But when I break my bread, I do not find myself marvelling about where it came from. I would be surprised if the Lord of Macragge, Throne be with him, is any different.'

Irritated, Fennick turned away from the high balcony overlooking the city. 'What is this report you have to make, colonel?' he demanded, sharp now, his eyes cold.

Boros stiffened. 'I meant no disrespect, my lord.'

They looked at one another. Finally, Fennick laughed.

'We have known each other long enough, you damn fool, that we can speak our minds freely – when we are alone together at least. Forgive my tone, Boros. Arguing in council is apt to sharpen a man's tongue.

'You and I remember when Zalathras was a mudbound settlement surrounded by a wood stockade, and beyond it the jungle shrieked and teemed with fear. What is it now, thirty years?' He turned and smiled. 'Long enough to wear away some of the formalities at least.'

Boros stumped towards him. With his right hand he snapped and unsnapped the strap that held his pistol holstered to his thigh. The tall-ceilinged chamber in which they stood made the gesture click out loud. Brutal Imperial architecture, grand but functional. Its design and dimensions were echoed on ten thousand other worlds across the galaxy, the imprimatur of the Imperium of Man. It seemed designed for giants – perhaps it once had been.

'I remember when we both wore sergeant's stripes, and were proud to wear them,' Boros said.

'I do not forget, Boros. I could never forget that,' Fennick replied. The two stared at each other again, and then at nothing, the memories in the eyes of them both.

Finally Boros coughed, and grinned sheepishly.

'I am about to complicate your day, my lord, and for nothing perhaps.'

'Go on then. My day can fit one more complication in, I'm sure.'

'There are rumours – barely more than that – coming from the border moons of the Chrisos System. A few outposts have fallen out of vox, and there is a claim that some addled enginseer picked up a strange signature on augur while on a sanctioned-trader bound out of Chrisannon.'

'What kind of signature?' Fennick asked. He was leaning over the long table that ran down the middle of the room. There, acid-etched into the hide of a jungle centaur, were the plans of his Zalathras – the city that currently existed, and the one that was still gestating. Upon the scaly hide of the map, roads yet unbuilt arced out towards satellite cities which at present were nothing more than stockaded hamlets. And all around the edge of the map, the deep jungle known on this world as the Tagus: unconquerable, perilous, source of both fear and wealth.

'Something big,' Boros said, still clicking his gunstrap. 'It is probably nothing.'

'The farther eastern outposts of the system were always at the limits of the vox's capabilities. You know that, Boros,' Fennick said irritably. 'Messages are relayed from station to station, they get lost, or misunderstood...' He stared at his guard commander's restless fingers and Boros lifted his hand from his holster.

'Is it the augur report?'

Boros nodded. 'It bothers me. The enginseer said it was a passing pulse, no more, but it was big enough to be a large vessel, or a lot of smaller ones. He might even have thought it to be a stray asteroid cluster, except that it seemed to alter speed and course. It was far out, but on course for the heart of the system. And, my lord, our enquiries show that no other Imperial ships were in the area at the time. That area of space is deserted, or at least it should be.'

'Perhaps it was an asteroid cluster after all then... How far away?'

'At normal cruising speed, many weeks, perhaps as long as two months from Zalidar.'

'Perhaps we should wait awhile before jumping to conclusions,' Fennick said dryly.

Boros bowed slightly. 'I thought it best to draw it to your attention, just in case.'

Fennick's eyes were ranging over the map on the tabletop. He seemed utterly absorbed by the representation of his city as it was, and as it could be.

'Quite right,' he muttered. 'Was there anything else, Boros?'

'No, my lord.' The leather-armoured soldier hesitated. 'But – well – I would like your authorisation for a long-range patrol of the system to be set up. I will need one frigate, no more, and the *Hesiod* is available. I checked.'

Fennick arched one black eyebrow. 'You should perhaps be consulting Rear Admiral Glenck on a fleet matter, Boros.'

'I did. He refused.'

Fennick straightened and looked Boros in the eye. 'So you decided to step out of channels, eh? And play on our friendship.'

'Yes,' Boros said, thrusting out his jaw.

'You think it is that important?'

'I think, my lord, that the universe is a dangerous place, and as you have said yourself, not all enemies are of this world.'

'But this is Ultramar, near as damn it.'

'And the Ultramarines have many claims on their time.'

'You have never liked Glenck, have you, Boros?'

Boros flushed slightly. Again, the outthrust jaw. Fennick had seen that expression on his friend's face many times over the years.

'He is a functionary, relegated to what he sees as a backwater, his career all but over. He may have been an effective officer once, but those days are past.'

Fennick smiled. 'Harsh words. I wish I could disagree with them.' He turned back to the map. 'Very well, Boros. I trust your judgement. Your instincts have saved my hide more than once, Throne knows. You shall have your patrol, and let us hope it is all for nothing. I will issue an executive order. It will do the *Hesiod*'s crew good to see something of the outer system at any rate.'

'Thank you, my lord.' Boros bowed, and turned to leave, but Fennick held up a hand.

'One thing, Boros. You know you are making an enemy of Glenck by doing this, don't you?'

Boros shrugged. 'He is not much of an enemy. We have faced down far worse, you and I.'

Then he left by the great double doors at the end of the chamber, his footsteps echoing off stone and plascrete as he went.

# THREE

THE CHRISOS SYSTEM lay even further out towards the Eastern Fringe of the Imperium than Zalidar. This far from Ultramar, humankind paid lip service to the Imperium without giving it much other thought. To meet a member of the Astra Militarum – the Imperial Guard – was a nine-day wonder, and the Adeptus Astartes themselves were nothing more than figures out of legend.

On these far-flung border worlds, men conducted their own affairs, prayed to the Emperor to keep them safe from the denizens of the void that surrounded them, and plodded through their lives, hardy, self-sufficient, and unaware of the great convulsions and upheavals that went on in the more populous sectors of the Imperium.

Chrisannon was a large moon that orbited Chrisos in an elliptic loop. Its seasons were long and harsh, bitter year-long winters giving way to arid summers. But there was an abundance of life on the world. Tall, iron-hard trees with spiked leaves reared up in thickets and forests, and there were subterranean seas that came to the surface now and again in roaring torrents. Moss and lichen grew in mounds as large as hills, and were fed upon by teeming herds of grazing herbivores, squat, bone-headed beasts that the first human settlers of the moon had quickly tamed and used for both fodder and transport.

Predating on the herbivores was a variety of more dangerous animals – therapods with clashing jaws and whipping tails that could cleave a man in two, and small pack hunters that ran on four legs and had enormous ears, and jaws as long and narrow as a sword blade. And in the green skies above them, raptors whirled on translucent scaled wings, swooping down to seize the river snakes that teemed iridescent as jewels in the waters.

It was a dangerous, raw world, but by no means lethal to humankind, and in the last millennium many of the restless and desperate souls that inhabited the Imperium had come this way and had settled here, some by design, some by chance.

Now there were towns upon the moon, and even a primitive spaceport, the landing pads fashioned out of crushed stone, sealed by the black pitch that the natives crafted by burning the ironwood trees and collecting the residue.

There was trade with Chrisos, the planet that loomed huge in the morning and evening sky, and now and again an enterprising trader would bring a ship in even from far Zalidar, whose governor had nominal authority over the Chrisos System as well as his own.

A hard life for those who lived upon Chrisannon, then. But not a bad one. Men struggled through far worse existences in the bowels of hive cities up and down the galaxy, or upon the deadly surfaces of worlds where every day was a struggle for survival against inimical flora and fauna. Chrisannon had peace to run its own affairs, and the scattered settlements knew no true central authority. There was a vox system in the moon's putative capital, Horesby, but communications out of the Eastern Fringe were proverbially bad, echoes of warp storms that raged in the void beyond the known galaxy sending disruptive ripples through the immaterium. Without a skilled astropath, one might as well set a paper boat to sail on a swollen river as try to get a message through to Ultramar and the Imperial-compliant worlds that surrounded it.

The green sky of the morning was paling into a peridot gleam, and Chrisos was becoming dull silver on the horizon as Gurian strode out towards the ironwood forests that were his hunting grounds. He was a short man, long in the arm, his black hair cropped to a bristle, and he carried a long-barrelled rifle at the trail. An old, kinetic weapon that fired snub-nosed rounds, it was highly decorated with silver studs along the black, gleaming stock, and the muzzle was wrapped in plastic against the damp of the morning.

Gurian was studying the ground, oblivious to the grandeur of the sunrise. In the long whipgrass he followed the dew-bright trails of the night, and smiled. Looking up, he peered into the darkness of the ironwoods before him. His head snapped up as he caught sight of a bright momentary flash in the sky above. A meteor, grazing the thick atmosphere of Chrisannon. He took it as a good omen, and toiled onwards, the grass sawing at his hide boots and soaking him to the knee.

Behind him, the lights of the little settlement from which he had come went out one by one as the light of the world grew around him. It was a perfect hunter's morning, the air hanging still and cold as the moon's long winter began to take a grip, the orbit of Chrisannon arcing away from the system's only star.

The night before, the borealis had been a bright cascade of light that swooped clear across the sky, a harbinger of winter. And there had been thunder in the distance, though not a drop of rain had fallen. Gurian had watched the flashes on the horizon and listened to the dull boom of the thunderclaps for an hour while his family had slept soundly in the cabin behind him.

He strode on now with the easy, economical stride of a man who has been walking across open country all his life. A flight of wide-winged raptors took off out of the ironwoods ahead, squawking and screeching. He followed the trail in the wet grass, gaze moving up and down, sweeping across the hillside. Once, he stopped and grasped a fistful of moss. He squeezed it against his mouth and sucked in the chill water it gave up, before tossing it aside.

Then he entered the shadows of the great trees.

It was much darker here. The ironwoods were like immense pillars of grey marble that soared up all around him, tall as towers. Their timber was as hard to work as stone, and as durable – and when it finally was made to burn it smouldered for days, glowing like molten metal, before melting into the black tar that was one of the chief exports of the moon.

Ironwood pitch could be turned into fuel, glue. It could be poured into moulds and then filed and sharpened when it had cooled. The shining black stock of Gurian's rifle was made of ironpitch.

One day, the Imperium would wake up to this resource, and Chrisannon would take its place on the trade lanes of the Imperium, but for now the moon was just another forgotten frontier world. And that suited a man like Gurian just fine. As long as he could hunt, feed his family and drink moss-beer in the town tavern, he was content with his life. One horizon was enough for him. One world was all he needed.

The trail widened, but now it was more distinct. The tri-cloven hooves of the solitary bull-grazer he was tracking sank deep into the emerald moss of the forest floor. Here and there the beast had stripped a patch bare and chewed on the green vegetation for water, even as Gurian had. It was an old, lonely animal, cast out of the herd. Gurian's bullet would end its wanderings, and he would harvest the choice cuts of the beast, the eyes and tongue and hump-fat.

The eyes, poached, were a delicacy on Chrisannon, the tongue a huge lump of fine protein, and the fat could be rendered down into oil and burned in lamps. The thick hide and sinews of the rest of the carcass rendered it almost unworkable without power tools. But the beasts of the forest would feast on it after Gurian was done.

He felt he was being watched as he picked his way through the immense trunks of the ironwoods. It was an odd feeling for one whose life had been spent in and out of the forest.

He stopped and loaded his rifle, stripping the plastic from the muzzle and feeding four rounds into the magazine that ran tube-like under the barrel, before clacking the feedbolt up and down to chamber one of them. The bullets were as big as one of his fingers, with hollow-cored points. He had seen a man blown clear in two by such munitions before now. One was sufficient to bring down the largest grazer, if it were put in the right place.

He stopped. The screeching and flapping of the birds in the canopy overhead had stilled. The forest was eerily silent. He turned slowly around, watching, rifle to the shoulder. There was something new here. The cacophony of the dawn chorus had been clamped down, as though the mindless raptors above were watching and waiting even as he was.

There was nothing. Irritated with his own uneasiness, he strode on again. He was a hunter of his people, respected and experienced in the ways of the forest. Most shunned the ironwoods for fear of the beasts that lurked in the shadows under the trees, but Gurian had encountered them all in his years of tracking and trading. He knew when to fight and when to run, when to stand still and silent and let the monsters of his little world walk on by. There were rules. You obeyed them, and you lived. You ignored them, and the forest would take your life. There was no mystery here. It was mere biology.

The trail he was following changed. The grazer had picked up speed. He saw the dull score on an ironwood where the creature's horns had slashed it, as though it had lunged at something and missed. And there were different marks in the moss. The green sponge of the forest floor had been trampled down. Other beasts had gathered here. He studied the ground, intrigued. And as he did, he saw at the toe of his boot a single bright green fungus with a globular top, a type he had never encountered before.

He knelt and drew out his old iron knife, levering the fungus out of the ground. It came easily. He touched the knife tip to it, and for just a moment he started back in shock. He could have sworn that the fungus had moved, writhing away from the blade.

Fascinated – it was rare, if not unprecedented, for him to find anything in the forest that he had not seen before – he picked up the fungus. It was oddly heavy, and when he sniffed at it he caught a powerful reek, as of some animal-type musk. Hardly of the vegetable kingdom at all.

It squirmed in his fingers.

'Throne!' He dropped it, and instinctively brought the heel of his boot down upon the thing, crushing it. In the broken fragments of the fungus, he thought for one moment he saw a shape, humanoid, curled up like a foetus. Then revulsion overwhelmed him, and he stamped on it again and again until it was a mere green paste on the roots of a tree.

The silence was all around him, heavy as fog in the mouth. He felt a momentary impulse to turn around and make his way back out of the woods, feel the wind on his face and see the roofs of the township beyond, his wife and son waiting for him. But that would be an absurd humiliation. What would he tell them – that he, Gurian, finest hunter of the northwoods, had been spooked by a mushroom?

One step, two. He walked on, the trail so broad and broken now that a blind man could have followed it. But now he kept the long rifle poised in his shoulder, the barrel following his gaze.

More of the green fungi, in ones and twos and globular clusters. There was no mistaking it now; they pulsed and throbbed like eggs in a frying pan. They were not of his world – he was quite sure of that. And he thought for some reason of the meteor streak he had seen earlier in the morning. Perhaps they had been brought here by some tumbled meteorite in the night.

They were no threat, at any rate. He crushed half a dozen underfoot as he padded along. They followed the trail in a scattered green line as though the grazer he tracked had been excreting them in its wake.

Now the silence was as loud as singing in his ears, and his own breathing seemed too loud to him. There was blood splashed on the moss at his feet. The beast he was following had been wounded and was bleeding freely. He cursed his luck. Like as not one of the forest predators had chanced across it and–

A noise in the great silence, an animal bellow. But it was not any animal he knew. It carried through the trees like fire in the night, and something old and elemental shivered in Gurian's spine at the sound.

There were words in that long roar, he was sure of it. Perhaps even a shred of Gothic. A beast that spoke? It was impossible.

He kept going. Curiosity drew him on, the bane and blessing of man's nature. The rifle, his hunting companion of twenty years, seemed far too heavy in his sweat-slick palms. He clung to it as a man on a cliff will cling to a thrown rope.

There was a small clearing ahead. He could see it by the light, which thickened and grew, green and bright with the rising sun. And in that clearing–

He stopped short, heart hammering in his chest. Slowly – so slowly his knees creaked – he knelt down in the moss. The rifle barrel dipped in his grasp.

He took in all that his eyes showed him of the scene ahead, but it seemed to him that his brain could not quite process the information.

He knew what they were – he had heard of such things. But they were... more, than he had ever imagined. Larger, more grotesque. Misshapen oddities brought to sudden, stark, terrifying life.

* * *

THE GRAZER LAY dead in the clearing, a grey mound, the body broken open and steaming, shredded to scarlet. And around the torn carcass stood creatures out of mankind's oldest nightmares.

They were huge, almost twice a man's height, and six feet across at the shoulder. Their arms were as thick as Gurian's waist, longer than their short, bowed legs. And on their corded shoulders were set massive fanged skulls with outsize jaws and cavernous eyes ringed by bone. The eyes glinted red, and red were their clawed hands, and red was spattered liberally over all of them.

They were tearing into the body of the dead animal at their feet like ravenous animals, but animals that wore armour, and belts, with wide cleaver-like blades dangling at their waists, and outsize squat-barrelled contraptions, which might have been parodies of firearms, holstered there too.

They were green, where the blood did not paint them, the same green as the fungi that had sprung up on the forest floor. But the shade of their hides ranged from the dark olive of stagnant water to the pale bile-brightness of new leaves. Some had painted their skin with crude glyphs and sigils that were meaningless to Gurian. Others had dark-inked tattoos, and iron rings that pierced ears and lips. One had an iron claw for a hand, but it opened and closed as if part of the beast, the steel cables that controlled it running into the very flesh of its forearm.

And they stank. Even thirty yards away, Gurian could smell them, a rank, foetid stink that filled the clearing and threatened to overwhelm his own senses. It was the smell of large unwashed animals, but underlying it was the reek of rot and mould.

They were gabbling and snarling at one another, a noise which was loathsome to hear, and which was not the mere growling of animals. It was indeed speech of some kind, a violent, guttural explosion of noise that nonetheless had within it elements of Low Gothic.

Words came through it to Gurian's ears. They were arguing over the taste of the animal they had brought down, quarrelling over the choice cuts. They seemed about to launch at one another's throats, and clashed their great tusk-like teeth and waved their broad-bladed swords in paroxysms of bestial fury.

These, then, were orks. He had seen them at last.

The Great Enemy of mankind was Chaos – every man and woman alive knew that, it was drilled into them all their lives. But orks were the green storm that rolled across the stars, leaving desolation in their wake. They infested worlds, consumed them, then moved on. They fought among themselves more than with any other species. They were cunning, brutal beyond belief, violent beyond the edge of sanity. And they knew no mercy, either for themselves or anyone else. There could be no negotiation with such foes; their minds worked on a different level of understanding to that of all other sentient races.

They were as relentless as a virus. They had to be stamped out, every last one, or a planet might find itself plagued by them for decades. They–

Now Gurian looked down in horror at the fetid little green fungi that dotted the ground around him. They were somehow connected to the orks – he was sure of it.

The thought turned his stomach, as if he had uncovered a secret charnel house in his own backyard.

The orks were busy shoving and lashing out at one another, throwing chunks of torn meat through the air. As Gurian watched, two of them fell to fighting in a writhing struggle of roaring fury. The rest of them stood back and cheered and bellowed and laughed. The sound hurt the ears.

The town must be warned, Gurian thought. I must go back. He thought of Mina and Mardian, his wife and son, in the hands of these monsters. It could not be contemplated – it was too horrible.

Know when to fight and when to run, when to stand still and silent and let the monsters of the world walk on by. Those are the rules. You obey them, and you live.

He rose to his feet slowly, knowing that a sudden movement drew attention like no other. His heart thundered in his chest, and seemed about to rise up into his throat. He was beyond fear. He knew that his skin was cold and pale. His body was sending all his blood to organs and muscles he would need if he were to fight or flee.

He backed away, one step, two. No fear of making a noise. The racket around the downed grazer would cover the approach of a tank, and the moss underfoot accepted his steps without a sound.

He had a tree between him and the clearing now, and his breathing came a little easier. It was hard to do, but he set his back to the orks and began picking his way back along the trail. He would strike off into the forest and find another way home. The beasts of the ironwoods held no fears for him, not any more.

He was perhaps fifty yards away from the clearing when he struck off to the right, away from the trail and into the depths of the great trees. There was little vegetation on the forest floor aside from hummocked mounds of moss, but some of these were higher than his head, a second, softer forest growing at the feet of the immense ironwoods.

There was light ahead, another clearing, and a smell in the air as of a great burning. He hefted the rifle and walked on, wondering what new horror was lurking in the trees. It was not the smell of a fire, but heavier. Smoke hung in the air, the acrid taint of smouldering ironwood, and underlying it was the scent of something else, a metallic taint utterly unfamiliar to him.

This clearing was many times larger than the one in which he had seen the orks, and all around it, stately ironwoods stood broken and toppled. Some were glowing, the blackened ends of them turning to black pitch, bubbling with heat. And there was the deep, dark fragrance of upturned earth also, as though someone were digging here, deep into the black loam of Chrisannon.

It was an enormous meteorite, lying amid the clearing it had smashed into the forest. As tall as five or six habs, it was burnt black, a massive rounded crag that had careered through the trees leaving a trail of destruction for fully half a mile to the north. A relic of the void, it sat steaming and smoking in the forest like some gargantuan beast resting after long labour. Gurian stared at it. In its own way it was as astonishing as the sight of the orks had been.

Things were scurrying about the black base of the rock. Not orks – they were far too small for that. Gurian, drawn by that irresistible curiosity, moved closer, keeping in cover.

It was like seeing a stone upturned and insect life come teeming out from under it.

These creatures stood no higher than his waist, and some reached barely to his knee. They were the same rancid green as the orks and they swarmed in the clearing like maggots in a corpse's eye. They set up a muttering, high-pitched cackling, as loathsome to listen to as the ork bellowing had been. Gurian saw spindly limbs, tiny clawed hands, bald green skulls surmounted by pointed ears. These were kin to the orks, had to be. Individually, they were not to be feared, but there were scores of them busy about the base of the meteorite. He saw them wielding hammers and chisels, carrying lengths of rust-flecked cable and fragments of machinery on their thin shoulders. They were as busy as a broken termite mound of old Terra, almost comical to behold. Orks? Surely not.

Something poked him from behind and he whipped round. One of the creatures was right behind him, holding a rod of black iron. Its eyes glinted red and its head reached barely to his belt buckle. It gnashed its teeth, cocked its green skull to one side, and snarled, baring its needle-thin fangs.

He did not think. He lashed out with the ironpitch stock of the rifle, smashing it into the bestial little face with all the disgust and fear of his adrenaline-fuelled muscles. He broke open the skull, saw the brains leap out. The little creature collapsed like a puppet whose strings have been slashed. Its blood was red and bright as new paint.

It was still moving. Even with its head caved in, the hands were scrabbling in the moss and the legs were kicking. Gurian brought the rifle stock down again and again, the blood spattering his clothes and face as he pounded the creature's head into mush.

He heard a high shriek from the clearing behind him. Turning, he saw more of the creatures closing in, jaws agape. They were pointing at him and gabbling, jumping up and down and waving their tools.

He fired one round from the hip, the rifle bucking in his hands. It splattered three of them to shattered pieces, tearing through their ranks. The sound of the gunshot was shockingly loud. He racked in another round and fired again, felling a whole line of them as the heavy bullet tore through the green flesh and hit the side of the meteorite, ricocheting off with a crack of sparks and a high whine.

There was a roar, and he saw a full-sized ork come raging through the crowd of its lesser brethren, throwing them aside and kicking its way through them. It seemed to have just materialised out of the side of the meteorite itself. Gurian's bowels turned to water at the sight of it. But he was a hunter, and he had faced down great beasts before.

He cocked the rifle again, and took careful aim this time. The ork powered towards him with a huge cleaver upraised in its fist, mouth agape and fangs shining.

He shot it through its open mouth.

The ork staggered. The heavy bullet had blown out the back of its head. Gurian saw the red eyes blink, the broken teeth clash. But it kept coming, while at its feet the smaller creatures of its kind hooted and cackled and gabbled in hate and alarm.

Like some hulking green monolith, the great ork loomed up closer in the rifle's sights as Gurian fired his last round at where the heart of a man would be. The huge beast was knocked backwards, but it kept its feet. It could not roar, for its tongue had been blown off, but it uttered a horrible wet gargling noise as it came on, shrugging off the heavy slug that had smashed into its chest. There was no life in its eyes, yet still the beast moved, sluggish but relentless.

Gurian, bewildered beyond terror, turned to run.

He crashed into something and fell on his back. For a moment he thought he had hit a tree, but when his vision cleared he looked up to see a second ork standing over him. It seemed huge beyond belief, armoured in crudely forged iron. Something like a smile was splitting its jaws. It stood on his arm as he reached for the fallen rifle, and Gurian screamed as his bones broke under the weight of its boot. It bent over him, and he gagged on the miasma that welled out of the tusk-ringed mouth. But there were words being spoken to him. He heard them distinctly, Low Gothic mangled by the beast's oversized jaws.

'*Fresh meat*,' it said. And then the jaws came lower, and closed over his agonised face.

# FOUR

LORD FENNICK STIFLED a yawn. The room was stuffy and hot, a long low expanse of desks and data-slates and flickering screens before which the planetary communications staff sat dutifully, sending messages out into the aether, receiving and recording them on old-fashioned plastape. Streams of it littered the floor, remnants of conversations that were not worth his attention. Even a small world such as Zalidar accumulated a bureaucracy over time, one that seemed to delight in talking to itself.

Thus do we justify our existence, he thought with an internal shrug. When the heavy lifting of establishing a settlement is done, it is a case of sitting back for a time and letting the lower orders of the world create and build and bicker and wheel and deal amongst themselves. Even the Imperium of Man cannot regulate everything. But we can monitor it at least.

He caught a fragment of his own thoughts. *The lower orders.*

I was one of them myself once. A man should never forget where he came from.

Idly, he picked up a plastape reel from a near desk, running it through his fingers to read the verbose Low Gothic that ran black along the tape. The township of Meriolus was short of iron ore and quicklime, and its praetor, one Vlad Municius, deemed these supplies vital to the arresting of jungle growth along his borders.

Fennick frowned. The jungle. They cut it back, burned it down, hacked it to the very roots, and still it sprang up again.

Here, around Zalathras, the native vegetation had been tamed, but a hundred miles to the south the Deep Forest still loomed large over almost every settlement. Zalidar was a fecund world, that quality part of what made it potentially a rich one, but the native flora had to be battled daily by those outside the city, beyond the cleared croplands that opened in a belt around it.

The great beasts that had haunted its past had withdrawn to the high mountains and the fastnesses of the Deep Forest, what men here called the Tagus, but the creeping trees still patiently struggled to reclaim the cleared, tilled country he had created. It would never end, not until the continent had been scoured like a dirty pan sanded clean.

He dropped the tape – some lower-level functionary would investigate further and decide whether good Municius' request was worth kicking up the ladder – and turned to view the map that hung framed on the moist, gleaming stone wall behind him.

He did so love a good map. They made the world clear and ordered and intelligible.

This one showed his beloved Zalathras as a hexagonal red dot in a pale expanse of open country, crossed by the brown slow waters of the Dromion River to the south, and then, fifty miles beyond that, the sea of green that was the Tagus, the great Southern Jungle that led down to the Pole, and the Morcault Mountains, at the base of the world.

Ghent Morcault, who claimed to have landed on those mountains and walked their slopes, was somewhere out there in his ramshackle ship even now. If not on the planet itself, then elsewhere in the system for sure, pursuing his crack-brained dreams.

The old man was eighty if he was a day, a legend upon Zalidar. Once a small-time trader, he had landed his ship in a small clearing on the banks of the Dromion some fifty years before and had named the river after his trading partner, a drunken ne'er-do-well long dead and famous only for the river that took his name. Then he had hopped all over the planet in his creaking little freighter, naming features and mapping the basic geography of the unclaimed world.

Not one mountain to my name, Fennick thought petulantly. And yet it was I who made Zalathras what it is today. I commissioned the building of the walls, the space port, the first of the hive-spires. And Morcault, the old miscreant, he has an entire mountain range named after him. Where is the justice in that?

Even the city itself had been named by Imperial edict, after Gaius Zalathras, who had been high up in the Administratum of Ultramar at the time.

We should have named it after a hero of the Imperium, Fennick thought. Something stirring, a name to catch fire and draw the eye of Macragge to the Eastern Fringe. We should have named it Sicarius, or Fabian, after the captains of the blessed Ultramarines. Or Calgar, perhaps.

But he knew that these ideas were presumptuous, absurd even. As jealous as the Adeptus Astartes were of their honour, they did not name planets after themselves. Their names lived on in the glory of their deeds, not in the words carved above some city gate.

He left the comm chamber with an eye on his wrist chrono. He grimaced as he paced the long echoing corridor towards his own offices.

Perhaps there will be a city named Fennick one day, the lord of Zalidar thought. His face twisted in self-mockery at the thought.

Probably long after I am gone.

His aides were seated in the anteroom, but sprang up as he approached. He smiled at them, remembering other young, earnest faces, all of them long dead. He closed the door to his offices and uttered a sigh. Sometimes he saw them yet, the faces of those dead.

FENNICK HAD NOT always been a lord. A soldier first, he had served in the Astra Militarum alongside Boros in the Thrax campaign, fighting Chaos cultists and all manner of teeming horrors. The Guard had been defeated by the Great Enemy on that unhappy planet, and the Adeptus Astartes had been called in.

Thirty-eight thousand of the Guard had fallen on Thrax, four full divisions torn to pieces in the space of a few weeks. The things he had seen there still haunted Fennick's nightmares. A young sergeant, he had been given a battlefield commission after all the officers in his company were dead. And Boros had been there beside him, older, more experienced, but lacking the latent tactical sense that Fennick possessed and that had kept the company from being entirely wiped out.

The two of them had handled the bloody withdrawal to the drop-ships when the order came to evacuate, and as they had lifted off to rejoin what was left of the fleet they had seen through the grimy viewports of the troop hold something that Fennick would ever after have burned across his memory.

A Space Marine battle-barge, miles long, bristling with weaponry, painted deep blue and adorned with the Ultima sigil of the Ultramarines. Marneus Calgar himself had come to the fray, along with three full companies of the Adeptus Astartes. They had dropped on Thrax like avenging angels, bearing fire and death.

But even that was not enough. The Chaos taint ran too deep. The Ultramarines had defeated the enemy on the ground – three hundred Adeptus Astartes accomplishing what sixty thousand of the Astra Militarum had failed to do. And still it was not enough.

The order had gone out – an Exterminatus, the destruction of all life on Thrax, even though the planet was a forge world, vital to the military economy of Ultramar.

From orbit, Fennick and Boros had watched an entire world die, the Ultramarines raining cyclonic torpedoes down upon it in a pattern that seared the surface of the planet down to the gutrock. Even the atmosphere had been burned away.

The concussions of its destruction rocked the transports in high orbit. There were millions burned up in that holocaust, men and women who still clung to life, struggling to survive in the swamp of Chaos that their home world had become. But they were expendable, mere kindling caught up in the fiery rage of the Angels of Death.

Thrax was now a dead thing, a globe of rock upon which no man had set foot since.

The world had been saved; the world had been destroyed. It was the same thing to the Ultramarines.

Boros was right, Fennick thought with something of a shiver. Sorrow follows them wherever they go, the Angels of the Emperor. They are not human, and they do not think as humans do.

After the Thrax campaign, Fennick and Boros had been shipped to Zalidar on garrison duty along with what was left of their decimated company. The world was a backwater colony upon which a few thousand settlers struggled to hack a living out of the jungle. Contact with Ultramar was intermittent, and life was harsh.

That had been thirty-one years ago.

It was no sinecure, this posting. Of all those men Fennick had brought to Zalidar from the Thrax campaign, only he and Boros now remained. The Tagus and the beasts had claimed the rest.

Fennick remembered one of his last veterans, doughty Jarik Samos – who had come through all the bloody carnage of Thrax – dying outside his own barracks from a snakebite. The white, disbelieving face of the dying man. To survive so much, only to be taken down by such a trifle.

As time went on, Fennick and Boros had taken the running of the colony into their own hands, for want of better candidates, and with the founding of Zalathras, orders had come through from the Imperial Administratum for Fennick to take over the planetary governorship on a pro-tem basis. He was an unknown young officer, but he had made his mark and had been rewarded for it.

Either that, he thought sourly, or no one of superior rank thought it a title worth holding. He was governor of what amounted to a small town, on a hostile planet at the very edge of human space.

But it was a beginning. And thus in name at least, the young lieutenant of guardsmen became a lord, and Boros was promoted to colonel of Zalidar's defence force.

Colonel of a few hundred badly armed militiamen. They were not much, by the standards of the Imperium, but they had sufficed – just – to keep the colony on its feet.

In time, the city had begun to grow, as more settlers arrived from all over the Eastern Fringe, and the beasts of the jungle had been thinned out by bloody killing drives, which both Fennick and Boros had led. Something like a true economy had become established, as opposed to the barter markets of old. And the Administratum seemed to forget that Fennick's promotion had been a temporary, stop-gap measure. The years went by, and they hacked farmland and towns out of the Tagus, and tried to attract as many settlers and colonists as they could to Zalidar, for they needed people above all else.

Manpower, and money. The pillars of success.

Zalidar had been largely left alone after that, a forgotten frontier world that had escaped the heavy tithes levied on long-established planets further to the galactic west. This oversight had allowed private enterprise to thrive to a surprising degree on an otherwise primitive world.

Fennick smiled. He remembered the day old Ferdia Rosquin had made planetfall with a shuttleload of clerks, to set up a branch of the first bank on the planet. He had known in that moment that they would survive, and, more than that, they would prosper. With loans taken out from Rosquin's bank they had brought in heavy machinery and materials, paid Vanaheim's construction company to begin the circuit of Zalathras' tall walls – they had seemed far too long, back then, for the population within them – and dug the foundations of Alphon Spire. Not because they needed to build upwards for lack of space – it was to make a statement. Zalidar had arrived. And Zalathras began at last to assume the trappings of a genuine city.

One day the Imperium would take note of it, and the planet would be called upon to make its contribution to the unending war effort, which taxed all of humanity amid the stars, but for now, Ultramar looked the other way, and Zalidar grew steadily.

Ghent Morcault had turned up again around the time of the wall's building. A rogue trader with a talent for tracking down elusive cargoes, his help had been invaluable in those early years. But as Zalathras expanded and the city's needs burgeoned, his little ramshackle freighter – the *Mayfly*, he called it – had proved inadequate in both tonnage and reliability, and Morcault had made it his business to set off on what he called his expeditions, in a quest to map the surface of the planet and explore the system surrounding it.

Fennick and Boros helped him out from time to time, with repairs and supplies, and in return, every time Morcault returned to Zalathras they were able to fill in a little more of the blank space on Fennick's beloved maps. The trader had spent decades doing what an Imperial survey vessel could have accomplished in a few months, but there were no survey ships available, not for Zalidar, and so Morcault's eccentric quest had a use of sorts.

But in the last few years his wanderings had become more and more unpredictable, and he seemed wrapped up more in his own personal obsession with the planet and the system it inhabited, rather than any systematic methodology of survey. Ninety per cent of Zalidar was explored now, thanks to him, but there were times when Fennick traced his fingers over the features on his charts, and wondered just how reliable the old space-tramp's data was.

One day, Zalidar would be mapped properly by a dedicated Imperial survey team of the Administratum, but for now, Morcault's discoveries were the official version of the planet's geography, for good or ill.

A KNOCK ON the tall doors behind him. It made him start, he had been so lost in his own memories.

'Yes,' he barked.

When did I begin to sound so much like a bad-tempered sergeant major? Fennick wondered to himself.

An aide put his head around the door. 'My lord, Rear Admiral Glenck requests an audience.'

Fennick sighed, and waved a hand. 'Show him in, Pherias. And fetch some wine. The good stuff, mind.'

'Yes, my lord.'

He had been expecting this. Fennick took a seat behind his desk and adjusted his scarlet sash of office. He touched for a second the Silver Starburst he had won on Thrax, which bore the gems of two wounds upon it.

Those were simpler days, he thought. But when one is young everything seems simple, even life and death.

Glenck was a broad, heavily built man with a wide, florid face. In his own youth, he must have been formidable, but the muscle had softened, giving him a look of pink, unbaked dough. Two eyes blinked in that slab of a face, black as broken coal. Fennick had never heard him laugh, not once in the five years since he had been seconded to Zalidar.

The two of them were of an age, but, through no fault of his own, Glenck had seen very little combat. Rising up through the command tree over the dead bodies of his more combative colleagues, Glenck was one of those men who get promoted because no one is sure what else to do with them.

He knew this, and it rankled him. He resented his posting to quiet, forgotten Zalidar. He resented the fact that someone of his rank had only half a dozen obsolete ships to command. He resented the way his life had panned out. That resentment had made him into a sour martinet, but he was still able to play the system as well as any. Fennick could not afford to antagonise him too much; the Administratum did not like annoyed rear admirals sending memos and missives from the back of beyond.

'My dear Glenck, how happy I am to see you.'

He stood up, shook the naval officer's clammy hand, and gestured to a chair. Pherias, bringing in the wine, covered up the admiral's lack of reciprocity.

Five years, Fennick thought, steepling his fingers together behind the wide desk. A long time to be sitting on one's rump, letting the self-pity turn to bitterness.

'You know why I am here, my lord,' Glenck said. He did not touch his wine.

'Do I?' Fennick sipped his own. It was warm, like everything else on Zalidar. But he had grown used to drinking alcohol that was blood temperature.

'One of my ships has left orbit and is powering off to the back of beyond on your orders, thanks to the meddling of Colonel Boros.'

'Ah, the *Hesiod*. That is correct, admiral.'

Glenck did not blink. 'That is an unwarranted and irregular intervention on your part. Orders to the fleet come from me, and I alone am responsible for ship dispositions. They shall hear of this in Ultramar, I assure you.'

But will they care? Fennick wondered wearily.

'Colonel Boros put a convincing case–' he began.

Glenck snorted. He had a face well suited to a snort, like that of a snub-nosed pig. 'I heard Colonel Boros' case. Some vague rumour which was probably nothing more than an augur shadow, and the usual vagaries of the vox. And for that he came crying to me for the loan of a Sword-class frigate and a four-thousand-man crew – a skeleton crew, mark you – to send them out to the edge of the system and sweep in circles until doomsday. It was arrant nonsense.'

'A long-range patrol of the system does not seem so fantastical to me,' Fennick said mildly.

'We have a patrol,' Glenck snapped. 'I do my job. Zalidar is protected by a combat patrol night and day.'

'Short-range fighters, admiral. The Furies extend our sensor knowledge half a million miles beyond high orbit.'

'I work with what I have, my lord. Had we a fleet worthy of the name I would be happy to institute long-range standing patrols, but we do not have the resources. Even our existing ships possess only a tithe of their proper fighting complement. If you would requisition Ultramar for better ships, more trained personnel–'

'Yes, yes.' Fennick held up a hand. This was old ground. And besides, Glenck was in the right of it.

In the last ten years, Zalidar's population had quadrupled, but the armed forces that guarded it had remained stuck at a level more suited to an outpost. The militia – some twenty thousand soldiers – was all very well, but the planet needed orbital defences, deep-space vessels and anti-air missiles. Six ageing frigates and destroyers and a few dozen orbital fighters would barely slow down a determined adversary, especially since the two larger ships, the Sword-class vessels, were undermanned and underequipped with munitions.

'Admiral, you know I am one with you on this issue. I have sent request after request to Calth, and Lord Joule has been very polite, but uncooperative. There are ongoing incursions within Ultramar itself, and the Ultramarines have companies scattered all over the sector fighting half a dozen wars. Orks, eldar and the Great Enemy itself – they are all exerting pressure on Imperial resources at present. Our system is quiet, and has been for decades. We are at the bottom of the list; it's as simple as that. We were lucky to get the two frigates. I lobbied for years to obtain them.'

Fennick held up his hands and smiled like a reasonable man, though inwardly he was both irritated and bored by Glenck's whining. What a great child the man was! No wonder he had been shunted off here to this backwater. The thought of him in charge of a proper combat fleet was one to chill the blood.

'Then if we are to work with what we have,' Glenck snarled, 'I must at least insist that you allow me to issue my own orders to my own command. Shipmaster Relisch came to me after he received your orders, and since they bore your imprimatur, I allowed the mission to proceed. But this flouting of the chain of command is wholly unacceptable, my lord. It breaks down discipline, injects an element of uncertainty into the command process, and–'

'And it makes you look bad,' Fennick drawled.

For a second he thought Glenck would lean over the desk and strike him. He almost hoped the man would. He would have him arrested, confined to quarters, and one source of headaches would be removed from the day-to-day running of the planet. But Glenck was too wise for that. His jowls quivered, and the pudgy fist remained clenched.

'I find that comment offensive,' he snapped.

You find everything offensive, you fat bore, Fennick thought. But what he said was, 'I apologise, admiral. I spoke flippantly. We must at all costs work in harmony, you and I. You are quite right, of course. But perhaps we could see the *Hesiod*'s mission as a training mission, if nothing else. The fleet has done little but remain in a standard orbit these last eighteen months.'

'They remain there to safeguard the security of this planet,' Glenck said stubbornly.

'They are not numerous enough or well enough equipped for that task. They are perhaps more valuable as intelligence-gathering assets. And surely their captains should jump at the chance for independent command.'

*Away from your interference,* Fennick added to himself.

'I am the best judge of what my captains need in terms of mission and training,' Glenck barked. 'Your place, my lord, is to tell me your broad strategic needs. I decide how those needs shall be met by the fleet.'

My place? Fennick thought. And he felt the anger rise in him.

'Very well,' he grated. And he let Glenck see the anger this time, staring into the fat-framed black eyes.

'My needs, admiral, include a standing long-range patrol on the edge of the Zalidar System, to give us early warning of any incursion into Zalidari space. I will have that put in writing before the day is out. You may forward that to the Administratum if you please. I certainly shall.

'Commander of the Fleet you may be, but I am planetary governor here, and have been for the better part of three decades. You will obey my orders, or I will replace you with someone who does. Do we have an understanding between us?'

Glenck's face was flushed red. He stood up.

'I understand you perfectly, Fennick,' he said, his voice dripping hatred. 'But let it be said here and now, if your meddling in the affairs of my command results in any kind of setback or unfortunate incident, I will pursue redress of the matter all the way to Macragge itself if I have to.'

'I expected nothing less,' Fennick said. He pressed a button on his desk. 'Pherias, Rear Admiral Glenck is leaving. See him out.' And as the young aide opened the tall doors behind Glenck, he said, 'My compliments, admiral, to you and all those who serve so devotedly under you.'

You damn fool, he added to himself. And he was not sure if the thought was meant for Glenck or for himself.

# FIVE

THE VOID. IT was a frightening thing, all that black; an absence of everything that was necessary for life. One might term it empty, except that it was not. There was life in the void, organisms barely known to Imperium science that drifted on the faint pulse of solar winds and somehow subsisted in the vacuum, garnering all that was needed out of the nothingness for their tenuous existence.

The void was mystery, and fascination. A man who looked too long into it could well find something staring back at him. The immaterium beyond the material universe – the deeper blackness beyond black, which housed things no man should ever see.

But men had gone there, many never to return. The peerless warriors of the Adeptus Astartes had fought wars in that place and come back again, their enhanced intellects protecting them from the madness of the journey. But even they had been lost to the darkness, time after time. Entire Chapters, gone. It was a dark legend of the Imperium. And it was fact.

The immaterium stared out of the blackness with a cackle and a grin, daring those who plied the void to look into it and indulge that horrible fascination. The fascination for the cliff edge, the impulse towards self-immolation that existed in all men.

Ghent Morcault knew more of the void than most, for he had been travelling it these sixty years. During that time he had blazed trails across the Eastern Fringe and carried cargoes between worlds that were mere names on Administratum star charts, far beyond Imperial compliance.

All over the Fringe there were forgotten little moons with men struggling to survive upon them. They invoked the Emperor's name, they told tales of the titanic wars of the Imperium, they spoke in whispers of the Great Heresy. But for them the true reality of existence was bounded by the horizon they could see and the sky above it. All else was lights in the night, far unknown stars upon which their fellows strove to keep the flame of civilisation alive. And in the dark between the stars, there were monsters.

Monsters, Morcault thought. Well, they are no legend. They exist, more fearsome than any nightmare of the dark.

They are here. I am looking at one right now.

'The anatomy of the creature is singular indeed,' Scurrios was saying. He bent low over the carcass on the gurney, and the overheads played back in flashes from the array of surgical blades that were arrayed to one side. Scurrios was bent over the flayed flesh like a child burning ants with a magnifying glass, his rat-like face drawn tight with concentration.

'Look here, Ghent. It's the first time I have seen it.'

'I prefer to remain where I am,' Morcault said dryly, leaning on his stick. He tapped the pitchthorn on the deck, and poked aside a tiny globe of green that had tumbled there from the tabletop. His mouth twisted in revulsion.

'We will have to open the vents when you are done and blow this compartment. I want none of this filth on my ship.'

'Yes, yes, of course. Though I doubt any of the spores would grow in this environment. They are fungus-like. They need moisture, and, I would hazard, a minimum of nutriment. Soil-based, of course.' Scurrios grinned his little rat-faced grin. 'Not much of that on a starship.'

'What about a corpse – would that be enough?'

Scurrios blinked behind the thick lenses he wore. 'Why yes, I should think so.'

'So they could grow out of their own dead. Throne, what a thought.'

'They are an amazing species.' Scurrios straightened as far as his hunched spine would allow. He stepped back, and Morcault saw the full horrible glory of the body the little man had been carving open.

An ork.

A small one, by their standards, only some six and half feet tall. Scurrios had carved it clear from skull to knee, flaying the green flesh from the bone and laying open the thoracic cavity. Morcault felt his stomach give a brief twinge, and the bile rose in his throat.

'Notice the lack of recognisable internal organs,' Scurrios said with unforgivable enthusiasm. 'Its very flesh is, in effect, one large digestive tract, and whatever vital systems it possesses are not centralised, but distributed through the body. Only the brain is as we might expect it, and it is well protected.' He gestured to the empty skull-case that lay like an oversized bowl on a side table. 'I would hazard that its skin is capable of limited photosynthesis also, meaning–'

'I know what it means,' Morcault said irritably. His joints ached. He popped a stimm from the pouch in his pocket.

'Yes. This is only supposition on my part, you understand, but it seems to me that while the ork can ingest nutrients in the usual mammalian way, it may well be able to top these up by utilising light itself as an energy source. And the spores–' Scurrios picked up a marble-sized green globe from the gurney in his black-gloved hands and studied it, his eyes bright and huge behind his lenses.

'The beast sheds them more or less continually, but especially, as we have seen, at the moment of death. These spores could be each and every one a little ork in the making. They start out as tiny creatures which seem almost harmless, but every record I have consulted emphasises that the ork never – never, Ghent – stops growing.'

He studied the green mushroom-like globe in his fingers. 'Given a few centuries, this nondescript object might bloom into a mighty chieftain, an enemy to be reckoned with, the leader of armies.'

He crushed the globe in his gloved hand. Was it his imagination, or did Morcault's old ears hear a tiny, high-pitched scream?

Scurrios dusted off his gloves. 'What we have then, is a creature which has been genetically engineered. There seems to be no evolution involved here that I can see. The ork may even be an artificial creation, born through the application of some science long lost to the known artifices of the galaxy as we understand it.'

Scurrios rubbed one lens, leaving a green smear.

'In sum, it is a species which is fearsome beyond belief, bred to war, and incredibly hard to eradicate.'

'What is the best way to kill it?' Morcault asked impatiently. 'That's the rub. It's why I have allowed you to turn my sick bay into a charnel house.'

Scurrios smiled. 'For which I am duly thankful, captain. It is a long time since I have had the privilege of dissecting such a perfect specimen. How to kill it?' He began to strip off the elbow-length rubber gloves that encased his hands and forearms.

'Simply put, one blasts the hell out of it.' He giggled, but sobered at the look on Morcault's face. The huge eyes blinked behind the green-smeared glass lenses.

'The ork's nervous system is so effectively distributed that the usual targeting strategies would be rendered almost ineffective. This beast could lose a limb and barely feel it. You could burn out its chest with concentrated las-fire and it would probably be able to keep fighting for quite some time.

'No – headshots are most effective. The creature's brain is anatomically similar to that of any basic humanoid, contained wholly within the skull – a very thick skull, mind – and with its destruction, the ork should, finally, fall.'

'And when it does, these... spores pop out of its hide,' Morcault said with a sigh. 'I thought they were boils or warts, all this time.'

'In death, the ork seeds its very corpse with the makings of new life,' Scurrios said. 'Not just new life, but a new ecosystem. Not all the spores are the same. I would hazard that many, if not all creatures of ork biology are hidden in these, for I have identified at least five different types. Left unhindered, one ork corpse could engender an entire new host of the creatures and everything they need to subsist and prosper.'

'They are like a virus,' Morcault said with disgust.

'No, captain. They are an incredible fusion of plant and animal. They have more in common with a mould.'

Morcault laughed. 'A mould! The great scourge of our galaxy, the green storm that has toppled Empires – a mould!'

Scurrios did not smile. 'What could be more effective? Captain, these things have been bioengineered to be the perfect fighting animal, almost impossible to eradicate once they have been introduced into an ecosystem. They make it their own. Only prolonged exposure to complete vacuum can wipe out all traces of them – as it killed this one – that, or a firestorm so complete that it destroys almost all other forms of life alongside them.'

'An Exterminatus perhaps,' Morcault said. His lined old face was even grimmer than age had made it.

'Well,' Scurrios said with a trace of nervousness, 'that might be a little on the drastic side. But a planet which has known an ork incursion must be prepared for further troubles in years to come – not from without, but from the spores that have incubated on its own soil.'

Morcault nodded to himself. 'In half a century, I have not seen them so far into the Eastern Fringe. And this fellow you carved up was only a scout. If his engine had not failed, who knows where he would have ended up?'

'Ork technology is unreliable at best,' Scurrios said, blinking like an owl of old Terra.

'But surprisingly effective. They maintain space fleets, armoured vehicles and heavy weaponry. How can such stupid creatures grasp warp technology?' Morcault's white eyebrows shot up. 'It seems bizarre.'

'They do not understand technology as we do, it's true. But if you read up on the history of interactions between humanity and their kind, it seems plain that in some orks the mastery of machinery and technology is an inbuilt skill, as much part of them as a gene. There are orks for all occasions, captain. Some are psykers of sorts, others crazed kinds of physicians. They do not learn these trades – they are born to them.'

'And are some born to lead, Scurrios?'

'That I do not know. Orks will keep growing larger and stronger until fate or ill luck cuts them down. The largest orks are the warleaders and chieftains that are the scourge of our galaxy. I would guess that a few centuries of constant warfare create a kind of low animal cunning at the very least. And history tells us that when they gather in large enough numbers something happens to them, as though they are somehow psychically attuned to the prospect of massive, all-out conflict. It is then that they are at their most cohesive, and their most dangerous.'

'They are always dangerous,' Morcault said quietly.

'You have encountered them before, captain?'

'More times than I would wish. I have seen what they can do, Scurrios, and it is as ugly as all hell.' He tapped the pitchthorn stick on the metal deck of the sick bay.

'I want you to wrap up here. Bag the body and scour the sick bay for all remnants of it, then clear the place out of everything that is not nailed down, and we will vent this filth into space.'

'Captain, may I keep some samples, for scientific enquiry?'

'You may not, Scurrios. It is too dangerous.' Morcault set one blue-veined hand on the little stooped fellow's shoulder. 'I am sorry, but the risk is too great, my friend. You have done sterling work here. I had suspected some or all of what you have told me, but it is something to have it confirmed at last. By keen scientific enquiry, no less.' He smiled, but Scurrios still looked glum. The little scientist was brilliant, in his way, but sometimes his keen mind was blind to certain consequences. He knew so much, and so little, at the same time.

'And the ork craft?' Scurrios asked.

'Gortyn is out setting charges to its hull as we speak. We'll blow it to shreds and leave the debris for the void.'

'Captain, that craft was not long-range–'

'I know, Scurrios. Another reason why I want this wrapped up quickly. This area of space has become unhealthy. And besides, we must get the *Mayfly* back to Zalidar and bear this news to Fennick.'

'Is the vox still down?'

'The vox is always down when there is something important to send on it,' Morcault growled. 'And Zalidar has no astropath worthy of the name. So we must make our best speed. I am no magos, but if there is one thing I have learned about the orks down the years, it is that where there is one, there are many. They never hunt alone.'

Morcault regained the bridge, leaning on the pitchthorn and grimacing at what it cost him to make it up the metal stairs. The blast-shutters were raised from the viewports – old-fashioned titanium, for the *Mayfly* had not the power for full-time void shields – and he could see a wide expanse of almost starless space, dark beyond the blinking glimmer of the consoles.

Hester was in her chair, murmuring in Low Gothic that was spiced with elements of binaric terms, and the two servitors plugged into the *Mayfly*'s cogitators went about their arcane business without pause. Morcault patted one on its bald, wired scalp, as he always did, and took the captain's chair in the centre of the bridge, glancing at the surrounding data-slates and monitors to make sure his ship was as it should be.

'Gortyn will be back shipside in fifteen minutes, he tells me,' Hester said. 'Twenty-minute delay on the charges. I take it that we are going back to Zalidar?'

'As fast as she can run,' Morcault agreed. 'And keep trying the vox.'

'Damn the vox,' Hester snapped. 'I might as well climb out on the hull and try some semaphore.'

Morcault chuckled.

'The void currents are strong out here,' Hester went on. She turned to Morcault and her bionic eye gleamed blue in the low light of the bridge. 'The immaterium is close to our plane, this far out, Ghent. It is not a place to linger.'

'No, it's not,' he conceded. 'But that ork rattlebag came from somewhere. A scout ship if ever I saw one. You can bet there is heavy metal somewhere out there, Hester.'

'Long-range augurs have come up empty. I've had the servitors sweeping constantly since we stopped. Not so much as a squeak. The ork ship was in a dire state, Ghent. Perhaps it was just puked out by the warp. I've seen it happen.'

'So have I. But not with orks, my dear. And never with a ship that small.'

Hester turned back to her screens with a grunt. 'First time for everything.'

Morcault sat back in his chair and let his tired old eyes range over the bridge. Everything was as it should be. Hester knew the *Mayfly* as well as he did himself. Twenty-five years, give or take, she had been first mate on his crew. Longer than many marriages, and more successful than most.

This bridge – this ship – was the closest thing in the world he had to a home and a family. He had spent his life chasing first glory, then profit, and finally knowledge, and the *Mayfly* had been with him every step of the way. A tiny craft by Imperial standards, she displaced only a few thousand tons, and though she was older by far than Morcault himself, Gortyn the chief engineer kept her running like a well-built chronometer.

With the odd hiccup, of course. But she had not failed him yet. Not totally, at any rate.

'How long to Zalidar at full burn?' Morcault asked Hester.

'You go full burn all the way, and you'll make Gortyn weep,' she retorted. 'The ship can't take that kind of abuse any more, Ghent.'

'How long?' Morcault repeated.

Hester punched her console with impatient fingers.

'Forty-six days, give or take a few hours.'

'Damn.'

'Want to take to the warp?'

Morcault thought about it. 'How is Jodi?'

'Same as always. Drunk.'

'Damn.' Jodi Arnhal was their Navigator. Brilliant but erratic, he sometimes doubled as the ship's cook, a whim of his they had not thought to contradict. Psykers were fearsome, unpredictable creatures all in all, and even years aboard ship had not divested Arnhal of his innate strangeness.

'We'll have to get him sobered up. We may have to chance the warp. Orks in the system – it's news that needs to travel fast.'

'Maybe he could get word to Ultramar.'

'He's not an astropath, Hester. We have to contact Fennick as soon as we can. Zalidar is the only world worth raiding in this part of the sector. The blasted place should have had an astropath of its own well before now.'

'Beggars would ride, if wishes were horses,' Hester said.

'You've never even seen a horse, Hester.'

'Hey, I can read.'

Morcault smiled. He was about to say something else when the comm crackled and they heard Gortyn's voice.

'All right, chief, I'm inboard. Charges set to blow in eighteen minutes and counting. Time we made some distance between us and that ork wreck.'

'Acknowledged,' Morcault said crisply. 'Hester, get us under way. And vox Scurrios. See how he's getting on in sick bay. I want that compartment vented as soon as possible.'

'One thing at a time, old man,' Hester said. She punched some buttons and pulled back gently on the black yoke that rose from her console.

'Give me power.'

The nearest servitor garbled in binaric. Morcault caught some elements of it, but he had forgotten more of the machine language than he had ever learned. He felt the ship shift and turn under his seat as the gravitics compensated for pitch and roll, and there was a faint pressure on his chest as they picked up speed.

'Leaving it behind, and good riddance,' Hester said quietly.

'We were lucky to chance across it out here,' Morcault told her.

'Lucky you still like to investigate every piece of flotsam and jetsam you come across,' Hester replied.

'Old habits die hard.'

Hester's one human eye narrowed. 'Bad habits especially.'

'I know. A symptom of age. Let me know the second the vox clears up. I'm going to have a word with the ship's cook.'

'He's in his bunk doing his tortured soul act,' Hester said irritably. 'That means freeze-dried mush for dinner, I shouldn't wonder.' She paused. 'Sometimes I feel that third eye of his, as though he is looking through all of us.'

'That is the way of his kind, Hester.'

Another buzz on the ship's comm. 'Captain, this is Scurrios. Sick bay is all set to blow. Vent when you're ready.'

'Stand by,' Morcault said. He looked at Hester, and nodded. She lifted a fail-safe cover and flipped one of a series of brass switches above her head. 'There she blows. Repressurising in about four minutes,' she said. 'I hope Scurrios wasn't in sick bay when he made that comm.'

'Not even he is that absent-minded,' Morcault told her, though they shared a look. Scurrios was brilliant, in his own way, but there were days when Morcault felt he shouldn't be let out alone.

He left the bridge, easing down the metal stairs where once he would have slid down the handrails that bounded them. He knew Hester was watching him, and hated the thought she should see him so frail.

Ghent Morcault was eighty-one years old, and despite a small fortune spent on the best rejuvenating procedures the Imperium could boast, he felt it.

He could still get about, and his mind was as sharp as it had ever been, but he knew that his days were near an end. When his time came, his crew would consign his remains to the void, and Hester would be the new captain of the *Mayfly*. That much he had impressed upon her, though she refused to speak of his end. *We'll have to take you out and shoot you to get rid of you*, she always said.

Arnhal was not answering his door. Morcault rapped harder with the bulbous end of the pitchthorn stick.

'Jodi, open the damned door or I'll get Gortyn to kick it in.'

There was a mumble, and the lock went green.

Arnhal's stateroom stank of cheap grain alcohol – the Navigator's poison of choice. The smell of it always brought back vague, brightly coloured memories to Morcault – he had given up alcohol himself some twenty years before, a battle that had taken a lot of winning.

'Jodi, it stinks in here.'

The ship's Navigator was on his bunk, a lean, cadaverous young man with the sunken black-flecked eyes of the psyker. They were red-rimmed as cherries. He wore a black bandana to conceal the third eye that was the mark of his calling. Beside him a data-slate blinked and flickered with the navigational information that the *May-fly* updated every few seconds.

Arnhal always liked to know where he was. If there was one thing that terrified him, it was the thought of being lost. Once a Navigator lost his bearings, it was said the immaterium drew closer to him, and the barrier that separated this universe from the howling chaos of the other thinned. It was how so many of his kind went mad. They looked into the abyss, and found its invitation irresistible.

Some echo of that struggle, some... taint of the darkness hung around Arnhal, as it did about all of his kind. Morcault had always made an effort to treat the Navigator as just another member of his crew, but it was never easy. The sense of the other was always there. That darkness.

'I hate it this far out,' Arnhal said, throwing his forearm across his bruised-looking eyes. 'The Astronomican is a faint gleam, no more. A silver note in the black.'

'Where's your sense of adventure?'

'In the bottle. Pour me some more.'

'You've had enough. I have to get a message to Ultramar quickly, and that may require a warp translation. The vox frequencies out here are as addled as a rotten egg.'

Arnhal sat up. 'That's impossible, captain. The currents of the immaterium are so strong here that–'

Morcault looked away from the psyker's unsettling eyes. 'Spare me, Jodi. I need you to do your job. We have to get back to Zalidar, and speed is of the essence.'

'Then avoid the warp. We might get there in a matter of hours, or it could be months. Something has stirred it up of late. There has been movement here, Morcault. I sense the ripples of it all around.'

'You can do this thing, Jodi. It's what I pay you for, after all.'

'Then respect my professional opinion. That ork scout ship was not here on a whim, nor was it brought by an errant bubble of the immaterium. There is a large presence out there in the black, beyond our augurs, and it has kicked up huge eddies in its wake.'

Morcault leaned on his stick, frowning. 'A fleet?'

'Perhaps.'

The old rogue trader swore under his breath. 'You damned psykers, always coming up with hints and riddles. I want facts, Jodi.'

The young man shrugged his narrow shoulders. 'Facts are a luxury few can afford out here on the edge of the Fringe. But I have other abilities beside Navigation. That is my curse. I will tell you what I know, Morcault. You're the captain. But I would not enter the warp anywhere near here – and that is my last word on it.'

Morcault tapped the pitchthorn on the deck. 'Very well.' He stood lost in thought. Arnhal watched him with the bright, inhuman stare of a raptor staring into the sun. He swung his legs off the bunk.

'Very well. What is this urgent message Ultramar must hear?'

'That there is an ork presence in the system. That vox is stymied for an unusually long interval, even by the standards of the Fringe. You may add to that your own suspicions about this… this fleet, or whatever it is you have sensed. Taken together, the two things are disquieting.'

Arnhal nodded. 'I hear them, Ghent. Like a vast host of babbling minds. They are incoherent, and yet focused.' He waved a hand. 'It comes and goes, but it is no chimera. There is something out there, sure as I sit here.'

Morcault believed him. A drunk Jodi Arnhal might be, but there was no doubting his abilities. He had steered the *Mayfly* through the warp times beyond count in the last eight years, and saved the ship and all their necks more than once.

'Remember when the Chrisoni pirates jumped us last year, and you pulled off that warp entry right under their noses?' Morcault asked him.

Arnhal took a slug from the neck of his bottle and wiped his mouth. 'I try to forget it. We were right between the fire and the pan, and it was sheer luck we did not end up cast clear across the segmentum.'

'Your instincts were sound then. So I believe you now. We will proceed under conventional burn. But the moment you think the currents have calmed enough for warp entry, you must let me know. A lot could depend on it, Jodi.'

'You have my word, captain.' Arnhal swirled the cheap alcohol around in the bottle, staring into the amber depths of it like an augur seeking clues to the future.

'And lay off the booze. It won't do you any good. Believe me, I know.'

The Navigator smiled thinly, showing yellow teeth. 'It's all that lets me sleep.'

'Get some food in you – it'll do you good.'

'I eat the darkness in my dreams, captain. I have not much of an appetite for anything else.'

Again, the inhuman stare. Morcault felt that to meet Jodi's eyes for too long would be to send some part of his own soul on a journey from which there could be no return.

The Navigator smiled sourly, then saluted him, and Morcault left the foul-smelling stateroom with a grimace. The lock went red as soon as he was out of the door.

He wondered how much Jodi had left in him, how much longer the young man would be able to bear staring into the blackness. Navigators burned out fast, this far from civilisation.

Morcault set his palm on the closed door. The boy had such raw talent, and psychic abilities beyond those usually possessed by his calling, but he had never had much in the way of training. The techniques and conditioning that his kind learned on more sophisticated worlds would have saved him from this torment, or ameliorated it at least.

House Arnhal was a Nomadic House, Morcault knew, one of the Beggar Houses of the Navigator caste. Jodi never spoke of what had driven him this far from the civilised space lanes of the Imperium, this far from the comforting guidance of the Astronomican. He did his job, sometimes brilliantly, sometimes with a casual carelessness. But he had always come through for them. And it took a toll; navigating this far out on the Fringe was a taxing occupation.

As it was, Jodi needed a rest, a long one. Perhaps when they got back to Zalidar a place could be found for him in the planet's Administratum, for a while at least. Fennick would no doubt leap at the chance to take on an experienced deep-space Navigator, no matter how damaged. It would mean no more warp translations for the *Mayfly* of course, until a replacement could be found. But Morcault doubted there was one with Jodi's talent within a hundred light years.

'Hang in there, you little drunk,' he said quietly. And then he stepped back and began making his way aft, towards engineering.

HERE, AT LEAST, he stood on firmer ground. Jon Gortyn and his servitors kept the *Mayfly*'s drives humming like a hive. Most of the time, anyway. The chief engineer looked up as Morcault clicked his way into the drive section, and finished replacing one of the ship's precious vacuum suits on the wall-mounting.

Behind him, the drives reared up, two huge cylinders resting on their sides, each twice the height of a moderate hab and surrounded by a jungle of cables and wiring. They thrummed and vibrated so that all this section of the ship seemed to quiver with a life of its own. One was for real-space travel, and the other was for the warp.

The three servitors that helped maintain Engineering went about their business with the deliberate implacability of their kind. Morcault had obtained them twenty years before, by means mostly foul, and Hester had recoded them to work on the *Mayfly* – and had also obliterated all records of their previous service.

Morcault did not like to think about the risks they had taken back then – and even these days, were an agent of the Adeptus Mechanicus to examine the trio it would mean an instant death sentence for all on board. Grand theft of Imperial property, to say nothing of sacrilege. The Adeptus Mechanicus were sticklers for that kind of thing.

Despite this, or perhaps because of it, there was a small shrine by the door of Engineering in which a tiny votive light flickered. Gortyn was not a follower of the Machine-God, the Omnissiah, but he did say the odd prayer, and sometimes, when they were about to career into an especially tight spot, he had been known to anoint the drives with holy oil and mutter a few incantations. Every little helped.

'Hester tells me you want full burn all the way back to Zalidar,' Gortyn said, tapping a few keys and grimacing at what the slate told him.

'Could be. I want speed, at any rate, Jon.'

'Jodi drunk again?'

'Yes. But he has real concerns about the state of the warp in this part of the system. We may try a jump further in.'

Gortyn grunted. He was a huge man, black-haired and bearded, his back as hairy as his chest. He had always reminded Morcault of nothing so much as one of the irascible king-bears of the northern Zalidari forests. His hair was shot through with grey now, and his face was as lined as an empty waterskin, but he still had the arms of a longshoreman.

Despite this, his hands were deft and delicate in their movements. Morcault had seen him rewire an entire drive cogitator using nothing more than pliers, his teeth and the fifty years of expertise that resided in his thick head.

He could build almost anything, given a lot of spare parts and a little time, and he had an intuitive feeling for the operation of the warp drive that amounted almost to a kind of mysticism. Morcault wondered sometimes if his old friend had a little of the psyker in him. In any case, he and Jodi Arnhal made a fine team, though to all intents and purposes they despised each other. Many times, Morcault had had to separate the two when they seemed almost about to come to blows. The Navigator and the engineer.

In some ways, they were more similar than either would ever have admitted. Both saw their jobs as part of their very being. Both were touchy and needed careful handling. Both liked to drink more than was good for them.

'You keep her at full power for more than a day or two, and we'll end up dead in the air,' Gortyn said. He waved at the massive bulk of the thrumming drives. 'These things are the better part of two hundred years old, Ghent, held together by spit and solder and outright prayer. I won't answer for them if you mean to push them like that.'

'You'll keep them together, Jon. You always do.'

'What are we in such a hellfire hurry for anyways? It was one lost ork wreck, not a battleship. Like as not the muddle-headed swine just outran his fuel and was on the drift for who knows how long.'

'I hope that's true,' Morcault said. He sat down on a metal stool, about as comfortable to his old bones as a rock.

'But we can't be taking chances, not with orks. They are not the solitary type. Where there is one, a host will follow. I feel it in my bones.'

'Throne knows, your old bones pick up the oddest things.' Gortyn sighed, rubbing his big knuckled hands together as if washing them. He turned to a bank of monitors and watched the scrolling numbers, reading them as easily as other men read a book. Then he tapped a few keypads and slid the throttle agitators upwards.

The tremble of the drives took on a keener note, and Morcault felt the *Mayfly* give a little jump under his feet, like a horse that has been kicked in the ribs. He stood up and peered at the dials near Gortyn's console, translating their numbers into speed, trajectory and timings in his own head. Then he thumbed the ship's internal vox.

'Bridge, we are at eighty per cent main drive power. Increase velocity when ready.'

'Already on it,' Hester crackled back at him. 'I'll speed her up easy, Ghent. Don't want to rattle this old girl apart.'

'She'll be just fine,' Gortyn snapped. He did not like anyone, even Hester, mocking the ship. He was like a jealous husband when it came to the *Mayfly*.

They would have to close the bridge shutters now, and Morcault could hear the rasp and clank as Hester retracted the augur array. Even the smallest morsel of space debris could drill right through the more delicate parts of the ship's anatomy at this speed. A fair-sized fragment might even puncture the hull.

Morcault had survived an emergency decompression once before, as a young man. Surviving something like that was as rare as living through a lightning strike.

And it was still safer than warp travel.

Morcault's mind filled with a picture of the system and the worlds that wheeled within it, their places in orbit about the central star. It was not often he took the *Mayfly* out this far from Zalidar and he winced as he thought of the untold millions of miles that loomed black between his little ship and the planet that was their goal. Only Chrisos and its moons were farther out from Imperium space than this. They were on the edge of the known galaxy, and in the great black beyond the known star lanes there were Throne knew what kind of xenos lurking.

The monsters in the dark.

He prayed to the Throne itself that Scurrios' ork was a lone wanderer, nothing more.

# SIX

'HERE? HE'S HERE, in the Fringe?' Fennick asked, incredulous.

'It came by priority bulletin not an hour ago,' Boros said. 'You were in Council. A vox transmission relayed from Iax, just letting us know as a courtesy. It means nothing, Lucius, not to us here on Zalidar. His ship will not be coming within a system of us. We are to proceed with normal security measures, and that's all.'

Fennick bit his thumb. 'Marneus Calgar himself. I'll be damned. Boros, what's his route – do we know?'

'You think they'd let slip something like that over the vox? We do know that he'll be visiting a couple of Guard garrisons in the Salem System, and probably the fortress-moon of Gascan. No other details.'

'I wonder if we could...' Fennick's head snapped up. 'Pherias!'

The young aide popped his head round the door. 'Yes, my lord?'

'Who is our best vox specialist?'

'On the staff, sir?'

'Yes, on the staff, damn it.'

Pherias' forehead furrowed. 'Why, it would be Lieutenant Yeager, sir. He's–'

'Get him to the main vox transmitter and await my orders.'

Pherias saluted, thoroughly confused, and left.

Boros began to laugh. 'You're not serious!'

'Why not? We've just completed the space port, Boros. He wouldn't be landing on some mud-covered waste like we used to. I could turn out the entire city for him – think, man – think what it would mean to those millions toiling down there in the manufactoria and the farm-plants – Marneus Calgar himself, here in Zalathras! It would be a coup to end all stories. Do not tell me you would not relish it.'

'Relish it?' Boros' eyes flashed. 'Think of what you are saying, Lucius. We live on a forgotten world, out here on the Fringe, mostly left to our own devices – and you think it would be a fine thing if the Adeptus Astartes came calling? No, Throne help me, I do not relish that prospect. The Angels of the Emperor are not to be lightly invoked.

'Lucius, be careful, I beg you. You are playing with fire when you so much as mention the Lord of Macragge's name on the vox. It makes ears prick up. You might garner the sort of attention we could do without. Lord Joule, for one, would be incandescent at the thought of a backwater like Zalidar hosting the Lord of Ultramar.'

'You're talking like a politician, Boros,' Fennick said with a grim smile. 'I didn't know you had it in you.'

Boros shrugged. 'It is all one. You will be lucky to receive a bare acknowledgement of the request – you know that. The chances of it actually happening are close to nothing.'

Fennick's fey mood dampened somewhat. He set a hand on Boros' shoulder. 'Of course I know that, my friend. But it will be something to have tried, at least.' He smiled again. 'And if it should be let slip amid the officers of the militia that Macragge may be coming to Zalidar, then what's the harm? It will do amazing things for their discipline.'

'For a while. And then when he does not turn up–'

'Trust me on this, Boros. The mere fact that they knew he was asked will be a cold shock to every man-jack of the army, not to mention Vanaheim's agitators. You think they'll dare foment another strike when they hear the rumour? They'll be quaking in their boots.'

'You are the governor,' Boros said ruefully. 'I'm glad my meat and drink is the army, nothing more. I just kill things, and I don't have to issue invitations first.'

IT TOOK MOST of the day for Fennick to get the wording of the communication right. He sent it to Iax, to Espandor, and even managed to get it relayed to Macragge itself, via a tenuous link-up with Parmenio, the Ultramarines' training world. By the time he was done Lieutenant Yeager was thoroughly frazzled and they were both trying to blink away the after-images of the bright scrolling text from their eyes.

For good or ill, it was out there now. The Lord of Macragge had been officially invited to land on Zalidar.

It remained to be seen whether Marneus Calgar thought it worth his attention.

FENNICK HOSTED A dinner a week later in the Governor's Mansion at which all those who mattered in Zalathras were present – even Rear Admiral Glenck did not refuse the last-minute invitation, for word of Fennick's doings had travelled fast, Lieutenant Yeager having been told to be as indiscreet as he liked with it.

They trooped into the great chamber, several score of the richest and most influential people on the planet, their clothing agleam with gold and silver, adorned with gems that had cost the lives of dozens to mine from the western ranges of the Morcault Mountains.

They were preceded by three preachers of the Missionaria Galaxia who walked slowly into the banqueting hall with their bare feet slapping on the stone, swinging incense holders as they came that lent a blue smoke to the humid atmosphere.

On either side of the entering throng were lines of serfs in the livery of the Administratum; shaven-headed, collared and anonymous, they were indentured servants, petty criminals and the irredeemably poor. All had undergone rigorous conditioning, and they hung their heads in apprehension, forbidden to so much as glance at the guests.

The blessing of the Emperor was invoked by a preacher, and they all stood for a moment in silence before the places set at the immensely long table that ran down almost the entire length of the banqueting hall. Zalidar was not an especially rich world, but Fennick had made an effort for the evening, and the tabletop was a blaze of silverware. Melted down, it could have bought a starship.

They took their places, the serfs sliding the heavy chairs in behind every guest, scurrying back and forth to the kitchens on the level below, pouring blood-warm liquor into glasses and goblets of stone-crystal. From a gallery above, a blind choir sang quietly. Their song was so soft it was almost one with the drifting fragrance of the incense.

Rich people watching each other, smiling with their mouths, clinking glasses, eating careful bites of food that had taken days to source and prepare. Along this table were arrayed friends and enemies, co-conspirators, business partners, bitter foes. All of them stuffed to bursting with ambition and egotism, the driving engines of every society. Outside the battlefield, this was the other kind of war. It spilled less blood, but often had as profound a consequence for the future of a world as any meeting of armies.

Fennick sat at the head of the table in his scarlet sash with the Thrax medal on his breast. He had made sure that a couple of empty-headed ladies of no consequence were to his immediate right and left, so as not to show favouritism to any of the important families present. The real movers and shakers of his world were farther down the table, with Boros planted in their midst to listen in to what was going on.

The choir sang, sightless children with voices pure as the dawn. The courses came and went in a blaze of silver and spice. The glasses were filled and emptied. The room grew hot, the glims a stuttering of yellow glows.

Fennick studied his guests. Many rich families sat at that table, but only three really mattered.

The Vanaheims, father and sons, were the richest conglomerate on the planet. They had financed the building of Kalgatt Spire, on the condition that they should have a veritable palace of their own on the top of it. The head of the family, Kurt Vanaheim, was a capable, black-haired man very like Boros, only paler. He had been many things in his youth, it was rumoured, not all of them legal, and he had moved to Zalidar lock, stock and barrel to get ahead of angry creditors, and even, it was rumoured, the Adeptus Arbites themselves.

Setting up a logging operation deep in the Tagus, and then diversifying into the Ballansyr Quarries, he had amassed a vast fortune, an ugly wife and three ambitious sons who hated each other almost as much as their father despised them.

They had grown up soft, handed life on a plate, and Kurt Vanaheim was anything but soft. But he indulged them, for he wanted them to be gentlemen, part of a caste he had been struggling to enter all his life.

And yet, for all his riches, he had no title to pass down to them – that was what he craved, above all else. Were Zalidar to move into full Imperial compliance, then the Administratum would surely award his industry and power with some bauble. It might mean little to other men, but for Vanaheim it would be the crown of his career. The coming of the Adeptus Astartes to Zalidar might mean many things to different people, but to Kurt Vanaheim it would be seen as an opportunity, first and foremost. Men like him grew fat on war and all that came with it. They created industries that fed it, and in return, the Imperium protected them. In the galaxy that mankind struggled to survive within, everything must ultimately oil the cogs of the great machine, the monster that consumed them all. War was the natural state of things. Just because it had not yet visited Zalidar did not mean that the planet could remain untouched by it. Imperial compliance would mean a whole gear change in the way the Administratum operated. Fennick was prepared for that eventuality. He knew that the industrialist was, too.

Vanaheim raised his glass to Fennick now, and sipped at the blood-warm wine, the glim-lights shining through it. Fennick answered him. They were competitors, in a way. Fennick had authority, Vanaheim money, and sometimes it was hard to tell which mattered most.

Fifteen years before, Fennick had ordered the chief businessmen and landowners of the planet to turn over their private armies to the militia for Boros to command, and Vanaheim had done so without a murmur – five thousand men, just like that.

He had been counting on retaining their loyalty, and hence a power base in the army itself. But Boros had worked hard and long, and eventually won them over – they were his now, body and soul, proud to serve in the First Zalidari Regiment, the most senior formation in the armed forces. Vanaheim had miscalculated, and neither he nor the other kingpins of Zalathras could now hold the threat of armed insurrection over the Administratum of the planet.

The Vanaheims worked in other ways after that, through the labour organisations, always three steps removed from the angry workers their agents incited to riot. Their aim was not to destabilise the Administratum, but to remind it of their power, to be called upon to mediate. It was an open secret that Vanaheim aimed at the governorship for one of his sons one day, Fennick being unmarried and childless. He had links leading all the way to Ultramar itself, it was rumoured, and was already greasing the process.

But at the height of the labour disputes, Fennick had beaten Vanaheim's striking malcontents with the swift efficiency that the Astra Militarum had taught him. After a dozen of the ringleaders had been taken out and shot, the strikers had faded quickly away, and Vanaheim's schemes had gone back into the shadows.

In the meantime, Vanaheim's companies had bought everything he could lay his hands on, and he went into construction with every asset he possessed. Rosquin's bank – the old man was here now, and Fennick raised a glass to him also – and Vanaheim's construction gangs had built the city walls. The main southern entrance to Zalathras was called Vanaheim Gate in recognition of this, and, as if to do justice to his namesake, Vanaheim had fortified it with looming towers and a huge barbican – old-fashioned, but immensely strong.

And now Kurt Vanaheim was entirely respectable, a senior member of the Council, a politician and grandee. The gangster who had first come to Zalidar was no more.

Everyone gets something named after them except me, Fennick thought with a tinge of self-mockery. Well, if the Lord of Macragge turns up by some happy chance, I will be remembered as the man who brought him here. That will last longer even than a name carved in stone. It will be worth more than riches, or a palace on a spire.

Vanaheim and Rosquin – these were the two richest families on Zalidar, and the most influential. Ferdia Rosquin must be seventy years old now, but he had a mind like a steel trap, and his bank had branches in half a dozen systems in the Fringe.

Why he had transferred his headquarters here was still something of a mystery to Fennick, unless he saw in the jungle-clad planet some of the potential that Fennick himself saw.

Zalidar was young. There was land here for the taking, billions of hectares of it for those who were hardy enough and brave enough to claim it. Rosquin financed new settlers and in return they mortgaged their claims to him. Already, he owned the equivalent of a small continent, the claims of those who had defaulted on their payments reverting to his bank. For many had died out there in the Tagus while fighting to clear the land and fend off the jungle beasts. Rosquin took the land of these dead pioneers and resold it. The gift that keeps on giving.

He too had sons, square, unimaginative bean-counting men, but he did not crave titles for them. He seemed to find money an end in itself. Fennick's Administratum was hip deep in debt to the Rosquin bank, and the old man seemed to like it that way. Boros commanded the army, but it was Rosquin money that paid their wages.

The last of the triumvirate of powerful families on Zalidar were the Lascelles. Only ten years on the world, they owned a shipping company that dominated all trade between Zalidar and the other scattered planets of the Eastern Fringe. Their patriarch, Gram Lascelle, had only been seen on Zalidar once, back when the foundations of the spaceport had been laid. He was a flamboyant but shrewd man, flash and substance combined. Without his expertise and advice, Fennick doubted that the spaceport would have been built at all. Inevitably, it was going to be named after him. Lascelle's Landing they called it down in the lower city, and the name had stuck.

He had left his son, Roman Lascelle, here to keep an eye on this branch of the company his own grandfather had founded, and the son had turned out to be a rake and a dandy, a fighter of duels, popular with women and loathed by their husbands. Not a man to cross lightly, even though he was not yet thirty. Perhaps Gram had thought the son could be kept out of trouble here on this frontier world. Or out of the way, at least.

Fennick raised a glass to Roman Lascelle, also, and the stunning courtesan he had brought to the table. Lascelle always had a hint of mockery in his eyes, and he grinned now as he raised a glass in answer – a feline young man who also delighted in hunting, and was a skilled pilot. He found Zalidari society to be something of a bore, and left the business side of his father's company to the clerks and accountants while he spent as much money as he decently could and lived large on the generous stipend his family allotted him. Even so, his gambling debts were the stuff of open gossip, and the Rosquin bank had offered him loan after loan to keep him afloat, for his father was one of their chief investors.

Roman Lascelle was one of those gifted, cursed young men for whom life would always be a bore and a chore, who would squander their gifts for want of a proper outlet.

Well, he did, at least, lend a certain vitality to the table.

Fennick sighed, looking down that table at the finery and the chatter. His own meat – as fine a haunch of gruebuck as had ever been grilled – congealed on the plate before him. While he felt that he was building something lasting and worthwhile here on Zalidar, there were times when he thought he understood that old nomad, Ghent Morcault.

To be one's own master, subject to no one – not the orders of the Administratum, or the intrigues of ambitious businessmen... Perhaps the old man was not such a fool after all.

But the feeling passed. He was governor of an Imperium world, an Imperium he had bled for, a system he believed in. If he were not here to politick with the Lascelles and Vanaheims and Rosquins of the world, someone else would take his place, and the lower orders, the little people who quarried stone and raised crops and fought in the militia – they would be the poorer for it.

He sat here for them as much as for himself. And he would never forget that, no more than he could forget the scars he carried, and the black memories of battle that haunted his dreams.

Let us see him here, just once, he thought. Marneus Calgar, that most puissant of lords – the greatest living of the Adeptus Astartes.

And then all the dealing and wheeling will have been worth it, and the poor people who built this city with their bare hands will have something to tell their grandchildren. A story that will endure down the generations.

Throne, let it be so.

Boros would have told him to be careful what he wished for.

It had been a long time since the destruction of Thrax, since Lieutenant Fennick had watched in awe and horror the immense power of the Adeptus Astartes ships laying waste to an entire planet. The wider Imperium was a place perpetually on the brink, consumed by the struggle for survival in an inimical universe where nightmares stalked the dark. Those on Zalidar thought they knew danger in the cries that echoed out of the Tagus, in the deadly fauna of the jungles. But these things were nothing compared to the horrors that flooded the space between the stars. Zalidar had been forgotten, even sheltered, in its brief history of human settlement. The Planetary Administratum had been largely benign, because it could afford to be so – there were no crippling tithes of men and materiel to be forwarded at rigidly stated intervals to Ultramar. Not yet.

That would no doubt change, if the Lord of Macragge ever set foot on the planet. Zalidar would be admitted as a full member of the Imperium, with all the prestige and hardship such a step entailed.

The reality of this black and bitter universe would then be brought home to these aristocrats and dilettantes. And Fennick for one looked forward to it.

'My lord governor!' Roman Lascelle called up from the middle part of the table. 'Have you received back any word from Macragge about this invitation you have sent to the Ultramarines Chapter Master?' The young man's eyes danced with devilment.

'That is a matter for the Administratum, for now,' Fennick said, a smile easing the sharpness of his tone.

'It has been all over the city for the past week. The Lord of Macragge himself, asked to set foot on humid little Zalidar! Was this a notion of your own, or did the Council agree on it?'

Fennick's smile curdled on his face. Two of the most powerful Council members, Kurt Vanaheim and Ferdia Rosquin, were seated not six feet from Lascelle, and were now watching the exchange with a less than discreet interest.

'That is a matter for the Administratum,' he repeated levelly.

'Come, Fennick – the prime movers and shakers of the planet's Administratum are all seated about this table! Why organise such a well-attended dinner if not to broach the good news to us. We are eager to hear – has Macragge responded to your gallant request?'

'Not yet,' Fennick said. His smile was now a rictus.

'Ah, a pity.' Roman Lascelle pursed his red lips and shook his head. 'Still, what could one expect of such presumption? I applaud your initiative, Fennick, I truly do. But it would be something of a humiliation if not even a reply were forthcoming, would it not? No doubt Lord Joule will commiserate with you on the failure of such a brazen initiative.'

'No doubt,' Fennick said. He collected himself, raised a glass to Lascelle – though he would rather have thrown it at the handsome rake's face. 'But it is something to have tried, is it not?'

'It is,' Lascelle said. He smiled, and raising his glass in reply he bobbed it in a kind of salute. 'It is good to know our governor is a man of such risk-taking enterprise.'

'We are all risk-takers here,' old Ferdia Rosquin spoke up unexpectedly. He looked up the table, his face as dry and lined as a withered apple. His eyes glittered like those of some nocturnal rodent. 'Else we would not be out here, on the Fringe, in the first place. But to take a risk is one thing. To open oneself to humiliation is quite another.'

'Which is why I issued the invitation personally,' Fennick said, raising his voice a little – though the chatter around the table had fallen as the guests listened in on the exchange. 'Your name, Rosquin – and

Vanaheim's too for that matter – were not connected to it. If there is any fallout from my... presumption, it will be on my head alone.'

Rosquin shared a look with Kurt Vanaheim opposite. He smiled a little. 'So be it,' he said.

WHEN THE PLATES were taken away they rose from the long table with glasses of the black cordial that had been fermented on Zalidar from the time of the first settlement – a bracing, bitter liqueur, which Fennick drank at a gulp, needing the astringency and fire of the alcohol in his brain. The party made its way to the great balcony that overlooked Zalathras, and they looked out at the warm night, the teeming lights of the city below. It was a sight that always calmed Fennick and put things into perspective.

He found Lascelle at his elbow, the perfumed courtesan left behind. The younger man sipped his black drink and grimaced. 'Nothing more than jungle juice,' he said. 'I have never acquired a taste for it, not in ten years,'

'Give it ten more. You'll grow to love it,' Fennick told him.

'I would have done the same,' Lascelle said, that cat-like smile upon his face.

'What?'

'Your invitation. It was reckless, impulsive. Men like Vanaheim and Rosquin would never have signed off on it, but it will sit well with the lower orders. The streets are still running with the rumour of it. Bravo, my lord Fennick. You still have the capacity to surprise.'

Fennick looked at him. Roman Lascelle was a hard man to quantify. The rake and the dandy were out there for all to see, but there was more behind that sneering face than met the eye. A kind of hunger that Fennick half understood.

Was it for fame? Glory? He did not care about money, except for how it served his purposes. And he possessed a name already, one widely respected across the Fringe and in Ultramar itself. If he chose, he could be more influential than anyone else in the room, but he did not play politics, except when it amused him to do so.

'One must keep grasping at passing stars,' Fennick told the younger man. 'Otherwise–'

'Otherwise a man dries out – as Ferdia Rosquin has,' Lascelle said. 'I understand you more than you know, my lord. You are no mere manager or accountant. You have a real passion for this primitive little world of ours. I respect that. Sometimes I wish I shared it. It would make life infinitely more diverting.'

'You don't much care for Zalidar, do you, Lascelle?'

Roman Lascelle stared into his black drink. 'I am in exile here. Zalidar is my punishment, my prison. My father sent me to this world so that I might not disgrace his name in more important places.'

He shrugged, and emptied his glass, mouth twisting on the bitterness of it.

'I had my suspicions.'

'Rumour flies ahead of truth, every time,' Lascelle said.

'So why not engage with your gaolers?' Fennick asked him. 'Make something of yourself on Zalidar. You have the ability, I know that.'

Lascelle looked at him, mouth still twisted ruefully. 'And try to be the son my father wants? I would not give him the satisfaction, Fennick. He packed me off here to rot, and rot I shall.'

'Zalidar is too small for you – is that it?'

'Something like that.' Lascelle looked into his empty glass. 'As you say, give it another ten years. Perhaps Zalidar will grow on me. Or perhaps I shall find something here to care about. Stranger things have happened.'

He stared out over the sea of lights that were Zalathras below, and beyond the cleared plains, the howling darkness of the Tagus, that limitless forest which encroached upon their world.

'I hope you succeed, Fennick,' he said. 'I hope Marneus Calgar himself comes here, sets foot on our forgotten little planet. That is something I would like to see too. A glimpse of something greater.'

He patted Fennick on the shoulder, and, before the governor could reply, he was away, gliding through the congregated crowd at the balcony, ignoring the stares, the attempts to draw him into banter and conversation. Fennick watched him go, frowning.

Boros joined him, wiping the sweat off his broad face.

'That popinjay,' he said. 'If he were less of a name, I'd have cut him down to size myself before now.'

'You think you could, Boros?' Fennick asked the colonel.

Boros snorted. 'That whelp?' Then his eyes fell. 'Well, perhaps. He is damned quick with a blade and a sidearm, and I suppose I am not as young as I once was.'

Fennick smiled. 'We are none of us as young as we once were. But that boy, Boros, is a better man than we think. I believe that, given the right circumstances, he could be a decent man.'

Boros laughed. 'You surprise me, Lucius. Are you taking a shine to him?'

'I wouldn't go that far. He's the sort would set a city on fire to see how bright it would burn. He is made for other things.'

'He's a damn nuisance.'

'Let us hope he finds some way to channel his energies before too long, or I fear he could become an enemy – and a fearsome one at that. And he would not become so out of spite, or conviction – but because to work alongside us would bore him.'

'Well, let's hope his gambling and his whoring keeps him fully occupied then,' Boros said.

'Indeed. We have troubles enough as it is.'

Boros snorted. 'Troubles!' He and Fennick looked at one another. Finally the governor smiled.

'I know, my friend. Sometimes I forget what trouble truly is.'

'They have never known it, not here,' Boros said, his broad face cast in a sneer. 'You and I have seen whole regiments seared to black meat by the flames of monsters, Lucius. The folk here – they have no idea of the reality of the Imperium. They think it all some kind of grand game for their amusement and enrichment. I sometimes wish–'

'No,' Fennick said quickly. 'Do not wish for anything, Boros. Trouble always comes calling, in the end. There is no point in wishing for it to come sooner.'

# SEVEN

'We are somewhat scattered,' the Lord of Macragge said mildly, looking at the multicoloured holographic map that floated above the plinth in the middle of the room. It turned slowly, in time with the slow convolutions of the spiral arm in which Ultramar floated.

A vast region of space, full of teeming worlds as bright as jewels, and between them the orbital fortresses of the Ultramarines, layer upon layer of them, set amid minefields, bristling with armaments, all protecting the trade lanes and serried worlds that owed Macragge their fealty.

And at the centre of them, Macragge itself, with its populous cities, its green coasts and howling mountains, its snowbound polar fortresses, as well as the immense donjon that housed their Chapter: the Fortress of Hera – with the Temple of Corrections and great Guilliman's shrine at the heart of it.

A holy place, a place built to survive the convulsions of the ages. A place of pilgrimage, and an arsenal of war.

But they were a long way from Macragge now.

'Second Company with the *Victus* task force is confident that their campaign will be brought to a successful close within four to five Terran months, my lord,' Veteran Brother Orhan said. 'The *Deo Volante* fleet with Third is still heavily engaged in the systems beyond Iax and will be for some considerable time. The traitor forces there are proving stubborn.'

'Has Fabian asked for reinforcements?' Calgar demanded at once.

'No, my lord. He is confident that with the Guard divisions assigned he can mop up resistance on the cleansed worlds and still proceed with the offensive on schedule. Third has taken only minor casualties thus far and the *Deo Volante* reports that no capital-class enemy ships have been encountered.'

'Very good. What of Fifth?'

'Fifth Company is still in close pursuit of the eldar craftworld Karan-Ske in open space beyond Bathor. Our last vox reports from Task Force *Cestus* suggest that the xenos will make a fight of it, but only on ground of their own choosing. They are displaying the fickle cunning of their species, with hit and run raids on the fleet, but as yet there has been no major engagement.'

'There will not be,' Calgar said. 'Not if I know the eldar. They will draw Galenus out as far as they can before they stand and make a fight of it – that is their way.'

'Shall I set a limit on the pursuit, my lord?' Brother Orhan asked.

'No. The Karan-Ske is a threat to our flank which cannot be ignored. Tell Galenus he is to pursue to the death.'

'Yes, my lord.'

'What of Second? Still no word from Sicarius?'

There was a pause, slight but perceptible. Orhan was chiding himself for a fault that was not his. Calgar smiled inwardly, though his face remained as impassive as always. Very little that went on in his mind showed upon his face. It was something that centuries of service had bred into him.

'Second Company and Fleet *Ignis Deus* have sent no word in eleven

Terran day-cycles, my lord. When they last reported, the bulk of the armada was on course for Golsoria, in the Fringe, still in desultory contact with that tau incursion.'

'The tau are known for their facility with jamming communications. They are probably flooding the vox and degrading the signal,' old Proxis said with a grunt. His hands shifted in the sleeves of his robe, as though his massive fists were clenching under the dark blue fabric.

'Agreed,' Calgar said. 'There is no cause for concern as yet. The *Ignis Deus* fleet is strong enough to take on any force the tau care to throw at them. Sicarius will get something through, if he has to. Brother Orhan, what of Seventh?'

Orhan tapped some buttons on the plinth before him, and the bright holographic map shifted round.

'Seventh Company holds its station four light years out from Prandium. Captain Ixion reports that the border with the Fringe is quiet, and he remains in a position to reinforce Second if called upon.'

'He'd like that,' Proxis growled with some humour. 'How long have they been out there, Orhan?'

'Some eight months, my lord.'

'He'll be getting bored, I shouldn't wonder,' Proxis said.

'He will stay in reserve,' Calgar said quietly. 'He is the only reserve we have at the moment, barring Guard formations. And even they are based far to the galactic west. Signal Ixion this day, Orhan. Impress upon him the need to remain at full readiness. It is wearisome, but necessary.'

'Yes, my lord.'

His mind juggled the various factors, the several campaigns that his beloved Chapter was engaged in. He saw in his mind's eye the myriad fleets out there in the darkness, all intent on violence, all proceeding into the belly of war.

It was as it should be. The enemies that threatened Ultramar were all being met head on, far from the ordered realm which was his particular responsibility. Billions of men and women upon the worlds that comprised it knew little or nothing of the wars that were being fought on their behalf out in the spaces between the stars. That also was as it should be.

*Thy will be done,* he thought. And he bent his head in a moment of silent prayer, while in the briefing chamber around him the members of his staff stood silent also.

Marneus Augustus Calgar raised his head at last. The others stood stock still with the iron discipline of their kind. This was an informal briefing, and they were all in the deep-hooded robes that the Adeptus Astartes donned for prayer and contemplation. Towering shapes – giants, they would be, to a normal human being – they were like ancient statuary from a bygone age. The briefing chamber rose up around them in buttressed arches, like the space in some ancient temple of worship – but the walls and pillars were of titanium and ceramite, and the space thrummed with the low tenor of the drive engines.

They were on board Marneus Calgar's personal transport, the *Fidelis*, and beyond these walls and bulkheads wheeled the infinite dark of the void.

Proxis broke the silence. As the Ancient of the honour guard he was one of the few in the Chapter who would speak in the presence of his Chapter Master as easily as he would with the lowliest neophyte – and Calgar valued him for that, amongst many other things.

'The last time we were this far out in the Fringe, we were chasing Behemoth,' he said, and he met Calgar's eye. 'It is a long way from Macragge, my lord.'

'And yet we are still within the bounds of Ultramar as it was once understood,' the Chapter Master answered. 'I want to see for myself how the Fringe is faring, Proxis. The xenos destroyed so many worlds, but on others mankind is thriving. It will do them good to realise that the Imperium has not forgotten them.

'I want to see for myself what has become of the Eastern Fringe in the last half-century. Our rebuilding of Ultramar's heart is complete, but we have neglected this far corner of Imperial space. Too often, the only time men see the Adeptus Astartes on their world is when that world is on the brink of destruction. We are the guardians of mankind, and yet we are known as the Angels of Death.

'I would not have the Ultramarines viewed that way. Guilliman would not have wished his descendants to be mere figures of terror. Other Chapters may see things differently. But in this, I adhere to the teachings of our primarch.'

Proxis bowed slightly. 'My lord, I would never gainsay your wisdom. I only wish to point out that we are a single vessel, far from home in a remote region of the Imperium, and on board we carry the Chapter Master of the Ultramarines. That is a precious cargo.'

Calgar did allow a smile now. 'What's wrong, Proxis? Have you lost your taste for adventure?'

The Ancient cocked an eye at his Chapter Master. 'Never. Lead on, lord, and whither thou goest, I goest.' Then he quoted the old saying: '*We are the Pilgrims, Master. We shall go always a little farther.*'

They had fought together time out of mind. Proxis had been one of those who had carried Calgar from the smoking hecatomb of Cold Steel Ridge. Calgar simply nodded in response. No other words were necessary.

THE FIDELIS WAS a small craft by the standards of the Imperium. Less than half a mile long, the hull was based around the engineering compartment of a falchion-class destroyer, with the drives of that class. But it carried much more in the way of short-range armament. Batteries of lasburners dotted its hull, and it had a pair of torpedo tubes as well as an array of plasma cannons in its angular bow.

It had been designed for speed and endurance, and was only lightly armoured, though its generators were the most powerful that could be fitted in such a small hull, and provided power for a series of heavy void shields that could absorb a tremendous amount of punishment.

The human crew of the vessel numbered some eleven hundred, not counting the numerous servitors, and most of these lived their lives upon the ship. In the belly of the *Fidelis* were hydroponic farms and a small munitions manufactorum. It could, if needed, operate independently of the fleet and remain in deep space for months, even years. But it was designed primarily for swift inter-system travel, not combat. In the launch bays were half a dozen Thunderhawks and an array of unarmed shuttles, but though there was a hand-picked company of Astra Militarum on board, the only Adeptus Astartes were Marneus Calgar himself and his entourage: barely two dozen Space Marines in all.

The *Fidelis* was part ceremonial yacht, part command centre; its communications array was as powerful and well staffed as that of a capital ship and it had some of the best astropaths in the segmentum to back it up.

Usually it had a squadron of destroyers as escort, but Calgar had sent these off to reinforce a Guard offensive against the Fringe pirates some weeks ago, and now the vessel travelled alone.

It was not unprecedented for the Chapter Master of the Ultramarines, Lord of Macragge, to travel with so little fanfare, but it was unusual, even within Ultramar itself.

Calgar preferred it that way, at least for now. His Chapter's fighting companies were scattered all over that broad region of space of which he was suzerain, and he had been visiting what combat formations he could, both Adeptus Astartes and Astra Militarum, to gain first-hand intelligence of their various campaigns – and also, it had to be admitted, to boost morale. The *Fidelis* travelled faster alone in any case, and now that the destroyers had been left behind, its peerless Navigator, Geyr Van Brandt, could proceed on warp jumps without worrying about the other ships.

It was as good a time as any to nose out beyond the more well-travelled space lanes, and hear the pulse of the Astronomican grow ever fainter as they travelled into the sparse worlds of the Galactic East. There were planets out there that belonged to the Imperium in name only, whole systems that had been left to fend for themselves for decades.

Scattered news came through, of course, carried by traders and caught on vox, and there was some commerce with the border worlds. But no real interaction. The fading pulse of the distant Astronomican was one reason. The wars that had passed over the region were another. Hive Fleet Behemoth had scoured untold Fringe planets clean of human life, and although the Chapter had eradicated that filth, the scars remained.

We serve mankind, Calgar told himself. That is the Codex. Some Chapters come close to forgetting that. The Ultramarines will not. Not so long as I lead them, and the Emperor wills it.

The bridge of the *Fidelis* was a long nave-like space flanked by banks of cogitators, data screens and rank on rank of murmuring servitors. Calgar strode down it as one would down the length of a great planetbound cathedral, towards the dais at one end above which reared void-shielded viewports.

He was clad now in the plain suit of Mark VI armour that he wore on ship, with a long-familiar Corvus helm mag-locked to his hip. The ancient battle artefacts in which he had fought on battlefields beyond count were on display in the vessel's chapel for all the crew to visit, attended by a pair of tech-priests whose sole task was to maintain and repair them, for they were priceless. The Gauntlets had been worn by Guilliman himself, and the artificer power armour was almost as old, repaired times beyond count, and reverenced as a relic from a bygone age. One did not strap on such holy objects in everyday use; they were reserved for the glory and cataclysm of war alone.

Gothically carved balustrades and buttresses arced fantastically above Calgar's head, many gilded and garishly painted, as he strode down the nave. There were alcoves wherein votive lights flickered, a softer light than the blinking of the endless consoles, and rivers of cables coursed like pythons of old Terra in protective channels. Colour-coded and painted with runes, they shone with supplicatory oils, and in the air was the blue scent of incense. The ship's tech-priest, Masala, knew his work, and kept the machine-spirit of the *Fidelis* placated with proper ritual, aided by a small staff of underlings and servitors. He and the shipmaster, Martyn Tyson, worked well together.

They had served the vessel together these twenty years, and Calgar felt no need for the *Fidelis* to have an Adeptus Astartes commander. The Ultramarines needed every battle-brother in the fighting line, now and always. It was not for them to see to the minutiae of the fleet. They gave orders and saw to it that they were obeyed. They did not concern themselves with the warp and weft of voidsmanship, though there was in their ranks an enormous level of expertise in that particular skill.

Tyson bowed as Calgar approached the dais, and Masala inclined his hooded head, the ocular implants in his face shining red. Around them, banks of servitors hard-wired into the ship systems muttered to themselves in binaric, and two enginseers sat immobile on tracks, their heads twitching back and forth as information was relayed to them in floods of data.

As well as these, there were several human officers, fleet lieutenants by their badges, and a pair of armsmen with laspistols strapped to their thighs. The dais was large enough to accommodate them all with ease, for it had been built with the Adeptus Astartes in mind, and the floor under their feet was not metal or alloy, but the stone of Macragge itself, brought here and embedded within the ship, a fragment of the home world. It was smoothed and pitted by the passage of centuries of feet – for the *Fidelis* was old, by the terms of normal humanity. In comparison to the millennia-old cruisers that the Ultramarines fleet possessed, though, it was a mere parvenu.

'My lord, I am glad to have you back aboard,' Tyson said. He was a short, burly man with a shaved head and a cogitator implant behind one ear, the better to stay linked to the running of the ship.

'I trust the Guard welcomed you with suitable fanfare,' Masala said. His mechadendrites were folded inside his robe. Save for the face, his form was almost human under the scarlet robe of the Adeptus Mechanicus.

'It was satisfactory,' Calgar said briefly. The Astra Militarum outpost on Istria VI had paraded before him for half a morning, two full divisions of Ultramar-recruited men who would remember that morning for the rest of their lives.

But to Marneus Calgar it was just one more ceremonial occasion. He had learned more from the briefing by the colonel in charge. All was well. All was quiet. This sector of the Fringe had not seen a xenos incursion of any strength since the Behemoth wars. It was well garrisoned all the same, as were most of the Ultramar border systems.

Most. Not all.

To defend everything is to defend nothing. Calgar knew that. And yet he had spread his forces thin in the last two years or so. His strategy veered towards risk, even hubris. If another tyranid fleet appeared, there would be a scramble of weeks, if not months, before a powerful armada could be gathered to counter it.

One of the gambles he made in defending a vast sea of space with limited resources. The same might be said of the entire Imperium of Man. It had been thus since the Heresy. It had been thus since the Fall itself.

'My lord, we have received a vox communication, relayed through Parmenio,' Tyson went on. 'It is somewhat irregular, from a border world far into the Fringe. Zalidar. I confess I had to consult the data archives to even find the place. Its governor, one Lucius Fennick, has extended an invitation to you personally.

'It would seem this Fennick has just completed the construction of a functioning spaceport, the first in that system, and would–' here Tyson cleared his throat as if embarrassed – 'and would be honoured if you would make personal inspection of it and the world he is entrusted with. Zalidar is not yet fully Imperial-compliant. It is a jungle planet, and–'

'Fennick,' Calgar said thoughtfully. His mind worked on the name, roaming over masses of data in the blink of an eye.

'He fought in the Thrax campaign with the 387th Armoured. A battlefield commission, and then transfer to Zalidar with a single company. Zalidar is a new world, settled barely a half-century. But it was not ravaged by Behemoth. Fennick did well. It is why I confirmed him as governor. A temporary expedient which I have not yet seen fit to revise.'

'A mere Guard lieutenant?' Masala asked in his clipped, metallic tone.

'He showed promise. And from what I could gauge, he cared more about his responsibilities than his ambitions. Such men are unusual – and thus valuable.'

Masala bowed.

'So, he wants me to see what he has made of his planet, does he?' Calgar said, and his face lightened a little. 'The man is enterprising.'

'He borders on insolence,' Tyson said. 'The vox did not go through channels, but was widecast to several of our bases. Lord Joule seeks your permission to chastise him for his presumption. The security risk alone–'

Calgar held up a hand. 'Lord Joule will do no such thing. And as for security, shipmaster, do you really think that my presence here in the Fringe is still a secret? No.' He paused a moment. In his mind he was calculating revised timings, possible warp trajectories, and overlaying them with his timetable as it currently stood.

'If we make best speed for three days we will be able to spare sixteen hours on Zalidar before making a warp jump for Seventh Company. You will make it so, shipmaster. It will do no harm to have a look over what this Fennick fellow has achieved on Zalidar. The planet must be in good shape, or he would not have been so keen for me to see it.' He smiled thinly. 'Are we agreed?'

Tyson bowed. Masala's oculars glinted. 'Your calculations are correct,' the tech-priest said.

'I am relieved to hear it,' Calgar said dryly. 'They have no astropaths on Zalidar, or I miss my guess. Get a vox relayed there. Let this Fennick fellow know that in three days we shall make planetfall.'

'You do him too much honour,' Proxis said.

'It is not a question of honour, brother,' Calgar told the Ancient warrior. 'I am not unaware of what my office means to others. I am a name in this part of the galaxy, one which men recognise. Sometimes men's hearts need to be lifted by a bolt from the blue.'

'Ultramarine blue,' Proxis said, and he bared his teeth in a fierce grin. Marneus Calgar actually laughed.

THE FIDELIS PICKED up speed and altered course for the Zalidar System. At the same time as it was travelling through the Fringe from the Galactic West, so from the far darkness of the East something else was moving through the serried systems and scattered, isolated worlds of mankind.

A cloud, a shadow, it appeared at first on the augur scopes of far-travelling freighters and cargo-tramps. As it drew nearer, so it thickened. It solidified into what seemed to be a cluster of ragged, mismatched asteroids, hundreds of them wheeling through the Eastern Fringe in a formationless skein of dots and blobs that lit up the sky.

There were no astrophysicists in this part of the Imperium to theorise on it. Perhaps a far-flung moon had disintegrated under the tidal gravitics of the stars and was now bound on a long, slow sweep through the universe. Except that the asteroids were moving quickly, and now and then an energy bloom would flare up within them. Two alloy-rich meteors smashing together in their dark transit perhaps. It was an interesting phenomenon, but not a unique one. Many strange things were seen and told of this far out from the heart of human space.

No one on any world of any consequence followed the path of the asteroid cluster, so they did not note that it changed course from time to time. Some asteroids left the main body and crashed down on sparsely populated moons and worlds that it encountered in its path, but the main body of the cluster remained together.

It travelled in an unerring line, and if a voidsman of any skill had taken out a galactic map and plotted its course, they would have found that it led squarely through the Zalidar System, and that it would make up the distance in a matter of a few Terran days.

But no one took any note of it. Those that had were all dead already. The asteroid cluster left darkness and silence in its wake, worlds going quiet as it passed them. Such was the unreliability of the vox in this part of the galaxy that their voices were not missed – not yet.

The creeping silence came on unremarked, unnoticed. The massive asteroids with their momentary energy blooms coursed through system after system, and cohered as they came, drawing together. Their course steadied. In a matter of days, they would be in the skies of Zalidar itself.

# EIGHT

IT WAS SOMETHING to be vindicated. Fennick had overseen the hanging of the banners on the Vanaheim Gate himself. Sixty-five feet long, they were deep blue, with the sigil of the Ultramarines near their crest. Crowds had come to see them hung, and more massive hordes cheered the governor now as he walked among them, hemmed in by the escort from the First Zalidari, all white-faced and sweating under their helmets. His grav-car was waiting just inside the gate, ready to take him to the spaceport. Ready to meet Marneus Calgar himself.

There was a quivering apprehension about Zalathras that he had never known before, an almost religious sense of anticipation that was three parts outright fear.

He felt it himself. And he wondered again at his own temerity.

I did this, he thought as he walked down the broad Avenue of Dromios towards the gate. And Throne, I hope it does not blow up in my face.

The cheering crowds were out in their hundreds of thousands. Not just from Zalathras itself – half the surrounding countryside was within the walls of the city also. The news had run across the planet like wildfire.

In between the cheers, that sense of wonder, of awe. Despite the troops on the streets, there would be no public order issues here today. Fennick knew that. The crowds stood like an assembled army. They did not quite know what to expect, but they knew the legends of the Adeptus Astartes, written in terrible letters across a thousand rumours and tall tales. Mercy was not a quality associated with them. There would be no unseemliness here today.

WORD HAD COME through from the *Fidelis*, the personal transport of Marneus Calgar, not three days ago. The Master of Ultramar would be touching down on Zalidar this morning. A small part of the most glorious history of the Imperium of Man would be written upon this long-forgotten world, if only for a few hours.

Now, Vanaheim, Fennick thought, waving at the crowds, how do you like that?

Boros was waiting for him, and there were other grav-cars there. They had all, Fennick noted, been repainted in Ultramarine blue. The Council members stood by theirs, waiting for him. There was Kurt Vanaheim, with a face torn between excitement and thunder; Ferdia Rosquin, who was as inscrutable as always, but who dipped his head to Fennick as though in a momentary little salute; Rear Admiral Glenck, who did not acknowledge his governor with so much as a nod. And Roman Lascelle, who was not a member of the Council but whose lineage could not be ignored. He was the only one to leave the line of speeders and stride out to meet Fennick. He had a rapier at his hip, and a deep blue sash under his belt. He held out his hand.

Fennick could hardly hear him over the baying of the crowds, but he could read the two words on his lips as they shook hands.

'Well done,' the young aristocrat said, with something like a genuine smile.

They clambered into the grav-cars. Behind, the more ungainly wheeled transports of the militia brought up the rear, a hand-picked regiment in their finest uniforms. A full division was already lined up at the spaceport, no doubt already sweating buckets in the heat of the morning.

'I hope he's not late,' Boros said, as he and Fennick relaxed in the back of the grav-car. A shadow passed over them as they travelled under the immense fastness of the Vanaheim gate.

'If he is, will you reprimand him?' Fennick asked with a smile.

'I'm thinking of the men on the landing pads. It will be baking hot out there.'

'Of course.' Fennick realised with a tiny shock that he had forgotten about them, he who had once been a sergeant of the Guard.

I really have changed, he thought. The men in uniforms – they do not mean what they did to me. They are not brothers in arms any more, but mere pawns and window dressing. Is that what it means to become a politician? Throne, I hope not.

'Take the salutes, Boros,' he said to his companion. 'Enjoy it while you can. For this one day, we are the cynosure of the entire Eastern Fringe, of Ultramar itself. Today, history comes calling.'

'May the Throne be merciful,' Boros said in a low whisper.

'THIRTY SECONDS,' BROTHER Markos said over the shipboard vox. 'Initiating launch sequence. Thrusters armed, clamps retracting... now.'

There was a series of clanks and bangs up and down the long, angular hull of the Thunderhawk *Alexiad*. Marneus Calgar sat back in the immense cradle that supported his armoured form and closed his eyes for a second. He was bare-headed, the better to display himself to the people of Zalidar, but arcing over his skull was an Iron Halo that crackled slightly with the protective field it generated. He wore artificer power armour of such antiquity that no one had ever been able to date it reliably. It was conceivable that parts of it had been worn by Guilliman himself. A thing of beauty as well as brutal utility, the armour resembled a Mark IV pattern, but had been repaired and embellished so many times over the millennia that he doubted a single plate of the original ceramite remained. It was a relic of the past, but still fully functional, and combined with his scarlet cloak it looked suitably impressive.

Other elements of the Chapter Master's wargear were stowed in the stern compartment. The Gauntlets of Ultramar were too bulky for use in any environment other than a genuine battlefield, but he took them everywhere. His helm was here with him, a simple Mark VI Corvus with a gold wreath and enhanced vox capabilities.

That was all. He would be on the ground for only a few hours, and Zalidar was a peaceful world. There was no need to be bringing an arsenal down to the planet. Two Thunderhawks, the *Alexiad* and the *Rubicon,* would make the journey while the *Fidelis* orbited above.

The *Rubicon* was piloted by Brother Dextus, and in addition to the ship's Ultramarine crew there was a half-squad of battle-brothers inside. But the majority of its passengers were Guardsmen of the Astra Militarum, a platoon of thirty Imperial storm troopers of the First Ultramar Guards, packed in the *Rubicon*'s hold like bolter rounds in a magazine. Cadian-trained, they were as good as wholly human troops could be, and would fulfil most of the security details that came with the presence of the Ultramarines Chapter Master. Their officer, Lieutenant Bran Janus, was a career soldier whose rank belied his varied combat experience.

CALGAR GLANCED DOWN the cavernous belly of the *Alexiad* at the other occupants of the hold. Close-up security for the Lord of Macragge was provided by Calgar's own battle-brothers. Only two members of his honour guard, Orhan and Proxis, were present on this trip, both in the ornate winged helms of their calling, both bearing power axes that had seen torrents of blood in their time. They, too, were in artificer armour, sealed and blessed and streaming with prayer scrolls.

In battle, Proxis was entrusted with the Chapter Banner – it was back on Macragge at present – and was one of the oldest remaining battle-brethren in the Chapter. He had been a member of First Company for a time, and he had his Terminator badge,but his secondment to the honour guard had saved his life when all of First Company died shoulder to shoulder during the Behemoth campaign. He had almost broken down, the day the first relief teams found his dead brethren. Now he had few intimates in the Chapter save for Marneus Calgar himself, who owed him his life several times over.

Brother Orhan had been seconded to Mars for Techmarine training, but had left of his own accord after the Chapter was attacked, and made his own way back to Macragge in time to join in the destruction of the hive fleet. While not a Techmarine per se, he still had a vast knowledge of the workings of the various systems and machinery that were used in the Chapter, and his expertise had proved useful time and again. He was a perfectionist, and took failure of any kind hard, constantly striving to better himself, in knowledge, in fighting prowess, in strategic insight. There was a captaincy in his future, Calgar had often thought, perhaps even Master of the Forge, but Orhan had never evinced interest in advancement, content to remain in the honour guard.

The rest of the Adeptus Astartes contingent was made up of aides and specialists and line warriors. Brother Valerian was an Epistolary Librarian who had fought in the Behemoth and Thrax campaigns. Young for his station, his psyker abilities were in the Alpha range, and he was a new addition to Calgar's retinue. He sat now with his hood pulsing blue light, his eyes closed, his face oddly troubled.

Brother Mathias was the party's Chaplain, and he wore the tar-black power armour of his calling. His helm was a white skull of sculpted ceramite. A fierce advocate of Codex orthodoxy, he was also an inspiration in battle. His rosarius glimmered round the neck of his armour, and in one gauntleted hand he held the crozius arcanum of his calling, the eagle-topped stave which was both badge of office and deadly weapon.

Brother Parsifal was a study in white and blue. The Prime Helix on his shoulder guard marked out his vocation. An Apothecary of incredible skill, he had been largely responsible for saving Calgar's life after Cold Steel Ridge. He wore plain Mark VI armour and a Corvus helm, which turned to Calgar now in the red light of the Thunderhawk interior, and nodded slightly.

Mathias and Parsifal and Proxis were among the oldest remaining brethren of the Chapter, and regularly accompanied Calgar when he went off-world. They had come up together, and formed an immensely powerful trio of courage and experience; by virtue of long association they were entitled to address Calgar as familiarly as they would any battle-brother of the line companies.

It warmed Calgar to look upon them. Their faith and dedication was always heartening to him. They were creatures of indomitable will and unflagging devotion. More than that, they were his friends.

The rest of the entourage on both Thunderhawks was made up of a reinforced squad drawn from the veterans of the Ultramarines First Company. The brethren of this company held an election every few years to vote for those members who should have the honour of joining the Chapter Master's personal detail. Those who won were, quite simply, the outstanding warriors of their time, and a tour of duty on the *Fidelis* was an almost certain route to sergeant's stripes.

Their First Sergeant was Brother Avila, who had started out in Sixth many decades before – a quiet, somewhat morose veteran of countless campaigns who was as dogged in defence as he was ferocious in attack. He had led the escort squad for thirty years, and his prowess in battle was legendary. In another few years, if he survived, Calgar contemplated promoting him into the honour guard itself.

If one included the crew, then the *Alexiad* housed some sixteen Adeptus Astartes in all, and there were eight more in the *Rubicon*. But they were the apex of the Chapter, the best the Ultramarines could produce.

Whole worlds had been conquered with less.

'Ten seconds,' the *Alexiad*'s pilot, Brother Markos, intoned over the vox. He had a co-pilot, a gunner and a navigator, but in the main, the responsibility for flying the *Alexiad* was his alone. He went through the last items on the checklist yet one more time. The flight was routine, as was the landing drill. Once on the ground, the gun-servitors stowed in the side bays would follow the rest of the detail out and set up a perimeter, which would be checked and rechecked by the *Rubicon*'s storm troopers before the Chapter Master himself and his immediate companions disembarked from the *Alexiad*. The routine never varied, not even for the most secure Imperial world. Every landing was treated as hostile. No precaution was ever overlooked.

'Launch, launch, launch,' came over the *Fidelis* vox, and there was a shunt, a clank, and Marneus Calgar's huge armoured bulk rose in its restraints as the gravitics in the launch bay switched off and the Thunderhawk nosed out of the hull of the barge and into open space.

'Clear away,' Markos said. 'Main engines in three, two, one–' The *Alexiad* jumped under them, like a horse of old Terra that has felt the spur. Calgar closed his right eye, and through the enhanced optics of his left he brought up the visual feed from the cockpit. Lines of figures ran down in his sight, absorbed, documented and analysed without conscious effort.

Plugged into the Thunderhawk's cogitators, he could have flown the ship himself without leaving the hold. But Brother Markos was peerless as a pilot, and he had trained the battle-brothers of his crew up to a standard which few others in the Chapter could attain. Calgar monitored the info-feed, the augur relays, and sat relaxed in the launch cradle that stopped him from floating weightlessly away from the bulkhead supporting his back. All was going according to plan. All was–

'Chapter-Master–' It was Brother Markos. 'We have what appears to be a meteor shower approaching from the planet's terminator, rounding the dark side now. Low orbit, skimming the atmosphere. Some appear to be losing altitude and falling planetside. Their speed is unusual, and they are on an intercept course.'

Calgar frowned. 'Analyse,' he said tersely.

'They appear to be–'

'*Alexiad, Rubicon* – this is *Fidelis*.' The ship's vox interrupted him. It was Tyson himself, the shipmaster. Calgar tensed at once, reading the man's tone even over the crackling vox.

'Meteor cluster is travelling at high speed on intercept course with our location. Augur detects energy blooms within the cluster consistent with drive engines. My lord, it is a ruse. Those–' He grew muffled, as if he had turned away from the vox-mic.

'Enemy fleet, enemy fleet approaching. Those are no meteors. Battle stations. *Alexiad* and *Rubicon*, come about at once and dock. We have incoming torpedoes, thirty thousand miles out and closing.'

'Acknowledged,' Markos said.

'Belay that order,' Calgar barked. 'Tyson, take evasive action. You can't dodge torpedoes if you hold for docking procedures. Brother Markos, Brother Dextus, make full speed for planetfall.'

'Acknowledged, lord,' Markos said.

'Tyson?' Calgar asked.

There was a pause. Finally the shipmaster came back online. 'My lord, the risk to you–'

'Protect the *Fidelis*,' Calgar snapped. 'We will take care of ourselves. Relay enemy strength and composition as soon as you are able. Fight with your ship, Tyson, and give me more information as soon as you can.'

'Acknowledged, my lord,' Martyn Tyson said. 'I will try to head them off and draw them away.'

'Throne be with you. Calgar out.'

The man did not need his Chapter Master breathing down his neck over the vox, not in the midst of a battle. Calgar put the fate of the *Fidelis* out of his mind, studying the stream of information being relayed by the *Alexiad*'s cogitators.

An ambush – or mere coincidence? It mattered not. The Thunderhawk rolled and wheeled under him as Markos threw it about in the void.

'Energy signatures consistent with ork ships,' Markos said. 'Firing chaff, and taking evasive manoeuvres. Smaller craft are now launching from the larger meteors – I mean ships. Landers are heading down to the planet. I see also Onslaught attack ships breaking free of the main body. My lord, this is no mere raid. This is a major incursion.'

And they have caught us wholly by surprise, Calgar thought, the fury simmering in him.

'Get us down on the ground, brother,' he told Markos. 'We cannot survive up here, not in the middle of all that heavy metal.'

'Acknowledged. Going for emergency orbital insertion. *Rubicon*, follow us in. All crew, brace for turbulence.'

The dorsal gun was firing now, up on the superstructure of the Thunderhawk, and Calgar could register the thrumming vibration of the heavy bolters in the sponsons. They must be close. He logged into the battle-array and saw a cloud of scarlet lights surrounding the *Alexiad* and *Rubicon* and the farther bulk of the *Fidelis*. Ork tactics were crude but effective. They charged in close and fast and hammered away with everything they had. Even as he watched, he saw a red strike on the *Fidelis*, but refrained from voxing Tyson. The man's hands were full enough.

'A ramship just struck the *Fidelis* amidships,' Markos said, spitting out the words like a curse. 'Launch bays look heavily damaged. More are closing.'

Calgar watched the augur feed, analysing with cold calculation. It was impossible; the *Fidelis* could not weather this storm.

'Planetary defence fleet is moving in on the enemy flank. I see a frigate and a squadron of Furies.' There was a pause. 'They have no chance,' Markos said with weary disgust.

'*Fidelis*, this is *Alexiad*,' Calgar said. 'Do you read?'

The vox came back with a series of explosions stunning it. Calgar winced at the shrill squawk of them.

A sizzling, intermittent comm. 'We read you.' It was not Tyson.

'Break off, repeat, break off and make an emergency warp jump. You cannot stay here. Jump and make for Seventh Company if you can. Do you acknowledge?'

No answer.

'*Fidelis* is burning,' Markos said in a low voice.

There was a crash in the stern and the Thunderhawk was shunted forward as though given an enormous slamming kick from behind.

'Fighter-bombers on our tail,' the dorsal gunner said. 'I count eight, no, nine–'

Then an immense explosion struck the *Alexiad*. Calgar was thrown forward in his restraints, then back again. One of the Ultramarines further down the hold was knocked partially free of his harness. Proxis grabbed the battle-brother's arm in his own massive gauntlet and held him fast.

'Losing atmosphere in the hold,' Calgar said calmly, studying the readout in his bionic eye. 'Helm up, prepare for vacuum.' He locked down his own helm with its corvid beak, and it immediately took over the relay feed. He could see more clearly now. The compartment was filling with smoke.

'Emergency landing, brother,' he said to Markos. 'Put her down anywhere you can.'

'Main engines offline,' Markos came back. 'We're working with retros only. Dorsal gun gone. My lord, I have failed you.'

'We will discuss that later,' Calgar said.

The atmosphere hit them like a wall, and the battered Thunderhawk bucked and leapt under them. There was a series of tearing crashes, and Calgar watched the readout and noted with approval that both Markos and Dextus were launching every missile they had, lightening the two gunships and ridding them of dangerous ordnance. The ramshackle ork fighter-bombers were trying to stay close, but even as he watched the feed, he saw three of them wink out, no doubt battered apart by the rough orbital entry.

'Stand by for crash landing,' Markos said over the *Alexiad*'s vox.

Calgar watched the shimmering data feed inside his helm, the altitude warnings roaring a red klaxon inside the compartment. The ork fighters were peeling off, what was left of them. They were trying to regain orbit, their systems being shredded by the thick atmosphere of Zalidar. And it was the *Fidelis* they were after, most of all. A single pair of Thunderhawks was poor pickings.

They don't know I am on board, Calgar realised. Well, thank the Throne for that at least.

The readout went dark. Calgar blinked, but it was dead – the onboard cogitator systems had failed. He was as blind as the rest of those inside the hold, a mere passenger being rattled around a punctured, broken tin can that was hurtling to earth almost uncontrolled.

His enhanced hearing still caught the shriek of the airbrakes, and the grating roar of the forward retros. Markos was trying to bring her nose up. His suit systems noted a change in the outside atmosphere and automatically shifted from vacuum mode to save power. The air in his helm tasted different, and was warmer. He was breathing the air of Zalidar for the first time.

'Brace for impact,' Markos said over the Chapter vox, and Calgar repeated the phrase out loud for the sake of the storm troopers in the bow, raising the volume with his suit speakers. Even so, he was not sure they would have heard over the roar and rattle of their headlong descent.

Gravity and G-forces were clamping him down – he could feel them even through the artificer power armour he wore.

A crash forward, not an explosion, more as if they had hit something yielding. The nose was up – Markos was working wonders with the crippled ship – and then another thunderous bang. Thank the Emperor's mercy that the prow of the Thunderhawk was heavily armoured.

Then there was a sensation as though an immense hammer had slammed into them. Calgar had a glimpse of broad daylight as a chunk was torn out of the bow. The ship cartwheeled and whirled in a dizzying series of leaps and crashes, the massive craft tumbling like a stone tossed downhill. He glimpsed vegetation, green, then blue sky, then the limbs of trees torn off and sent flying through the compartment.

A final, withering crash, and then all was black and silent.

# NINE

THERE WAS BLOOD in his mouth. He swallowed it. His auto-senses fizzed a little, and he lay there, taking stock as he had so many times before on so many battlefields. It took only a few seconds to realise that he was whole, and relatively uninjured. His body's superb auto-repair systems were already at work, and the suit he wore worked with them, administering stimulants and painkillers, clearing the fog of concussion from his mind.

He cast off the tattered restraints, and caught himself as he fell from the uptilted hull of the *Alexiad,* his six-hundred-pound frame making a hollow boom as he landed on his feet. Some suit systems were flashing red in the heads-up display within the helm, but by and large the damage was minimal. Calgar's ancient armour had seen much worse.

Other figures were stirring in the tumbled mayhem of the hold. He saw the gleam of gold on Proxis' helm as the veteran unclipped himself and punched the side of his own head. The vox crackled.

'My lord?'

'I am fine. See to the others, Proxis. Get everyone out. I am going outside.'

He stepped over strewn equipment, bolters, and broken plating. The battle-brethren of his entourage had fared well despite the violence of the crash, protected by their superlative armour. He saw that brother Parsifal was already administering to those who were lightly injured, and blinked upon the Apothecary's sigil on the vox.

'I want a casualty list as soon as you are able, brother,' he said. 'If the *Rubicon* came down as hard as we did, Janus' Guardsmen will have suffered severely.'

'It shall be so,' Parsifal told him. 'I must find my narthecium.'

'Make it fast. I want everyone out. Proxis?'

'Yes, lord?'

'A perimeter, as soon as we are on our feet. And then an inventory of all surviving stores and armaments. Valerian?'

The Librarian came over the vox. 'Yes, lord.' His vox feed broke, then steadied.

'Outside, now. I need you to find out where we are and what is around us. Let us be at it, brothers. Time is not our friend.'

His brethren went to their duties with the smooth economy of men who have seen it all before. Sergeant Avila was barking at his squad, and they were searching in the wreckage for their weapons, which had been blasted free of mag-lock by the impact of the crash.

Marneus Calgar clambered over the wreckage at the bow ramp – the landing had bent the adamantium shell open like the lid of a can – and set foot on soft, black earth that was still smoking from the *Alexiad*'s landing. The forward retros had burned a blackened clearing out in front of the wrecked craft and there was a trail of destruction stretching for fully half a mile behind it.

It would have been a superb feat of flying, that final, almost unpowered approach, had not the Thunderhawk struck a massive forest tree in the last moments, slashing it onto one side. The tree was cloven in half three hundred yards back and its smouldering branches lay all about, entangled with shards of metal and broken plating. Through his auto-senses, Calgar could smell the deep reek of the jungle, even over the carbonised stink of the wreck. He looked up and saw Zalidar's star, still not quite at its zenith. It was hot, and getting hotter, and there was a thickness of moisture in the air, which his suit systems immediately adjusted to.

Figures were piling out of the wreck behind him. To his side, Valerian appeared. His armour was scored and dented and there was a gout of brown dried blood down one side of his face, but his eyes were clear, except for the black flecks floating within the iris that spoke of a life spent fighting the immaterium and its perils.

'My hood is dead, my lord,' the young Librarian said. 'I will be able to bring it back online, but it will take time.'

'Get to it,' Calgar said. He touched his own thigh, but the mag-locked bolt pistol was gone. He was weaponless for the moment, but that would be remedied presently. He strode around the downed Thunderhawk, past the angular prow, so he could look into the shattered cockpit.

It was a mess in there. Brother Markos had been decapitated and his crew dismembered by the jagged limbs of the trees they had crashed through. Leaning in, Calgar set one hand on the dead pilot's shoulder guard for a second.

'You did well, brother,' he said quietly. 'May you have peace now. In His name.'

He straightened, looking around. The crash had stilled the jungle noises for a while, but now they were starting up again, a cacophony of hoots and screeches from creatures unseen in the eaves of the towering canopy all around.

'Well, here we are,' he said, still in that same quiet tone.

Lieutenant Janus could be heard shouting hoarse orders off to the left – so he had survived. Looking over, Calgar saw that the *Rubicon* had come down hard perhaps four hundred yards away. The escort gunship had flipped onto its back on the final approach, and looked even more mangled than the *Alexiad*. Janus' surviving Guardsmen were hauling the dead and wounded out of the wreck, and beyond them, a half-squad of Sergeant Avila's battle-brethren were already fanning out across the clearing, weapons raised. Their armour was scored and dented, scraped down to the bare ceramite in places, but the bolters they held were loaded and cocked. It was in hand.

Orhan and Proxis joined Calgar at the *Alexiad*'s cockpit. Their parade finery seemed out of place in that setting. They had discarded the ceremonial scarlet cloaks, but the gold ornamentation of their armour caught the light. They both bore bolters and had their power axes locked to their thighs.

They looked down on Markos' ruined corpse, faceless masks of blue and gold. There was no need to say anything.

'We need to know where we are,' Calgar said. 'We must also leave the crash site as soon as we have salvaged everything from the gunships that we can. There is no telling what is in these forests, or what may be dropped on our heads at any moment.'

'What of the *Fidelis*?' Proxis asked.

'Heavily damaged, when last I saw. I told them to make a warp jump. If they succeeded, it will have sucked in or damaged most of the enemy ships surrounding them. That may buy us a little time. That, and my conviction that they do not know who was on the *Alexiad*.'

'Are you sure of that, my lord?' Orhan asked.

'Nothing is sure in this world except birth and death,' Calgar told him. 'All that lies between is uncertainty. But they would have pursued the *Alexiad* with everything they had if they knew I was aboard. That much I know.'

'I suppose we should try and contact the planetary authorities,' Orhan said. But Calgar held up a hand.

'No long-range vox, for now. The orks are primitive, but they are not above monitoring the planetary frequencies. We do not want to draw them here any sooner than the crash already has.'

He looked up at the bright sky. 'My guess is they think the crash left no survivors. They will arrive here at some point, if only to pick over the wreckage. But at present I think they have other things on their mind. This is no mere raid, brothers. It is an all-out invasion.'

Eleven of Lieutenant Janus' storm troopers had been killed in the *Rubicon*'s crash, and four more were too injured to walk. These wounded were loaded on two of the tracked gun-servitors that had survived. Two more were laden with every scrap of ammunition and provision that could be saved from the two downed Thunderhawks. Brother Parsifal administered the Emperor's Peace to two of the critically wounded whose condition was hopeless, murmuring a prayer over each before ending their agony with opiates from his stores. The dead were buried outside the clearing the Thunderhawks had created in the jungle, and Proxis and Orhan felled several trees over the shallow graves with their power axes, the better to protect their bones.

The Thunderhawks enginseer had died in the crash along with Markos and his crew, so it was up to Mathias and Orhan to help Calgar on with the Gauntlets of Ultramar. Massive power fists, they radiated a shimmer of might, and had storm bolters attached to their undersides.

Calgar cocked these powerful weapons with a blink on his heads-up display, and the artificer armour he wore readjusted power levels to maintain the extra energy drain. He could not keep the fists at full power indefinitely; they would drain even the superlative power pack of the armour over time. But for now, he flexed his fingers in them and for a moment let the anger in him flood his brain.

He thought of Brother Markos and the four other dead Ultramarines of the gunship crews, whose gene-seeds were now in a capsule on Parsifal's belt. He thought of the storm troopers who had died unworthy deaths in the chaos of the *Rubicon*'s crash, good men all. And he thought of the *Fidelis*, burning in the void. All down to the implacable hatred of the orks.

Hatred, he thought. I will show you what it is to arouse the hatred of the Ultramarines.

There would be a reckoning for this. He looked forward to it. He wanted it as keenly as if he were some neophyte out to prove himself in his first skirmish. That feeling never left him, and not even the fault line of tiredness in his psyche could dampen his fury. The difference now was that his anger was cold, analytical, a searchlight shone upon every tactical and strategic situation. The anger lit up the way for him. Occasionally it took him wrong, as it had upon Cold Steel Ridge, a half-century before. But he had learned to trust it all the same.

He flashed up a map of the planet in his mind. It was crude and incomplete, the result of amateur surveys carried out over a period of decades, but it was the best data he had. There were no satellites left overhead to guide him, but he studied the Zalidar star, measured its distance from the horizon and overlaid it with a star map of the system. Then he factored in the re-entry angle of the *Alexiad*, the craft's speed and angle of descent. Some rough calculations, a juggle of longitudes and an approximation of latitude followed. And he had their location to within a hundred miles or so.

All this he did in the space of a few seconds.

They were far to the south of the capital, Zalathras, deep in what the natives called the Tagus, the primary rainforest of Zalidar.

Calgar looked around. Sergeant Avila's reinforced squad of Ultramarines was holding a loose perimeter, each of the battle-brothers weighed down with packs of extra ammunition and other stores. Janus' surviving Guardsmen were standing by the tracked servitors that bore their wounded comrades and the heavier equipment. Closer to, Proxis, Orhan, Mathias, Valerian and Parsifal stood waiting.

They were nineteen Space Marines and fourteen unwounded human soldiers in total. Not much of an army, but it would have to suffice. Calgar smiled inside his helm.

'Brothers,' he said, 'follow me.'

He slashed the vegetation out of his way with the power fists, the ancient artefacts emitting a humming crackle as the disruptive field about them shattered creepers, vines and minor trees. Insects sizzled in the field and died in tiny white sparks of flame. Calgar lowered the energy input into the fists and used more of his own brute strength to hack a way forward. At the same time, he opened up the receivers on his suit's vox systems and listened over the aether for any nearby transmissions.

The rest of the company tramped behind him in silence. Proxis and Orhan were at his back, as they had been for so many years, and then Sergeant Avila and a half-squad, then the servitors and guardsmen. Mathias, Valerian and Parsifal came next, and another half-squad of Ultramarines brought up the rear under Brother Gamelan, who bore a combi-bolter-flamer and had the wound-seal of the Behemoth campaign painted on one shoulder guard.

They made just over a mile in the first hour, the ground under their heavy armoured forms sinking into a moist mire. Soon the bright ceremonial gold of the honour guard's armour was obscured by mud and sap and green dust from the trees, and the Guardsmen's uniforms stuck dark and soaked to their backs as they helped the heavy gun servitors follow the path that Calgar blazed.

No one spoke. The wounded had been tranquillised by Parsifal, and the rest were too disciplined for idle chatter. Calgar consulted his chrono, paused and looked back. Seconds later there was a boom that shocked the jungle, muffled by distance and the suffocating vegetation. The self-destruct charges they had laid on the *Alexiad* and the *Rubicon* had finally gone off. There would be nothing left of those noble Thunderhawks now save smoking shards of metal. The orks would find no booty at the crash sites, and with luck the explosion would help conceal the origin of the path that Calgar was slashing through the undergrowth.

They marched on. The trees grew taller, becoming giants of their kind, and overhead the canopy drew together, until the company was walking in a dim twilight. There was less vegetation growing here, and they made better time. Proxis took over on point, power axe in hand, and Calgar dropped back down the column to keep an eye on things.

They marched for five hours before the Chapter Master called a halt. The Guardsmen were staggering with fatigue, drained by the heat and the moisture-laden air and the pace that the Chapter Master had set.

It was becoming darker. Night was approaching, and around them the jungle noises took on a raucous intensity, howling in the canopy of the immense trees. They had made a good pace, considering the terrain; Calgar had been counting his strides and knew that they were now some seven miles from the crash site.

'We will set up camp here,' he said. 'Sergeant Avila, I want half your squad at full battle readiness at all times during the night. Two-man posts in a fifty-yard perimeter, optics set in passive infrared. Lieutenant Janus, your men will not stand guard – they need to rest. They also need water. You will find that by slashing the thicker vines it can be obtained in some quantity, with patience. Brother Parsifal, how goes it with the wounded?'

Parsifal's blue and white helm stared at him. 'Fading fast, lord. The climate is enervating, and their injuries are putrefying with remarkable speed.'

'Do what you can. Brother Valerian?'

'Yes, lord.' The Librarian's hood was once more glowing pale blue, but it flickered every now and again, like a candle flame in a draught.

'I want some information, brother. Anything you can give me.'

'What I can tell you, my lord, is not much more than I am sure you already know. I have a distant impression of souls in conflict and torment, far to the north, a great flux occurring in the immaterium, that which is always associated with large-scale warfare. I believe that the main settlement of this planet, Zalathras, is under heavy attack.'

Calgar took off his helm. At once, his bionic implant took over the input and automatically switched to infrared in the dimming light. The company was gathered together in a rough circle at the foot of a gargantuan forest tree, and Avila's squad were already setting up firing positions around them, scraping low depressions in the thick humus of the jungle floor and clearing fields of fire. The red eyes of the gun-servitors gleamed, and the wounded moaned faintly as Parsifal administered to them.

'That much I could have told you myself,' Proxis grunted, leaning on his axe. He too had doffed his ornate helm, and the implants in his organic eyes glittered now and then as his head turned, studying the jungle.

'This is perfect terrain for them,' he said in a low grate. 'A jungle world, thinly settled, but rich in life and organic material. All the building blocks.'

'Is it a Waaagh!?' Calgar asked Valerian quietly.

The Librarian shook his head. 'Not yet. An ork Waaagh! is like a veritable psychic tsunami. Their forces have not yet made that crucial step. But it is close, I feel it. Soon the enemy host will reach critical mass. The more of their hordes they drop upon the planet, the greater the infestation becomes. We do not have much time, my lord.'

'Zalathras is the key,' Calgar mused. 'They will concentrate their best forces there. As long as the city can hold out, there is hope for the planet. Tell me, Valerian, how do you rate your chances of getting a message through to Seventh?'

The Librarian grimaced. 'I have been trying all day. My hood is still damaged, and the violent currents in the immaterium are disrupting the aether.'

'Continue to try, then. Captain Ixion must know what is afoot here, and the news must make its way to Macragge itself. An ork Waaagh! is a serious matter. It could engulf several systems before our forces even know what is going on.'

*We are too scattered,* the thought came to him. *I have spread the Chapter too thin.*

He cast off the thought. Regret was the most worthless emotion in life.

'Can you tell if the *Fidelis* got away?' he demanded of Valerian.

'I can tell you that it is gone, my lord,' Valerian replied. 'That is all.'

'Tyson is a good man. He'll have got the ship out,' Proxis said.

Calgar was not sure that Tyson had still been alive during the last vox exchange with the ship, but he said nothing. Without firm evidence, there was no use in speculating. He said a quick, silent prayer, raising his eyes to the limbs of the primeval trees, and glimpsing the first stars in the tiny gaps between them.

'Night routine,' he said briskly. 'No lights, no sound. I will allow thirty minutes for eating, drinking and all else that is necessary. After that, we will await events, and hope that the orks were sluggish at picking up our trail.'

He stayed awake in the night, standing at the base of the great tree that dominated their campsite. All vox frequencies were silent, but he monitored them anyway as he stood there, an immobile giant. The Astra Militarum slept the deep slumber of tired men, but the Adeptus Astartes needed no sleep, and thanks to their power armour and their adamantine constitutions, they would not need it for some time to come. They held their positions in the jungle, barely moving, the blue of their armour faded to black by the night. Now and again a glitter of metal on a bolter would catch the light of some errant star, but the only sound in the camp was the occasional moan of one of the wounded.

Calgar could smell the wounded men's blood on the air. To his enhanced senses it seemed as clear as a scarlet flag in the night. When Proxis drew close he contacted the Ancient on their private frequency.

'If some animal approaches the perimeter, it is to be killed silently. Blades and fists, Proxis. I want no gunfire.'

'Acknowledged, lord. I will pass it along.'

The night hours passed. Once, something large and dark padded all around the perimeter, sniffing loudly, but when it came close one of Avila's battle-brothers rose to meet it with his combat knife and, as the massive Ultramarine reared up out of the forest floor before it, the beast took fright and slunk away again.

One of the wounded sank near to death during the night. Calgar had Brother Parsifal release him from his last struggle just before dawn with drugs from his narthecium. As the light grew, Janus and his surviving comrades buried him, scooping out the grave with their bare hands. Then they stood and saluted silently, grim-faced and filthy, as the sun came up. Brak Justani of Macragge, twenty-six years old. Many Adeptus Astartes commanders would not have taken the trouble to learn his name, but Calgar knew every one of the *Fidelis'* crew, human and otherwise.

They moved out again with the swift and quiet efficiency of men who know their duty, and so the trek continued as the heat rose under the trees, and the insects rose with it, biting and buzzing in gauze-like clouds. The jungle came to life around them once more, the hooting and screeching growing with the climb of Zalidar's hot yellow sun.

By the morning of the fourth day all the wounded were dead and buried, and one of the gun-servitors was throwing its track every few hours, entailing hurried and makeshift repairs. A competent Tech-marine or even a decent enginseer would have been able to fix the servitor properly in a couple of hours, but neither was present, nor were the tools they used. But the stricken servitor was fitted with a heavy bolter, and was thus too valuable an asset to simply abandon. Calgar chafed at the delay. He estimated that they had marched over forty miles from the crash site, but the Tagus loomed as high and thick and unchanging as ever around them.

It was one of Sergeant Avila's brethren who noted it first. The rear-most Ultramarine, Brother Antigonus, informed them that he thought they were being followed. He said this matter-of-factly, and was firm in his conviction despite all evidence to the contrary. After that, Brothers Valerian and Mathias remained in the rear with him, but nothing materialised, and as they went into camp that night, Proxis made a caustic comment about brethren who had too much imagination for their own good.

But Marneus Calgar had never been one to ignore the instincts of his own kind, so he was not entirely surprised when, around noon on the fifth day, a shattering rattle of automatic bolter fire erupted from the rear of the column.

'All-round defence. Deploy heavy weapons,' he snapped as he powered up his gauntlets and ran towards the sound of the firing.

Proxis and Orhan came with him, snapping free their mag-locked bolters and cocking the weapons with blows of their fists. Calgar's auto-senses brought to him the reek of cordite, and, below that, the thin splash of spilled blood. But not the blood of his own people.

The gunfire came and went, single shots, and then a long, sustained burst. Then there was quiet again. Calgar found Mathias kneeling behind a tree with his crozius in his fist, Valerian beside him, and on the ground in front of them Brother Antigonus was crouched, changing his magazine. The jungle had fallen silent.

'Movement, forty yards back, lord,' Antigonus was saying. 'Large movement, bearing round our left. I'm sure I hit something.'

'Orks?'

'They returned fire.' Antigonus gestured to the divots torn out of the ground to his front. 'Stubber rounds.'

Calgar stood still, waiting. The sudden silence was deafening, eerie. It was if the jungle were watching them.

'Valerian?'

The Librarian nodded. 'Orks. Quite a few.'

'They have good skills, to remain silent so long,' Proxis said. 'Usually they roar their lungs out when the firing starts.'

'They have been tracking us – for days perhaps,' Calgar said. 'Brother Antigonus, I was wrong to doubt you.'

Antigonus shrugged. 'It is of no matter, my lord.'

There was suddenly a lot of movement out there a dark riot of shapes that flickered through the vegetation. And now they could all hear the grunts, the growled orders, the soft clash of metal off in the trees. Calgar's head snapped to right and left.

'They're on both our flanks. Looks like they're going to try and surround us.'

A far bellow, like that of a great angry beast, and a chorus of other voices gargled out a medley of rage and bloodlust.

'That's more like it,' Proxis said wryly.

The Chaplain, Mathias, stood up and hefted his crozius.

'May the Lord of Battle bless us with His grace,' he said gravely.

'Here they come,' Valerian told his brothers.

Calgar raised his voice to a shout. 'Ultramarines!' he cried. 'We have enemy incoming!'

Suddenly the jungle to their front and on all sides reared up in a wall of charging figures, roaring monstrosities as green as the jungle, taller even than the Adeptus Astartes before them. They came through the trees in a stampeding mass that made the earth quiver under them, dozens of flailing, snarling monsters firing wildly as they came, waving great swords and cleavers and axes, their maws agape and tusks protruding.

'Short bursts. Fire at will,' Calgar said over the vox, the Gauntlets of Ultramar clenching and unclenching on his fists, and from the embattled circle of the Ultramarines the bolters began to bark out, jumping against the shoulder-guards of his battle-brethren. The heavy bolters roared in staccato bursts, and amid their bright tracer-hedges lanced out the carmine-bright lasgun fire of the Guardsmen.

'Head-shots, brothers,' Proxis said. He sounded as though he were smiling as he said it. 'Don't waste ammunition on tickling these scum. I want to see their brains jump.'

There was laughter in the firing line, a low dark murmur of it as the Space Marines lined up their targets in their helmet displays and the deadly muzzles of the bolters jumped up blazing fire in their hands. The first wave of orks was brought down thirty yards from the firing line, and as the xenos died, so the Ultramarines stood up, switched to three-round bursts and began sweeping the second wave that was now charging forward over the humped bodies of their own dead.

The orks came on with a diabolical fury that had in it no notion of fear, no hesitation. One used the body of its fellow as a springboard to leap high in the air and come down almost within the perimeter, but Brother Gamelan wheeled round and turned it into a burning torch with a bright blast from his flamer. It wriggled and struggled until he put a bolt-pistol round through its skull, and the light from the burning ork lit up the Ultramarine position as though they were fighting around a central bonfire.

The second wave died. But there was a third, following on right after, and this made it right up to the position, and all around Calgar his brothers were firing point-blank into the gaping maws of the creatures. One Space Marine was lifted into the air by the foe but he stabbed the muzzle of his bolter into the creature's eye and opened up with a burst that blasted the thing's head clean from its shoulders, dropping him on the ground again to fight on, his blue armour painted vivid steaming scarlet with ork blood.

It was hand to hand up and down the line, and in the close-quarter battle the strength of the orks told. Calgar saw a Guardsman torn open like a rotten sack in the fists of one roaring xenos, seconds before Proxis' axe clove it from shoulder to crotch. It fell in two struggling pieces to the ground and the Ancient slashed it up further, as calm as a man chopping wood.

Now Calgar allowed himself to step into the fray. A wide burst from his storm bolters cleared the front of the position, the heavy rounds dismembering half a dozen of the enemy, and as more hurtled towards him he set up a great, joyous shout, and with the Gauntlets of Ultramar pulsing and shining on his fists he plunged into the thickest part of the melee.

The artificer armour magnified his own immense strength, and the disruptive field that encircled his fists tore the foe to pieces in his hands. 'Guilliman!' he shouted, and he hurled the orks aside left and right in bloody gobbets and broken steaming remnants. He broke clear through the attacking line, shattered it like some blue juggernaut of slaughter, and cast aside his enemies like so much chaff.

Even the mindless savagery of the orks could not withstand that blinding blur of murder. The enemy broke and began streaming away from the Ultramarines, and up to Calgar's side came Proxis and Orhan, wielding their power axes to terrible effect. The three of them pursued the fleeing orks, tearing them off their feet, slashing them apart and trampling their dying faces underfoot.

Finally, Calgar caught sight of a lone trio of larger creatures to the rear of their attacking line, a huge ork chieftain and his bodyguards. As the ork saw Calgar it opened its jaws and bellowed hatred and defiance, but there was recognition in the savage scarlet eyes also. As Calgar pointed the Gauntlets' storm bolters at it, the ork chieftain shoved its underlings into harm's way and took off at a sprint. The storm bolters roared out and chewed up the two unfortunates into bright spattered gore, but their leader ducked behind a tree, and became a shadow flitting through the jungle. Calgar followed it with well-aimed volleys, but the ork had luck on its side, and the Chapter Master ceased firing to conserve his weapon's precious ammunition, watching the shadow disappear into the shocked silence of the fetid jungle.

The attack fell apart, the orks broken and running in ragged knots and skeins that were methodically shot to pieces by the Ultramarines. A last few barking rounds, and then a quiet fell, strange and unlooked for after the roaring chaos that had gone before. Calgar drew a deep breath and shook his dripping gauntlets free of clotted blood. A momentary flick of the disruption field and the ork filth was burned off them completely, leaving them inviolate again.

'Re-form perimeter,' he said over the vox. 'Reload, and watch your arcs. Proxis, I want a headcount. Watch and shoot, brothers, watch and shoot.'

The Ultramarines resumed their firing positions, changed magazines, and scanned the surrounding jungle. All around them the bodies of their foes steamed and twitched. There was a single shot as one was finished off by a watchful Space Marine. The only sound after that was the crackling of the burning ork carcass in the centre of the position.

'All brethren accounted for,' Proxis said a minute later. 'Three minor wounds. That is all.'

Lieutenant Janus' young voice piped up. 'Two dead, two wounded, my lord.'

Calgar stood like a statue of some war god made incarnate, smoke still issuing in a thin ribbon from the muzzles of his storm bolters. Beside him, Mathias unhelmed, and kissed his crozius arcanum, whose power field he had switched off at last. 'Blessed be,' he said. 'This was a good accounting.'

'One of many to come,' Calgar said quietly.

# TEN

THEY SHIFTED AWAY from the battlefield while Parsifal tended the wounded. Sergeant Avila took out a half-squad on a sweep all around the camp, and when he came back he reported that by his count some eighty-six of the enemy were lying dead about them. By the trails that led away, he estimated the strength of the warband that had attacked them at some two hundred.

'That will grow,' Calgar said thoughtfully as the brother-sergeant stood before him, helm off, pale skin glistening with sweat in the heat.

'How are we for ammunition, sergeant?'

Avila's face remained impassive except for a slight frown that creased his forehead. 'My lord, we possess some fifteen full magazines for each battle-brother. But we are low on belts for the heavy bolters and power packs for the plasma gun.'

Calgar nodded. It was as he had suspected. A few more engagements like the last one would see them reduced to battling with knives and fists.

'How far do you think we are from Zalathras, my lord?' Mathias asked him, leaning on his crozius.

'By my best estimate, at least three hundred miles.'

Mathias whistled softly. 'My lord, we must pick up the pace, or we will be swamped before we are halfway there. This attack was only the beginning. The orks are on our trail now. The attacks will be unrelenting from here on in.'

'I am aware of that, Brother-Chaplain,' Calgar said.

'My brethren are marching far more slowly than they are capable of, lord,' Avila said. Calgar stared at him, but the sergeant did not meet his eyes.

'The servitors and the Guardsmen,' Brother Mathias said with a low sigh.

'I know what it is you are thinking, Mathias – it has been on my mind also,' Calgar said. 'If we were Ultramarines alone, we could march day and night, and at double the pace. But I will not abandon Janus and his men. I would be leaving them to their death. Other Chapter Masters might do it without a second thought – but I am heir to great Guilliman, and do you think he would countenance such a dishonourable act?'

'I think he might consider the greater good that would be served by your own survival,' Mathias said. 'Lord, we will be weeks on the trail at this rate, and Zalathras could well be lost by the time we struggle out of this infernal jungle.'

Calgar turned away. Mathias had always seen the dark logic behind every command decision more clearly than most, and like Proxis he had known his Chapter Master long enough to be able to speak his mind freely. The question had been gnawing at Calgar since the very first day's march.

'I will think on it,' he said.

'Do not think too long, lord.'

* * *

They policed the battlefield quickly, and even the Ultramarines, aware of the ammunition situation, were not above rummaging through the ork carcasses to stock up their dwindling supply. Very few of the xenos used bolters, and the rounds within those that existed were crudely made, some downright unstable, but they might be glad of them one day hence.

As they marched away from the scene of the fighting, Calgar looked back, and saw to his disgust that all around the piled carcasses of the orks, hordes of tiny green fungi were already springing up. The seeds of another warband had been sown in the very soil of the planet. Such was the unending scourge of the orks.

They were attacked twice more in the next three days. Both times the assaults came out of nowhere, but were crude and uncoordinated, even by ork standards. Both attacks were beaten off with only minor injuries, but the expenditure of ammunition was becoming a real problem. As the Ultramarines manned their perimeter at night, the battle-brothers took turns unloading bolter rounds gleaned from the ill-made magazines of the orks, and wiping them down, rasping off the rough edges, then reloading them into empty magazines of their own. Many were ill-fitting, and they would no doubt cause jams aplenty, but they were a lot better than facing the enemy with brute strength alone – even Adeptus Astartes could not hope to win out against the enemy they faced if it all came down to hand-to-hand combat.

There were times, at night, when Calgar left the perimeter and walked out into the jungle alone, surprisingly quiet despite the huge bulk of his armoured form, stepping as lightly as a half-ton shadow. He looked up in rare gaps through the canopy overhead, and studied what stars he could find, aligning them in the map he carried in his head, constantly regauging their position.

There were stars that were not stars, and he watched them too, battling the fury in his hearts. Ork ships circled up there, dominating the skies of the planet and landing troops at will. He saw one once that grew into a bright torch as it descended through the thick atmosphere and landed somewhere to the east of them, lost in the jungle for a moment before coughing and blazing up into the night sky again in a flare of stuttering afterburners. The planet was being infested with the creatures, and every day that passed saw the odds against Calgar and his brethren lengthen.

THEY PICKED UP the pace. Janus' surviving storm troopers divested themselves of all equipment save their lasguns and handed it over to the Ultramarines to carry. The crippled servitor was finally abandoned, left with a single belt of ammunition so that it might go down fighting with the heavy bolter that was part of its anatomy.

They heard the long, distant rattle of it later that day, far to their rear. There was no mistaking the precision of Macragge-crafted munitions, not for the attuned ears of Ultramarines at any rate. A few minutes it fired, burst after burst, and in reply came the ragged stutter of ork guns, rising in volume until the noise suddenly cut off, and there was only the rancid chatter of the jungle creatures again.

The company marched on, the Guardsmen white-faced with fatigue at the pace now set by the Space Marines. There were times when a human trooper would faint with the extreme exertion in the shattering heat, and would regain his senses to find himself borne along in the armoured limbs of Brother Proxis, or Orhan, or occasionally carried on one arm of the Chapter Master himself. On the eleventh day, Lieutenant Janus went down, having pushed himself to the extremes of endurance ever since the crash, and he woke from a stunned stupor to find himself in the arms of Marneus Calgar. He looked up, astonished, and Calgar glanced down with a smile. 'My lord, I must apologise,' the young lieutenant managed to stammer.

'Save your breath, lieutenant. Think of what a story you will have to tell one day.'

The Ultramarines were the model for the Adeptus Astartes all over the galaxy, the backbone of the Codex. Their own primarch had written it. Since that time, ten thousand years before, the various Chapters of their kind had proliferated and grown away from Roboute Guilliman's strictures, some in small ways, others more completely.

But the Ultramarines held to the traditions of their founder, and were proud to do so. Guilliman had emphasised a side to the Adeptus Astartes that many Chapters had seen dwindle – their humanity. Superhuman the Space Marines might be, but in the last analysis they were still men, still part of mankind itself, not a species apart. And they did not look down on their fellow man as many other Space Marine Chapters did, but embraced what was left of their humanity. They did not despise the weak, or consider them expendable. That teaching above all endured in their ranks, and so it would remain.

So the hollow-eyed troopers of the Astra Militarum were not left behind. They were set a punishing pace, and they were carried when they fell, but they were not abandoned. To do so would be to violate the teachings that made the Ultramarines what they were.

They began to make night marches, for the impatience was growing in Marneus Calgar with each passing day, though to all outward appearance he was calm and impassive as always. Only those who knew him well, like Proxis, could see the intense self-control of the Chapter Master rein itself in further.

He was the overlord of a vast region of space, suzerain of a dozen worlds. He commanded great fleets and armies and his name was known and renowned clear across the galaxy among men and xenos alike. But here he was, leading a small, lost party of hounded fugitives through the depths of an unending jungle, on an unimportant world far out on the fringe of Imperium space, as cut off from his responsibilities and his command as if he had fallen through a pit in the warp.

It was maddening. It filled him with a dull, brooding anger and a raging frustration. But he clamped down on those emotions, as he did on so many others. To set an example. More than that – to discard that which could not be helped. But as he marched along in the screaming, steaming jungle day after day, a strategy began to grow in Calgar's mind, based upon what had gone before, and what he knew of the mentality of the orks.

If, as seemed possible, the assault upon Zalidar grew into a Waaagh! then it was not only this far-out system that would be at risk. So widely separated were the fighting companies of the Ultramarines at present, that were the Waaagh! to consume Zalidar speedily enough and move on, then it would find the outlying regions of Ultramar itself before it, and heavily defended though Ultramar was with its orbital bastions and minefields and divisions of Astra Militarum, it could do untold damage before the Ultramarine companies could be recalled to repel it. More than that, the wars that the Ultramarines were currently engaged upon would have to be abandoned – some on the very brink of a successful conclusion – and that work would all have to be done again. A decade of Imperial progress could be set back.

No, the orks had to be held here, for as long as possible. They must be made to bleed, here on Zalidar, made to send in all their strength, commit everything to the taking of this world.

The world itself was not important enough to warrant such a massive commitment. Waaaghs! swept through whole systems like a storm. They did not concentrate on single planets.

Unless there were something on Zalidar that could draw them here, like iron filings to a magnet.

Something. Or someone.

If they know I am here, they will stay and fight, Calgar calculated. My name is worth something, even out here on the Fringe. Any ork warlord would be willing to risk his entire army for the chance to fashion a drinking cup out of my skull – it would make him a legend among his kind, a name across the galaxy.

Eventually, the orks must learn that Marneus Calgar is here, on Zalidar. Once that information leaks out, the Waaagh! will concentrate here. My head is worth the conquering of a dozen border worlds. I must draw them to me, and I must make a stand here, long enough for Seventh to come, for a relieving armada to be assembled.

I must become bait, pure and simple.

And if the bait is swallowed whole, well then–

Then he would still have spared Ultramar an ork invasion, safeguarded the people he had sworn to protect. If he could hold the orks here, even if he died doing it, then he would have done his duty. Great Guilliman himself could not but approve.

On the thirteenth day the orks attacked, not from behind but from in front, and it was no mob of a warband that assaulted blindly this time, but a coordinated attack preceded by a fusillade of shoulder-mounted missiles. The barrage caught the front of the column in a storm of fire, felled several of the giant trees and sent wooden shrapnel clicking and slicing through the company along with its metallic counterpart. Proxis, on point, was hurled backwards ten yards by the blast and the ornamental wings were torn off his helm. Brother Castus was hit full on by one speeding missile and blown to shreds of flesh and shattered ceramite. His head, still in its helm, went flying down the column and killed one of Janus' Guardsmen like a cannonball of old Terra.

As the dirt was still falling in showers from the explosions, so a tight-knit mob of larger orks powered forward, firing stubbers from the hip and yowling in triumphant rage. Behind them came a crowd of their lesser brethren, firing autoguns, flamers and the occasional bright lance of a melta weapon. There were hundreds of them, advancing under the trees in a mass as thick as a moving carpet.

The Ultramarines went to ground and returned fire with all the discipline and efficiency of their kind. They placed well-aimed head-shots all up and down the line, and the orks started to crumple in mounds – but there were far too many of them, and they had no notion of breaking or running this time, not so long as the larger of their kind, the leader orks, came hurtling on in a fearsome phalanx, laying down a thicket of heavy fire…

'Brother-Sergeant Avila,' Calgar said on the vox.

'My lord?'

'Hold here, at all costs. Use grenades if they close, but try to keep them at a distance for as long as you can.'

'Acknowledged.'

'Proxis, Orhan, Mathias, with me.'

They were at his side in moments, Proxis staggering slightly. His ornate honour guard armour was sheared and battered and blasted down to the bare metal, but still seemed to be functioning.

'Brothers, we will flank them, come in from the left and take apart their leaders. Close combat – do not stop to fire but pitch straight in. Now follow me.'

Calgar led them back out of the front line and then took off at sprint in a wide circle to the rear of the Ultramarine position. He opened up all the energy reserves in the artificer armour, and flew across the ground at enormous speed while the other three Space Marines of his entourage struggled to keep up behind him. He saw the power sigils flicker red in his helm display, but threw energy into every system regardless, especially the Iron Halo – he would need all the protection it could give, shortly – and charging up the Gauntlets of Ultramar.

This assault had to be broken, or it would prove fatal to the company. It was larger and better equipped than any that had come before. The orks had finally become aware of the threat they faced in the depths of the Tagus and they were throwing a major formation at it.

The four Adeptus Astartes covered the ground with unbelievable speed, slashing aside a few stragglers that appeared in their path. Finally, Calgar raised a gauntlet, and they halted. He could hear his brothers panting over the vox.

'Now, move in with me, and keep close. We want the leaders, brothers – and ware those heavy weapons.'

He lit up Avila's sigil. 'Brother-sergeant, we are coming in on the left. Be prepared to shift fire.'

'Acknowledged.'

Even with auto-senses engaged, the roar of gunfire was enough to stagger the ears. The orks were flooding forward, leaving dozens of dead in their wake, but closing their ranks and howling en masse and sending out a torrent of fire that was chopping up the forest before them, felling whole trees, bringing branches clattering down in shattered clouds. The Ultramarines and Guardsmen to their front hugged the ground or crouched behind fallen timber, shifting position after each shot to keep the orks guessing. But all around their positions the incoming ordnance ploughed the wet ground into a mire and filled the air with debris. They were close to being pinned down. When that happened, the orks would charge in to close combat, and it would be over – for not even Space Marines could match the strength and numbers now advancing.

'Throne be with us,' Calgar muttered. Then he plunged forward as fast as the ancient armour he wore could go. He let loose one devastating volley of storm-bolter fire that flayed a dozen of the enemy, then lit up the Gauntlets of Ultramar, and in seconds was right there in the midst of the ork ranks, in among the leaders, their heavy weapons a clumsy hindrance at such close range.

He punched clear through the hide and entrails of the orks before him, ripping out their innards as he withdrew his fists. The Iron Halo that arced above his helm flashed and flamed as it deflected blow after blow, and he spread his fingers and chopped the enemy to pieces, the concussion of his own strikes running up his forearms and jarring his bones. He took apart six of the leaders in mere moments, felt a tug as one tried to wrench off his head, and tore that ork's arm clear from its shoulder.

He moved in a welter of slaughter, and behind him were Proxis and Orhan, wielding the axes of Ultramar, cleaving the foe into twitching pieces. Guarding their back was the terrible, black skull-faced figure of Mathias, who swung his crozius arcanum until it flew with blood that sizzled and steamed on the energy field that encased it.

The four of them were as close-packed as the fingers in a fist, and they blew the ork leaders apart, killing them where they stood, their helms blank masks of Imperial hate, power armour whining with the workload, sigils lighting up in their displays, power-packs smoking at maximum yield. The ork host split around them, the lesser of its members drawing back and opening up with autogun fire, and a blast of flame that enveloped them all for a few seconds before they smashed their way clear of it. Still burning, the Ultramarine armour shrugged off the flames, and the four of them opened out. Calgar blinked on the storm-bolter sigil again and strafed the ork lines like a man scything wheat, the intense fire chopping down any group of xenos that was trying to stand and rally. He felt incoming rounds impact on the artificer armour, punching through the protective field of the Iron Halo, and saw a missile flash past his face.

'Take out their heavy weapons,' he said over the vox. 'Sergeant Avila, advance by bounds. Let us finish this thing, brothers.'

Avila's squad came up to join them, the battle-brethren moving by twos, adding their fire to the slaughter, and behind them Janus'

Guardsmen followed, unwilling to be left out of the fight, awed by the example of their liege lord.

The jungle caught fire and flamed up around them. The ground burst up in a concussive series of grenade blasts. Brother Orhan was knocked to his back and a great ork pounced on him, gargling hate. He plunged his fingers into the thing's eyes and ripped the great bony skull in two pieces, then stood up and threw the shattered bone remnants of the ork's head back at its fellows. Retrieving his axe, he leapt once more into the fray.

The ork host was in a great crescent, and the Ultramarines were at the concave belly of it. The wings were closing in, about to surround the Ultramarines and Guardsmen who were all in a compact mass now, Janus' men dodging nimbly between the struggling giants all around them. Just as the two horns of the crescent were about to close, the last gun servitor rumbled up, its tracks spraying muck, and let loose with a torrent of heavy bolter fire that broke off one horn of the crescent and sent it buckling back in on itself.

With that, the fight finally began to leave the orks. While many still continued to charge forward, immolating themselves under the guns of the Ultramarines, and more sniped from a safe distance, a great mass of them began to back away, still howling.

'Follow them up, brothers – with me!' Calgar cried. The storm bolters cut down swathes of the enemy as he advanced, and finally clicked dry. He sprinted forward into the mass that was retreating before him and laid about himself like a prizefighter drunk with violence. Red sigils were flaming all over his helm display, but he did not hesitate. The thing was in the balance now – it could go either way.

'Keep the pressure up!' he heard Proxis shout. 'Break them, brothers – they are almost there.'

And then the orks could take no more. Even their mindless savage courage had its limits. They broke. Scores turned and ran, the stronger trampling the weaker, the unhurt shoving aside the wounded. Their formation was scattered and became a horde of running individuals.

'Single shots,' Avila said. 'Conserve ammo.'

'A home for every bullet,' Mathias said, and there was laughter over the vox, the dark, hard laughter of men on the cusp of victory.

Even the dampness of the jungle could not dim the flames. Gouts of promethium still blazed here and there, bright in the shadow of the rainforest, and in the air was the reek of fecund broken earth, while banks of smoke floated low above the roots of the trees, like a ground fog.

The enemy lay in heaps. Here and there one wriggled and struggled under the body of its fellows, until a bolter barked out and took off its head.

The Ultramarines reloaded what ammo they had left, saw to their own wounded and policed the battlefield.

Calgar watched his brethren at their work. He was weary, he who rarely knew true physical tiredness, and his armour was injecting his mighty frame with analgesics and stimulants. The artificer armour had preserved his life in the thick of that mayhem, aided by the Iron Halo, but all the same he saw upon it the thick dents of bullet strikes, the deep scars of energy blades mere increments from his own flesh, sparks flashing and spitting out of several rents in the ancient ceramite. In his helm display several sigils still blinked red, while others had settled into steady amber. He reloaded the storm bolters with the last of their ammo and flexed his fingers.

Proxis limped over, axe on his shoulder. Very little trace was left of honour-guard finery now. All the ornamentation that had once bedecked his power suit had been torn and blasted off, and he was as mud-coloured as the bloody ground on which he trod. He doffed his battered helm and lifted his eyes to the canopy above, darkening now with the beginnings of night.

'For a moment there, I thought we might be in trouble,' he said, and grinned.

Calgar set a hand on his friend's shoulderplate.

'For a moment there, I think we were.'

Mathias joined them. The Chaplain's skull helm was stained with ork flesh and viscera. 'Emperor be praised. We do his work–'

'And that is its own reward,' Calgar and Proxis said together, finishing the proverb.

'They fled north,' Calgar said thoughtfully after a moment's silence.

'To what, I wonder,' Proxis said.

'Chapter Master, our injuries are minor, our losses light, all things considered. But we have no logistical back-up, no resupply,' Mathias said. 'In short, we do not have the means to fight another such skirmish.'

'I am well aware of that, brother,' Calgar said.

'We've been using some ork rounds in the bolters, but they jam the firing mechanisms too often when used in automatic,' Proxis said, a snarl flitting across his face.

'Then we will fire single-shot from here on in,' Calgar told him. 'And we will gather what heavy weapons have been left in the hands of the enemy dead. I know that ork weaponry does not function well in the hands of others, but there is Imperial hardware lying around here too, brothers, looted during some older campaign of these xenos. We will make it work. We will break trail in the dark and make a camp off to the west of our route, and spend a few hours working on what weaponry and ammunition is worth scavenging.' He paused.

'We will fight on, brothers, for as long as it takes. I for one do not intend to end my days in this jungle.'

'It is a tiresome spot,' Proxis agreed with a crooked smile. Then he laughed again. 'Picking over ork ammunition as though it were made of gold, scrabbling for a few rounds to cram into our bolters – my lord, I think of the massive arsenals of Hera's Fortress on Macragge, and I do not know whether to laugh or weep.'

'Whatever you choose, do it in your own time,' Calgar said tersely. 'For now, there is work to do.'

They sat in a ring, in the darkness some five miles west of the battlesite, every Ultramarine surrounded with what looked at first glance like a mound of scrap metal, battered and ill-cared-for weapons and magazines, most of Imperial mark, all being gleaned for anything useful. For now, Janus' surviving Guardsmen stood sentry over the industrious battle-brethren as they worked to scavenge what they could, while Calgar stood watchful with them.

Lieutenant Janus had aged twenty years in as many days, but his eyes were still bright and hard, and he went up and down the thin line of his men with a word for every one of them. Calgar watched him approvingly. Such a soldier might have been worthy to become a neophyte in the Adeptus Astartes, if only he had been found young enough.

Such were the massive genetic and surgical modifications made to a would-be Space Marine that only the young could hope to accept the process and bear it to fruition. It was rare indeed for anyone over fourteen years of age to survive that brutal initiation, and yet tens of thousands tried every year, volunteers from the great families of Macragge and hopefuls from all across Ultramar. Out of those myriads, perhaps a dozen finally managed to bear the Ultima sigil on their shoulder one day and took their place among the battle companies, gaining for their families everlasting honour, and for themselves, a life of discipline, endurance and endless warfare.

'Your men are bearing up well. You should be proud of them,' Calgar told Janus quietly as the Astra Militarum lieutenant came over and saluted him.

'Thank you, my lord.' The young man's face lit up for a second, the exhaustion leaving it. 'There are only eight of us left, but we will never let you down.'

'I believe you.'

'My lord, may I speak freely?' Janus' face had settled into fear and stubbornness. Calgar knew what he was about to say.

'The answer is no, lieutenant. Your men may not stay behind. We do not abandon our own. That is not our way.'

'We are putting your survival in jeopardy, lord. None of us want that.'

'You will obey orders, lieutenant. And for now, your orders are to fight side by side with the Ultramarines. There is no more to be said on the matter.'

Janus saluted him again, and their eyes met. There was in the young man at that second such pride shining out that Calgar knew in his hearts he would have made a fine battle-brother. He knew also that Janus would not survive this campaign – his sort never did. Willing as horses, faithful as hounds, they would fight on until they died, and would do so without a word of complaint. As all soldiers should.

Later on, Calgar stood alone and watched over the camp in the night. Everyone in the company had been ordered to sleep, even the Ultramarines. They needed only a few hours in as many days but had now been awake almost constantly for two weeks, and Calgar wanted everyone rested for what he was sure would be a hard day in the morning.

The clouds had thickened overhead, and there was not a star to be seen. A hot heaviness was in the air, which even nightfall could not lift. There was a storm coming. He could feel it, smell it in every ion. The morning would bring it upon them, and he stood there alone and figured it into his plans. There might be a way to use it – to resort to stealth instead of this brute battering at a closing door.

Calgar was not alone for long. The pale blue glimmer of the

Librarian's psychic hood came through the dark towards him, and he nodded at Valerian as the psyker approached, sensing in him a pent-up excitement.

'My lord, I have news, perhaps good news.'

'Then share it, brother.'

'I have been monitoring the vox constantly since the crash. All I have been able to pick up thus far are the floods of gibberish the orks produce. They saturate the aether like sewage. But now and then I have gleaned some nuggets that make sense, and I have been building a picture of events across the planet. It is not detailed, or particularly coherent–'

'Spit it out, Valerian, before I grow old standing here.'

Valerian bowed slightly. 'It would seem that there are many ork tribes involved in the invasion, and it has not yet metamorphosed into a Waaagh! – the psychic signature of such an event would be unmistakable. There is one supreme warlord who is directing operations, however. It has not yet made planetfall, but will soon – all the other ork tribes are in fear of it – and when that happens, I believe the momentum will be there for a Waaagh! to be created.'

'And then things will become interesting indeed,' Calgar said.

Again, Valerian bowed. 'There is more, my lord. Zalathras, principal city of this world, has been assaulted, but for now at least, it is holding. Fresh ork forces are on their way from orbit even as we stand here. The city is under siege, surrounded, but its defences are formidable for such a border world, and the orks are hard at work constructing siege lines and preparing for another assault, one to be made with overwhelming force.'

Calgar stared out into the night, his bionic eye shining red. 'Your information is invaluable, brother. I thank you for it.'

'One last thing, the most important perhaps. The planetary fleet has been all but wiped out, as might be expected, but I have established intermittent contact with a psyker aboard a ship in low orbit, a vessel which has been evading the ork squadrons for some days now.'

'What kind of ship?' Calgar asked sharply.

'A rogue trader, lord, of no military consequence. But the psyker – he is the ship's Navigator, but he possesses minor telepathic ability – thinks that it may be possible for them to pick us up, if we can find a suitable landing site somewhere in the jungle. We could then be ferried to the capital in minutes, instead of…' Valerian trailed off.

'Instead of fighting our way through fruitless battles, hundreds of miles from our goal.' Calgar's interest quickened. 'Can this psyker be trusted, brother?'

'I do not know, my lord. If it is a ruse, then it is one whose subtleties are beyond the usual brute cunning of the orks.'

'You must have some sense of the man's psyche.'

'I do. It is troubled, damaged even. But I sense no taint of the Great Enemy. If I were to make a guess, I would say that he is genuine.'

Calgar stared at the Librarian, hope flaring in his hearts. But it was heavily leavened with scepticism. In this universe, luck was more often bad than good, and he did not like the idea of committing his fate to such an unknown element.

'If we go down this route, brother, then we risk everything.'

'I know that, my lord. But, forgive me, are we not in a position of great risk as it stands?'

Calgar said nothing for a long moment, weighing up the new information, plugging it into his map of events. Pondering on luck, both good and bad. And analysing the weather change in the air.

They could not fight their way through to Zalathras. Even if they were able to break through the ork forces now massing in their path, by the time they made it to the city walls, the city would be a burning shell – he was sure of that now. It would take weeks, if it were possible at all.

This new thing – it might be their salvation, it might be an attempt to flush them out of the jungle, but either way, it could not be ignored.

The risk had to be taken. This time, he would chance something to luck, and the Emperor's Grace.

'Contact this psyker of yours tonight,' he told Brother Valerian. 'Give him our location and ask him to direct us to a suitable landing spot for his ship.' He paused. 'Does he know that I am here with this party?'

'He knows only that there are Adeptus Astartes among us, lord.'

'If he has any brains, he will have guessed as much. My coming here was no secret. But we must hope that all concerned believe I was still on the *Fidelis* when it was attacked. Do not reveal my presence here, Valerian, but get this ship to us, as soon as you can. There is not a moment to lose.'

He looked out at the dark hooting depths of the rainforest that surrounded them – dripping, dank, full of the stink of rot. But there was a sense of change on the air. A storm was coming.

He would not leave his bones in such a place. If he had to die on this world, then it would be at a place and time of his own choosing, and this was not it.

# ELEVEN

THE THUNDEROUS RATTLE and roar of flying a spacefaring craft through the chop of a heavy atmosphere had to be heard to be believed. It was not just heard; it was felt in every bone, and the very fabric of the ship seemed to moan and protest at the buffeting it was getting.

'Bring her in low and slow, Hester,' Morcault said, raising his voice to be heard over the din. He was tapping his pitchthorn stick on the steel decking of the *Mayfly*, and suddenly grew irritated by the nervousness that the tic betrayed.

The entire crew was on the bridge; even owl-eyed Scurrios had left his lab for the moment, and Gortyn had abandoned the drives for the seldom-used engineer's console on Morcault's left. He swept his gaze over the dials and readouts of the cogitator at his station now and then, but the hirsute engineer was as gripped as any of them by the drama of the moment, despite his perpetual scowl.

Morcault looked over the augur display, his heart thumping, afraid that at any moment it would crowd with red lights. Under him, the *Mayfly* danced and lurched as it powered through the thick atmosphere of Zalidar, like a Terran ship making heavy weather of an ancient sea.

'Jodi?'

The Navigator sat at his station beside Hester, eyes closed. But through the thick fabric of his bandana the glow of his third eye could be made out, blinking every so often. His presence on the bridge was unsettling; usually he only came up here during a warp translation. But now Arnhal was intent on other things.

'They are at the rendezvous, but they have been pursued. The orks are closing in on all sides.'

Morcault cursed. 'Hester–'

'I know what I am doing, old man,' his first mate shouted at him. 'Leave me be, unless you want to take the yoke yourself.'

Once, Morcault had been the finest pilot in the sector, a daredevil, a voidsman of singular talent. But his reflexes had slowed with age. He was still a cut above most, but he could not match Hester's skill now, though he itched to take control of his ship in his own hands.

'Fifteen miles to landing zone,' Scurrios called out, pushing his bottle-thick spectacles up his nose. Every time the turbulence shunted the ship, they fell down again.

There was a loud clank from the stern of the *Mayfly* somewhere, and Gortyn raised his eyes to the deckhead of the bridge and swore as Morcault had done.

'She's not built for this, Ghent.' The airframe screeched around them as if to agree with his words.

'It won't be for long, one way or another,' Morcault told him grimly.

'Nine miles,' Scurrios said mechanically. Then the little man looked up from his screen. 'Augur has caught three contacts closing fast to our rear.'

'Those damn fighter-bombers again,' Morcault growled, leaning forward in his chair. 'Countermeasures.'

The ship leapt under them, twisting, battered by dense cloud. The viewports were a grey blank, streaked with rain and illuminated by the odd lightning flash that lit up the entire bridge.

'If they can home in on us through this, then they're better pilots than I am,' Hester snapped. 'Gortyn, airbrakes – give me thirty per cent.'

The ship shuddered as though it had been struck. Morcault was lifted momentarily out of his chair and then thrown back into it again. He dropped his stick and clicked his restraint harness in place about his chest.

'Reducing speed. Countermeasures away,' Hester said, 'though much good they'll do in the middle of all this muck.'

'Four miles,' Scurrios told them. There was a shake in his voice. One hand was clamping his glasses to his face.

'Disengaging hold door locks,' Gortyn said. 'I'd better get down there to welcome our guests. Jodi, you'd best be damned sure of yourself. I don't want to be opening the bay doors for a mob of orks.'

'They are in place, waiting for us,' Jodi said in a faint voice, hardly heard over the chaos of the storm. 'They are fighting now. The orks are in the clearing.' His hand scrabbled at the arm of his chair as though seeking a glass. He licked his dark lips.

'Perfect,' Gortyn snarled. He threw aside his harness and left the bridge, lurching as the ship yawed under him. 'Be ready for my signal,' he called out to Hester as he left.

She did not reply. Her good eye gleamed as bright as the mechanical one as she worked the yoke and the throttles, and studied the altimeter and the trim dials. 'Like flying through soup,' she muttered.

'Landing zone in twenty seconds,' Scurrios said shrilly. 'Fifteen seconds.'

'Hold on,' Hester said, and she slammed on the retros. There was a pummelling roar that echoed throughout the ship and the *Mayfly*'s nose came up, while it jerked and lurched under them like a running dog coming to the abrupt end of its leash.

The fabric of the vessel groaned and screamed, and a spray of sparks spat out of the drive console. One of the servitors, unhurried and calm, extinguished it with a spray from his bio-mechanical arm, and the other ranged over the cogitator circuits, tapping in adjustments to the power feed, easing the pain of the ship, placating the machine-spirit with an influx of coolant.

'Red line,' he creaked in one of the few binaric phrases Morcault still understood. 'Adjusting.' Then he went silent. His fellow joined him, and they worked the consoles as though playing some delicate and intricate musical instrument. For all their work, red lights were flashing on all the boards.

'Taking her down,' Hester said, her voice a harsh rasp.

The retros thundered, and the ship shook like a rattle in the hand of a child. A child having a tantrum. Morcault unbuckled and retrieved his pitchthorn, grasping for every safety rail he could find.

'I'm going aft,' he told Hester.

'Mind your way,' she admonished him. 'Take-off will be even funnier.'

THE SHIP CRUNCHED down as Morcault was making his way to the hold, nearly hurling him to his face. Swearing and praying alternately, he tapped his way towards the stern. There was fresher air back here – the bay doors must be open. He made it to the gangway over the cavernous hold and slammed shut the airlock door behind him.

Rain and vapour were streaming into the belly of the hold ten yards below. He could see Gortyn at the loading console, his black beard dripping, and the roar of the downpour beyond the yawning hatch vied with the thunderous bellow of the *Mayfly*'s atmospheric engines.

And beyond that, the crack of gunfire, single shots and bursts.

Morcault ducked instinctively as a volley of bolter fire arced into the hold out of the rain, tracer rounds careering about too fast for the eye to follow. Then came running men, half a dozen of them in what might once have been Astra Militarum uniforms, but were now little more than muddy rags. They dragged two of their kind with them, trailing ribbons of blood across the plasteel decking. The gunfire grew to a tearing climax outside.

And then came a giant, following them.

In all his travels, Morcault had never seen one before, and he grasped the gangway railing and knelt, staring, everything else forgotten.

Almost eight feet tall, it was a man, or man-like, clad in bulky armour that had been scored and battered and was plastered with muck and wet soil. Once, it might have been blue, and there was still the remnant of a white sigil on one immense shoulder-guard. It looked up at him at once, and the muzzle of the bolter followed its gaze – the blank inhuman mask of it – then it looked away again.

'Hold secured. Proceed,' it said, the metallic, toneless voice filling the air. It took up a firing position with the rain streaming from it, and loosed off a series of aimed shots out into the storm of rain and wind beyond the ship.

More of them trooped in, dripping titans, firing as they backed up the ramp. Ten, fifteen – their feet resounded on the sturdy metal of the *Mayfly*. They seemed like things from another world – and they were. One fired a blast of promethium back the way he had come, and, for the first time, Morcault heard the other voices outside the ship, the gargled bellowing of the orks. He heard gunfire clatter off the ship's hull.

A nightmarish giant in black armour with a skull for a face counted the others in. He carried a huge stave-like weapon with a skull-headed eagle at its crest. Beside him were two more with fragments of glittering gold still clinging to their armour. They carried axes nearly as tall as a man in one fist and fired bolt pistols with the other, aiming with the unhurried care of creatures that did not know the meaning of fear – though Morcault could see the dark ranks of the orks outside now, storming forward, voices raised in the hellish cacophony of their kind. The front ranks were barely two hundred feet from the loading ramp.

Gortyn stood shocked and wide-eyed at the loading console, fist poised over the red locking lever. Tall and burly though he was, he looked tiny compared to the giants that had come aboard out of the downpour.

And last of all, one marched aboard who was greater than all of these.

Bare-headed, a thorned crown of iron rising above his skull, and one eye shining scarlet, a huge shape came striding out of the rain and into the crowded hold of the *Mayfly*. It turned and let loose a withering, deafening volume of fire from bolters hung beneath its fists, chewing up the advancing orks and toppling them in an avalanche of sundered, smoking meat.

'You may seal the hatches, shipmaster,' it said, in a voice that stunned the air. Gortyn, still staring, yanked down on the locking lever, and the loading ramp began to come up while the bay doors slid closed. A clatter of explosive rounds spattered on the heavy plasteel doors as they came together, and then there was a resounding thump, and the green light went on above them.

Gortyn thumbed the ship's comm. 'Get us out of here!' he shouted at Hester on the bridge, and it was a matter of seconds before the *Mayfly* answered. With a shattering jolt, it leapt up under him, the frame of the ship protesting, keening like some great overworked animal. The G-force flattened Morcault and the Guardsmen down on the deck and sent Gortyn tumbling from the bulwark, but the giants in their midst remained standing, balanced easily on the plasteel plates, rainwater running from their armour in filthy streams. Their leader, the only one whose face was visible, looked around, and finally caught Morcault's eye as the old man remained pounded by the ship's ascent, flat on the gangway above. He smiled.

'That was well timed,' he said.

'The ork fighter-bombers have drawn off – they can't see anything in this and their airkeeping abilities are even worse than ours,' Hester said. 'Everyone aboard?'

Morcault sat down in his chair, blinking. His old flesh was aching and bruised, but more to the point his mind was still dealing with the shock of it.

'Ghent, are you all right?'

'I'm fine. Stay low, Hester. We don't have to worry about being pursued, not in this weather. The storm was a blessing.'

'You look as though you have seen a ghost.'

Morcault shook his head, shaking out of his daze.

*He is here – on my ship.*

'Make for Zalathras, and – be careful, Hester. We cannot afford to go down, not now.'

'I prefer not to crash at any time, Ghent. Who are our passengers? Jodi here won't tell me a thing. I hope it was worth almost getting us all killed for.'

'Oh, it was worth it,' Morcault said, and he felt an absurd urge to laugh, but rubbed his bony hand over his face.

Jodi Arnhal turned in the Navigator's chair and stared at him. 'Is it true, Ghent? Is it him – is he aboard?' The young man's eyes were painfully bright.

Morcault nodded.

Jodi sank back in his seat. 'I was not sure if I could believe myself. I sensed it, just as we were landing, but I could not be sure.'

'You should have told me.'

'No. Telepathy is overrated, and my version of it is wholly unschooled. I was not certain until now – truly, Ghent.'

'What are you two babbling about?' Hester asked irritably, eyes still fixed on the pilot console and the information from the cogitators that rolled across it in streams. Visibility was nil, and she was flying the *Mayfly* by instrumentation alone. There was sweat on her face and her coveralls were soaked with it.

'Our passengers are Adeptus Astartes – Ultramarines,' Morcault said with quiet wonder.

Hester did not reply, but blinked rapidly as she sat guiding the ship through the storm.

'And their leader is here with them. Their leader, Hester. Marneus Calgar, Lord of Macragge, is aboard our ship.'

He had to stoop to enter the bridge, and twist sideways to make it through the doorway. When he straightened, it seemed that the *Mayfly* was not big enough to contain him. Like a huge obelisk he stood there, water dripping from his battered ancient armour. His face was long and pale, the bones pronounced and laced with the white lines of old scars. His hair was cropped short; it might have been a golden yellow. His bionic eye shone with the same red that was in Hester's, but the other was grey as the blade of a knife.

He looked as calm and at ease as though he were on the bridge of a battleship, instead of crammed into the bow of a tramp trader. There were rags of purity seals hanging from his torso, and his armour was scraped and pitted and clodded with the muck of the jungle, but where it was undamaged it shone a lustrous blue, and ran with forged patterns as beautiful as the swirl of oil in water. He said nothing, and no one on the bridge said a word as Marneus Calgar stood among them, staring out at the blank roll of the storm clouds the ship was battering through.

At last, he spoke. 'What is our position and course, shipmaster?'

Morcault cleared his throat. Gortyn was down in the drives, as though too shocked by events to come out. Scurrios was treating the wounded Guardsmen. Only he, Hester and Jodi Arnhal were on the bridge, along with the two servitors. Jodi stared at the Ultramarine Chapter Master as though he had forgotten how to blink, but Hester kept her gaze fixed rigidly forward at her controls.

'My lord,' Morcault said hoarsely, 'we are currently some two hundred miles south of Zalathras. We will be over the city in some twenty-five minutes.'

'Very good. When you contact the authorities there for landing permission, do not mention who you have aboard. We do not know who may be listening in.'

'Of course.'

'What is the status of Zalathras at present?'

'It is... it is besieged, sire. The ork host is encamped before the walls, and their aircraft conduct daily bombing runs.'

'Orbital bombardments?' Calgar asked sharply.

'None, my lord. There are rumours that orbital fire has been used further north, but it was crude and ill-aimed and largely ineffective. These particular orks do not seem to have mastered it, thank the Throne.'

'Indeed?' Calgar said, raising his eyebrow. His voice had a strange resonance. It was not particularly deep, but it seemed to have an echo of its own that filled the bridge.

Then he looked down at Morcault. It was hard to bear his gaze, but Ghent forced himself to hold it.

'This is your ship, is it not?'

'Yes, my lord.'

'Then you have my gratitude, captain, you and all your crew – but especially your Navigator here. Were it not for him we would still be battling hip-deep in orks down below. You have done the Imperium a valuable service. It will not be forgotten, not by me and mine.'

Jodi Arnhal's pale face flushed. His mouth moved, but no words came out.

'We would have done it for anyone,' Morcault found himself saying. 'No man should be left to the orks, no matter his station in life.'

Calgar nodded. The stone-hard visage softened. 'I quite agree,' he said.

It felt wrong to be sitting in his presence, but Morcault kept his seat; it was too small to be offered to him anyway, and the *Mayfly* was still dancing through turbulence. He felt he should say something more, but he was acutely aware of the two Imperium-coded servitors on the bridge, working away, blind to their guest. Stolen property, even if it were from a long time ago. But such things would be beneath Marneus Calgar's attention, surely.

'Your name has cropped up in reports from the Fringe from time to time,' Calgar said.

'I hope it was good news,' Morcault told him, and then gulped at his own presumption.

'It was certainly interesting. From what I can tell, Morcault, you know Zalidar better than almost anyone. You have made the system your life's work, as it were. My own geographical data on the planet is largely gleaned from your own explorations.'

'It has become something of an obsession,' Morcault admitted.

'Why? What is so special about Zalidar?'

'It was a virgin world when first I set down on it,' Morcault said. 'But no death world. It had simply been overlooked by man and xenos alike, left to evolve into a rich, balanced ecosystem.' He hesitated.

'It was… pure. I was the first man to set foot on so many mountains, to taste the water of unknown rivers, to see sights that no other member of my species had ever known. I became protective, even possessive, of the place. My lord, I think it just got under my skin.'

Calgar's organic eye narrowed. 'And now the orks are here, to infest and despoil it. I will need your knowledge of this planet, Morcault.

You have shown yourself to be a survivor, and such men are rarer than you think. When we land in Zalathras, you will remain with me as an aide. I hope you find that acceptable.'

'Of course, my lord. But my crew–'

'Your crew will of course stay with you, and your ship may well prove to be a useful asset.'

Something in Morcault bridled at the easy way Calgar laid claim to his friends and his ship all in one breath. 'My lord, I am not so sure that–'

'If you have a problem with that, you may tell it to the orks,' Calgar said shortly. 'Let me know when we are one minute from landing.' He turned to leave the bridge.

Morcault slumped. 'I will.'

Calgar paused, stooped in the doorway. He smiled slightly. 'Impressive servitors, by the way. Such models must be hard to come by in this part of the Fringe.'

Then he was gone, his heavy tread echoing in the companionway beyond.

JODI ARNHAL SPOKE up, his voice a little unsteady. 'Morcault,' he said, 'I have some advice for you. Try not to piss off the Chapter Master of the Ultramarines. For all our sakes.'

Morcault wiped sweat from his forehead. 'I shall bear that in mind,' he said.

Hester had not looked up from her console once. 'Approaching the ork lines. Let's hope their anti-aircraft batteries are asleep.'

Morcault thumbed the vox and slid his fingers slowly across the frequencies. Squawks and screeches echoed through the bridge, the grunted gargle of the orks, here and there the desperate transmissions of men cut off from the city. A world of pain flashing out into the aether. At last he settled on the code for Zalathras' military. Fennick had given it to him years before, the better to ease his comings and goings into Lascelle's Landing. But the spaceport was outside the walls now, overrun no doubt. The *Mayfly* would have to alight somewhere else.

'Zalathras air defence, this is the *Mayfly*, inbound to your location in figures two zero. Respond please,' Morcault said hoarsely.

They came back at once. 'This is Zalathras air control. State your entry code or stand off. We will fire on you if you do not validate.'

'This is Omega Mark Six Three Two, *Mayfly* civilian transport inbound your airspace in figures one nine, Ghent Morcault commanding. Please give us a landing site. Urgent. Acknowledge.'

There was an interminable hiss of static. The three of them sat on the bridge watching the blank, rain-battered viewports to their front while the ship bumped and swayed under them and lightning strikes flashed up in the thunderheads all around. But there were other lights in those clouds now also, bright yellow and red flares flashing silent in the storm, like lightning streaking up from the ground below. One exploded five hundred yards ahead in a black flower, and as they arced through it they heard the tink and clatter of shrapnel bouncing off the ship's hull.

'Ork flak guns. Someone down there has their eyes open,' Hester said tautly.

At last Zalathras came back on the vox. 'Omega Six Three Two, your code is confirmed. Set down on Dromios Square. Do not deviate from your current course or we will fire on you.' A pause, and then a different voice.

'Morcault, is that really you?'

'Fennick?' Morcault asked incredulously.

'I can't believe that tin can of yours is still in the air,' they heard the governor's voice say.

'Only just. Listen, Fennick, we have a priority cargo on board. Request you meet us in person on landing.'

'Impossible. You do realize there is a war on?' The attempt at humour sounded flat and forced. Fennick's voice was blurred with tiredness and tight with strain at the same time.

'It will be worth your while, my lord governor, I guarantee it,' Morcault told him.

'Very well. But if I find you have wasted my time, Morcault, you will live to regret it...' There was a sigh. 'Sending course corrections now... It is good to hear a friendly voice on the vox, Ghent. We thought we were all alone.'

'You are not alone, not by a long shot,' Morcault said. 'Landing in figures one six. I will see you soon, Lucius. Morcault out.'

'Friendlier than usual,' Hester said.

'A friend in need,' Morcault told her.

'Strap in, old man. We have another delightful landing ahead of us.'

They came in as low as they dared, cutting a fine balance between impenetrable raincloud and clusters of anti-aircraft fire. For Morcault, the two or three minutes they spent on the final approach to the city were among the longest of his long life. They were guided in by air traffic control on the Alphon Spire, and directed to land right in the middle of Dromios Square at the foot of the hive. As they flashed over the city, Morcault could see the broken buildings and ruins smoking in the rain, the craters of artillery bombardments, and here and there a fire left to burn itself out. Zalathras had been taking a pounding, but the walls were intact, and the massive Vanaheim Gate, once considered a mere vanity project, was now reassuring to see, towering over the formations of ork infantry that were teeming across the muddy plain to the north of the Dromion River.

Their numbers were numbing. Morcault's old eyes could not quite take in the full spectacle of the ork army, but they were at the very least in the many tens of thousands, the host straggling for miles back down to the river and swarming up to the very walls in places. He thought of the solitary specimen that Scurrios had dissected aboard this very ship, and the spores that it carried. There would be millions upon millions more now dropped upon the fertile soil of Zalidar. The world he loved would never be the same again.

The *Mayfly* dodged through the desultory barrage of flak that lanced up from the ork encampments – the enemy did not seem to think that the little freighter was worth firing upon – and Hester brought her down gently upon the paved expanse of the great square that dominated the Alphon district of the city.

As the retros died away and the ship settled on her gear, Morcault sank back in his seat with a sigh. It was done then. He had brought Marneus Calgar to Zalathras. The rest was up to others.

As he had promised, the governor of Zalidar was out there with a large escort of militia, all standing in the rain with their weapons ready, surrounding the ship as if they thought it might at any moment disgorge a horde of orks.

Morcault unbuckled. 'Come on, you two,' he said to Hester and Jodi. 'I want to see Fennick's face when he finds out who we have aboard.'

The cargo bay doors were just grinding open when Morcault and the others joined the rest of his crew in the hold. The Adeptus Astartes stood watchful, bolters poised, and at their head Calgar himself was poised, a lethal giant. Looking at him, Morcault understood for the first time why the Space Marines, upon landing amid primitive societies, were often worshipped as gods.

The rain swept in and there was a crack as the ramp came down on the rockcrete paving of the square. Calgar strode out of the ship with his brethren behind him, bolters levelled, and in the rear the Astra Militarum came bearing their two wounded on makeshift litters.

Morcault and his crew stood at one side. Hester pulled a raincloak over the old man's shoulders and he thanked her absently, all the while watching Lord Fennick's face. It was white and livid in the lightning flashes that came and went, and the militia were dumbfounded.

Several dropped their weapons and held up their hands as though surrendering. Gortyn gave a smothered laugh at the sight.

'Governor Fennick, I presume?' Calgar said, his voice somehow amplified – it must be the armour he wore. It carried easily over the hissing rain and the crump of artillery that rumbled under the storm.

Fennick's reply went unheard. Morcault saw the man master his shock, and then the wild flash of hope that lit up his eyes as he stared at the Chapter Master and the towering Ultramarines who stood with him.

Macragge had come to Zalathras at last.

# II
# THE SIEGE

# TWELVE

FENNICK THOUGHT HE understood now why Imperial architecture was so brutally massive. He stood before the map table in the palace and that great chamber now seemed perfectly proportioned to those who stood within it.

Marneus Calgar bent over the maps and studied them with an eye that missed nothing. Behind him, two more Ultramarines stood rigid as statues, power axes at their sides. Their ornate armour was scored and pitted and dulled with hard usage, but there was still an archaic sense of grandeur about them. These were members of the honour guard, veterans of a thousand battles.

But more unsettling even than them was the Adeptus Astartes Chaplain who was off to one side, his helm a white skull, his armour black as night. He had not spoken since entering the room, but stood resting his fists on his staff of office. None of the ordinary humans in the room would so much as look at him.

All of the Ultramarines radiated brute physical power, and it was difficult not to be cowed by their mere presence. And their lord was in a different class even from these.

Taller and broader in his artificer armour than any of his brethren, Marneus Calgar was the only one of them who was unhelmed, his own helmet maglocked to one thigh, a bolt pistol on the other. The massive power fists he had worn on arrival had been removed, the Space Marine Chaplain standing guard over them now as they sat upon a table at the corner of the room.

Calgar spoke quietly, did not raise his voice, and saw no need to assert his own authority over that of the Imperial governor. He simply assumed that he would be taking over control of the city, and Fennick did not for one moment feel like contradicting him. The sheer authority that emanated from the Lord of Macragge brooked no questions, allowed for no doubt.

This, standing a mere few feet from Lucius Fennick, one-time sergeant of the Guard, was one of the great figures of his time, one of the few names that were known and renowned across the entire human galaxy.

I finally got him here, Fennick thought. I never for a moment imagined it would be in circumstances like these, though.

Now he knew that Zalidar and Zalathras would at last make their mark upon the chronicles of man, not because of what they were, or what had been achieved here, but because this giant figure had come visiting, and had stayed to fight.

'And so the city is entirely invested on all sides, yes?' Calgar was saying in that calm, resonant tone of his. Fennick collected himself.

'Yes, my lord. The main force of the enemy appears to be opposite the Vanaheim Gate, but they have warbands all around the circuit of the walls. Their artillery is emplaced several miles to their rear, and they have also been working on what we believe is a landing pad for supply ships. Our own spaceport is outside the defences and was largely destroyed in the initial fighting. Our guns overlook the ruins.Nothing could fly in or out of there without being brought down.'

'What about the garrison – what do we have to work with?' Calgar asked.

'Boros?' Fennick said.

Colonel Boros stepped forward. He was less stocky than he had been; his broad face had become gaunt and his tan had faded. He wore standard Imperial body armour over his old leather harness and was as down-at-heel-looking as a private soldier except for the grimy badges of rank upon his shoulders. He stared up at Calgar from sunken eyes.

'We had a full division lined up to welcome you, my lord, as the initial assault took place. That worked in our favour. We were able to throw them straight into the fray and hold off the enemy long enough to secure the walls, but we lost heavily those first days.'

A trace of impatience showed on Calgar's face. Boros went on hurriedly.

'At present, we have inside the city the elements of five divisions of militia, but all of them are hugely understrength, with only light to medium weaponry. We number some sixteen thousand trained troops in all, and last week we opened the armouries and conscripted thirty thousand male citizens to make up our numbers. But these are soldiers in name only. They have received almost no military instruction, and can be counted on only to stand upon the wall and fire a lasgun.'

'Artillery?' Calgar asked.

'We have a battery of six Basilisks, only four of which are currently operational. We are trying to repair the other two as we speak. Also, a dozen Centaurs with heavy stubbers, and some sixty mortars, all of which have been emplaced at strategic points near the midpoint of the city, so they can bring fire down in any direction to protect the approach to the walls. We also have one Colossus heavy gun, but at the moment it is little more than a wreck. I have my artificers working on it.'

Calgar frowned. 'What about wall guns? What do we have in the towers?'

'There is a defensive tower every two hundred yards along the wall, my lord, and in each there is emplaced a heavy bolter, an autocannon or a multi-melta.'

'Vehicles? Do we have the means to make a sortie?'

Boros cleared his throat. He could not keep the keen penetrating gaze of Calgar's sword-pale eye.

'Sentinels and Chimeras, a dozen of each, of which two-thirds are runners, the rest–'

'Undergoing repair. I get the picture, colonel. You are not overly resourced on this planet, and no mistake. What about the fleet? Do any ships survive?'

Boros was about to speak, but now Rear Admiral Glenck stepped forward and interrupted him.

'The fleet, my lord, was largely destroyed in a valiant effort to aid your ship, the *Fidelis*, on the first day of the invasion.'

'And yet its commander stands intact before me,' Calgar said, and there was something in his tone which chilled them all. Glenck's flabby face went as white as marble. 'I was on the ground, my lord, coordinating. We managed to salvage a squadron of Furies. These now are stationed on the main avenues leading up to the Alphon Spire, hidden in the shells of large buildings.'

'No transports, light lifters, scout ships?'

'None worthy of the name. A single Sword-class frigate is still at large, somewhere in the system. It was detached from orbital duties by… by me before the assault began. We have not as yet been able to re-establish communications with it.'

'Make that a priority,' Calgar said. 'At present, any and all means of communicating the situation here to Ultramar must be utilised.'

'What of your own ship, lord?' Fennick asked.

'You know as much as I do, my lord governor. When last I was in contact with the *Fidelis*, the ship was about to make a warp translation for Ultramar.'

'I believe they may have succeeded,' Glenck spoke up. 'Certainly, something disrupted the enemy fleet long enough for some of my Furies to get away.'

'To make it into the warp is one thing. To get out again, after such an unscheduled and hurried entry, is quite another,' Calgar said. And his granite visage hardened further.

'We cannot count on the *Fidelis* getting through. It could be lost in the warp for months or years, if it survived the translation at all. No, gentlemen.' He straightened from the map table and loomed over them all. 'We must rely on our own ingenuity and will, if we are to prevail here on Zalidar.

'My absence will not have gone unnoticed, but the fighting companies of my Chapter are engaged in their own separate campaigns as we speak, and it will take time for them to disengage and redeploy. We are talking weeks, if not months, before we can hope for relief on this world.' There was a pause as this sank in. Calgar looked around them all – Fennick, Boros, Glenck and the cluster of young militia officers who stood stiffly to one side. Each commanded a division. Each looked barely old enough to need a shave.

'In the meantime, we must endure, and if possible attack the orks with all means necessary. A passive defence does not suffice when fighting greenskins. They will engulf us. We must be ready to strike out every time we see an opening, and keep the enemy off balance.' He paused, and once again let his cold stare range over the humans who stood before him.

'You have done well, these last weeks, to hold on here as you have. But this thing is only beginning.' He looked at Fennick. 'What is the population of Zalathras?'

Fennick blinked, grasping the numbers from his head.

'Some eight million, my lord.'

'And how do we stand for weaponry in the city arsenals?'

This time it was Boros who spoke.

'We have light weapons only, lord. All the heavy stuff is already up on the walls. I daresay there are enough lasguns to arm another couple of divisions' worth, but no more body armour or uniforms or vox equipment.'

'Men with guns, colonel,' Calgar told him. 'That is what we want, as many of them as we can get. It does not matter what they wear – it is not even crucial that they have good communications. We have a large perimeter to defend, and every inch of it must be covered by fire. If the orks gain a lodgement within the walls, then it is all over. Take volunteers first – young, able-bodied. My presence here should galvanise a few who were missed by your initial wave of conscription. Start instructing them at once in weapon use. You must establish a training cadre of experienced men – Lieutenant Janus and his surviving Guardsmen will help you.'

Boros bowed.

'I want the Basilisk battery to be made fully operational as soon as possible, and I want it keyed to my personal vox. It will be part of our reaction force. Six Basilisks will be a great help in disrupting any advance the enemy makes. The other vehicles will report to Lieutenant Janus. He will form a regiment of men who will become firefighters, ready to reinforce any threatened portion of the perimeter at a moment's notice. Are we agreed?'

They all nodded.

'What manufactoria do we have in the city that are germane to the war effort?'

Fennick was ready for this one. He consulted a list. 'The manufactorum district lies here in the shadow of Alphon Spire. We have three facilities for the production of light ammunition and power cells, and enough raw materials to keep them running at full capacity for eleven weeks.'

'And what is full capacity, Lord Fennick?'

'Four thousand cells a day, my lord, plus a hundred thousand bolter rounds.'

'It is not enough. It is not nearly enough.' Calgar frowned. 'The manufactoria must work round the clock, and the production of bolter ammunition must be quadrupled, at the very least. What of artillery ammunition?'

Fennick grimaced. 'We have no facility on the planet capable of making it.'

Calgar shook his head slightly. 'What store do we have?'

'A quarter of a million shells of all types.'

'We will burn through those in a matter of weeks. You must find a way to make more, Fennick. The Basilisks and mortars must be able to fire without rationing their munitions. Promethium?'

Fennick consulted his list again. 'Two thousand gallons.'

Calgar said nothing. He set one fist on the map table and the stout timber creaked under it.

'I see we have our work cut out for us,' he said at last, in that quiet tone of his which made them all straighten their spines a little – even the Ultramarines who stood behind him.

There was a silence. Finally, Calgar bent and studied the map table once more, and the gauntleted fist unclenched.

'Lord Fennick, I look to you to be my quartermaster. Your responsibility is to keep the troops supplied with arms, munitions and the means to sustain life. From here on in, every single commercial and industrial activity on this city will be geared towards the war effort. Every workshop capable of turning out a screw, every mechanic who can tinker with an engine – they all work for you now, and are as much under your command as my battle-brethren are under mine. The city is from this moment on under martial law.'

He looked at Fennick. 'Equip the men, my lord governor, and I will see that they are trained, and I will lead them in battle. Is that acceptable to you?'

'Of course, my lord.' Fennick felt his shoulders sag a little with relief. There was a tiny part of him that resented the way Calgar simply assumed command, but mostly he was glad to leave the decision-making to the Lord of Macragge.

The last two weeks had been a hellish series of improvisations and mistakes and bloody setbacks. Eight thousand men lost already – they barely even counted the bodies any more – and he had not had more than two hours' sleep a night since the first day of the invasion. Nor had Boros. The two men looked at one another now and he saw in Boros' eyes that same conflict of resentment and relief.

Calgar missed nothing. A tight smile played across his face. 'This is what happens when you invite the Adeptus Astartes to come calling, gentlemen,' he said. 'As I have noted, you have done well, but my people and I are trained for this, bred for it. You must trust me – I have been here before.'

Fennick met Calgar's steel gaze. He nodded. 'We are most grateful to you, my lord,' he said hoarsely. 'I am only sorry that my invitation has brought you to this place at such a time.'

'Places like this, times like this – they are what I was made for,' Calgar replied. Then he tapped the vellum map that sprawled across the table before him.

'Now, let us go into the detail,' he said.

The word went out all across the sprawling expanse of the city, a rumour that seemed to grow wings and flit the length of Zalathras' great walls, permeating every district, spreading through the exhausted workers in the munitions manufactoria. In the low-level slums below the towering hive-spires, it ran like wildfire. Marneus Calgar had landed, and was in Zalathras with the Ultramarines.

The news mutated as it travelled, and his escort grew from a dozen Ultramarines to a company, and a regiment of the famed First Ultramar Guards. People who had been under artillery barrage for days lifted their heads and began to hope again, and at the offices set up throughout the city men began to queue up to enlist in the new militia divisions that were forming, whilst in the crowded taverns others spoke of having seen the Ultramarines themselves marching through the city or upon the walls, blue-armoured giants that spread awe and hope in their wake.

Broadcasts were made across the city vox system, and Fennick finally announced publicly that the Lord of Macragge had come to Zalathras to share and lead their fight. Now the struggle would begin in earnest, and the orks would be broken before the tall walls of the city, as Marneus Calgar had broken their armies countless times before in campaigns that spanned the galaxy.

There was a sense of a great fist taking hold of life in Zalathras. Things became organised. The frantic improvisation and inefficiency of the first days vanished almost overnight. Militia patrolled the streets, rounding up every artisan and mechanic they could find and delivering them by the thousand to the great Vanaheim trade warehouses below Kalgatt Spire. Here a long series of workshops was set up, and men began constructing from scratch the machinery necessary for turning out the sinews of war, while in the long-established manufactoria, shifts of workers laboured round the clock. Production doubled in the first week after Marneus Calgar's arrival, and doubled again in the second.

To save fuel, the long trailers of raw materials that drove daily out of the city arsenal and other warehouses were now drawn by teams of petty criminals and deserters, harnessed to the long vehicles like draught animals a hundred at a time.

Those who protested or tried to evade their duties were taken aside and shot out of hand, and after the first few dozen had met this end the rest grew rather more cooperative. Mercy, like fuel, was in short supply.

But there was at least a sense of purpose, of order. As the rainy season drew on, and the downpours washed across the muddy plain before the Vanaheim Gate, so the tired inhabitants of Zalidar took hope and began to scan the grey overcast skies as if at any moment they expected an Imperial fleet to arrive in their relief.

And beyond the perimeter the encampments of the orks grew day by day, and desultory artillery barrages continued to sweep across districts of the city. But the Zalathi picked their dead out of the ruins and went about their daily business. The walls would hold, now that they were manned by the Ultramarines, they said. Zalathras would not fall, could not fall. Marneus Calgar would see to that.

'HOPE IS A wonderful thing,' Roman Lascelle said to Fennick.

The young nobleman was no longer the dandified gentleman he had been. Appointed captain of a militia company, he had seen his share of fighting on the walls already these last weeks, and now he wore plain camouflage fatigues and body armour. The only remnants of his old life seemed to be the rapier he still bore at his hip and the sneer he wore on his mouth.

'Long may it last,' Fennick replied.

'They can't dig trenches, not at this time of year,' Ghent Morcault told the other two. He pulled his raincloak tighter about his shoulders, though there seemed little point; the rain was blood warm, and in the end it saturated everything. In the gaps between downpours the air was filled with steam as moisture rose from the warm plascrete walls.

Down in the city, they were growing mushrooms on every vacant plot, and the fungi were already becoming a staple of the daily ration, along with anything else that could be grown quickly and harvested with a minimum of effort. Meat was already at a premium, and there were enterprising teams of men who worked in the sewers beneath the streets, snaring the great rat-like rodents that thrived there and bringing them up to sell in the bazaars, neatly gutted and skinned. Private enterprise: it was a wonderful thing.

Fennick, Morcault and Lascelle stood now on the walls of Zalathras, looking south. To their right loomed the huge barbican of the Vanaheim Gate, thirty storeys high and bristling with gun emplacements, half of which were empty. The barbican was blackened and pitted from four weeks of wild shellfire, but such was the strength of its construction that it was essentially undamaged. Kurt Vanaheim had made it to be his monument, and he had built well.

There were over a thousand men stationed within the Vanaheim Gate, and the enemy had launched assault after frontal assault upon it. All of these had been broken at little cost to the defenders. Now the orks were spreading out beyond effective range of bolter and autocannon, and formations were constantly on the march to the north, circling the huge walls of the city at a safe distance. They were harassed by intermittent fire from the city's mortars, but every tube had a strict ammunition schedule to follow at the moment, and the orks seemed unperturbed by their attentions.

Zalathras possessed three other gates besides the Vanaheim, positioned at the cardinal points of the compass. To the north, the Cascari, to the west, the Rosquin, and to the east, the Buridian, all named after the noble families whose funds had part-sponsored their construction. But Vanaheim's was the strongest, the most imposing. Fennick had filled in the other gates in the first week of fighting, pouring liquid plascrete behind the entryways so that they were now as solid and impenetrable as the walls they were set in. Only to the south did he leave the gateway intact, for he had intended to draw the orks in to attack it, and had largely succeeded. Until now.

'Half a dozen Basilisk batteries would tear them to pieces,' Fennick said, thumping his fist on the wall in frustration. 'As you say, they can't dig in, not in this weather. They're just milling about out there in the rain. I never knew orks could be so patient.'

'They have a leader who knows what he is about,' Ghent Morcault said. 'And he seems to be in no hurry. A singular type of ork indeed.'

'He lost thousands in the first attacks,' Lascelle said. 'They rushed the walls before they even had all their forces on the ground. Now they are just rotted mounds in the mud, all those corpses. He will have to try something different to take Zalathras – the walls are too high and strong.'

'Orks are aggressive to the point of mania, but they are not as stupid as many would like to make out,' Morcault told them. 'He is up to something, in those camps down by the river. You mark my words.'

'The river is in full spate, and the ground is a quagmire,' Fennick said. 'Zalidar works for us. As long as the full force of the rainy season is in play, I do not believe he can launch another major assault. And if he does, it will have to be here, at the Vanaheim. Only here do the gates still open. And the walls are too high to scale with ladders, and over a hundred feet thick. To blast a way through would take weeks.'

'Well, that is comforting... I wonder how long it will be before the Angels of Death come to the aid of their Master,' Lascelle drawled, looking up at the impenetrable sky. 'And if any of us lesser mortals will still be standing when they arrive.'

He smiled. 'I used to think my father had sent me off here to fester in a dead-end spot at the back end of nowhere – no offence, Fennick.'

'None taken.'

'And now I find myself wearing uniform and commanding men in what may be one of the more notable wars of our times. Fighting alongside Marneus Calgar himself, no less. I wonder what my father would make of me now.'

'He would be proud of you,' Morcault told him, 'or he is no kind of father at all.'

Lascelle gave the old voidsman a look almost of gratitude, but covered it with a harsh laugh.

'You do not know him.'

'I've heard enough of him, down the years, Lascelle. How you conduct yourself in the coming days will affect your family's name forever. Your gambling and whoring will all be forgotten, as will all our lives prior to the arrival of the Lord of Macragge. In the years to come, all that will be remembered of us is that we were here, now, and that we fought alongside him. That is a kind of fame few men are allowed.'

'Let us hope we live to enjoy it,' Lascelle said.

# THIRTEEN

THEY CAME IN the night, and they struck at the Vanaheim Gate. But they did not come rushing across the body-strewn swamp before the walls. They came hurtling out of the dark, rain-filled sky, a cloud of tiny lights bearing down on the defences like a shower of errant meteors.

They were all over the battlements before anyone even raised the alarm. Ork assault troops, lighter-framed creatures of their kind wearing jump packs, came swooping out of the darkness and landed like a hammer on the upper works of the Vanaheim. By the time the alarm klaxons were ringing out they had already overrun half a dozen heavy weapons emplacements and were turning the guns on their erstwhile owners. A reinforcing company of militia was cut down as it pounded along the battlements to take on the invaders, some eighty of them blown to shreds by the fire of their own autocannons.

A hard, bitter, utterly confusing fight began at close quarters on the upper storeys of the barbican, as the orks fought their way into the massive structure of the gate itself. Once inside, the assault wave jettisoned their jump packs and closed with the defenders in the corridors and passageways of the fortress, tearing the defenders limb from limb in the confined spaces below.

But those who fought and died there bought time for their comrades, who shut the heavy blast doors that guarded the covered ways to the gate mechanisms and the very heart of the Vanaheim. The orks, stymied, massacred every one of the defenders in the upper levels, while to the south of the city a massive warband, five thousand strong, began advancing on the walls. From the entire southern circuit of Zalathras, the fire began to flash out from every defensive tower and from the newly recruited militia companies who were holding the battlements. A huge explosion rose up from the Vanaheim, smoke billowing out of the interior as the orks set charges against the blast doors within.

The entire city came awake, shocked by the sudden fury of the assault. Lieutenant Janus' firefighting regiment clambered into their vehicles and thundered down the broad expanse of Dromion Avenue towards the south, Sentinels out in front, the bipedal war walkers striding along like woken monsters. Behind them thundered a long convoy of squat Chimeras, their tracks squealing and rattling on the paved road.

In a single modified vehicle with an open top, Sergeant Avila and five Ultramarines of his squad rode easily, their helmed heads sweeping the streets of the city to their front. Avila blinked on the command vox sigil in his heads-up display.

'Attack on the Vanaheim. Looks like an aerial insertion. Word from the walls is that a host on the ground is following up. Heavy fighting within the barbican. We will debus there and work our way up to the roof.'

'Secure the gate mechanisms,' Calgar's voice came back. 'That is the priority. Once they are safe, then proceed with clearance.'

'Acknowledged,' Avila said. He looked at his brethren, who all nodded at him one by one.

The Ultramarines jumped off the Chimera a hundred yards short of the gate. Janus' Sentinels had already established a perimeter and the other Chimeras were disgorging troops, while their turret guns ranged back and forth, seeking targets. Avila found Janus studying the barbican through a pair of magnoculars.

'We will go in first,' he told the Guardsman. 'You follow up. Hold every junction and doorway in force. Defence in depth. Nothing must get through.'

'As you say,' the lieutenant said. He smiled. 'Good hunting.'

The massive Ultramarine sergeant nodded. The two had known each other for years, and did not need to speak further. Janus was as indoctrinated in Ultramarine fighting methods as any ordinary man could hope to be, and he had proven his worth many times.

'First Company!' he shouted. 'Form up on me. Prepare to move out. Flamers to the front.' Beside him the half-dozen survivors of the *Fidelis* platoon stood in militia uniforms with the sigil of Ultramar painted on their body armour. The rest of the militia companies gathered around these veterans.

Avila and his brethren ran into the deeper shadow of the gate, the rain shining on their armour. The postern here had not been made for his kind, and he had to stoop to enter. Once inside, the schematic of the interior popped up on his helm display, and he followed the fastest route up to the gate control room, spurning the large elevators and pelting up the stairwells with his squad on his heels. The Space Marines took the steps four at a time, as fast as a lean man can sprint. Up they went, into the maw of the fighting above, and they switched to infrared as the smoke thickened around them.

Marneus Calgar studied the readouts on the vid-slates arrayed around him. The green arrowheads of his own forces were congregating on the area around the Vanaheim, whilst beyond the walls the ork host massed in its thousands. Clearly, the storm boys' mission was to gain control of the gates and open them for their fellows outside. By his reckoning at least five hundred of them had dropped upon the barbican and the walls next to it, and they were now in possession of the upper three storeys of the massive fortress and fighting their way down level by level to the gate controls on the twenty-fifth. The Zalidari militia could not hope to match the orks in a fight at close quarters.

They were being slaughtered.

'It looks like being one of those nights,' Proxis said behind him.

'Indeed. Avila will need to be reinforced. The situation is more critical than I had supposed. Proxis, take the balance of his squad and go there.'

'It shall be my pleasure, lord.' He turned to go.

'Wait.'

Proxis paused.

Calgar scanned the screens. The fighting was two miles from where he now stood, high up in Alphon Spire. Clearly, this location was too far away from the heart of the matter to be an effective command post, despite the excellence of its communications hub.

Or is it just that I want to be down there in the thick of it? he wondered.

Ordinarily he could rely on his own brethren to handle any tactical situation, but they were so few here on Zalidar that his own presence might be worth more in the front line than up here. He scanned the rest of the perimeter. The orks had opened up with their artillery, but by and large the rest of the city was unthreatened. The Vanaheim Gate was clearly the point of main effort tonight.

'I will go with you,' he told Proxis as the Ancient lingered there.

Then he turned to Fennick and the rest of the Zalidari staff, who stood mute. 'Full mobilisation. I want every man up on the walls. I do not think this is a diversion, but we cannot take that chance. I will monitor the command vox frequency. Inform me at once if an assault materialises anywhere else along the line.'

Fennick bowed. Before he could say anything, Calgar had swept out of the room with Proxis in his wake.

Sergeant Avila sent the blast of promethium into the face of the nearest ork, and, still depressing the trigger of his combi-bolter, he walked the white fury of the flame to left and right, engulfing those who were spreading out around it. The foremost orks burned like torches, shrieking and bellowing and clawing at their cooked flesh. He booted one aside, drops of promethium burning on his own armour, and strode on.

'Twenty-fourth floor. One more to the gate controls. Let us hope they sealed the door. Brother Gauros, Brother Surian, you're up. They're massing up the corridor.'

The passageway was full of acrid smoke, and bolter rounds were zipping down it. One clanged off Avila's shoulderplate. Another snapped back his head as it gouged a furrow in the ceramite of his helm.

'Suppress these scum, brothers. We have stood here long enough.'

The corridor was wide enough for three Adeptus Astartes, and now two of Avila's brethren flanked him, both bearing heavy bolters. They opened up, the massive weapons jumping in their hands, the 20mm rounds whining as they sped through their belts from the magazines on their backs. A torrent of tracer fire sped over the burning orks and the far end of the corridor erupted in shrieks and the multiple slaps of the rounds exploding in flesh.

'Well enough,' Avila said. 'Forward by twos. There should be a stairwell on our right sixty yards ahead.'

More gunfire, a hellish racket. Rounds thumped into the three Ultramarines with flat smacking sounds. Shards of ceramite and plasteel sparked through the smoke. Avila saw Brother Gauros' sigil blink amber a moment, but neither he nor brother Surian backed so much as a step. They laid down a flood of bolter fire and followed it up with gouts from the flamer, blasting almost blind into the smoke, following the bright shapes that came and went on the infrared.

'Gauros, are you hit?' Avila demanded.

'Light wound,' Gauros grunted. 'Systems nominal. I've had worse in training.'

'End those scum. We must move forward, brothers. We cannot allow the xenos access to the gate controls.'

The corridor was solid reinforced rockcrete, but the bolter fire was shredding it into powder, deepening the fog of smoke that billowed within. They stepped over ork bodies that had been chewed up by the heavy bolters, blood and dust making a red mud under their feet.

'Here is the stairwell,' Brother Surian said. And then, 'Grenade!' Without hesitation he threw himself on top of the hissing little cylinder that had tumbled down from the stairs above. It went off with a dull crump that blasted his body four feet into the air. His shoulder plate clanged off Avila's helm. In the readout, Surian's sigil flashed crimson.

Avila dashed into the stairwell and ran up the stone steps with every ounce of speed his body and power armour could give him. Halfway up he saw a dark shape and fired a long burst, heard a bellow of agony, and stood, the targeting cogitator in his helm lining them up – three orks with bolt pistols and chainswords. They came charging down the stairs at him and died one after the other. He set his boot on the wriggling back of the last one as it lay wounded and blew out its skull with a single point-blank round.

'Stairwell clear. Move up. How is Brother Surian?'

Gauros' voice came back at him. 'Gone, sergeant.'

Avila paused a second, then said, 'Make haste, brothers. With me – we are almost there.'

He had known Surian for twenty years. They had served together on the *Fidelis* for six.

'Farewell, my brother,' Avila murmured. Then he raised the

combi-flamer he carried as more orks appeared on the stairs above him.

Calgar jumped off the roof of the Chimera that had borne him through the city and led the Ultramarines into the smoking hell that was the Vanaheim Gate. As he pelted up the stairs he engaged his storm bolters, and the chainlinked belts that fed them clicked and chimed as they swung from the dorsal ammo well. No more worrying about ammo. Not today.

Sergeant Avila's voice came over the vox. 'We are at the gate control room. The door is still sealed. Heavy enemy presence on this level. We will go firm here and defend the door.'

'Acknowledged,' Calgar said. He scrolled through the formations in his helm displays, saw that one of Avila's squad was dead and three were nursing wounds. He had been right to come here. It was the main effort of the enemy, and its strategy was close to success.

He felt the rage rise in him. I have been complacent, he scourged himself. I underestimated the guile of the orks. Their leader is more formidable than I would have believed.

Up the stairs he went, so fast that he left Proxis and the rest of the squad behind. He passed Brother Surian's body and ran up the last staircase with the sound of fighting raging above.

He came out on a wide landing, fifty yards to a side. It was full of dials and monitors and data screens; the control panels for the elevators and the fire control systems were here.

The space was full of orks.

Wide blast doors, as heavy and formidable as those on the entryway of a missile silo, rose to one side, and in front of them Sergeant Avila and his brethren were fighting hand to hand now. A burst of promethium blossomed out, engulfing an Ultramarine, and the battle-brother fought on while he burned. The rage rose in Calgar's throat until he thought he would choke on it.

'Guilliman!' he roared, augmenting his own voice with the suit speakers. His battle cry rippled through the smoke, and as the orks turned he pointed his fists at them and opened up with the storm bolters.

He felt the savage, satisfying jump of the weapons' recoil through his forearms, and saw the nearest orks disintegrate as the heavy rounds blasted clear through them and into the flesh of those that stood behind. Then he surged forward, lighting up the Gauntlets of Ultramar, and powered bodily into the mass of orks before him.

His fists swept out and the disruption fields that cloaked them tore the enemy apart. He shrugged off the strike of chainswords, feeling the teeth of them snag and grind into the superlative ancient armour that protected him. A chop of his right wrist beheaded one ork that was snarling almost in his face. He grasped the protruding lower jaw of another and tore it out of the creature's skull.

As quick as the blink of an eye, he switched back to the storm bolters and slammed out a volley, the muzzles of the weapons almost touching his foes. They sizzled with burning ork meat.

He raised his power fists, strode forward, and pitched in again, his arms slamming back and forth, a blur of mayhem. A bolt pistol was fired at his helm, and for a moment the concussion of the impact blinded him, and his display fizzed and darkened.

He struck out on instinct, switched back and forth between power fists and storm bolters, blasted the enemy back, and booted out at grappling claws that sought to tear him down.

His helm display steadied, though there was a line of white broken static buzzing across it now, and the Iron Halo rune was greyed out. He felt the suit inject him with an analgesic in the side of his neck, though he did not mind the pain. He welcomed it. He welcomed the blood that painted his armour, the clots of ork flesh that festooned it and hung dripping from his fingers. Moments like this were what he was born for – to bring death to the enemies of mankind, to serve his Emperor and his Chapter, to fight for his brothers.

He clamped down on the battle rage, stepped back with another roar of storm-bolter fire. The enemy was thinned out. They were peeling away for the broken doors at the back of the chamber. Calgar looked around. Proxis had been fighting at his side, guarding his back in the melee, and for those few minutes of slaughter he had not even been aware of the Ancient's presence. And Sergeant Avila was moving up with his entire squad now. There were a dozen Ultramarines standing together, and the orks knew they stood no chance against such a force. They were streaming away, yowling with hate and frustration, turning to fire wild bursts as they withdrew towards the stairwells.

'Brother Jared, Brother Antigonus, stay by gate control,' Calgar said, breathing deep. 'The rest, follow me. Let us cleanse this place, brothers.'

They fought upwards, level by level, room by room. Calgar fell back and let Avila's brethren gut the place, a grenade through every doorway followed by a volley of bolter fire or a blast of the flamer. The passageways were choked with ork dead, the big xenos lying in mounds that the Ultramarines had to clamber over and pull aside in order to get through some of the narrower doorways. It was bitter, close-quarter fighting, and Proxis barely had room to swing his axe in places, but he snapped off rounds from his bolt pistol, head-shots every one.

The ork assault troops had nowhere to run to, so at the last they stood and fought and died where they stood, or else they charged the Adeptus Astartes warriors in a savage attempt to bring their superior strength to bear.

When they closed with Avila's brethren, Calgar and Proxis stepped up and broke them apart, hacking them down. They waded through blood and flame and thickets of autogun fire that careered in mad screeches off the walls and tumbled with clangs and sparks off the armour of the Ultramarines.

Two more of Avila's squad went down, struck by lucky shots that came out of the smoke and chaos, but both were alive, and now, coming up behind the Ultramarines, Lieutenant Janus and his men worked to pull the injured battle-brethren clear of the fighting. It took four or five of them straining and grunting to drag each huge warrior out of the melee, while the rest of the squad fought on without pause, grouped around Calgar and Proxis.

Up again, more stairways, more grenades raining down on them, to be kicked out of the way or thrown back into the faces of the orks before they went off. Finally, Calgar noted a change in the air. The smoke was being sucked out by wind from the outside. They were on the topmost level of the Vanaheim, and the orks were pulling back onto the roof itself, a two-acre expanse that was lashed by warm rain and pitted by the fighting of the initial assault.

They were under the sky at last, and the fight opened out here, the heavy bolters brought up again to hose down the scattered ranks of the enemy. Avila's squad ducked into shell craters that had been blasted into the thick rockcrete roof, or settled into empty weapons emplacements, dozens of dead Zalidari militia lying scattered around them. From here they picked off any ork that raised its head, methodically working their way across the roof.

Beyond the Vanaheim, the night sky was lit up with explosions and tracer. Calgar ran over to the battlements and saw, three hundred feet below, the great mass of orks that had gathered at the foot of the barbican, like seaweed washed up there by the waves of a sea.

He thumped his fizzing helm and blinked on the Basilisk sigil. 'Beta Primaris, we have target in the open, massed formation at the south wall. Defensive fire on location grid alpha one, fire for range. Fire now.'

'Acknowledged.' The Basilisk battery had been waiting.

'All reserve tubes, same grid. Fire now.'

He waited, as the fight went on around him. Looking up at the rain-dark night he thought he saw a faint brightness on the horizon – it would be dawn soon.

Proxis cut in half an ork that tried to charge him, and held up his axe as the ork blood sizzled on the power field that enclosed the blade.

Calgar barely registered the deed. He was looking out from the walls, south across the beetling plain where the enemy massed in untold thousands. The big formations were many miles away, hardly to be made out even with the enhanced optics of his armour and bionic eye. But here – right here – they were packed tight in anticipation of the Vanaheim Gate opening. They would pay for that presumption.

He could see the ork host beginning to break away from the walls. They had failed – by a narrow margin, but they had failed, and knew what must be coming. Now they were retreating to their camps.

But they had left it too late.

He heard the earthshaker shells in the air, a roar like passing freight haulers. They impacted six hundred yards south of the Vanaheim Gate, throwing up huge fountains of earth, and the shockwave staggered the air and sent the rain flying sideways.

'Beta Primaris, all tubes, on target. Fire for effect.'

All over the southern districts of the city, the mortar teams of the militia were dropping bombs down their tubes. He could see the spark of them rise up into the air, dozens of the squat bombs propelled skywards, a sight beautiful to behold. And above them, the high parabolic arc of more earthshakers inbound.

The ork warbands below were trying to scatter, but the torrent of mortars found them while they were still packed too tight to miss. The plain south of the Vanaheim erupted in a forest of explosions, and down came the earthshakers to break it up in cataclysmic fountains of mud. Calgar glimpsed dozens of ork bodies tossed skywards before the flash of the explosions greened out the infra of his optics.

'On target, repeat, on target. Fire schedule Primaris and Secundus.'

He saw the hellish light of the barrage reflected in the black lenses of Proxis' helm, fountains of fire rising in the night. His auto-senses dulled the noise of it to protect his hearing.

'All call signs, walk your fire south on axis alpha two. Enemy in the open. I want promethium shells mixed in.'

Confirmation came back in a score of flickers in his vox display. The fizzing damage of his helm was irritating him, so he took it off, and breathed the unalloyed reek of Zalidar's air, thick with smoke and slaughter. He felt the rain on his face, refreshing despite the warmth of it.

Proxis unhelmed also. Behind them, Avila had brought his squad forward and they were manning such heavy weapons as had survived on the summit of the Vanaheim. Janus' troopers fanned out behind them, a hundred militiamen, most of whom had never seen an ork up close until tonight.

The sky was growing bright, and in it lights could be seen coming up from the south.

'Flight of enemy fighter-bombers inbound,' Calgar said automatically. 'All anti-aircraft batteries, engage at will.'

The Hydras on the defence towers roared out along half the perimeter, and the growing dawn light in the sky was striped with an intense cloud of tracer, bright skeins of it in a concentration so thick that it illuminated the underside of the rainclouds above.

The incoming aircraft ran into a wall of fire, but kept coming. Four were shot down before the walls were reached, their broken flaming carcasses spiralling down into the hordes of orks still fleeing from the artillery barrage below. Two more were shot down over the city and came down in districts close to the Alphon Spire, exploding in bright globes of fire.

That was not the end of it; a series of secondary detonations went off, larger than the initial impact. A whole block of habs and warehouses was destroyed in a rippling flash that lit up the district and thundered out across the city in pulsing shockwaves.

The last fighter-bomber was crippled, but its pilot managed to guide it on a suicide course until it smashed into the side of the spire itself. Calgar watched the Alphon Spire burn, its head lost in cloud, lights all over its massive slopes, and the bright boil of the crash flickering in its flank.

He turned to regard the swathe of ruin below the spire, the explosions still cooking off, and frowned.

After that, no more attacks were launched. It was full daylight by that time, and it was possible to see the dismal spectacle that surrounded them.

Out on the shot-torn muck of the plain, the carcasses of thousands of orks lay, most steaming in bloody ragged fragments. A whole army had been destroyed there. The ork dead created a mire of blood-filled craters and mounded meat.

But the city had suffered too. The top half of the Vanaheim Gate was largely gutted. It was a monolithic blackened hulk that towered over the walls, smoke still streaming from its gun-ports, the roof of it a reeking wasteland of the dead and dying, wrecked armaments, broken emplacements and the low-hanging fog of cordite.

And at the base of the Alphon Spire and the districts around it, the fires still burned. Hundreds of tiny figures were fighting the flames. Others were demolishing whole streets of habs with heavy vehicles and explosives, so that the fires might not spread. The steady crump of these concussions boomed out in dull succession, like a minute-gun at a funeral.

Calgar felt suddenly weary. Not in body – in the secret place within his mind where the faultline lay. But he fought it, battled against it with anger and prayer. He breathed deep.

'Well, Proxis, I suppose we must start clearing up this mess.'

The Ultramarines carried a variety of war gear during the Zalidar campaign, all of which was superbly artificed with their insignia and honour markings

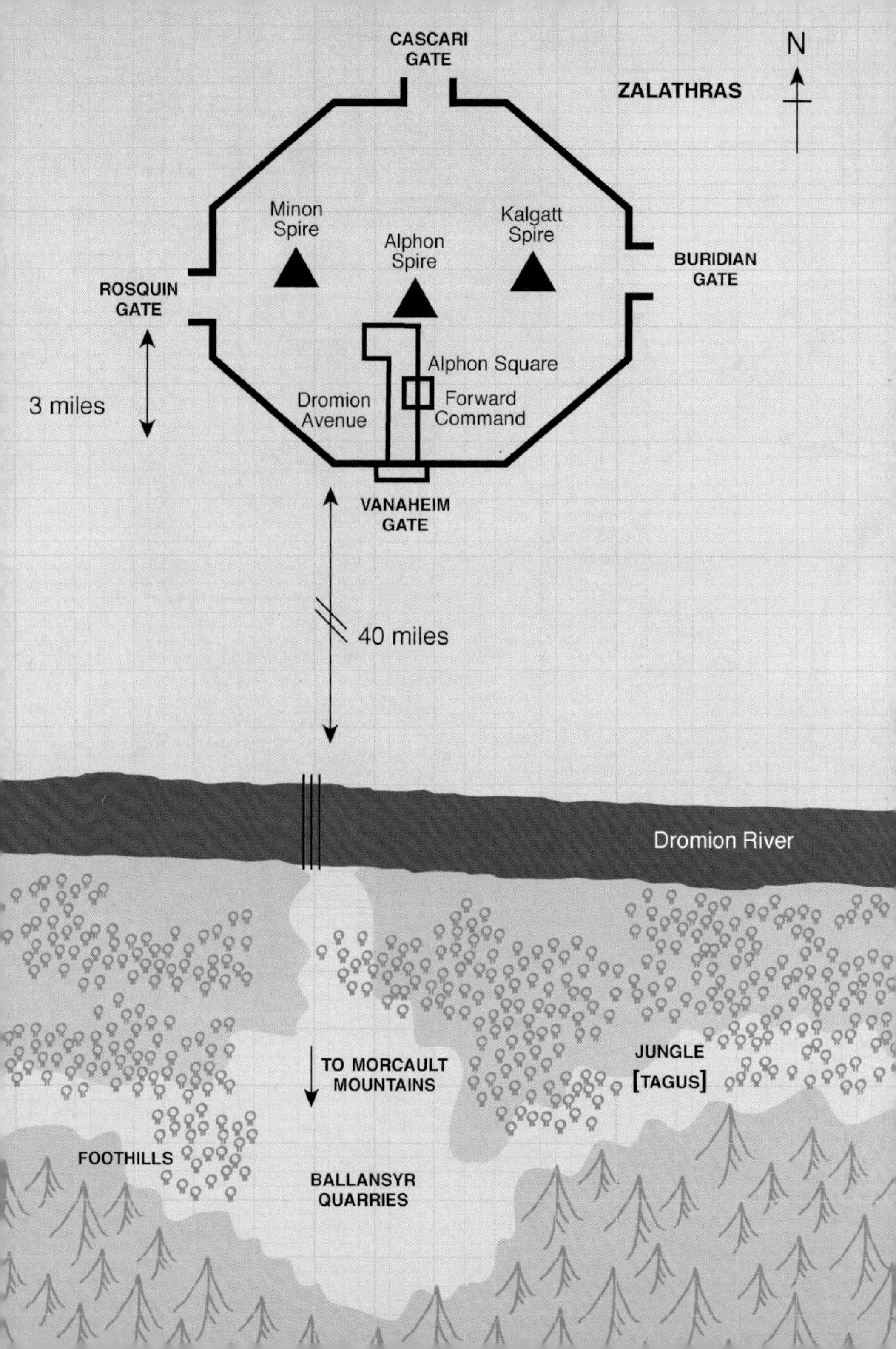
CASCARI
GATE
N
ZALATHRAS
Minon
Spire
Alphon
Spire
Kalgatt
Spire
BURIDIAN
GATE
ROSQUIN
GATE
Alphon Square
3 miles
Dromion
Avenue
Forward
Command
VANAHEIM
GATE
40 miles
Dromion River
JUNGLE
[TAGUS]
TO MORCAULT
MOUNTAINS
FOOTHILLS
BALLANSYR
QUARRIES

# FOURTEEN

'THE ENEMY IS more enterprising than I gave him credit for,' Calgar said harshly. 'That error is mine alone. I had no idea he could muster so many assault troops for an aerial attack.'

'Well, he doesn't have them any more,' Proxis said with relish.

'The attack was seen off with massive ork casualties – that is the main thing. I congratulate you on your victory, my lord,' Admiral Glenck said.

They were all gathered in the map room of the palace, all the high command. Calgar glanced impatiently at the fleet officer, but did not comment.

The Lord of Macragge had taken off his armour and was clad now in a simple hooded blue robe without sign or sigil. It had been run up hastily for him by seamstresses in the lower city. His armour was undergoing repair. Brother Orhan was working on it, aided by the best artificers in Zalathras. The ancient power armour had taken a beating during the battle that even its superlative construction could not shrug off, and the dorsal magazines were being reloaded with bolter rounds fashioned here in the city's manufactoria.

All the Ultramarines were taking advantage of the momentary lull to reload and refit and repair, and the wounded of Avila's squad were being seen to by Brother Parsifal in a special apothecarion that had been set up in the palace itself. One of the Ultramarines, Brother Tarsus, had been badly burned and would not return to the front line for some time to come, but the others were coming along more quickly. The incredible genes and implants of the Adeptus Astartes rendered them hard to kill and quick to heal.

'It was a victory, sure,' Governor Fennick said, 'but last night we burned through almost a third of our artillery munitions. Shells for the Basilisks, in particular, are in very short supply.'

Calgar regarded the governor, his pale eye cold as winter. 'My lord Fennick, you must remedy that situation.'

Fennick met his gaze squarely; with repeated exposure to Calgar's presence, the initial reverential awe was wearing off. He spoke now with respect, but less of the outright fear that had characterised their first interactions. 'It takes time to start up a whole new heavy industry, my lord. It will happen – the machinery is being retooled even as we speak. But until we can manufacture our own heavy shells, we must be careful in their expenditure. Another barrage like last night's will see our reserve almost exhausted.'

'We should perhaps throw rocks at the orks, or ask them nicely to run away,' Proxis said, his square mouth skewed with contempt.

Fennick faced him boldly, though he was very pale. 'I only tell you the facts of the matter. It is for you to make of them what you may.'

'Very well,' Calgar said, holding up one hand. 'From now on, all harassment and interdiction fire of the enemy will cease. All mortar and artillery ammunition will be saved for genuine assaults, at least until we have the new manufactoria up and running.'

Proxis bowed his head, frowning.

'Colonel Boros, I believe you have some reports to relate to us,' Calgar went on. He sat down in a huge chair that had been fashioned out of ironwood. It looked very like a throne, and even sitting down, his head was on a level with those of the ordinary human officers in the room.

Fennick watched the Ultramarine Chapter Master covertly while he gathered up his papers from the map table, and tapped closed the files running on his data-slate. Was it his imagination, or did the Lord of Macragge look... tired? No, it was not that. He was somehow listless, like a man being told things he already knew. A man who was waiting for bad news.

Boros stumped forward, holding a list. He read it off somewhat mechanically, not looking up. He was still apprehensive of the Adeptus Astartes in the chamber, as were most of his officers. Only Roman Lascelle, standing behind him, seemed uncowed by the sheer raw presence of Calgar and his brethren. The aristocrat stood balancing one fist on the hilt of his rapier, observant and thoughtful.

'We lost upwards of six hundred men last night,' Boros said. 'Most were from our original divisions – good, trained soldiers it will be hard to replace. The Vanaheim Gate is essentially intact, but many of the heavy weapons which defend it were destroyed in the ork assault – I have a list here–' He held it out. Calgar took it, a scrap of parchment, tiny in that massive, seamed fist. His eye ran over it in seconds, and his face darkened.

'Almost half of them.' He handed it to Proxis.

'We will miss those autocannon,' Proxis muttered.

'Yes, my lord,' Boros went on doggedly. 'If the Vanaheim is to be restored to its former strength, then we will have to withdraw weapons from other locations, principally the defence towers. That will leave portions of the perimeter defended only by the lasguns of my men, and the range of a lasgun...' He trailed off. The Ultramarines regarded the standard sidearm of the militia with something close to derision. Las-fire was all very well against human foes, or even the more delicate anatomy of the eldar, but against the robust brutishness of the orks it was an inefficient tool.

'The Vanaheim must be restored to its former complement of heavy weapons,' Calgar said. 'Colonel, you will remove them from every other defence tower on the northern perimeter and have them transported south to the barbican. I want them emplaced there by tonight, along with their crews. Lieutenant Janus' firefighters are currently garrisoning the Vanaheim. They must be relieved so they can return to the reserve. Pick your best men. And I want Hydras on the roof, to guard against any repeat of last night. It is unlikely, but it cannot be ruled out.'

Boros bowed.

'Next,' Calgar said.

This time it was a newcomer, a black-haired man in opulent civilian clothes. He had a hard face, but all the same he looked utterly out of place in that sober gathering, his cloak embroidered with gold and silver thread. Calgar cocked his head to one side and brought his bionic eye to bear on the finely dressed figure.

'You are the man we have to thank for the Vanaheim Gate,' he said.

Kurt Vanaheim bowed deep, the hem of his cloak whispering on the floor.

'My Lord Macragge, it is an honour.'

'You built well, Vanaheim.'

'I only did my part for the good of Zalidar.'

'Is there something else now you would like to do for the good of Zalidar?'

Vanaheim swallowed. Fennick watched him, fascinated. He had never before seen the swaggering, arrogant businessman so cowed. He had to fight his own features not to smile at the sight.

'My lord, Governor Fennick has seen fit to place me in charge of husbanding the raw materials needed to feed the war machine. I own a whole series of warehouses full of the material that supplies our manufactoria.' He hesitated, and now Fennick started to feel the beginnings of alarm at the fear on Vanaheim's face.

'I am sorry to report to you that one of the ork fighter-bombers that was brought down in the night crashed full square into that warehouse complex. A chain reaction was set up which resulted in a series of–'

'How much was lost?' Calgar demanded, his eye flashing.

Vanaheim clasped his hands together, eyes fixed on the floor.

'The most critical loss was to our store of heavy metals and minerals. Of our palladium reserves, we have lost some eighty per cent of the stockpile.'

Calgar stood up, and instinctively they all backed away from him. He began to pace up and down the room. 'Some among us may not be aware of the uses of palladium. Enlighten them, if you please.'

'The… the manufacture of munitions requires a very particular menu of raw materials. Steel, copper, even ceramite, we can still produce in quantity within the city foundries – the ores for these survive in their hundreds of tons. But the palladium, which is used in the detonator mechanism of every shell and bolt-round, is rare. It was our stores of this element which were largely destroyed in the crash and the subsequent explosion of ordnance on the ork craft.'

He raised his head and spread his hands. 'My lord, we can still make the bodies of artillery shells, once the new manufactoria are up and running, but not the detonators which will set them off. And we can no longer make much in the way of ammunition for bolters, either the heavy ones in the defence towers, or those of your own Ultramarines.'

'Throne,' Proxis swore softly.

'What do we have left in the arsenal?' Calgar asked Fennick. He seemed unmoved by Vanaheim's tidings, though the rest of the human officers present looked sick with dismay.

The governor thumbed his slate. 'Some three-quarters of a million rounds.'

'The city can burn through that in one day's fighting,' Proxis rasped.

Calgar stopped pacing and stood with his back to them all, facing out over the balcony that looked down on the rainswept sea of buildings below.

'I had a feeling, when I saw the ork craft go down…' he murmured. Then he raised his voice with the accustomed snap of command in it.

'The fact of the matter is that this material is required for the survival of the city,' he said. 'Therefore more of it must be found. Where can we get it?'

Vanaheim cleared his throat. 'I own a complex of quarries far to the south of Zalathras, beyond the Dromion River, in the foothills of the mountains. We use palladium in the mining charges. The quarry is almost played out, but there are stores of the element there in an underground facility which may well have escaped the attention of the orks. It was left there for safety reasons, and because I was moving my base of operations to a new site.'

'How much?' Calgar demanded.

'Several tons, my lord. Not enough to replace all that was lost, but enough to keep arms production running for a few weeks.'

Calgar breathed out slowly. 'And is that all there is?'

'There are scraps of it here and there, even in the city, but that is the only place on the planet where it exists mined and refined in any quantity.'

A silence fell in the map room. Calgar looked them over, his own brethren, and the human officers. He saw the same shattered, hopeless look on all their faces. Only Proxis seemed unperturbed, but then Proxis had always taken disaster in his stride.

He smiled at them. 'Then the course of action is clear. Somehow or other, we must go to these quarries of yours, Vanaheim, retrieve the palladium, and bring it back here.'

'My lord, we do not possess the means–' Fennick began, the first of a chorus of naysayers.

'We do not have the transports,' Rear Admiral Glenck protested.

'I do not have the men – trained men – to spare for a sortie, my lord,' Boros said.

'I'll go.'

It was a different voice, from the back. The ranks of military officers parted to reveal the old man, Ghent Morcault, sitting there leaning on a pitchthorn stick. His lined face was calm and set below the shock of white hair which thatched it.

'I'll take the *Mayfly* – it's only a couple of hours' flight to the Ballansyr Quarries,' he added.

'You'll never make it through, Ghent,' Fennick said.

'Do you have a better idea, Lucius?'

Again, the silence. Calgar strode up to the old man and stood towering over him.

'Can your ship make the journey?' he asked.

'It'll be nip and tuck, all the way,' Morcault said, 'but I believe I can evade the orks, as we evaded them on the way here. Yes, my lord, the *Mayfly* can get through, given a little luck. It's what else we may find at the quarries besides the palladium which is the problem.'

'The orks have overrun all the southern Tagus,' Boros said. 'The odds are they will be waiting for you, Morcault.'

'Then perhaps some Ultramarines should go along also,' Proxis spoke up. He shrugged. 'Just to keep an eye on things.'

Calgar strode across to the balcony again.

'If we do nothing, the orks will be over the walls in a week,' he said, and paused to let this sink in.

'We have no choice.'

He turned to regard Morcault. 'Proxis will go with you, and also Brother Valerian. His abilities may be invaluable. I will also detail others of my brethren to accompany them. Three or four is all I can spare.'

'I can add a platoon of militia,' Colonel Boros said. 'You'll need strong backs, and a couple of tracked lifters.'

'With your permission, colonel,' Roman Lascelle said, 'I would like to volunteer for command of that platoon.'

'You?' Boros asked incredulously. He looked at Fennick, and the governor nodded.

'Very well,' Boros said.

Calgar looked Lascelle over, his gaze missing nothing. 'I had thought to send Lieutenant Malleus, but he is needed here. If you vouch for this officer, Lord Fennick, then go he shall. Morcault, when can you leave?'

Morcault stood up. He looked very lean and frail in his stained voidsman coveralls, but his eyes were as bright as those of a much younger man.

'We'll wait until dark and make a course for the north before doubling round. The orks have their own anti-aircraft batteries positioned mostly around their camps to the south of the city.'

'Anything you or your ship need, you shall have,' Calgar told him. 'Are you sure your crew will be as keen to undertake this mission as you are?'

Morcault smiled. 'They are my crew. Where I go, they go.'

Calgar nodded. 'That is as it should be.'

FENNICK CAUGHT HIM as the meeting broke up and he was limping towards the conveyor terminals in the lobby of the palace.

'Ghent, what is this – some last death or glory stunt? You're too old to be pulling off things like this.'

'I've been pulling them off for sixty years, Lucius. It's become something of a habit.'

Fennick set a hand on his arm. 'You don't need to go personally. The Ultramarines can do this on their own.'

Morcault shook his head. 'The *Mayfly* is my ship. Besides, no one knows that rough country down around Ballansyr like I do. They're not called the Morcault Mountains for nothing.'

Fennick snorted a kind of laugh. 'You old goat. Is this one last attempt to get yourself written into the history books?'

'It's one last chance to prove myself useful.' Morcault thumbed the elevator button and his head sank down on his chest. He tap-tap-tapped the pitchthorn stick on the floor.

'I'm not long for this world, Fennick. If I am to go out, it might as well be on this trip as any other.'

Fennick looked at him. 'Then I wish you well. For all our sakes.'

The old man stepped into the elevator as the doors opened. He turned around and grinned. 'I should think so. From the sound of things, if I don't come back, you'll be following me before very long. Stay alive, Fennick. Look after my world for me.' Then the doors closed on his face. Fennick set a hand upon them.

'Stay alive yourself, you crazy old fool,' he murmured.

ALL THAT DAY the ork hosts remained within their camps, but shuttlecraft of all shapes and sizes came and went constantly some twelve miles south of the city. The observers on the walls of Zalathras tracked them through the clouds by the bright glow of their afterburners, but had no way of impeding the traffic to and from the ork fleet in orbit.

The main body of the xenos armies stayed clear of the noisome swamp that now lay before the tall walls of Zalathras. There were a few artillery barrages that snapped out with a distant rumble and slammed down into outlying districts of the city, but the inhabitants were now as accustomed to these as they were to the weather, and they did not seriously interfere with the reconstruction work on the Vanaheim Gate, or on the thousands of conscripted workers who laboured in the wreckage of the munition warehouses.

The debris of the artillery strikes was methodically cleared away, the main avenues of resupply and transport kept open, and in large habs all over the city the newest recruits to the militia were run through weapons training, tactics, communication protocols and basic field-craft by the training cadres set up on Marneus Calgar's arrival. The parlous state of their ammunition reserves was kept a secret from all but the high command, and the myriad citizens of Zalathras knew only that a great assault had been beaten off from the Vanaheim Gate, with ruinous casualties to the orks.

The green storm had receded once again, and the Zalathi fell back into their new routine, one dominated by the waging of war, with all its backbreaking work and thin rations and stultifying boredom. It had been over a month now, and they were becoming used to it.

THE MAYFLY HAD been given a once-over by the best void mechanics in Zalathras, much to Jon Gortyn's resentment. But his anger was eased by the sudden influx of new parts for the drives, replacement instrumentation, and a new Navigation cogitator that was installed in a matter of hours. At the same time, a small but powerful generator was set up in the hold and linked into the hull superstructure, giving the ship limited void-shield capability. It would not protect the *Mayfly* from shipborne armaments, but it would deflect autocannon fire and perhaps even guided missiles.

'Do you think they'll let us keep it, after?' Gortyn asked Morcault, and the old man had laughed like a drain.

'Jon, if we make it through this, they can plate the hull in solid adamantium for all I care.'

Roman Lascelle whistled softly as he led his militia platoon into the hold of the little tramp freighter, his men followed by two heavy tracked lifters.

'Morcault,' he said, 'you've been flying in this thing for fifty years?'

'Nearer sixty.'

'You're a braver man than I am.'

Last to come aboard were six Ultramarines, clanking up the ramp in single file like weather-beaten giants. Their blue armour had been beaten and scraped and stained until it was all a uniform nondescript shade, like that of the *Mayfly*'s hull itself. But their bolters were clean and shining, and their red eye-lenses gleamed darkly as the brutal helms turned this way and that.

The last two Adeptus Astartes up the ramp were the Librarian, Brother Valerian, and Proxis, Ancient of the honour guard of Marneus Calgar himself. The militiamen in the hold shrank away from all the Ultramarines, as dogs cower in the presence of a wolf. Proxis banged the handle of his axe on the deck.

'All present? Very well. Then let us shut the door and get on with it.'

# FIFTEEN

Proxis had not wanted to go, and had fallen back on protocol and tradition. The Ancient of the honour guard should remain close by the Chapter Master, he had protested – but Calgar had overruled him. He wanted someone on the *Mayfly*'s mission with combat instincts that matched his own, and Proxis was the closest he could come to going himself. Also, he was the best close-quarter fighter in the Chapter. If anyone could hack a path through a horde of orks, it was Proxis.

But he missed that steady, sardonic presence at his side, he had to admit. It would not be for long – no more than a day, with luck and the Emperor's Grace – but the days and nights in Zalathras were long now, and every hour was measured out in the blood of the defenders.

He had sent Brother Valerian along for a different reason. For a long time now, the Librarian had been trying to contact other members of his calling in the distant line companies of the Ultramarines, specifically the Epistolary, Brother Carimus with Seventh. Librarians were not astropaths, but their psychic skills still allowed them to project messages at great distances.

But Brother Valerian had been foiled at every turn. The psychic signature of the ork armies was growing, cohering, and its proximity, just beyond the gates of Zalathras, interfered with his attempts to contact his brethren. He feared that the moment of critical mass, when the xenos tribes would finally come together in a Waaagh!, was fast approaching. By getting him clear of the city for a while, Calgar hoped that he might be able to get through the crude psychic storm that the orks were generating. It was something of a long shot, but then all the shots were long right now.

THEY HAD SET up a forward command post a mile from the Vanaheim Gate, in the mansion belonging to the council member and banker Ferdia Rosquin – who had been persuaded to vacate the place for the greater good. Here, Colonel Boros' vox specialists had run comm cables and set up a link to the main augur network in Alphon Spire, relaying all the information from the map room up there to a series of data-slates and old-fashioned plasreel printers.

From the outside, the only thing that looked different about the Rosquin compound was the profusion of antennae that had sprouted from the roof of the mansion, and the heavy cables that ran out to a back-up power generator humming in the garden.

The population of Zalathras still peered up at the cloud-hidden summit of Alphon Spire and believed that Marneus Calgar was up there, looking down on them, when in fact he was located just off the main arterial north–south highway of the city. This had been cleared of all but military traffic, however, and under martial law, all those who had no work to do or rations to collect were directed to remain indoors, stay off the grid, and hunker down while listening to announcements from the vox-casters that had been set up on hundreds of street corners.

Boredom and fear, the two common elements of all wars. Millions of ordinary people endured them now within the circuit of the defences, as Zalathras entered its second month of siege.

The mansion was austere, old-fashioned and capacious, though still a little cramped after the cyclopean architecture of the Governor's Palace. Boxes of data-slates, plasreels, and good old-fashioned paper files had been brought down from the Alphon and arrayed around the walls of the central atrium, and Fennick had hung his beloved maps around the walls, displacing artworks worth a small fortune in the process. He was supervising the unpacking of the files as Marneus Calgar – fully armoured again – stared at a huge blueprint of the city that covered almost half of one wall.

'Lord Fennick, a word, please.'

Fennick stood beside the Chapter Master. He was staring at the wall-mounted plans intently.

'I have not seen this outlay before. It is different from the ones we studied up in the Spire. Why is that?'

Fennick looked more closely. 'This is an old plan, my lord, superseded by later building work. What you see is the city as it was perhaps twenty years ago – the red corrections are the improvements made since.'

'And what is this?' Calgar asked, stabbing a finger at a dotted line that ran south out of the city, straight as ruler's edge.

'That? It's the old sewer outlet. At one time it ran all the way down to the Dromion River, forty miles. We blocked it up a dozen years ago, and now the city has new outlets which feed directly into caverns delved below us, which in turn drain into the bedrock of the planet. The Dromion was prone to flooding, and the sewers would back up in the rainy season… My lord, is there a problem?'

'How was this older structure blocked off?'

'We blasted it closed, and then poured in rockcrete, at least fifteen to twenty feet thick...' Fennick trailed off.

'Is it guarded?'

Fennick found it hard to speak. 'No.'

Calgar clenched one fist. 'I should have been made aware of this, my lord governor. This old outlet represents a chink in our defences which should have been looked into long ago.'

'My lord, it is as good as destroyed–'

Calgar ignored him. 'Sergeant Avila!'

The Ultramarine was by the door in a second. His helm was off – the first time Fennick had seen his face. It was a square, shorn countenance much like Calgar's own, with metal studs implanted in the flesh of the temple and a shine to the eyes that spoke of ocular augmentation.

'Yes, lord.'

'You will gather together a small task force – a half-squad of our brethren – take Brother Parsifal – and a company of the militia with demolition equipment. Lord Fennick will show you where to go.'

Calgar turned to the governor. 'Let us hope the orks are as ignorant of these tunnels as I have been.'

THE DAY DREW on. The distant crump of artillery came and went, and with it, more meaningless deaths in the southern districts of the city. On the broad avenue beyond Rosquin's compound, the vehicles of Lieutenant Janus' firefighters remained lined up under cameleoline tarps and in the shadow of buildings, while the men of the regiment sat in trenches that disfigured urban gardens, and cannibalised whatever materials they needed for overhead protection. It was safer in the rain-filled trenches than in any hab; across the city, thousands of civilians were slower to learn than the soldiers, but backyard trenches and shelters were now common all the same, a place to run to when the klaxons sounded.

On the walls, the guns were silent, and the Vanaheim stood like some ominous blackened ruin frowning across the broken plain below. Once, a flight of ork fighter-bombers swept towards it, but a sudden storm of Hydra fire made them veer off and return to their bases. A heavy silence hung in the air between the artillery strikes, and to Fennick at least it seemed that the planet was as tired as he felt himself, beaten and battered in the endless rain and reeking of death.

His beloved Zalathras still stood, but the city had lost all trace of the busy, thronged metropolis it had once been. Whole districts were well-nigh deserted now, their inhabitants having fled the vulnerable regions near the southern walls. They were holed up now in the base of the three hive-spires that rose up out of the plain and lost themselves in rainclouds, man-made mountains which had once been the pride of Zalidar.

Part of Fennick's everyday duties was to manage the accommodation of the dispossessed, and their numbers grew by the hour, cramming into the undercity of the spires and living as tight-packed as meat in a can. Five thousand militiamen had been taken off the walls to police those slums, though they were mainly home to women and children, the old and the sick. All able-bodied men were subject to conscription now, and if they could not be armed, they could fight fires, create firebreaks, clear rubble and tend the vegetable gardens that now covered every patch of earth and vacant lot within the perimeter.

A great Imperial city mere weeks before, Zalathras' economy had been brought down to the level of a primal village. Barter and prostitution were rife, and the gangs of the undercity had taken control of many streets and subterranean hab layouts, looking after their own and preying on the weak.

It happened in every war, and Boros' militia were thrown into it by the regiment to root out those who did not contribute to the defence. But as soon as one gang was destroyed, another sprang up. It was part of existence now as much as the rain and the ork attacks.

* * *

'They are massing for another assault,' Colonel Boros said, lowering the magnoculars. He turned to his aide. 'Pherias, send word to Fennick. Ork formations growing to our front, and they seem–' Here he peered through the magnoculars again, striving to pierce the veil of rain that swept across the plain. 'They seem to have heavy vehicles. This could be something new.'

Pherias bent over the vox-station and began keying in the text of the message. They sent most non-combat comm this way now, for it was more secure and more reliable than a crackling voice down the line.

Boros looked up and down the walls. He stood in the central roof bunker of the Vanaheim Gate, a structure which had seen much death in the last month, and which still bore the marks of it. It was an unpleasant place, reeking of decayed flesh and stained with the blood of those who had died within it. But its view of the plain below was unmatched, and the thick roof had yet to be pierced by any shell.

In the casements that ran along it were half a dozen autocannon, some meltaguns and several missile launchers. Pride of place, however, was given to two lascannons – the best anti-armour weapons the defenders possessed. There were only a dozen of these on the planet, and their charge packs were rationed out with the utmost care, for there was no way of creating more on Zalidar.

Thirty shots each, that's it, Boros thought. If the orks come at us with a mass of armour, then the thing is as good as over.

The rain thinned a little. All along the walls the sentries stared out and hefted their lasguns and found their mouths suddenly dry and their palms sweating. Twenty-five thousand militiamen guarded the southern perimeter, but most of these were in bombproofs within the walls themselves, getting what rest they could. The sentries would not call their fellows below up onto the catwalk until they were told, or until the alarm was sounded.

Boros was sweeping the far-off ranks of the ork host with the magnocs when he stopped and cursed in a low, fluent flow of profanity.

Amid the boiling, crowding mobs of the enemy he could see even more massive, boxy shapes lurching and swaying as they advanced over the rough ground, and the orks made lanes for them in their ranks. The rain came and went in a blur, but there could be no mistake.

'Looted Leman Russes and ork Battlewagons. They have heavy armour.' Boros sounded bitter, as though his own fears had given rise to the advancing tanks.

'Pherias, sound the stand-to. And give me the vox.'

The young lieutenant punched the red klaxon button on the wall of the bunker and handed the vox mike to Boros. All over the city, the vox-casters droned out the dull blare of the alarm; this was not the tearing whine of the air-raid siren, but the more ominous repetitive thud of imminent ground assault. There was not a citizen in all of Zalathras who did not know the difference.

Along the twenty-mile length of the walls, men began thundering up the stairs from the bombproofs below, white-faced, silent or cursing. Some of the newer recruits vomited, but were shoved onwards by those behind them. At their rear, hard-faced militia noncoms from Boros' original divisions barked at them to hurry, laspistols drawn. Militia they might be, but those who had survived from the beginning of the siege were as good as any veteran Guardsman now, or they would have been dead already.

All across the city, civilian life came to a standstill. The barter markets in the lower southern districts broke up, the taverns emptied, and even in the looming hive-spires people instinctively sought the core regions, moving away from the vulnerable flanks of the structures. The ork fighter-bomber that had crashed into the side of Alphon Spire had killed upwards of two hundred.

They packed now into the centres of Alphon and Kalgatt and Minon Spires, and huddled together there in every square and roadway and corridor, snarling at anyone who tried to make them move. Traffic came to a halt. The spires became congested flues packed tight with humanity.

'Fennick, you there?' Boros spoke into the vox impatiently.

There was a crackle – moisture in the caster. Boros shook the thing with a grimace and tried again.

'Yes, yes, I'm here. What's to report?'

'New attack in the making. They have armour. I have counted a dozen Leman Russes and other heavy armour, though there may be more.'

'Good luck to them getting through the swamp in front of the gates.'

'My thoughts exactly. But all the same, I would like more lascannon down here around the Vanaheim. Do I have your permission to move a few from the northern walls?'

'Not my decision, my friend. Lord Calgar has specified that all redeployments of heavy weapons must be made through him.'

Boros cursed. 'Well, where the hell is he?'

'Not so far away, colonel.'

His bulk blotted out the daylight as he stooped through the rear blast doors of the bunker. Those manning the casemates set up a mutter that was both joyous and apprehensive. Some stared, some looked away, some became busy with their weapons.

Marneus Calgar looked around. He spoke quietly, but his voice filled the dank air of the bunker all the same.

'We have four lascannon in the southern circuit. That will suffice. I will not denude the rest of the perimeter, colonel, not at this time.'

Behind Calgar were his skull-faced Chaplain, an honour guard Ultramarine, and two others.

'We will fight them from here, with what we have,' Calgar said, looking around. 'I know you men will not let me down.'

'It seems you have your answer,' Fennick said with something like dark humour in his tone. 'Good luck, Boros. Keep me updated on plas-printer.'

'Boros out,' the colonel said. He bowed to Calgar. 'My lord, it is good to have you here.'

The Lord of Macragge moved up to the deep-set viewing slits in the bunker. 'Effective range of the lascannon is over ten thousand feet. Effective range of the Leman Russ main gun is similar – but the tanks will be in motion, and the soft ground will slow them down. They will be good targets. But your men must aim true, colonel.'

'They will, my lord.'

'Then let us wait and see what the enemy can bring to this fight.'

Far below the lofty heights of the walls, in a cramped, subterranean world, Sergeant Avila and his brethren led the way down the dripping, moss-slick and noisome tunnel.

With him were four of his squad, and Brother Parsifal, the white flashes on his power armour livid in the dim light. And some way behind them, eighty sweating, splashing militiamen followed in a long file, bearing bulky packs of explosive.

The tunnel had been built to last, from massive granite blocks which still bore the marks of the masons who had fashioned them. The Vanaheim sigil was on every base-stone, though most were obscured by encrusted, writhing vegetation and fungi of all manner and description. It had been many years since the tunnel ran with the effluent of the city above, and yet it still stank. Avila could have shut out the reek with a blink-click on his auto-senses, but he chose to endure it, to savour it almost. Every sense was of use in war. Every sensation had to be utilised and endured.

Even the Adeptus Astartes were knee-deep in brown water, while it came almost to the crotch of the men. The Ultramarines waded through it slowly, weapons raised. The *Rubicon*'s pilot, Brother Dextus, was out in front, and behind him came Parsifal with a hand-held auspex more powerful than those which were built into every Space Marine's helm. He swept it back and forth, its data automatically relayed to his heads-up display. He tapped a hand on Dextus' power-pack, and the lead Space Marine immediately stopped and scanned the darkness ahead.

'I'm getting tremors above us,' Parsifal said. 'Getting stronger.'

'How far out are we?' Avila asked him.

'We're five and a half miles south of the Vanaheim Gate.' Parsifal looked up at the dripping masonry of the tunnel ten feet above his head. 'We are below the ork lines.'

They stopped, every man of the militia company behind them freezing in place, white-faced, looking up as though they expected the orks suddenly to come pouring through the ceiling.

'Can you hear it, brother?' Parsifal asked softly.

They all could, now. A dull, rumbling thunder far above their heads that seemed to be in movement, south to north. It travelled over them like the rumour of a distant storm.

'The xenos are on the move,' Avila said.

'I read more than that. Tank tracks. They are bringing up heavy armour,' Parsifal said, still in that same low voice.

'We should be on the walls,' Avila said. 'We'll be needed there.' His voice betrayed his frustration.

'We are needed here, brother,' Parsifal said calmly.

'How much farther to the block point?'

'Another mile.'

'I am inclined to blow the tunnel here and now, brother.'

'We were also detailed to discover whether the orks have infiltrated this structure,' the Apothecary said. 'We have not yet done so. We must go on.'

Avila grunted and checked the magazine in his bolter. He patted the weapon as though it were a favoured pet. 'Very well. Lead on then. But let us pick up the pace a little. The main event seems to be underway above us.'

* * *

'I count fifteen Battlewagons, plus a few dozen Chimera equivalents and a motley horde of wartrucks,' Calgar said. He had helmed up, and his fists flexed in the Gauntlets of Ultramar. 'Thirty thousand infantry, give or take. This is a major effort.'

Boros was staring out the viewslit of the bunker at the hosts of the enemy milling about on the vast plains below. The rain was easing a little, and there was even a brightness in the sky that spoke of far-off sunshine.

He could no longer remember what it was like to be rested and well fed and, above all, dry. The rainy season on northern Zalidar was a trial at the best of times, but to have to fight a war in it just stacked up the misery. His uniform was stuck to his flesh under the heavy body armour, and sweat was oozing down under his helmet.

But all that was as nothing now, compared to the prospect of the assault that was rolling towards them over the broken muck of the plain north of the Dromion River. The attacking forces extended for fully two miles, a beetling mass of orks whose roaring gabble could be heard now from the walls of the city.

He heard a new noise also: the whistling swoop of shells. The flash of the guns could just be made out in the distance through the drizzling rain, minute twinkles of fire.

'Incoming,' he said.

'They are overshooting, as usual,' Marneus Calgar said beside him. 'One can count on the orks for many things, and inaccuracy is usually one of them.'

'Sir, Governor Fennick reports heavy barrage striking the Alphon Spire,' Lieutenant Pherias said, reading off the vox-feed.

Calgar was also monitoring the feed in his helm readout. He keyed up Janus' rune.

'Lieutenant, mount up the firefighters and move closer to the southern wall. Be prepared to move out of reserve on my word.'

'Yes, my lord.'

'The Russes are firing,' Boros said. Even at this distance, he could make them out, towering over the ork infantry. They were Imperial tanks, looted from some captured depot and customised after the ork fashion, splashed with garish paint, with silhouettes all wrong due to ork modifications. But the Russ was a good weapon. It could take a lot of punishment.

'Shall I engage at extreme range?' he asked Calgar.

'No, colonel. Wait for my word. No one is to open up until they hear my command. We cannot afford speculative fire – we do not possess the ammunition.'

Ammunition. If they saw off this attack, then they would have exhausted most of the reserves. Boros knew that, but it was a detached piece of information that seemed to have little relevance now. All that mattered was the advancing horde.

'Ork aircraft inbound,' Lieutenant Pherias said. At least twenty-five craft, nine miles out and closing fast.'

'Seal blast doors,' Boros said, and a few seconds later the yellow warning lights whirled and flashed as the massive strike-proof doors of the bunker began to grind closed. It seemed to grow hotter almost at once. He looked up and down the dim confines of the casemates and saw the weapons crews peering out with sweat pouring down their faces, cutting lines in the grime.

Over two hundred men in the bunker, all of them adding their own heat and stink to the miasma, and below them the other levels of the Vanaheim were similarly packed with frightened, unwashed soldiers, most of whom had been mere anonymous civilians until a few weeks ago.

They would fight. They had no choice. The Vanaheim was sealed now, with nowhere to run to.

The Hydra batteries next to them on the roof opened up, a sharp tearing clatter of automatic fire that could be felt as a vibration in the heavy air.

'Beta Primaris, are you ready?' Calgar asked.

The Basilisk battery based down in the suburbs came back at once. 'Yes, sir.'

'All tubes, hold fire until my signal, and fire only upon prearranged coordinates. Not a round must go to waste.'

*A home for every bullet.* Calgar looked at Mathias, who was standing close by. The Chaplain's skull-helm nodded slightly.

'The Leman Russes are opening up. They're making heavy going of the ground,' Boros said.

Now the flash of the tanks' firing could be seen. Some were drawing ahead of the line; others seemed to be bogged down. When this happened, a huge mob of orks would grapple with the massive machine and shunt it bodily through the mire. Nothing brought home the brute physicality of the orks more than watching them manhandle fifty-ton tanks.

'One and a half miles,' Boros said, reading off the auspex. He wiped the sweat out of his eyes, but it kept dripping from his face onto the device like warm rain.

Calgar moved forward – he had been immobile all this time – and his battered wreath-crested helm turned this way and that. The fingers flexed at the end of the great power fists he wore as he bent and stared intently at the approaching enemy.

Above them, the first bombs went off, and they heard the screech of the ork fighter-bombers as they swooped through a cloud of anti-aircraft fire.

The heat and noise in the bunker was almost unendurable, but what was outside was worse. They felt the plascrete under their feet quiver as ordnance impacted on the summit of the Vanaheim, and there was one particularly savage boom which made the bunker shudder and sent little streams of dust sifting down from the ceiling.

'First wave has passed over. Another enemy flight inbound in forty seconds,' Lieutenant Pherias said in a harsh croak.

'Two Hydras destroyed,' another officer said. 'They're really pasting us.'

'They're in range!' Boros said, banging his fist against the bunker viewslit.

'Hold your fire,' Calgar told him calmly.

They rode out the storm, and the one that followed it. The men in the bunker ducked instinctively as bombs impacted on the roof above. The vox was a tattered mayhem of competing voices.

Boros studied what pict-feed survived, scanning the northern picters. Alphon Spire had been hit heavily and was burning in half a dozen places. The sky was alive with explosions and clouds of anti-aircraft fire, and ork artillery was impacting in the suburbs, flattening whole city blocks.

'My lord, surely–'

'Hold your fire,' Calgar said, and his suit amplified the command so that it rang out sonorously through the bunker.

Lieutenant Pherias rubbed dust out of his eyes. A shard of plascrete had opened up his temple and the blood was flowing down it in a bright stream, but he seemed unaware of the wound.

'Fifteen hundred yards,' he said.

The big Leman Russes were still lurching forward, firing as they came. Three had been left behind by the advance, either bogged down or broken down, but at least a dozen were still advancing on the walls on a frontage of almost a mile or so, headed straight for the tall gates within the Vanaheim.

Around them massed a huge formation of ork infantry, at least ten thousand roaring forward on that frontage alone, and in the midst of that packed murderous mob there stalked taller machines, bipedal, angular and with heavy weapons and pincers for arms. Scarlet banners flew from their backs.

'They have Dreadnoughts,' Boros said. 'I count... Damn it, I can't see.' He wiped his face free of muck and grime.

Calgar straightened.

'Beta Primaris, targets in the open, grid omega one zero. Fire for effect.' Then he raised his voice.

'Pick your targets, left to right. Aim for the tracks with your first round, then the hulls. Tanks first, Dreadnoughts later.' He paused, and the command roared out of his suit speakers.

'Open fire!'

# SIXTEEN

'THEY ARE FIGHTING at Zalathras. I can sense it,' Brother Valerian said. He clamped his mouth in a thin line, his flesh a pale preternatural colour in the light of his psychic hood.

'I take it you are like our Jodi then,' Ghent Morcault said. 'These things just seem to come up on your own personal augur.'

The Librarian looked at him through unsettling dark eyes, the black in them flecks that peered into some unknowable dimension of hell.

'My calling. My purpose is to sense such things, to fight against the ruinous powers and all their minions. To aid my brothers in any way possible. And right now, my brethren have need of me, and I am far away.'

'Your own Chapter Master sent you on this mission. He must have had a good reason. From what I've seen of him, Marneus Calgar is not subject to whim.'

They were on the bridge of the *Mayfly*, and the ship was as calm and dead as a tombstone in a cemetery. They had landed an hour ago, brought down by the storm and the passing swathes of ork attack craft that infested Zalidar's lower atmosphere. Now the ship sat battered by the rain on a rocky shelf amid the Morcault Mountains, over six hundred miles from Zalathras. And yet Brother Valerian seemed to know at least some of what was currently going on in that beleaguered city, despite the fact that they were off vox, every frequency shut down for fear it would give away their position to the enemy.

Hester sat at her station, studying the augur relays, while Jodi Arnhal sat beside her at the Navigation console, the chair skewed round so that he could face the Space Marine Librarian. He was studying his fellow psyker with a mixture of awe and yearning.

'The Lord of Macragge sent me on this mission to get me away from the psychic turbulence which surrounds Zalathras,' Valerian said. 'But here we are far from its walls, and still I find around me the baying fog of the ork psyche. It is as though the very planet itself has become one with it. It happens sometimes, when the orks come upon worlds such as these in great numbers.'

'Worlds such as these?' Morcault asked, puzzled.

'Jungle planets, thriving with life. It is my theory that the ork was first engineered into being on such a planet, perhaps even using the genes of an indigenous species as a template. The ancient forces which could work such wonders are long gone, but the ork remains, like the cockroach after the bomb has gone off.

'In any case, Zalidar suits this particular strain of xenos as the ocean suits the fish. This world, Morcault, will never be what it was, even if we prevail here. The taint of the ork is not as sinister as that of Chaos, but it is almost ineradicable, once introduced to a world like Zalidar. The jungles nurture it, conceal it and help it breed. Zalidar will never again be free of it.'

Morcault looked tired and beaten by the Librarian's words, an old man with not much road left in him. It was Hester who spoke up.

'This is our world. If we have to fight to keep it, we will.'

Valerian smiled. 'I applaud your determination. Let us hope we are equal to the test that has been set us here.'

The bridge doors opened and Proxis marched in. Rainwater was dripping in streams from his armour and he had unhelmed; it shone in the stubble of his scalp.

'How much longer, shipmaster? We have an errand to run, and little time to run it. The weather worsens outside.'

'Hester?' Morcault asked.

The pilot consulted her slates. 'There is still a patrol some nine miles north of us. If we took off now they'd be all over us like fleas on a dog.'

Proxis' face gnarled with anger. 'They are counting on us in Zalathras. My lord is waiting. I trust you have no aversion to risk.'

'If we had, we would not have plucked you and your lord out of the jungle,' Hester snapped, though she did not look up at the towering Space Marine.

Proxis cocked his head to one side. He shared a look with Valerian, and something like a smile flitted across his face. 'I take your point,' he said.

'Hester is the best pilot in the system. When she says we can make it through, we will take off,' Morcault said to Proxis. 'Better we are delayed than destroyed.'

'Very well,' the Ancient replied in a quieter tone. 'But do not tell me better late than never. In my experience, arriving late is often the same as never arriving at all.'

It was three hours before the ork aerial patrols thinned enough to let the *Mayfly* take off and launch itself northwards again. The ship had come in a great loop to the south, clear down to the mountains – forced far off its course by the proximity of many ork fighters and transports. Now they had to approach the Ballansyr Quarries from the south, Hester bringing the little freighter skimming low over the

Tagus and using all her skill to contour the ground in a craft which had never been built for atmospheric manoeuvres.

The storm had moved north, and they were trailing in its wake, the black mass of it darkening the world in front of the viewports, underlit by concatenations of lightning and the silver sheet of torrential rain. It cleared the way for them, a piece of luck which even Proxis had to grudgingly acknowledge, and Hester lifted the ship slightly, approaching the quarries from an altitude of six thousand feet – which for a star-going vessel was within spitting distance of the ground.

They saw the Ballansyr region grow under them like a vast scar carved through the jungle, an open ochre wound in the green flesh of the world. Stretching for perhaps twelve square miles, the works laid bare the bones of Zalidar in a series of interconnected excavations, massive deep-delved hollows a mile to a side with roadways spiralling down into them and clusters of buildings dotted here and there. Some of the quarries had become lakes, grey as gunmetal under the overcast sky. Others seemed almost bottomless, mere dark holes reaching into the bedrock of the planet.

'Behold the world as Kurt Vanaheim would make it,' Morcault said grimly. 'The greedy bastard.'

Proxis stared intently out of the viewscreens. 'Brother,' he asked Valerian, 'what do you make of it?'

The Librarian stood with his eyes closed, the cerulean blue of his hood quivering and a kind of hum in the air about his head.

'The orks have been here. Are still here. But not in huge numbers. I do not sense any direction to them. They may be deserters or stragglers, or merely those left behind to pick over the bones.'

Proxis' eyes narrowed. 'You know the coordinates,' he said to Hester. 'Set us down but keep the engines going. I shall take my brethren out first, and then the militia and the vehicles will follow if all is clear. Brother, let us go and get the thing done.'

He snapped his helm onto his head, and the two Adeptus Astartes left the bridge.

'Charming fellow,' Hester muttered, playing on the controls with taps as swift and delicate as the footfalls of a dancer.

'He has seen centuries of atrocity,' Morcault told her. 'I wonder only that he has any humanity left to him at all.'

PROXIS LED HIS brethren out of the *Mayfly* at a run, the Space Marines jumping from the ramp while it was still ten feet in the air. The six Ultramarines dashed for the buildings to their front, and the cavernous entrance to the mine that loomed up black behind. Even as they advanced, a clot of small ork creatures came piling out of the shacks around the mine entrance, shrieking shrilly and snapping off wild lasgun fire. Brother Kadare opened up with the heavy bolter and blew them away.

The ringing echoes of the bolter fire died away. The rain pattered down, a steady drizzle that slicked the Ultramarine armour and striped the dust and filth on it.

'Spread out, by twos,' Proxis said. 'Brother Kadare, with me. Brother Valerian, you take the right.'

Valerian walked out in front. He raised one hand at the huge mine entrance. 'Something in there, Proxis.'

The Ancient consulted the map on his heads-up display. 'Well, that's where we are going, brother. Five hundred yards in there is a shaft to the left, and down it are the stores we are here for.'

The Ultramarines went through the buildings one by one, kicking in the doors and nosing their bolters into every room. Nothing but the trash the orks had left behind.

'All clear,' Proxis said. He changed frequency.

'Militia, on me. Bring the vehicles. Morcault, keep an eye on the augur. If anything appears here, try to let us know. If it is in strength, take off and circle.'

'I hear you,' Morcault's old voice came back. 'Be aware the mine has been deserted for some time. The rain may well have destabilised the supports closest to the entrance.'

Proxis did not reply. Glancing at the chrono running in his helm display he saw that they were seven hours behind schedule. He felt momentarily tempted to call up Zalathras on the vox, but that would give away their position. He said a silent prayer, watchful.

'Brother Valerian, do not forget the other reason you are here.'

The Librarian nodded, frowning.

From the hold of the *Mayfly* rumbled two large six-wheeled heavy loaders. Equipped with hydraulic cranes and massive flatbeds, their original bright yellow had been hurriedly sprayed dark green. The barking engines seemed very loud to Proxis. Both vehicles were crammed with militia, hanging off the sides and packed into the cabs. In front of them walked the militia officer, Lascelle.

'Nice day for a drive,' Lascelle drawled, but his quick alertness did not match his tone. He carried a beautifully tooled bolter, a scaled-down version similar to those the Ultramarines carried. It looked old enough to be an heirloom. He scanned the surrounding cliffs that frowned over the quarry, rain running in rivulets down them. The earth here was not the dark clay of the jungle, but a paler, lighter material, and when wet it balled up quickly under the boot.

'Debus your men,' Proxis told him. 'One hit on a loader could take out half of them. We go in on foot, staggered file, vehicles at the rear – no one in them but the drivers. Clear?'

'Yes, sir,' Lascelle said, chastened. He shouted an order and the men leapt off the two loaders into the mustard-coloured muck.

'Brother Antigonus, lead off,' Proxis said.

The company began trooping forward into the darkness of the mine.

* * *

It was eerily quiet when they had gone in a hundred yards or so. There was no power here, so they turned on the lights of the loaders for the sake of the militia, and two men worked the searchlights on the roof of the cabs. The sound of the rain died away as they ventured into the dark, and there was only the dull thump of their feet, the murmuring engines and the steady drip of water from above.

'Tracks in the dirt,' Brother Antigonus said. 'Orks, big and small, vehicles.'

'Let us hope they have not found this store we are looking for,' Proxis said. 'I should hate to have come all this way for nothing.'

The auspex was clear. Brother Valerian studied it constantly as they advanced, sweeping the tunnel for five hundred yards in front. But the Librarian felt a tingling in the corners of his brain. They were not alone down here, of that he had no doubt.

They found the side shaft, and Proxis left Brothers Antigonus and Kadare to cover the intersection, before continuing. The shaft here was narrower, but still wide enough for the vehicles, and it sloped downhill some fifteen degrees. The drivers in the loader cabs had their feet hovering over the brakes, and occasionally the wheels of the big vehicles locked and slid forward through the pale dust. The cursing, blinking militiamen jogged forward out of the way, while up ahead the Ultramarines walked on with a good deal less noise, despite their bulk.

They came to the end of the shaft and found themselves before a pair of tall doors, as well made as any blast door in Zalathras. The metal of these was dented and scored and they were surrounded by broken rubble. Before the doors, half a dozen of the ork maggot-folk known as gretchin were cowering. They held up their thin hands, weaponless and screeching in what might pass for Gothic.

Proxis did not waste ammunition. He and his brethren cut down the little creatures with their combat blades, breaking their skulls under their boots. Lascelle and his militia watched without a word.

Brother Valerian found the combination lock and punched in the code. The doors began to lift into the ceiling, showering the Space Marines with dust. Proxis turned to Lascelle.

'You know what to look for?'

'I've been briefed, yes.'

'Then get to it.' He peered into the storeroom beyond the doors, a vast silent darkness in which rows of crates and steel drums filed away in rows.

'Brother-sergeant.' It was Kadare up at the intersection.

'Go ahead.'

'We have noise coming from down in the main shaft. Nothing on auspex.'

'We will join you in a moment, brother. Hold fast. Brother Valerian?'

'As I said, we're not alone down here,' the Librarian told him.

'Lascelle, get those vehicles up and loaded with all haste. We will meet you at the intersection. One load will do it, yes?'

'These things can transport ten tons each,' Lascelle told him. 'I'll take whatever is useful, besides what we came for.'

'Do not be too long at it,' Proxis said. 'Come, brothers.' He led the Ultramarines back up the steep slope of the shaft at a swift run. It was startling to see them move so fast, those shadowed giants.

Lascelle turned to his platoon. 'Bring the loaders into the storeroom. You all know the sigils to look for. Kenning and Norblau, break out the winches.' The engines of the loaders muttered and growled. The militia went to their work with a will. They did not wish to linger in that place; the shadows seemed ominous, and the cold killing of the miserable gretchin had chilled them all.

The Ultramarines reunited at the intersection. Antigonus and Kadare were facing into the mine.

'We will be here an hour, by my reckoning,' Proxis said. 'Nothing?'

'Listen, brother,' Kadare said, gesturing into the darkness with his bolter muzzle.

They waited. After a few moments it came to them all, a far distant sound, like the rumbling gurgle of some great intestinal system. It echoed up the tunnel.

'That is organic,' Proxis said.

'We should perhaps investigate it,' Valerian told him. 'I sense something I have not encountered before. I wish to know more.'

'Dangerous thing, curiosity,' Proxis grunted. 'Very well, brother. You and I shall go, alone. Antigonus, you and the others hold this position. The mission remains key here – see to it that the vehicles get out to the ship, whatever happens.'

The Ancient and the Librarian stepped off into the darkness. The tunnel in which they walked was at least sixty-five feet high, a semicircular hole buttressed by pillars of plasteel and roughly worked stone. The dust of the floor had seen a lot of coming and going, and it muffled their footsteps. They advanced with the swift wariness of their kind.

Once, Proxis stopped and picked up a fist-sized fungus which looked as though it had been dropped there – there was a trail of them.

'The beginnings of the infestation,' he said, crushing it. And after a moment, 'They eat them, too.'

'I know, brother. I too have fought orks before.'

Another two hundred yards in, and the two Adeptus Astartes saw movement slithering across the floor and sliding up the walls. They stepped close, and saw strange life-forms, a snout and tiny black eyes attached to a slug-like body perhaps ten to twenty inches long. Many of them were sliding and wriggling through the dust. Proxis set his foot on one and settled his weight upon it until the thing exploded with a splash of green mucus and flaccid flesh.

'More xenos filth,' he said thoughtfully. 'The lowest rung of all ork ecology. Another foodstuff. I wonder if they have made some kind of supply depot out of this place.'

'They have been up to something,' Valerian told him. He had muted the blue light of his hood and helmed up. He maglocked his bolt pistol and took out his chainsword, but did not yet push the ignite button.

Further in they went. The vox was silent. They passed increasing numbers of the orkish creatures and had to kick them aside, rolling them in the dust like turds in flour. There was that long, gurgling rumble again, unmistakably the sound of organic life. It flooded up the tunnel, and along with it came the reek of excrement, not the familiar filth of the orks, but something more pungent.

'There is something monstrous down here,' Valerian said in a low voice. 'A thing I have not encountered before.'

'I see light,' Proxis said. 'How far in are we now?'

'Eight hundred yards. The auspex is lit up like a torch. Somewhere up ahead there is a mass of the things.'

'Easy does it, brother. Discretion is the watchword here.' Valerian could hear the grin in Proxis' voice.

The two Ultramarines crept forward. The tunnel kinked here, then split into three tall entrances. They went to ground at the sight of movement in the darkness ahead. The reek in the air would have been almost unendurable without auto-senses to alleviate it.

A sandbagged position, and in it half a dozen orks manning an autocannon, or something similar. They were alert and watchful.

'They must have heard the gunfire earlier,' Valerian said.

'And yet they stayed at their post. They guard something important, then. What do your senses tell you, brother?'

Valerian reached out with his mind, gliding past the ork sentries, flitting down into the back tunnels behind them. It touched on others – some barely sentient, others a teeming gabble of primitive intellects, the lowest orders of the ork genus. They were present here in their hundreds – thousands, even. And finally it came up against a sudden wall of inchoate brute rage and physicality which staggered him.

'We must get out of here,' he said urgently to Proxis.

'What is it? What have you discovered?'

A flash of fury blinking across his mind, closer to.

'No time, brother. They know we are here. We must go – now!'

He straightened and was turning back up the tunnel when the orks at the autocannon set up a sudden roar and the weapon exploded into life. The muttering silence was slashed apart by the heavy rounds that arced towards them in bright lances of light. Valerian was shoved to his back by Proxis as they swept over the two Ultramarines and went shrieking up the tunnel.

But not all of them went high.

Proxis cursed, a profanity of Calth, where he had been born. An autocannon round had smashed the Ancient full in the chest, punching through his armour and knocking him backwards. Still swearing, he got to his knees, snapped off a few shots from his bolter pistol, and then levered himself to his feet again with the haft of his power axe.

'I believe you were right, brother,' he said. Over the helm vox his voice sounded as though his mouth were full of blood. 'I may need some help here.'

Then Proxis toppled into the dust with a low groan.

Brother Valerian felt his head swim with anger. Orks were pouring up the three tunnels towards them now. He could not see them, but he could hear their bestial cries and sense the infant simplicity of their feral minds. Those at the autocannon were swinging the weapon to bear.

'Throne take you,' the Librarian muttered. He reached out his hand and the hood above his helm flared bright blue.

'Now, burn,' he hissed, and he called upon the latent energy that was bubbling up bright and hot as a reactor's core in his mind.

A blistering white light sprang out of his fingers, veined like storm-bred lightning. It arced out of him and soared across the tunnel, grounding in the autocannon emplacement.

The orks there raised their fists to their eyes and shrieked. They burned from the feet up, the white fire consuming them, popping off autocannon rounds, careering off the tunnel walls and darting in blinding tendrils down the three other entrances. The packed earth of the tunnels quaked and broke and tumbled down in clods and boulders where it was not supported by the plasteel buttresses, half blocking the entrances. The earth smoked as the lightning ran through it, a thing almost with a life of its own, a mad, unshackled energy that ricocheted and sprang from wall to wall.

Valerian sagged, and staggered. He grabbed Proxis' arm.

'Come, brother. Things here are becoming far too interesting.'

The Ancient was hauled to his feet again. Valerian could see the naked torn flesh of Proxis' chest through the splintered ceramite of the artificer armour – the power cables that ran into the aquila plate on his torso were severed and sparking with energy.

'Turn down your power-pack, Proxis, or you'll fry us both.'

The Ancient grunted, a bitten-down world of agony in the sound. The dangerous flashing rune in Valerian's squad display steadied into mortal red.

'Do not die on me, brother,' he said as he hauled the Ancient up the tunnel. 'Lord Calgar would never forgive you.'

Hester raised her face from the augur readouts, alarm written all over it. 'Morcault, we have enemy craft inbound, heading straight for us and burning everything they have. They'll be in our laps in ten minutes.'

Morcault swore. He thumbed the shipboard vox. 'Jon, power up the engines for an emergency take-off. I don't give a damn for your red lines. Push it with everything.'

The engineer acknowledged with a click of the vox.

'Something else – I'm reading an energy spike underground, about a mile north-west. It just came and went,' Hester said. She started flipping switches. 'Get them out, Morcault.'

'We don't have time.' The old voidsman stabbed his finger into the console. 'Ground party, do you read?'

A crackle, and then Roman Lascelle's voice came back to them. 'Let me guess. Bad news.'

'Time to go. In ten minutes we'll have company – a lot of it. Get everyone out.'

'We're almost done, Morcault, but it'll take more than that to get these vehicles back up the tunnel.'

A new voice – one of the Ultramarines. 'The mission must be accomplished. Start the vehicles back up to the surface. We will cover the rear. There is fighting in the tunnel below us, and our brethren are involved.'

Morcault swore. 'No time for heroics. Where is Proxis?'

'Unknown. He is off vox. Leave him to us. Get the palladium out – that is the priority.'

Hester was shaking her head. 'Fighter-bombers and transports. They're really moving.'

Morcault rubbed his forehead. 'They caught us cold. Take off – now. Get us in the air, Hester.'

'But–'

'Trust me, and do as I say. Gortyn, I want all the power you have. Jodi, light up the void shields they gave us, and pray the damn things work.'

The *Mayfly*'s boarding ramp came up with a crash, but even before the hatch doors were sealed the little freighter was off the ground, the retros hammering the quarry mud into a fat cloud. The ship shuddered and lurched in the air as it soared skywards atop a plume of flame.

'Fifteen thousand feet. Eighteen thousand,' Jodi Arnhal intoned. 'We have an atmospheric breach in the hold.'

'Ignore it. We're not in vacuum,' Morcault told the Navigator. 'Haul back on those throttles, Hester. Give them a nice big signature to follow.'

Gortyn came over the vox from the drive compartment. 'We're losing her, Ghent – you have to ease back on power.'

'Spit on it, for Throne's sake. Flood the coolant, Jon – just keep her burning.'

'They've changed course – the fighters will be on our tail in about a minute and a half,' Jodi said, his voice shrill with fear.

'You're going to get us all killed, old man,' Hester growled, one hand juggling the yoke, the other white-knuckled on the throttles.

'Not for the first time – make for the storm to the north,' Morcault told the pilot, staring into his chair readouts. The cogitator was plastering the slate with numbers almost too fast to follow, and red lights were flashing all over the bridge.

'Lascelle, do you read?'

He heard the engine noise of the loaders in the background as the aristocratic young officer replied from the ground below.

'We're on the move – don't know where in hell the Ultramarines are – still down the tunnel. We have a full load, Morcault. What's your status?'

'We're drawing off the fighters, but there are at least two transports still inbound to your location. They're slower – you have about seven minutes. You have to hold on against whatever lands out of them. We'll try and get back to you.'

He heard the shock in Lascelle's voice. 'You'd better.'

Morcault leaned back. The G-forces were working on his old frame, pressing him back into the fabric of his chair, making his heartbeat thunder in his ears. *Don't go fainting on me now,* he scourged himself.

The *Mayfly* roared off to the north like an arrow with its flights aflame. Arcing out of the west and south in pursuit came a dozen ork fighters, the swiftest of their kind. Light craft, they were buffeted by the thunderheads they were barrelling through, jumping up and down in the turbulence like spiders on the end of a windblown web.

Ahead of them, the storm in the north reared up like a wall, black anvils of cloud rising up to thirty thousand feet with lightning flashing at their base. The *Mayfly* was hurtling towards it with every ounce of power the drives could muster, but the ork craft were faster; they were gaining.

'Missiles launched on our stern,' Jodi said, wide-eyed.

'Countermeasures,' Morcault told him, labouring to breathe. 'Hester, get us into that storm front.'

'It's as liable to break us apart as it is the orks,' she told him.

'The *Mayfly* can take it. She'll not give up on us now. But those fighters–'

'Throne, a missile – it's going to hit–' Jodi's voice rose to a shout.

And then the explosion struck the freighter full on the starboard side.

Valerian sowed the tunnel behind them with grenades, set for proximity. He clicked them out of his belt and tossed them in his wake as he hauled Proxis up the tunnel. Fifty more yards, and he felt a bright wash of relief at the sight of his own brethren coming down towards him.

'Get down, brother,' Kadare said, and Valerian let himself and Proxis fall to the floor as the heavy bolter opened up, a bright flare of death pouring down the way they had come, streaming over their heads and producing a chorus of snarls and screams. One, then another, of the grenades went off.

The battle-brethren took a moment, and sent a torrent of fire down the tunnel, aiming by instinct as much as by the targeting cogitators in their helms. Then Proxis was seized up, and the six Ultramarines backed up the tunnel, firing as they went.

'How bad?' Brother Antigonus asked Valerian.

'Autocannon. The wound has sealed, but there is extensive internal injury. He needs an Apothecary.'

'Enemy?'

'Unknown. But there are quite a few of them down there.'

'More above, from what I hear. The vehicles are on the surface, but the *Mayfly* is gone. Ork transports five minutes away.'

'The odds seemed to have turned against us, brothers,' Kadare said. He patted the heavy bolter he bore. 'But we shall not go down without something to say about it.'

They made as best time as they could up the tunnel, and it was not long before there was a grey light ahead, and they came out into the endless rain to find the two loaders parked before the entrance, piled high with crates, and Lascelle's militia platoon arrayed around them in a defensive perimeter. Lascelle was white-faced, tense, but in perfect control of himself, though many of his men were plainly terrified.

'We make a stand here, and await Morcault's return,' Brother Valerian told them. 'The orks are on their way. Our task is very simple – survive as long as possible and preserve the supplies on the vehicles. Take your positions, brothers. Lieutenant, see to your men.'

There was nothing more to say. When the ork transports appeared in the sky to the south-west, burning bright against the clouds, the defenders merely stared. Brother Kadare looked up at the pot-bellied craft with their ugly lines and garish paintwork, and laughed.

'Plenty to go around.'

THE TRANSPORTS TOUCHED down three hundred yards away, blasting up a choking wall of muck and rain. Their ramps crashed down, and out of their bellies poured a tide of orks. These were the big, well-armed killers of their race, dark green, howling, taller than the Ultramarines themselves. Perhaps a hundred leapt to the ground in the first wave and came charging towards the Adeptus Astartes and militia like a raging green avalanche.

Brother Kadare's heavy bolter opened up on full automatic, the belt at his hip whining as the rounds sped through it. He chopped down a great swathe in the foremost orks, and more of these were then consumed by a blast of promethium from Brother Antigonus.

The transports hauled off again, but there were two more in the skies behind them, lumbering in from the west.

The orks sped forward. Brother Valerian activated his chainsword even while he dropped the enemy with aimed single shots from his bolt pistol. The Librarian summoned his powers once more – severely depleted by the episode in the tunnels, but not yet gone – and searched out the brains and psyche of the leading ork mob. Into the primitive creatures he sent a wave of despair, a projected hopelessness, a black echo of the grinning pit behind the immaterium.

It did not stop them, but dozens of them slowed, and their eyes dulled and jaws went slack as the vicious darkness invaded their minds. The rank behind them crashed into the dazed leaders at full tilt, and for a few seconds the orks were in a tangle, some even striking and shooting their fellows.

The Ultramarines took advantage of the moment, and opened up with a barrage of blazing fire that destroyed dozens, the heavy bolter rounds exploding within the ork carcasses, taking off heads and limbs, blowing strewn ropes of intestines clear across the field. And in the middle of that bright thicket of fire, the lasguns of the militia snapped out, burning through the ranks, bringing other orks wounded and roaring to their knees.

'They're coming up the tunnel behind us!' one of the militia shouted out.

'Kadare,' Valerian said. 'Aim at the tunnel roof – a good burst.'

The Ultramarine wheeled round and sent a hundred rounds pummelling into the roof right at the entranceway to the mine behind them. There was a moment when nothing happened, and then a great chunk of masonry and rain-rotted mortar collapsed on the lead ranks of the orks. He fired burst after burst until, with a hollow roar, half the entrance to the mine fell in. A tall cloud of dust puffed out into the rain, engulfing the Ultramarines and militia.

Into that choking cloud the orks from the transports thronged, and it became hand to hand with them all down the line. Gouts of promethium flame billowed out, men screamed, orks howled, and the Ultramarines fought with silent, deadly determination.

Brother Gauros was set upon by three massive xenos that grappled with him and bore him to his knees. He stabbed his combat knife into the eye of one, drove his fingers into the maw of another. The ork bit down, but could not pierce the ceramite gauntlet.

More piled upon him. They punched and tore at the prone Ultramarine until at last with a loud crack they wrested his head, still in its helm, from his shoulders. Gargling in triumph, they sucked at his blood and smeared it on their faces – until a well-placed grenade from brother Antigonus blew them all apart.

The militia were slaughtered, torn to pieces and flung aside like soiled rags by the raging orks. One unfortunate was spitted on a bayonet and raised into the air high above the fight, where he wriggled and screamed like a living battle-banner until he died.

Brother Valerian fought over Proxis' body with the bulk of a heavy loader at his back, wielding the chainsword until its hissing song turned into a caterwauling of overstressed steel. He cut up one after another of the foe, and shot down more with his bolt pistol, his eyes glaring with a dark light. The others of his Chapter gathered about him, along with the surviving militia, and they fought there with the desperate tenacity of the doomed.

Brother Comus was pulled out of the tight knot of the defenders and engulfed by the enemy, shot, stabbed and torn to pieces on the ground. Valerian stumbled in the act of decapitating one great ork, and would have suffered the same fate had not Brother Kadare turned the heavy bolter on the enemy to his front, blasting them back from the Librarian, the rounds impacting so close that two of them clipped divots out of his shoulderplate.

'My thanks, brother,' Valerian said, regaining his feet.

'I am on my last belt. You can thank me before the Throne,' Kadare riposted, and opened up again to save two militiamen from being trampled by the foe.

Lascelle was there, pale and composed, firing bursts out of his customised bolter. Only a dozen of his men were still alive. The others were not even corpses, but mere body parts and stripped bones strewn all around them. Some of the orks were shot down in the act of eating the dead. Others impaled the limbs of the slain militiamen on their spiked armour as grotesque ornaments – and Valerian saw with a flare of fury that one particular ork had set Brother Comus' head on a stick, and was shaking it as a trophy.

It was the end – they were finished, and knew it. But they did not stop fighting. When Brother Kadare's heavy bolter ran dry he clubbed one ork with the now useless weapon and then fought on with knife and pistol.

But then a shadow appeared over them, massive and shooting flame. It came down with a mighty boom and the fire of its approach burned dozens of orks to seared meat. It crashed to earth with a tearing grate of overstressed metal, the muck exploding around it, the ground under their feet jumping with the impact.

The ork warband was dashed asunder by the impact of the *Mayfly*'s landing. More were flattened as its heavy cargo ramp dropped down, and in the hatch behind was Jon Gortyn, the ship's engineer, and Jodi Arnhal. They waved wildly to the survivors of the ground party, gesturing them aboard.

Valerian turned to Brother Kadare. 'Take Proxis – get him aboard.' The remnants of the militia had broken and were running for the old freighter. Some threw away their weapons in their haste. Valerian looked back at the heavy loaders behind them. No Ultramarine could drive one – he would barely fit in the cab.

'Lascelle!'

'I know – get your folk on board. I'll drive one.' Roman Lascelle had a mirthless grin plastered across his face, like a death rictus.

The Ultramarines started firing at the orks who were still standing and clambering to their feet and collecting what little wits they had. Overhead, two more ork transports were coming in with a bright flare of afterburners.

One of the heavy loaders started up with a savage roar, and Lascelle nosed it up the ramp. An ork sprang onto the cab and hammered on the glass, shattering it, but Brother Antigonus hauled the creature off and put a bolt round in its head.

They staggered aboard, those who still could, firing as they came, knocking back the furious orks. Brother Antigonus, Brother Kadare and Brother Valerian held the line while the loader was driven aboard, and Antigonus booted off the lip of the ramp those who tried to climb over it as it rose.

It slammed into place, and the hatch doors closed. Gortyn hit the vox. 'Now!' he shouted.

The *Mayfly* rattled and shook and seemed about to come apart as the drives kicked in. There was daylight in the hold, a yawning hole in the starboard side, which orks were even now trying to clamber through, until Valerian cut off their hands and arms and kicked them out.

The ship lifted, creaking, the very fabric of the vessel groaning under their feet. Gortyn ran out of the hold towards the drive section, but Jodi Arnhal remained there, staring. 'Is this all?' he kept asking. 'Is this all of you?'

The G-force of their ascent made even the weary Ultramarines stagger, and rain whipped in through the damaged hull along with the roar of the wind. Roman Lascelle climbed out of the loader cab, his face bloody where the shattered glass had sliced it open. He would have fallen, had not Valerian caught him.

'Thank you,' he said, as politely as if he were in a drawing room. 'I am not quite myself.'

# SEVENTEEN

'THE VOID SHIELD saved us,' Morcault told Brother Valerian on the bridge. The old man had a field dressing wrapped around his head and his white hair was bloodstained.

'It wasn't much, but it was enough to deflect much of the blast down the side of the hull. We lost a chunk of the outer plating and one bulwark was punched right through, but the rest of her held together.' He thumped his chair arm lightly. 'She's a tough old girl.'

Valerian had never quite understood why humans referred to their vessels as females, but that was of no account right now.

'How long until we are back in Zalathras?'

'We can't go back through that storm,' Hester said waspishly as she grasped the yoke and stared out of the viewports. 'The way she is at the moment, the *Mayfly* would be torn apart – we're hanging together with prayers and duct tape – and you can tell your big axe-wielding friend that from me.'

Valerian's eyes flickered darkly. 'My brother Proxis is gravely wounded. I command this mission now.'

Hester blinked rapidly. She did not look round. 'I'm sorry,' she said.

'Morcault,' the Librarian went on, 'time is of the essence here, for many reasons. I need your best guess.'

'Jodi?' the old man said.

The Navigator punched up charts of the planet on his slate, and overlaid them with the augur relays. Red lights sprinkled his board. He did some calculations, pushing lines through the scarlet clutter on the screen, studying the scroll of figures that his course corrections brought up.

'We could try going high,' he said at last. 'Take her up into a low orbit. Most of the ork fighters and interceptors between us and Zalathras are sub-orbital craft. If we can get above them, and yet stay below the main ork fleet, we have a chance.'

'Like threading a needle,' Morcault mused. 'The question is whether we would survive re-entry.'

'Captain, there is a rather large hole in your ship,' Valerian said.

'Exactly. But Gortyn is working on it,' Morcault told him.

The Librarian looked over the Navigator's shoulder. Then he blinked up the Ultramarine vox. 'Brother Kadare.'

'Yes, brother.'

'Help out the ship's engineer with whatever he needs to try and seal down the hold. But get the militia forward, out of that compartment. We are going to try for orbit.'

Kadare gave a mirthless laugh over the vox. 'It shall be so. I applaud the pilot's temerity, brother.'

'Brother Kadare and Brother Antigonus can withstand vacuum in their power armour. They shall remain in the hold to help out your engineer,' Valerian told the *Mayfly*'s crew. 'Brother Proxis is in your sick bay.'

'Scurrios will monitor his condition,' Morcault said, looking up at the dark-eyed Librarian. 'I'm sorry you lost some of your people.'

'Your physician will not be able to do much with Adeptus Astartes physiology. The sus-an membrane in Proxis' brain has activated as a result of his wounds, placing him in a state of hibernation. It will take one of our own Apothecaries to bring him round.'

Morcault shook his head slightly. 'I forget how different you are to us.'

'We are still human,' Valerian told him. 'Some may debate that, but in my Chapter at least, we are never allowed to forget it.'

He breathed out. *Still human*. That might well be true – but there was a gulf between his brethren and normal humanity, and it had never seemed so wide to him as it did now. Perhaps because he felt an unease at placing his fate and that of his brothers in the hands of these frail creatures before him.

Morcault and his crew had saved them, more than once. It did not sit well with Valerian to owe so much to ordinary men and women, but he had to fight such prejudices. It was in the Codex that his own primarch had written: the Space Marines were created to serve humanity, not the other way round.

He thought of the surviving militia, bolting for the safety of the *Mayfly* and leaving the object of their mission abandoned, and his mind flooded with fury at their cowardice, their utter uselessness.

But then he remembered the courage of Lieutenant Lascelle, who had stayed with them. Without him, the mission would have been a complete failure instead of the half-wrecked thing it was now.

Humanity. It infuriated and inspired. Men could not all be depended upon – perhaps most of them could not – but some rose above their failings. Just enough, perhaps, to keep some faith in humanity alive. It had always been thus.

They tore up the deck plates around the loader in the hold and Gortyn welded them over the gaping hole in the ship's side while Brothers Kadare and Antigonus held them in place, manhandling the hundred kilo plates as though they were made of card. While they were doing this, the *Mayfly* sat hidden in a small jungle clearing some forty miles west of the Ballansyr Quarries.

'We were lucky,' Valerian told Morcault. 'Most of the palladium was on the first loader – the one Lascelle drove out. At a guess I would say we salvaged at least four tons of it. The rear vehicle was loaded with mining charges and other material less vital to the manufactoria.'

'What was down there – in the mines?' Morcault asked the Librarian.

The Ultramarine frowned. 'I sensed a great bestial psyche – an animal. But one which was linked into the overall mind-bloom of the orks. There was a sense of staggering power in it – not intelligence, but raw brute presence. Whatever it was, I think the orks were there to guard it and look after it. The mine was its cage.'

'Let us hope the cage door stays locked,' Morcault said.

'No – it is not imprisoned there – it is merely being... managed.' Valerian's face twisted in a sour smile. 'Whatever it was, I believe that we shall see it before the walls of Zalathras before long. The orks do not put so much effort into housing and feeding such a phenomenon merely to keep it hidden. It is part of their war effort.'

VALERIAN LEFT THE bridge and stepped into the *Mayfly*'s sick bay. He nodded at Scurrios; the little medic's eyes were as large as those of some terrified insect behind his thick lenses. He was wiping bright red Adeptus Astartes blood off his hands.

'Your friend – sir, lord – I have made him as comfortable as I could – I had to lay him on the floor. I am so sorry – he collapsed the gurney. The weight... the armour. I did not like to try and get it off him. It is...' he faltered. 'It is *part* of him. The breastplate had cables running into his very body. I never knew... not for a moment did I suspect–' He swallowed. 'Are you, you Ultramarines...are you robots of some kind?'

Valerian felt the first spark of amusement he had felt in a long time. 'If only we were,' he said. 'We have been... modified. We have a symbiotic relationship with the power armour we wear, but by and large, we are flesh and blood just like you. We break, we bleed.' He set a hand on Proxis' shoulderplate. 'And in time, we die.'

'He is in a coma. His life signs barely register,' Scurrios said.

'Proxis is still in there. He has seen centuries of the Imperium come and go, and survived nightmares of folly and mayhem that you cannot even imagine. He will survive this also. Just make sure he is kept stable. We must get him back to Zalathras for our own Apothecary to work on.' Valerian bent his head. He muttered a prayer.

'I am glad you people are on our side,' Scurrios said, polishing his glasses. His face had a shrunken look when he took them off. The top of his head reached barely to the aquila on Valerian's breastplate.

They are such frail things, Valerian thought. How do they survive in this wilderness of pain? And yet they have spanned the galaxy. Their blood runs in our veins – in the veins of the divine Emperor Himself. In the beginning, we were all of us the same, and our hearts still beat to the same rhythms, the same furies and madnesses and flashes of nobility. There is courage in man, and his humanity stands alone in a universe of malice. That is why we were made, the Adeptus Astartes. Not to supplant man, but to protect him.

He had never really understood that before, but seeing Proxis lying there wounded and helpless, and the transparent compassion of the little medic who stood beside his great prone carcass, he felt the truth of it for the first time.

Our Lord knows this, he realised. Marneus Calgar has always known it. It is what has made him great. He holds still to the vestiges of humanity that reside in us all.

THE MAYFLY TOOK to the skies again an hour later. Brothers Kadare and Antigonus remained in the hold to keep an eye on the hasty repairs, but Valerian stood on the bridge while the ship's crew went about their business, their efficiency masked by quips, insults and mocking threats. They were a family, he realised. Only people who knew each other intimately could be so flippant to one another in such a serious situation.

And he thought of Proxis, making a bad joke in the midst of a hellish battle. We are not so different after all, he thought.

'One hundred thousand feet,' the Navigator was saying.

'How is the repair holding?' Morcault asked, and Brother Kadare came over the ship vox.

'It is hot, but in place. The hold is still not airtight – we are losing atmosphere somewhere. Trying to track down the leak to weld it over.'

'Re-entry will find that leak soon enough,' Hester murmured.

The heat of re-entry would do more than that. It would seek the hole, widen it, and flood the hold with fire, perhaps take down the ship.

'One thing at a time,' Morcault said.

Valerian engaged his magnetic bootsoles as he felt gravity left behind. As he looked out of the viewports he could see Zalidar now as it had appeared on their first sight of it: a rich green curvature filling half their sky with a thin haze of atmosphere clinging to it. And beyond, the star-filled dark of the void.

'Engaging gravitics,' Jodi said. He thumped the console. 'Start up, you bastard.'

In the centre of the ship the gravitic generator came to life, and Valerian felt his weight upon the deck again.

As he did, he felt something else, also. Or rather the lack of something. The battering screech of the collective ork psyche that blanketed the planet was no more. He was outside it, looking in. He felt his mind clear of that extraneous noise for the first time since planetfall, like sudden relief from tinnitus.

'Throne be praised,' he whispered. 'Captain, how long will we remain in orbit?'

'A matter of minutes. I'm going to plan for re-entry a few miles south of Zalathras.'

'We have ork ships on augur, forty thousand miles out,' Jodi said. 'They're big. Cruisers. Lots of traffic between them and the planet. I don't think they've picked us up yet.'

'Hold off on re-entry until you have my word,' Valerian said. Now – it had to be now. Once he was back on the planet, the ork gabble would fog his abilities once more.

'Why?' Morcault asked.

'Just do as I say.'

Valerian closed his eyes. His head tilted back in the blue-lit mechanics of the hood that enfolded his skull. He reached out into that cold, clear dark, his mind sending out a quicksilver tendril that quested over light years in seconds, sped past other, lesser minds by the million, and flashed past burning suns, past pockets of the immaterium close to the emptiness of ordinary vacuum. He was not navigating by stars, but by minds, and he followed the signature of one he knew, one of his own brethren.

'Brother Carimus. It is I, Valerian.'

He let his own identity saturate the images he sent wavering out into the void. He could not be specific – it did not work that way. But he lent his message a bright sense of urgency.

And felt the recognition in reply, faint and far off. It was a long way. Carimus was with Seventh Company, in the Battlefleet *Andronicus*. It was clear across the Fringe, and the invisible currents of the immaterium wafted and coursed between them, battering Valerian's psychic presence to tatters.

*Carimus.*

He let the memories and pictures slide through his mind, all dominated by Marneus Calgar, the Chapter Master. A great beleaguered figure, standing alone, and around him a sea of foes, and beyond them, the looming jungle.

He could not fine-tune the image further, but he put into it every ounce of emotion he could muster, a flashing series of vignettes which made sense only if half-familiar. Marneus Calgar. Orks. Jungle planet. He pushed those facts as hard as he could, willing the pictures to flame bright and urgent across the intervening darkness.

And at the end, there was an answering flash, a moment of realisation. He was sure he had not imagined it.

And then the connection was broken, and Valerian felt his consciousness whip back through the intervening light years, the awesome, unimaginable distances across the glittering dark, and he staggered as he came back to himself and the humming bridge of the little battered freighter in which he stood. Like swapping a view from orbit for that of a look through a microscope.

He oriented himself, breathed out slowly as he had been taught, and eased the hammering of his hearts. The secondary had woken, feeling the need for more oxygenated blood to course through his system and revive him.

He had been trained in astropathy, but it had never come easy to him, and it sucked something out of the body as well as the mind.

He had communicated something – he had sent some sense of events – he was sure of it. Carimus must work with it. It was up to him now.

'Well, captain,' he said, his throat dry, his tongue large and numbed in his mouth. 'Let us return to the planet.'

It had been done. He hoped it was enough. There was hope now; it flooded him along with the blood pulsing through his arteries. He had kept faith with his Chapter Master.

If we can only hang on, he thought, then Seventh will surely come to us.

'IF WE CAN only hang on,' Morcault was saying. 'Those repairs will not take a lot of abuse. I'm going for a shallow, powered re-entry. Hester, try not to get bounced back into space.'

The pilot was hunched over her controls. She had eyes only for her slates and dials. The two servitors at the side of the bridge worked silently, but occasionally one would utter a swift flurry of binaric.

'Ork ships closing on our position,' Jodi said. 'Twenty thousand miles. They're in no hurry – perhaps they think we're part of their fleet.'

The vox lit up with a grunted flurry of words that were half animal growl and half Low Gothic.

'I haven't heard that tongue in fifty years,' Morcault said. 'Anyone speak orkish?'

No one answered him. 'Well, let's hope we lose them on re-entry.'

The bridge door opened and Roman Lascelle walked in. 'The heat is building through the ship,' he said, wiping sweat from his face. It was streaked with a staple-sealed gash that gleamed in the bridge overheads.

A rumbling bang, and the *Mayfly* began to dance under them.

'We'll need a complete refit after this little stunt,' Hester muttered.

The ship plunged into the atmosphere, and Morcault brought down the titanium blast shutters that protected the viewports. Everything was shaking. Lascelle took a chair and buckled himself in.

'Been a long time since I felt this,' he said.

'May be the last time you feel it,' Hester said. 'Jon, give me more power in the forward retros.'

'You can have all you want,' the engineer said over the vox. 'We're falling like a stone, and we're damn near out of coolant. I might as well relieve myself on the drives.'

'You do that,' Hester snapped.

The ship leapt under them, then tilted sideways. Valerian's magnetic bootsoles gripped the deck, but even so, he had to grasp a safety rail to remain upright.

'We're getting an influx of heat here,' Brother Kadare's voice came up from the hold. 'We're stacking another plate on top of it, but it won't hold for long.'

'Come on, sweetheart,' Morcault whispered. 'Hold together for me.'

'Do you need help, brother?' Valerian asked Kadare.

'Negative. No point in us all getting roasted. Can't weld – too much heat. But suit systems are coping.'

The *Mayfly* plunged through the thick air of Zalidar like a meteorite with a flaming tail. For those inside the craft it felt as though they were careering down a rocky slope without brakes. Condensation began to drip from the deckhead, as though the ship were sweating around them.

'The orks have turned off,' Jodi said, running his sleeve across his face. 'One torpedo launch, but it burned up in our wake.'

'Small mercies,' Morcault grunted. 'Altitude?'

'Hundred and fifty thousand feet and dropping fast.'

'Retros have cut out,' Hester said, and banged the console as though it had insulted her. She uttered a sentence of binaric to the servitors, and they went about their business with unhurried calm.

'Restart,' Morcault said. He touched the bandage on his head. 'Jon, give the plasma engines a kick, will you?'

'She doesn't want to know,' they heard Gortyn say, and there was a metallic clank over the vox. 'Starting auxiliary power generator. It'll give us twenty or thirty seconds, no more.'

'Going to need some fancy flying here, Hester,' Morcault said mildly, though the strain was etched across his face.

'I know it, old man.'

'Jodi, get Zalathras on the vox. I'd hate to get shot down before we crash.'

No one spoke. The *Mayfly* groaned and lurched around them like a beaten animal. The heat became almost unendurable. Even Valerian had sweat pouring down his exposed face. He could have helmed up, but chose not to. He reached out with his depleted abilities and for a few moments it was as though he had left the ship and was watching it from the outside, seeing the fiery plume in the sky that they had become. The green jungle of Zalidar loomed up like a wall below them.

'Try it now,' Gortyn said, the vox crackling with interference.

Hester was wrestling with the yoke, trying to haul it back into her lap. 'Jodi... I...' she grated.

'I can't move.'

'Give us full retro, for Throne's sake.'

They could feel the G-forces working on them now. The crew rose in their restraints and the flesh of their faces writhed. It was Valerian who leaned forward and tapped the blinking button. At once, a massive roar thundered through the ship, and the *Mayfly* shuddered and shook. The streaming figures on the altimeter slowed, became legible again.

'One hundred thousand feet,' Jodi said, his lips pulled back from his teeth. 'She's slowing.'

The nose of the ship came up. Hester's hands were bleeding on the yoke. 'I have her.'

'Zalathras air defence, this is Omega Six Three Two,' Valerian said, linking his own vox into that of the ship. 'We are coming in for a hard burn landing.'

'Six Three Two, we have you on augur. Regulate your descent. You're coming in too fast.'

'Doing our best, Zalathras.' This was Morcault. Blood was soaking the dressing wound about his temples. 'Clear us a path, will you?'

'There are ork craft in our airspace, and thick flak. We cannot cease fire to let you in – you will have to navigate through it. Good luck.'

Morcault raised the viewport shutters. The thick plexiglass was darkened with carbon. Zalathras was ahead of them, coming and going through boiling masses of cloud, and lights were winking above the city, a spattered field of anti-aircraft fire. Smoke rose in thick columns from Alphon and Kalgatt Spires.

'There's an old saying about frying pans and fires,' Morcault said, awed and exasperated in equal measure by the spectacle.

'Airspeed coming down, retros functioning. We have forty seconds of powered flight left in her,' Hester said.

'Get us below the firefight,' Morcault said. 'We'll set down wherever we can.'

They flashed over a mass of orks on the ground, the earth alive with the creatures. Then the tall city walls went by. The ship rocked with a near miss. They flew through a pillar of black smoke, heard shrapnel rattle against the hull.

'We're going down,' Hester said. 'Gear down, retros on full, airbrakes open–' The ship screamed around them, as though it had finally had enough and could endure the pain no longer.

The crew were thrown forward against their straps as the *Mayfly* yawed and pitched in mid-air, her forward momentum brought to a halt at last. Then she came down – for a moment falling with all the unguided aerodynamics of a dropped stone.

At the last moment, Hester punched every button she could find on the retro panel and the dials lit and flickered. The ship bucked up, swayed, and descended more slowly, the very fabric of the little freighter moving under their feet, as though she were being slowly torn apart.

Then there was a final crash that rang throughout the ship, and a great stillness. The drives were dead, and the lights flickered, died, and then came on again, a rusty amber hue. The air in the bridge was rancid with smoke.

'Well, we've landed,' Hester said in a whisper, before breaking into a fit of coughing.

Morcault patted the arm of his chair. 'The good old girl. I knew she wouldn't let us down.'

# EIGHTEEN

IT FELT AS though they had been in the sour subterranean stink of the abandoned sewer for days, but it had only been some five hours. The militia company were straggling behind, the men tired, laden down with the demolition gear that each carried in a backpack. Their officer, a recently promoted lieutenant in his forties, looked ready to drop.

Sergeant Avila called a halt, listening.

There was no mistaking it now. Above them, the earth trembled and the muffled thunder of artillery was a constant barrage of sound. A particularly loud impact close by made the militiamen flinch and crouch in the waist-deep water and filth they stood in.

'That was an earthshaker shell, or I know nothing,' Avila told Brother Parsifal.

'If the Basilisks are firing, then it must be an all-out assault,' the Apothecary agreed.

'Where are we, brother?'

'Three and a half miles south of the walls – we must be right under the ork batteries.'

'I'm surprised the scum have guns that can fire so far,' Avila grunted.

'Another mile or so, brother, and we will be at the block point. We should start setting the charges in another four hundred yards.'

Avila demurred. 'I am going to start setting them now, one every thirty feet. If there is trouble up ahead, then I want them in place behind us, ready to be blown.'

'Good thinking. Though the militia will not be happy at the thought of trapping themselves down here.'

'The militia will do as they are told. Lieutenant Einar!'

The rotund militia officer came wading through the noisome brown water up the column. He was too old for his rank, but had once served as a corporal in the Astra Militarum, which had resulted in his current elevation. Prior military experience was at a premium in Zalathras these days.

That experience had been a quarter of a century before. Einar was an unfit relic now. But as he stood dripping in the shadow of the towering Ultramarines, Avila could see some remnant of the old discipline in the man's eyes.

'Sir?'

'Detail your men. The charges are to be placed from here on in, every thirty feet on both sides of the tunnel, just above water level. The detonators are to be keyed into frequency sextus. You will inform me when the last charge is placed. Clear?'

'Quite clear, sir.'

'Then get to it.'

Einar puffed away again.

'I am glad we do not grow old as they grow old,' Parsifal said. 'We keep our strength until it is time to lay it down in service to the Emperor, and then we are remembered in the Chapter for the warriors we were. Our kind do not become age-crippled shadows of ourselves.'

'By His Name,' Sergeant Avila said.

* * *

THEY MOVED OUT again, more slowly now. The Ultramarines drew ahead of the militia, deliberately putting distance between themselves and the human troops. Alone, they moved more quickly, despite their bulk, and they needed no light to see their way; the infrared filter in their helms was so finely tuned that even the pitch-dark tunnel was clear as evening daylight to them.

'Contact signal, two hundred yards ahead,' Parsifal said quietly. 'It would seem our lord's instincts were correct.'

'Brother Gamelan, up front with Dextus,' Avila said. 'I want them suppressed as soon as you see a target.' He called up Lieutenant Einar on the vox.

'What is your progress, lieutenant?'

The man was panting into the vox-bead. 'Thirty charges set.'

'Move back – set the rest to the rear of the first batch, back up the tunnel. And make haste, Einar. We have company down here.'

'Affirmative, sir.'

The charges would bring down almost half a mile of the tunnel once they went off – enough to block any ork infiltration.

'We must buy the militia a little time, brothers,' Avila told his squad. 'Let us chastise these xenos. In His name.'

A mutter went over the vox, that fine-toned mixture of eagerness and anger which Avila relished.

'One hundred yards,' Parsifal said. 'They're advancing fast up the tunnel. Should be coming up on helm auspex any second.'

And they did. But before even that, the Space Marines could hear them, and their finely wrought sense of smell could pick up the peculiar reek of the orks, a mixture of base animal stink and fungal decay.

The clink of masonry and the splash of water were interlaced with the clink of metal tools and the harsh gabble of the creatures, always one note away from open violence. Loathing of them rose up in Avila's hearts. Of all xenos, he hated the tyranids the most. But the orks were a close second. They needed to be stamped out, like the vile disease they were.

I am Thy instrument, he prayed. Guide my hand, Lord of Mankind. Let me send Thy enemies into the abyss.

Brother Gamelan's heavy bolter rang out, stitching the darkness with light. Beside him, Dextus' plasma gun erupted in a flare of light as it propelled a bolt of superheated energy out towards the enemy. Not for nothing were such weapons known as sun-guns. For a split second the flare of it greyed out Avila's auto-senses, as his armour protected his vision from the searing blast.

The screams of the orks rang down the tunnel, strangely high-pitched for such massive creatures.

'Grenades,' Sergeant Avila said, and threw two of the deadly devices over the heads of his battle-brothers. They had been keyed for delay, and thus went off just as the orks ahead recovered and came charging forward again. The double explosion plastered the walls of the tunnel with ork entrails and body parts, and the tone of the shrieks beyond grew lower, descending into the fury of the xenos.

'Back up, twenty yards, fast,' Avila ordered his squad. They obeyed him, and a flash of promethium fire burned up the spot where they had stood moments before.

The sewer filled with steam, as thick as smoke. Avila's helm readjusted. He went to infrared for a second, and the enemy to his front came up on his targeting cogitator. The orks were milling and snarling in their accustomed manner, and wild autogun fire came streaking up the tunnel.

Brother Dextus grunted as one round struck his shoulderplate and made him stagger. For a moment the plasma gun he carried dipped into the filthy water they were wading in, and the muzzle of the weapon sizzled. Then he raised it up again and sent another energy blast hammering down at the enemy.

'Damage nominal – systems repairing,' he said.

'Brother Gamelan, give them a burst,' Avila said on the vox. 'The rest, back again. You stand still too long, you die, brothers.'

The heavy bolter shredded the enemy, giving them no time to form up and target the Space Marines. Gamelan jogged back to rejoin his brethren. Autogun rounds were skittering down the passage, impacting on the walls, bouncing off the Ultramarines' armour and ricocheting past them. The sigils of Avila's squad were all flickering from green to amber and back again in his display.

'Lieutenant Einar, how goes it?' Avila demanded of the militia officer back down the tunnel.

'Sixty charges set, sir. I need ten more minutes.'

'Get clear all your men save those still bearing charges. The enemy is pressing us close.'

'Yes, sir.'

'Enemy advancing,' Brother Gamelan said. Fire filled up the tunnel to his front, shrivelling the vegetation at water level and boiling the water itself. The interior of the sewer became as humid and rank as an equatorial jungle.

Out of the flames burst a massive ork, so large he had to crouch under the masonry. And so dark-skinned he seemed almost black, his red eyes gleaming and his jaw agape. He was clad in a tatterdemalion suit of powered armour, layers of ceramite welded carelessly together and running with spitting power cables. An ork-made bolter snapped out automatic fire from one fist, and the other was a gauntlet encased in a glowing power field.

Brother Gamelan opened up with the heavy bolter at close range, but the ork took the fire and charged on, bellowing. Brother Dextus' plasma gun lanced out and blew the bolter and the hand that held it clean off, searing the armour black and burning off half the ork's rabid face. And still it came on.

It slammed full tilt into the two Ultramarines and the power fist it wielded came down on Brother Gamelan's helm. There was a thunderous crack, and the Ultramarine fell limp as his skull was crushed in, helmet and all. The heavy bolter fell into the water and disappeared. Brother Dextus was hurled backwards into the rest of the squad.

Avila battered past him, mag-locking his own bolter and activating his chainsword all in one split second. He rolled into the filthy water below the ork and stabbed upwards. The chainsword shrieked as it hit ceramite, and Sergeant Avila thrust it with all the strength and fury that was in him. The weapon caught a purchase on the plate, ate into it, and found its way through.

But then the beast's power fist came down again. It grabbed Avila's arm and hauled him up out of the water like a landed fish. The Space Marine felt the deadly crushing vice of its grip break his own armoured forearm, the claws of the ork gauntlet searing through the ceramite and fibre-bundles and eating into his flesh.

The chainsword fell from his nerveless grip. There was a wrench, and his arm was torn off completely at the elbow joint of the armour. Agony flooded his mind, but he blocked it off, reached into his belt with his remaining hand and clicked out another grenade. He stuffed it into a crevice in the ork's armour and rolled free in the thrashing water. It went off, a bright blast that shut down his auto-senses entirely. For several seconds he was deaf and blind, the only sensation in the world that of pain.

His armour came back online in twitches and flashes. He felt himself being hauled away, tried to struggle, but could not break free. He felt shrapnel wounds gnawing all over him, and he could taste the foul air in the tunnel, the stink of the gutted ork. When his suit systems finally rebooted he found he was at the rear of his squad, lying with his back propped up against the wall of the sewer. Parsifal had pulled him free of the fight and then rejoined it.

His helm display was an intermittent wall of static, runes flashing red all over it. His power-pack had been blasted from his back by the grenade, and the armour that encased him was running down, its internal supply also damaged. In a few minutes he would be closed inside a dead metal shell.

His head cleared somewhat, and he climbed to his feet, swaying.

Heavy fire ahead, his brethren closely engaged. The big ork was a broken mound of flayed meat and metal in the water at their feet. The tunnel beyond was full of the creatures, far too many. He cursed them with all the venom in his hearts, and keyed up the vox.

'Lieutenant Einar, status.'

'All charges set, sir – we're retreating up the tunnel.'

'Very well.' He flicked to the Ultramarine frequency. 'Brothers, fall back, best speed. Get yourselves out of here.'

They gave ground at once. He saw Brother Parsifal, his blue and white armour streaked red with ork viscera. 'Let us get you out of here, Avila,' the Apothecary said, taking his remaining arm.

'No time. My armour is dying. I'm too slow. Get the rest away – now, Parsifal. My brother, you must get out. I will fire the charges.'

'Fire them all you like, but you're coming with me,' Parsifal said grimly. And he hauled Avila half over his shoulder and dragged him away.

The remaining Ultramarines followed. Brother Dextus fired four more blasts from the plasma gun at the advancing orks to cover the retreat, then darted back as his brethren took up the fire. The orks staggered and were halted for a few seconds. The Space Marines used that brief respite to sprint away, down the tunnel in a welter of spray. They passed by the first of the explosive charges Einar had set on the tunnel wall.

Avila began to recover, his training and brute strength overcoming the agony of his injuries. He shrugged free of Parsifal. He could function, for a while at least.

'Lead them out, brother. Frequency sextus. Blow the charges when you are all clear.' He drew out his bolt pistol.

'I will not leave you – this is no place for you to end, Avila.'

'We end where we must – there is no choice in the matter. In a few minutes my armour will be out of power. I will stand here and hold them until you are all clear. Blow the charges before any of this scum gets up the tunnel into the city – they will be dismantling them as they find them. I must halt them in their tracks here, before the whole mission is compromised.'

Parsifal looked at him, a blank mask. They had known each other a long time.

'Our Master shall know what you did,' the Apothecary said. 'Farewell, brother sergeant.'

Avila did not speak again. He stood hefting his bolt pistol, then began wading down the tunnel towards the packed mass of the advancing orks.

# NINETEEN

THE EXPLOSION CAME through to the city, a dull distant boom, no more, just one more noise in a universe that was full of it. But Calgar knew. Even with the interference that was skewing all augur relays, he knew that Avila was gone.

Parsifal came up on the vox soon after.

'My lord, our mission is accomplished. We are making our way back up the sewer tunnel, and should be in the city in less than an hour.'

'Sergeant Avila?' Calgar asked.

'Gone. And Brother Gamelan also. I failed to retrieve their gene-seed. There were too many of the enemy.' Parsifal's voice was dull and toneless.

'We all bleed when one of us does, my brother,' Marneus Calgar said. 'You do not need to tell me how he died – I know that he would have ended well. It was in him.'

'It was.' Then Parsifal clicked off the vox.

Marneus Calgar closed his eyes for one moment. To take the rage and the grief and use it, like some kind of moral fuel. The conditioning of centuries let him do that. It did not lessen his grief – he had seen so many of his brothers die they were beyond count even to his superlative recall – but it let him move past it.

'He did his duty by us and by the Emperor. No one could have asked for more,' Mathias said at his side. The Chaplain had heard the vox exchange. 'Now we must make his sacrifice meaningful of something.'

'In His name,' Calgar said quietly. He came back to the present, the dust-thick heavy air of the bunker, and the battle below, which was approaching a climax.

The lascannons in the casements were flashing out bright streaks of energy that arced across the plain at the advancing tanks. Their barrels were glowing dull red and their muzzles were black with carbonised dust.

As he watched, Calgar saw one of the Leman Russes struck some four hundred yards from the gate below his feet. Smashed full on the turret by the high-energy weapon, the vehicle clanked to a halt, stood silent for a second, and then its hatches were thrown open and the ork crew began to scramble out of the smoking interior.

Lasgun fire from the walls cut them down, dozens of the red beams zeroing in on each ork. As the last fell, the abandoned tank brewed up, a muffled explosion lifting it clear of the ground. Then it exploded again, and the heavy turret was sent flying two hundred yards across the battlefield, flattening a whole rank of advancing ork infantry.

But other tanks were grinding up behind it, their tracks throwing up fountains of muck from the soft ground, the heavy vehicles lurching in shellholes, churning their own dead into the mire. They had come together here, a compact formation of some eight or nine aimed right at the tall gate that stood in the Vanaheim fortress.

'How is lascannon ammunition holding out?' Calgar asked Colonel Boros, who stood, a dust-pale ghost, to one side. The colonel tapped on his slate, receiving direct feed from every emplacement on the walls. He looked up with a grimace. 'We're down to a dozen shots a gun.'

'Beta Primaris,' Calgar said into the defence vox. 'I want earthshakers on grid zero right now. One round from each tube, then wait for repeat orders. Confirm.'

'Acknowledged,' came back the crisp reply from the Basilisk battery back in the city. 'My lord, one of our guns is destroyed – an ork aircraft. We have three currently ready to fire, and six earthshakers left for each.'

'I hear you. Fire when ready.' He raised his voice to resound through the bunker. 'Lascannon crews, hold your fire. We have ordnance inbound from our own batteries. All other weapons, take up the slack. Target their infantry.'

It was like sparring against a heavyweight foe. Flat-out punching would not be enough. He had to come in from different directions, keep the foe off balance.

Calgar pulled in extra mortar tubes from farther north in the city, sending Lieutenant Janus' Chimeras to fetch them south. The bombardment was unrelenting. The plain before the Vanaheim Gate stretched like some maniac's view of hell for fully four miles. Burnt-out vehicles, broken Dreadnoughts and shot-down aircraft were strewn across it like the broken toys of a mad child, and in between them the ork dead lay in mounds, in unmourned and stinking thousands

And through it all, the artillery of both sides continued to plough the blood-soaked ground into a morass, transforming it into another element entirely, a soup of filth and flesh and metal through which the orks waded with insane persistence, their losses only goading them to a higher pitch of bestial fury.

But the city had suffered too. Ork artillery had overshot the walls and hit the central districts of Zalathras, laying waste to whole city blocks. The immense ork shells had rained down on the spires, too. Alphon was burning from half a dozen severe hits, as was Kalgatt.

The civilian casualties were already in the tens of thousands, and would climb higher. In one shelter off Dromion Square alone, two thousand people had been entombed when it had received a direct strike from something resembling an earthshaker.

Grievous though these casualties were, they did not affect the fighting strength of the defences, and Calgar found himself once more thanking the Emperor's Grace that the ork guns were poorly pointed, their munitions badly made and unreliable. For every shell that exploded, another crashed to earth within the circuit of the walls and lay at the bottom of its own crater, inert or ticking ominously.

The militiamen defending the walls were standing at their posts, agri-hands and Administratum clerks and outright criminals, all holding a few yards of wall each. But a steady stream of these men were dying also. In the last three hours, Boros reckoned they had lost four thousand men, and already Calgar had redeployed an entire division from the northern perimeter.

Attacks were going in there too, but not on the same scale as here. They were probes, no more. This – this apocalypse in front of the gate – this was where the ork warlord was throwing the bulk of his armies, and it was here that the breakthrough would be made or foiled, and the fate of Zalathras decided.

'He must have lost fifty thousand,' Colonel Boros was saying in a shocked croak. 'How can even orks take such ruinous casualties and keep coming?'

'He has five times that behind them,' Brother Mathias said calmly. 'Orks do not lose heart at the sight of their own dead. In some ways it stirs them to greater efforts. The xenos are inspired by violence and war – it brings forth a latent strength in them, a berserker rage. The enemy warlord is utilising this. He counts on it.'

'Then when will he stop?' Boros asked.

'When we are all dead,' the Chaplain said simply.

The earthshakers were falling, so close to the walls that the spattered earth of their concussion plastered the stone of the defences. Ork body parts and corpses were hurled clear over the battlements, and upon them the militia cowered from their own artillery, and the shrapnel smashed scars and gouges out of the walls that protected them.

Two of the Leman Russes disintegrated in that great convulsion, but there were still six of them powering onwards, several trailing fire and smoke, one with its turret blown off and the ork crew visible in the hull. In their wake staggered a column of Dreadnoughts, stiff-limbed giants lurching through the muck. And behind that were mobs of heavily armed ork infantry, the elite of their kind.

The Russes fired, one after the other. Calgar felt the strike in the very stone under his feet.

'The gate is taking a pasting,' Boros said.

They had piled up masonry and girders against the gate, but they had not sealed it like they had the other entrances to the city. It was still a way in, and the orks knew it. The defenders had made a deliberate decision not to seal the Vanaheim completely, in order to draw the enemy to the strongest bastion on the walls.

They had succeeded too well, perhaps. The adamantium-faced gate below them was as strong as any Calgar had seen in Ultramar – Kurt Vanaheim had spared no expense, especially since the Administratum was footing the bill for its construction. But no gate could take that kind of hammering for long.

'Lascannons, resume fire,' Calgar instructed.

He longed to come to grips with the enemy, to unleash the rage that simmered in him, to grapple with the orks on the ground, hand to hand, and feel their lives give out under his fingers. But they had to be kept back, here. If they closed in on the Vanaheim, a breach would follow, as inevitably as night followed day. It could not be allowed. Calgar had only one card left to play.

'Governor Fennick, do you read?'

'Fennick here – yes, my lord.'

'I need the Furies, right now. Armour is almost at the gate. It must be destroyed, at all costs. Do you understand, Fennick?'

'Yes, my lord.' There was the sound of burning over the vox. Forward Command itself must have been hit. 'I shall see to it.'

THE FURIES SWEPT in low over the city, released from their secret hangars. Six of them had survived the initial fleet action and the bombardments since. Their pilots knew what they were up against and flew them like fearless veterans. Calgar heard the screech of their approach as they swooped down on the ork vanguard like vengeful angels.

They came down from the near-vertical, released their bomb loads, and then soared up again in tight curves that blazed against the dying light in the sky. Two were shot down as they came in, and they crashed full tilt into the ranks of the orks below. Calgar saw an ork Dreadnought flung half a mile through the air by the blast.

The rest did their job. The Leman Russes before the Vanaheim Gate were engulfed in a series of massive explosions that rippled around them and sent concentric shockwaves through the rain, radiating out to bounce in hollow booms off the walls.

None of them made it back to their hidden hangars. All were shot down in a flailing cloud of ork fire that spanned the southern horizon. Their pilots had known it was a suicide run and had taken off without hesitation.

There is hope for us yet, when these tyros can show such courage, Calgar thought.

Multi-meltas were blurting out brightly now from the casements, and one or two missile launchers. The ork armour was finished off there before the gate, blown to blackened wreckage. The Dreadnoughts staggered to a halt in the thick mud amid the blazing wrecks of the Russes and were picked off one by one. Calgar felt the balance of the thing shift. He looked up at the sky. There was a roseate glow in the west; the long day was ending at last.

The orks were retreating, like a tidal sea which has reached the fulcrum of its farthest point and now must ebb. Mortar fire followed them across the plain, taking a huge toll on the withdrawing troops. They pulled back sullenly, some turning to roar hatred and defiance at the walls of Zalathras as they went.

For three to four miles in a great arc along the southern perimeter of the city, the ork hosts marched in untidy mobs back to their camps north of the Dromion River. Calgar called a halt to the mortar fire; they had to conserve ammunition. The orks did not seem like an army that had been beaten, but more like one that had tried one tactic and found it wanting. They were not going anywhere.

'They'll be back,' Mathias said, echoing Calgar's own conclusion. In the bunker, the militia were cheering and embracing one another and Colonel Boros had a grin that stretched from ear to ear.

'I must take a look at the gate itself, Mathias,' Calgar said. 'Take over here. I want ammunition brought forward to the walls, and rations for the men. They may rest half a squad at a time.'

'Night is coming,' the Chaplain told him. As he looked out of the firing slot the red light of it gleamed in the lenses of his skull-helm. 'The militia should be allowed as much rest as they can get. You know how these kind are. They fight one battle, and believe they have won a war.'

'They did none so ill, brother,' Calgar said.

'For amateurs,' Mathias retorted.

CALGAR MET FENNICK at the rear of Vanaheim's great gate. The governor's usually dapper uniform was dusty and torn. He looked as grimed and tired as a common trooper.

It was dark by then, and a crowd of militiamen were busy within the shadow of the immense Vanaheim barbican. The bright flare of welding torches was glaring here and there, and flatloaders piled high with stone and plasteel girders were parked in a line down the street. The place was a hive of activity.

Calgar unhelmed and nodded at Fennick with a glint of approval. The man did not believe in wasting time.

'How bad?' he asked the governor, his gaze ranging over the piled mound of rubble behind the gates.

'They aimed for the hinges, my lord, and for once, they hit what they were aiming at. The entire surround of the gates has been badly weakened, and the adamantium itself has been holed and split in half a dozen places.

'There is little we can do for the moment except prop them up and fill in the space behind. Even if we poured liquid rockcrete in now, it would not be hardened for three or four days.'

'And we do not have that kind of time,' Calgar said thoughtfully.

'It was my decision to leave the Vanaheim Gate in working order,' Fennick said. He sounded like a man drained of all emotion, his fine-boned face as planed and hollow as a skull. 'The fault is on my shoulders.'

'It was a good decision,' Marneus Calgar said. 'You have drawn them to the strongest part of the defences, and they have been battering at it for five weeks – and taken immense casualties. I might have done the same thing myself.'

Fennick bowed. His thin mouth worked with emotion under his beard, but he said nothing.

'They know what they have done here today,' Calgar went on. 'They know the state of these gates – you may count on it. It will not be long before they attack again, and it will be here. The gate has become a totem for them, an end in itself. I have seen it happen to all kinds of armies, human and xenos alike. When enough blood has been spilled in one spot, the place assumes a significance beyond the strategic. It becomes somehow sacred. They will keep attacking the Vanaheim until they possess it. That is for us both a problem and an opportunity.'

'We cannot last much longer,' Fennick said tiredly at last.

'We must. The orks will not tire, it is not in their nature. They will not stop now until Zalathras falls or they are destroyed. It has become a very simple matter.'

And he felt it himself even as he spoke the words – the simplicity of it. In its way, it was a kind of relief. All his long life he had overseen the movement of armies, the deployment of divisions, brigades, regiments, and the hallowed companies of his own brethren. He had overseen a great realm of far-flung planets with men in their millions willing to do his bidding.

And it had come down to this. This one place, this broken gate, and the half-trained and untrained men who manned the walls around it.

The weariness he had borne within him for so long seemed to lift. There was very little left to think about. Just the brutal logic of the orks. They would attack, and he would defend. There were no longer the resources or opportunities for anything else.

'I want to talk to you and all the senior officers of your command tonight,' he told Fennick. 'In the palace. The orks will not attack again for a while. Even they must regroup and reorganise after a day like today. We will have a brief respite. We must use it.'

He looked up at the looming shadow of the Vanaheim Gate. For him, too, it had assumed a significance beyond the strategic. He had a sudden presentiment that he would die here – he, Marneus Calgar, Lord Macragge, Chapter Master of the Ultramarines. Here, on this far-flung border world of little significance.

Thy will be done, he thought.

Just before midnight, the *Mayfly* came in at last, the little freighter a smoking half-wrecked hulk that settled with something close to a crash on one of the wide streets leading off Dromios Square. Calgar was there within minutes of the landing, in time to see the heavy loader and its precious cargo towed out of the smoke-filled hold of the ship.

He was also there to see Proxis' prone form wheeled down the ramp.

'Parsifal, see to him,' he said tersely, and the Apothecary at once bent over the Ancient's body, and then had him spirited away to the apothecarion in Alphon Spire.

'He lives, my lord,' Parsifal said as he left. The helix on the Apothecary's shoulder-guard was almost invisible, scraped and dented and covered with clotted ork gore.

'See that he does.'

Morcault, Lascelle and Brother Valerian stood at the foot of the ramp, a mismatched trio that nonetheless had the air of having come through something together.

'How much did we get?' Calgar asked his Librarian.

'Some four tons, my lord.'

'Less than we had hoped.'

'The orks were there in some strength. My lord, I must speak to you privately.'

'Other casualties, besides Proxis?'

Valerian grimaced. 'Brothers Comus and Gauros.'

Calgar said nothing. They were being whittled down. Of the twenty-four Space Marines, himself included, who had crashed in the *Alexiad* and the *Rubicon*, eleven were still standing. Proxis and Brother Tarsus were gravely injured. The gene-seed of so many had been lost to the Chapter forever, brethren who were some of the best the Chapter had produced. It weighed on him, but his shoulders had carried this burden and others like it for centuries.

'We were lucky to make it out – Brother Valerian did all he could – as did we all.' It was Morcault. The old man leaned on his black stick and wisps of his white hair blew around the dressing that circled his temples. He stared up at Marneus Calgar and was no longer intimidated by the Chapter Master's imposing bulk. He spoke to him as one man to another. How things changed.

Calgar looked at the smoking hulk behind them that was the *Mayfly*. 'You did well to navigate through such perilous skies,' he said quietly. He nodded at Valerian. 'Brother, you and I shall speak presently. The material you brought out of the quarries is invaluable. It shall be sent to the foundries at once. Morcault, you have my thanks. Will she fly again?'

The old man gave a sad smile. 'Perhaps. But I doubt I shall be alive to see it.'

The lives of men were so short. This aged man was a mere child compared to the span of years Calgar had seen. He was younger even than Valerian, but his time was almost done. And yet he had risen through that frailty and given good service when it was most needed. He had volunteered himself for it.

Men's short lives were such a waste. By the time they learned something of life, they were ready to lay it down.

Calgar looked up at the battered ship, weighing other options. Then he stared at Morcault again. There was no fear in the man. He was too aware of his own approaching end. A fearless man was a valuable thing, an asset not to be cast aside.

'Come with me,' Calgar said. 'All of you.'

In the middle hours of the night they assembled in the map room of the palace, high atop Alphon Spire. From there, they could look out and see the districts of the city that were still burning, far below. They glowed through the clouds, and even the rain did little to deaden that light.

Calgar turned from the high balcony to stare at those assembled. Fennick, Boros, Glenck, Lascelle and the half-dozen divisional commanders who were still alive stood in a group. To one side sat old

Morcault, stooped over his stick. Then there were his own people. Mathias, Valerian, Orhan, and Brother Antigonus, who had taken over leadership of the squad survivors – six of them left now. Parsifal was still working on Proxis in the apothecarion.

Also present were Kurt Vanaheim, the industrialist whose manufactoria were fuelling the war effort, and Ferdia Rosquin, the banker whose compound was now the forward command post. He looked even more old and withered than Morcault, but he was a senior member of the planetary council.

Calgar felt he should inspire them with a speech, trot out some heady rhetoric about the repulse of the ork assault today. But such words came too easily. The silence spoke more eloquently of their position than anything Calgar could say, and he knew it. The city had survived the day, but its fate still hung by a thread.

'Vanaheim,' Calgar said at last, 'how goes it with munitions?'

The burly, dark-haired man consulted a slate. 'With the palladium brought in from the Ballansyr Quarries, we can go back up to full production. We are running the works day and night, and turning out some twelve thousand heavy shells and fifty thousand rounds of bolter ammunition a day.'

'How long before we exhaust the raw materials?'

Vanaheim did not look up. 'Four days, give or take.'

'What is the state of the reserves?' Calgar asked Fennick.

The governor needed no slate to consult. He faced Calgar squarely. 'We have some hundred and fifty thousand rounds of bolter ammunition left, and about a fifth of our original artillery shells.' He paused. 'We burned through a lot today – over half our remaining reserves.'

'What about other heavy weapons?'

Fennick seemed to slump, though he remained standing. 'There are fewer than a hundred charge packs for the lascannons still remaining in the city. The mortars are down to thirty bombs per tube. Promethium is almost exhausted.'

Calgar nodded. 'Colonel Boros – today's casualty list.'

Boros rubbed the stubble on his face. 'Almost four thousand dead or badly wounded. Civilian casualty figures are still coming in, but they are many times that.'

'Have we controlled the fires?'

'Those in the spires have been put out, but we are merely containing some in the southern districts. We do not have the capability to extinguish them. They will have to burn themselves out.'

They were tired. They felt themselves beaten. Calgar could almost smell the defeat off them, and it disgusted him. It was not in his nature or that of his brethren to give in to despair. The Adeptus Astartes died fighting to the end, and in their end they found the reason for their creation.

Battles were fought, wars went by, but the Imperium endured, and the Emperor sat upon His throne in far off Terra, a deathless husk.

It had been thus for millennia. It would remain so, no matter what happened on one far-off planet. Ordinary men did not often feel themselves connected to that larger picture, that greater universe.

And yet ordinary men, too, could die fighting, and die well. It was one of the traits of humanity that had sent them spanning the galaxy. These men before him – most of them, at any rate – they had faced down death at Zalathras, some of them many times. And they stood here now wanting only leadership, direction. Some kind of hope, no matter how slim.

And Calgar would give it to them. He looked at Brother Valerian, and he and the Librarian nodded at one another.

'We have done well here,' the Lord of Macragge said. 'I have seldom seen men fight better. We are near the end of our strength, but that does not mean we cannot prevail here on Zalidar. Weapons and ammunition are only part of what makes an army capable of resistance. The will of men – the determination not to give in – that is what leads to eventual victory.

'You fight here for your city, your world, your families and all that you hold dear. If the orks make it over the walls or through the gate, then all that is gone. Those who die quickly will be the lucky ones. The non-combatants will be mere foodstuff and slaves for the xenos. The planet will be razed to the ground.

'There is no negotiation, no reasoning with such foes. They understand only violence, and they will not give in until they are decimated or destroyed. But do not think that we fight them alone, here in Zalathras.'

Calgar had them rapt now. He looked them all over, gauging, weighing up their frailties and strengths, the resolve in their eyes.

'For we are not alone. We belong to the Imperium of Man, which is the lone light in a sea of darkness. It has burned for tens of thousands of years, and will burn for ten thousand more. We are part of that, brothers in arms, defenders on the wall. All of us, whether we are Adeptus Astartes or militia, soldiers or civilians.

'We are men, and we stand together in that darkness. We will never give in, for it is not in our nature to admit that final defeat.'

He stopped. He had not meant to give a speech. He had heard too many like it, voiced by friends and brothers who were all dead now. But there were some things that had to be said, which never lost their truth.

'And we are not forgotten here. The word has gone out. Even as I speak, my brothers are coming to our aid. The Seventh Company of the Ultramarines and their battlefleet is in the warp even now. I do not know when they will be here, but they are coming.

'Tell your men that as they stand upon the wall tonight. The Adeptus Astartes are on their way. We have only to hold on here a little longer, and there will be deliverance. I give you my word.'

He saw the flush of relief in their faces. Some of them grinned. Others looked as though they might weep.

His own brethren were stony-faced. That was as it should be.

Triumph and disaster – they had learned to take both in their stride. They would fight on no matter what the cost, no matter what the odds. It was what they had been born to do.

He had given his word. Marneus Calgar had never yet broken it. The thing was said.

And I will keep it, he thought. I will keep it or die trying.

# TWENTY

The orks milled about in their camps for five full days after the failed assault of their heavy armour. Their artillery continued to batter the city, and they finally seemed to be trying to zero in on the Vanaheim Gate itself. Their aim was still far from true, but at least one in every ten of the rounds falling came close to or hit their mark. The massive thirty-storey fortress had strong plascrete armour, but shell after shell chipped away at it, and the region around the Vanaheim itself became a blasted wasteland of shattered ruins and deep-delved shellholes as it was hit again and again.

Work on reinforcing the damaged gate went on regardless, and the militia engineers who struggled in the shadow of the barbican took heavy casualties at their labours, whilst the streets leading up to the fortress were littered with burnt-out and blasted vehicles that tried to run the gauntlet and bring building materials up to them.

But the fact remained; the gate was weakened. Fennick had left it unblocked because it would draw the enemy to the strongest defensive point on the circuit of the walls, but now that strategy had been turned on its head. What had been the strongest was now the weakest.

Everywhere else, the walls still stood, one hundred feet high and as many thick. They had taken damage in countless places, but were essentially intact. The men who manned them had been thinned out, however; the entire perimeter, all those rolling miles of battlements, was manned now by fewer than forty thousand exhausted troops, many of whom had undergone nothing more than cursory military training.

Thousands more were deployed in the city itself, to keep order, suppress the gangs in the undercity, fight fires and man the logistics convoys that rattled through the streets day and night. And in the manufactoria which had survived this far, a quarter of a million workers toiled round the clock to keep turning out munitions of all calibres, the blood that kept the beating heart of the city's defences alive.

Thus did Zalathras enter its sixth week of siege.

CALGAR DIVIDED HIS time between the walls and the forward command post, with occasional forays up to the palace to look in on Proxis and Brother Tarsus in the apothecarion. Both Ultramarines had had their power armour removed, and the junction points on their torsos that linked into their suits now had myriad tubes attached, which led to life support machines, some purely human, of necessity, other customised by Brother Parsifal with Brother Orhan's help.

Brother Tarsus was a fearsome sight, his features melted beyond recognition by the promethium that had engulfed him. But under the skin he was largely whole, and almost ready to return to duty.

For three days after the *Mayfly*'s landing, Proxis had remained in the coma in which his own enhanced physiology had placed him. On the fourth, Brother Parsifal brought him out of it. By that time the Ancient's own recuperative biology, along with Parsifal's surgery, had repaired the gaping hole in his chest and the catastrophic damage to one of his two hearts.

Calgar was there when he opened his eyes, along with the Apothecary. Proxis stared at the ceiling for a long moment, blinking slowly at the overheads and swallowing. Then he turned to his Chapter Master and recognition filled his gaze.

'I had the strangest dream,' he said, in a voice quite unlike himself. And then he blinked again, and his hand reached out to grasp Calgar's.

'My lord. I rejoice to see you.'

'And I you, brother.'

He looked past Calgar, saw Parsifal standing there in his blue and white armour, and raised an eyebrow. 'I take it this one has been plying his grisly trade.'

'He has indeed. He saved your life, Proxis.'

Proxis smiled slightly at the Apothecary. 'Well, it is not for the first time. And I doubt it will be the last.'

'I grow tired of patching you up, Proxis,' Parsifal said, coming forward. 'One of these days I will run out of patience and you will be clean out of luck.'

'Luck deserts us all, in the end,' Proxis told him. He looked at Calgar. 'That is why we are born with brothers who never do.' His forehead creased with pain.

'My lord, the mission–'

Calgar tapped the Ancient on the chest. 'It was a success, though barely.'

'Who did we lose? I can see it in your eyes.'

'Brother Comus, and Brother Gauros.'

Proxis' face gnarled with anger. 'I failed them, getting myself shot like that – as foolish as a neophyte.'

'You saved Brother Valerian, from what he tells me. And that may have proved the most vital aspect of your mission. He got through, brother – he contacted Seventh. Ixion is on his way with the *Andronicus* fleet.'

Proxis closed his eyes again. He gripped Calgar's gauntlet. 'Throne be praised.'

Calgar straightened. 'Another ork assault is coming. I want you on your feet for it, brother. We need you on the walls.'

Proxis made as if to get up, but Calgar pushed him gently back down again.

'They are not at the gates just yet, Proxis. Take this time we have. Become strong again. Brother Orhan has effected repairs to your armour. It is ugly, but functional.'

'Much like himself,' Parsifal said.

'I will be with you, lord,' Proxis said. 'It is my place, after all.'

'It is. Where would I be without you to watch my back, my friend? Now I will leave you. Obey Brother Parsifal in everything as you would me.'

'My axe–'

'It waits for you, as I do. Take this time to heal, Proxis. There will be more work to be done soon enough.'

Brother Orhan joined him as they left the apothecarion. 'He is as hard to break as the armour he wore.'

'And how is that armour, Orhan – in fact, how do you rate all our wargear? You are the closest I have to a Techmarine on this world.'

They took one of the great conveyors down into the heart of the spire. Orhan seemed to be running a checklist in his head.

'Everyone has sustained minor damage of some sort. It has all been easily patched up, though it is not perfect – I cannot restore our equipment to perfect functionality without our own tech-priests and a good, trained Techmarine, which I am not, my lord, despite your generous appraisal of my abilities.'

'You trained on Mars.'

'Not for long enough. And besides that, some of us wear and fight with gear that was created by technologies now lost to us. I think of your own power suit, and my own, and that of Proxis. Such ancient equipment is still robust enough to take minor repair, but the systems within the bare plate – if they are damaged, there is little I or anyone can do to bring them back online. Ideally, they should be sent back to Mars itself for full-scale evaluation and restoration. They are artefacts from a lost time.' He touched the aquila on his own breastplate.

'They are all we have on Zalidar. They will have to serve, as we do ourselves,' Calgar said. 'Work with what you have, Orhan. This lull in the assaults will not last much longer.'

'Of course, my lord. Where to now?'

'To Morcault, and his ship. I must speak with the old voidsman. I have…' Calgar let it trail a moment. 'I have a favour to ask.'

The honour guard Ultramarine had something else to say – Calgar could sense it. As the conveyor continued on its interminable descent, Calgar said, 'What's on your mind, brother?'

Brother Orhan was a conscientious soul, utterly lacking in any kind of flamboyance. Calgar sometimes thought that something of the Mars tech-priests' clinical attitudes had rubbed off on him. He was a formidable strategist, and a master of detail, but he seemed sometimes a little outside the brotherhood. Someone who could stand outside the Chapter and look in. It was for these reasons that Calgar kept him in the honour guard. Orhan never failed to bring a sense of objectivity to any proceeding.

'I was thinking on Seventh Company, my lord.'

'Yes?'

'They have taken to the warp to get here, and I know that their Navigator, Fell Grimstone, is more than capable. But the warp is fickle, above all at times like these, when there is a great bloodletting to disturb the currents of the immaterium. It seems to me that

Captain Ixion could be here within a few days, or he might take much longer to arrive.'

'That much is merely obvious.'

'My lord, if he is long delayed, then he will almost certainly arrive above Zalidar to find the planet overrun – we will all be dead and the orks will be in complete control of this world. Is that not so?'

'Yes.' Sometimes Orhan's relentless logic took a long route to arrive at the conclusion, and he liked to build it up in unassailable blocks. It was an irritating but valuable asset. Calgar knew where it was headed.

'Our policy, when a planet is irredeemably lost to the xenos, has been to issue an Exterminatus. It has been thus since the Behemoth campaign, has it not?'

'It has.'

'And in your absence, Captain Ixion will, I suppose, adhere to Chapter policy.'

'He will, Orhan.'

'You did not mention this to any of the planetary authorities.'

'Would there be a point? If it comes to that, they will all be dead anyway.'

'You sought to spare them this knowledge – that their world might end up as dead as Thrax did, thirty years ago.'

'I sought to keep their backbones straight. Ultramarine strategy is to defend until the last, and to destroy that which is lost rather than leave it in the hands of the enemy. Is that all, Brother Orhan?'

'Yes, my lord. I am not questioning you. I just like to have these things clear in my mind. Forgive me if I spoke out of turn.'

'There is nothing to forgive, brother.'

They rode the elevator the rest of the way down in silence.

The message came through towards the end of the next night, at that time when the body is at its lowest ebb, the dark hour before the dawn.

Valerian sent it, in a burst of Ultramarine battle-code. And with it, everything had changed, and nothing had.

When it arrived, Marneus Calgar was in a small half-ruined Imperial shrine a few blocks from the forward command post, on his knees, with the rain spattering down cold upon his bare head.

He knelt there and prayed to his primarch, great Guilliman, for insight and guidance. He prayed to his Emperor in far-off Terra, half a galaxy away. And he prayed to the dead brethren whose faces he still saw in his sleep, a long parade of them stretching back over the years.

He prayed that he might be worthy of their sacrifices, their loyalty, and the honour they had brought to the Chapter.

The little chapel had been beautiful once, and now that it was half a ruin, it might be more beautiful still. Even as Calgar knelt there, the endless rain finally let up, and a cool wind blew through the darkened streets of the city. And there were stars overhead, the first he had seen in a long while.

There was still traffic to be heard on distant roads, and a kind of hum that spoke of human concourse. There were millions contained within the walls of Zalathras, and even in the straits of a war as desperate as this, they went about some shadow of their usual business, striving for scraps of normality in the face of so much horror.

Far off, he heard the scattered crump of ork artillery. It was as much a part of life here as that human hum, that ticking-over of humdrum activity. War never could be forgotten, not here, not anywhere else. It was the state of all existence. The universe turned around it.

On that implacable wheel whole worlds were broken. Calgar knew this – he had seen it many times. But he retained enough of his humanity to feel grief for the loss and waste. That grief would never stop him from doing his duty, but it left its mark on him, as he suspected it had upon his mighty primarch, and upon the Emperor Himself when that puissant super-being had walked the galaxy as one man amongst men.

Humanity had to be protected, guarded and led. Sometimes that path led to the annihilation of innocent billions and the extinction of whole worlds. That was the nature of the universe they inhabited.

'By Your will,' Calgar whispered, a lone supplicant under the stars, kneeling in prayer as his ancestors had done before him in millennia beyond count.

He was not surprised by the flickering message-rune that lit up in the field of his bionic eye, though it might signal his deliverance, and that of the city itself and the world around him. Nor did he raise his head when almost at the same time the klaxons began to sound from vox-casters all over the city, a thumping urgency that signalled imminent ground assault.

He had seen it coming. He had known, somehow, that it would be today, on this morning. Great events had their own gravity. They drew together in lines of fate entangled.

Lord, in Thy glory and Thy goodness, Thou hast sent me Thine enemies to kill. Let me be worthy of Thee, bright father. Today, let me be Thy instrument.

Then he rose to his feet, flexing his fists in the Gauntlets of Ultramar. Orhan and Proxis were waiting for him, and beyond stood Mathias, Valerian, and all the surviving brethren he had brought down to Zalidar. They were thirteen Adeptus Astartes in all, brothers in name and in blood, living embodiments of faith and courage and honour.

'Brothers,' Calgar said, smiling, 'Let us go to the gate.'

# III
# THE GATEKEEPER OF ZALATHRAS

# TWENTY-ONE

THE SUN ROSE, and for once there was clear sky above the wrack of cloud that hid the horizon, a delicate green that deepened into blue as Zalidar's terminator moved steadily across the planet.

The ork bombardment had stopped, and the world seemed an eerily quiet place as the dawn came reaching towards them. A hush spread out over the blasted mire that extended to the south of the city for so many miles.

Not even the carrion eaters of Zalidar picked at the corpses out there. The wasteland was complete, churned clean of all indigenous vegetation, the roads which had run across it obliterated, the landmarks gone, replaced by wrecked vehicles and the strewn heaps of the ork dead, incubating their replacements in garish fields of green fungi.

The encampments of the orks were a scab that stretched across the land to the south, and there was movement out there, massed formations of the xenos moving out and beginning the long march up to the walls. They were in numbers such as the defenders had not seen before.

Marneus Calgar stood on the shell-shattered summit of the Vanaheim Gate with his brethren deployed around him. Beside him stood Governor Fennick, Colonel Boros, Rear Admiral Glenck and Lieutenant Roman Lascelle.

'I wonder if they know,' Fennick said.

'I doubt it,' Glenck snorted, his jowls quivering. He had lost weight everywhere but his face these last few weeks, and was shrunken, an admiral without a fleet. Or nearly so.

'It seems almost too good to be true, after all that has happened,' Colonel Boros said, shaking his head.

'Brother Valerian has confirmed the message the *Hesiod* got through,' Calgar told him. 'He has established communications with Seventh Company's Librarian, Brother Carimus.

'The *Andronicus* battlefleet re-entered normal space last night on the outskirts of the system. It will reach orbit around Zalidar in two planetary days. My brethren were skilled – and fortunate – in their navigation of the warp.'

'The orks must know,' Roman Lascelle said, wondering. 'They're coming out to fight, to try and get the thing done before your people arrive, my lord.'

'That is the orks for you. Nothing if not stubborn,' Calgar said. But his tone belied the lightness of his words. 'A lot can happen in two days, gentlemen. They know that as well as we do.'

'There is something different in the air,' Fennick said. 'Can you feel it? Like the heaviness before the break of a storm. It sings in my head like a song I cannot get rid of.'

They watched as the orks massed across the plain in their tens of thousands, summoned by wardrums whose bass thump carried across the intervening miles in the morning quiet, a steady, ominous beat.

'We have the resources for one more all-out fight,' Colonel Boros said. 'After that, we're done. We'll be fighting with lasguns and knives.'

'We will fight with those, if it comes to that,' Calgar told him grimly.

He scanned the towering walls that stretched out east and west from the Vanaheim Gate. The battlements were full of militia. He had brought south as many as he dared, denuding other sections of the perimeter. The orks had remained fixated on the Vanaheim from start to finish. They would not attack anywhere else now; the place had for them become symbolic of victory or defeat.

'I did not know there were so many,' Rear Admiral Glenck said, awed by the sight of the marching thousands.

'Then you should have spent more time on the wall,' Boros said sharply.

'Lord Fennick, have all my instructions been complied with?' Calgar asked, ignoring the exchange.

'Yes, my lord. Every available heavy weapon in the city is now concentrated in this sector, and the ammunition stockpiles are even now being shifted south for quick access. We could not move them earlier, because of the bombardment.'

Calgar nodded. 'Very good. Where is Morcault?'

Fennick seemed surprised. 'As far as I know he and his crew are still trying to repair his ship.'

'He has been given every cooperation in your power?'

'Yes, my lord. I detailed the engineers myself. But I am still not sure why.'

'The *Mayfly* may not yet be finished as an asset.'

Fennick looked at Calgar strangely. 'Does – does Morcault know that?'

'I spoke to him a few hours ago.' Calgar did not elaborate.

'What of our other repair job?' Colonel Boros asked.

'It is done,' Fennick told him. 'The vehicle is operational and is in place. But we have only a single shell for it.'

'One will have to be enough,' Calgar said, his face impassive, giving nothing away.

'My lord, I would feel better if you included me in your planning,'

Fennick said, thrusting his bearded chin out. 'I do not know all that is going on.'

'Just keep the munitions coming, Fennick,' Calgar said. 'Colonel Boros, I want the reserves moved up closer to the southern wall. If the regiments there begin to fold, there will be little time to reinforce.'

'Yes, my lord.'

Calgar studied the advancing orks. His gaze ranged across the broken battlefield, estimating numbers, studying the approach. The wardrums thumped endlessly, like the heartbeat of some vast distant beast buried out of sight.

'Today will be the hardest,' he said to those around him. 'Today, they will come at us with everything they have left.'

'All they have left is infantry,' Admiral Glenck said. 'My lord, their aircraft have been decimated, their armour destroyed, their aerial troops massacred. All they have left are footsloggers.'

'They have more than that,' Calgar said. 'The orks always save the best for last. Brother Valerian?'

'It is not yet here, my lord,' the Librarian said. 'I confess myself puzzled. I do not sense its presence anywhere.'

'What presence?' Fennick asked, irritation overcoming his customary courtesy towards the Ultramarines.

'The orks have brought to the planet a last weapon, one of the greatest in their arsenal,' Calgar said with unwonted patience. 'Brother Valerian discovered it at the Ballansyr Quarries. It is a great beast, the likes of which is seldom seen, the very pinnacle of their barbarous ecology. It will be the centrepiece of their assault. Governor Fennick, I want every anti-aircraft gun you have to be manned and ready. If we are attacked from the air, the enemy craft must not be allowed to range over the city – that is imperative. Do you understand?'

'Yes, my lord, of course... but–'

'I want no surprises in our rear. Let them come at us as they always have. I have detailed Lieutenant Janus' firefighter regiment to be on stand-by. Their command is left to you. There is a good chance I shall be very busy in a little while. Janus has received a warning order to move on your word alone.'

Fennick bowed slightly.

'They're coming closer,' Admiral Glenck said. His glabrous face was white as chalk.

The drums picked up, a sonorous booming that carried from one end of the plain to another. The orks were advancing steadily now on a broad front.

'There must be sixty or seventy thousand of them out there,' Lascelle said, awed by the terrible spectacle.

'Closer to one hundred thousand,' Calgar informed him.

There was silence along the city walls, but out on the plain the ork masses had begun to set up a sound, a repetitive chanting that could not quite be made out. They were still some two and a half miles away, but the noise of their combined voices carried clear to the walls of the city, a dull murmur, punctuated by the relentless drums.

Calgar had read extensively on history, on the Imperium, the Great Heresy, and back before even that, the scraps and remnants of story that pertained to the origins of them all, ancient Terra herself.

There had been a place there, a city before which had stood a flat plain ideal for the massed movement of troops – and so often had armies contended on that soil that the plain had acquired a name. The city had been called Thebes, and the plain had become known as the Dancing Floor of War.

He looked out now at the chanting orks and the tortured earth that trembled under their feet. It seemed fitting here, also.

'All artillery and mortars to hold fire until I give the word,' he said.

'What are they saying?' Glenck demanded, listening to the thunderous voices of the ork host with fear and apprehension warring across his broad pale face.

'Does it matter?' Colonel Boros asked him.

Calgar clicked his battered Corvus helm with its wreath of gold from his thigh. He knew what they were saying, as did Brother Valerian.

'It has come,' the Librarian said in a quiet voice. 'They have finally cohered. I can feel it, my lord.'

'As can I,' Calgar said calmly. He placed his helm upon his head and clicked it shut on the collar of his ancient armour. At once, read-outs and runes sprang up in his vision.

'Gentlemen, brothers; the orks have become a Waaagh!. They have finally buried all divisions of tribe and clan and have united under their warlord. He is out there now, in their lines. Today they will give battle under a single command, and we can expect them to fight with a fury beyond that which we have known hitherto. They will not retreat. They will keep coming until we have broken them apart again, or they have slain all of us.'

The chant drew closer, rose up against the lightening sky. As the sun broke out over the passing clouds, so the word that the orks were chanting became clear to all those on the summit of the Vanaheim. The human officers there looked down in horror. The Ultramarines stood, giants of stern discipline, unmoved.

'Calgaar, Calgaar, Calgaar,' the orks chanted, making a mockery of the name. It carried clear across the city, horrible to hear out of the fanged maws of xenos.

Proxis stepped up, and tapped the haft of his axe on the ground.

'They shall pay, for uttering that.'

'That they shall,' Calgar said. He checked his rangefinder, looked at the sky, as clear and blue as a summer's morning on Macragge. He missed the mountains, the clean snow of his homeworld.

But one did not choose where one fought. There was only the battle ahead to think of. It was all that mattered now.

'They know I am here,' he told the others. 'They know that the Lord of Macragge stands upon these walls. They will come for me, for the name I carry. For what I represent.

'It may be I shall be able to use that against them.'

He keyed the vox. 'All guns, range thirty-three thousand feet, axis one eighty, targets in the open, wide spread. Fire for effect.'

'Now,' he said to those beside him. 'Let the dance begin.'

# TWENTY-TWO

MORCAULT HEARD THE battle open, and raised his head to listen. The air was full of fire, shells arcing up out of the guns and mortars of the city to streak south in high parabolic arcs. The sound of their impact carried north from the Vanaheim, a heavy thunder that sullied the air and tore apart the quiet of the morning. The storm had come at last. The final days were upon them. One way or another, the siege of Zalathras would soon be over.

The streets had cleared of all but military convoys and personnel, and now millions were cowering in bunkers and shelters and the basements of the sturdiest habs. The three hive-spires of the city rose up out of the sea of buildings and rubble, and for the first time in a long while were visible all the way to their sharp summits.

A haze of smoke still hung about the city and could be tasted in the mouth, but the sun was shining through it in wands and bars and lines of bright, bitter beauty. He was glad he had seen it again, glad to turn his face to the light.

Hester stumped down the ramp of the *Mayfly* towards him, head cocked, her black hair pulled back in a greasy ponytail and her coveralls rank with oil and smoke smudge.

'So they're at it again,' she said.

The rest of the crew joined her, while past them filed the mechanics and engineers who had worked on the *Mayfly* all through the night. White-faced, their stations were now up on the wall, and the hell that awaited them there.

'How does she stand, Jon?' Morcault asked his engineer.

The big man was wiping down his blackened fists with a strip of cloth. 'She'll fly. For how long is anyone's guess. She's not vacuum-ready – you take her out of the atmosphere and she'll fall apart like a pack of cards. What are you up to, Ghent? Macragge himself was here last night. I saw you talking to him.'

'It may be I need to make one more trip in the old girl,' Morcault said with a smile. 'But it will be a short one. I will not be going off-planet, Jon.'

'Where are you taking us this time?' Hester demanded sharply.

'Not us, Hester. This time I go alone.'

They stared at him. 'We're your crew,' Gortyn said. 'Where you go, we follow.'

Morcault looked them all over. Jodi Arnhal and little Scurrios stood silent, Hester had her hands on her hips, scowling. And Gortyn was wiping his hands mechanically, as though he had forgotten about them.

'Sometime today or tomorrow, I aim to take the ship up myself,' Morcault said. 'You are all released from my employ, as of this moment. Find yourselves a safe place to hole up until this thing is over. If Zalathras is still standing at the end of it, Marneus Calgar will see to it that you are all well compensated. I have his word.'

'You sound like a man on a one-way trip,' Hester said.

'We are all on a one-way trip, Hester. That is what life is.'

'What has that monster persuaded you to do?' she demanded. 'You've done enough for him already.'

'I do this not for him, or for the Ultramarines or the Imperium – I do it for my own planet, for the world I love. There is nothing more to be said.'

'And if we refuse to leave you?' Jodi Arnhal spoke up.

'You are all younger than I, by some distance,' Morcault sighed. 'I will not have your lives tied to mine any longer. Jodi–' He set a hand on the Navigator's narrow shoulders. 'Where I am going, you cannot follow. Not yet.'

He limped slowly up the *Mayfly*'s ramp, his stick clicking on the plates. 'Look after one other,' he said, and punched the ramp control. The ramp began rise.

'You are the best folk I have known, the best crew I have ever flown with.' His voice broke. The ramp slammed shut on his face, leaving them standing there, dumbfounded.

The ork hosts broke into a charge and came careering across the plain with a roar that rose up into the morning like the fall of a stony avalanche. They carried scaling ladders, runged metal poles slotted to fit together, and at the vanguard of the formations were huge armoured orks bearing all manner of heavy weapons.

The Basilisks and mortars of Zalathras sent a hail of fire to meet them, the plain erupting in geysers of muck and water as the shells struck home in the leading formations. Hundreds fell, but the attack was not even slowed.

As soon as they came within range, the heavy weapons in the wall casements added their fire to the carnage. Heavy bolters, autocannon, stubbers and meltaguns blared out, streaking tracer and fire.

The entire first wave of the orks was chopped to pieces, but still the armour-clad vanguard came on. Some of these huge orks lifted their fellows and held them bodily in front of them to soak up the torrent of fire that was raining down. When the corpse was shot to pieces they picked up another lesser ork and it began again.

They were five hundred yards from the base of the wall, and now their own heavy weapons began to bark out. Ork weapons teams went to ground in water-filled shellholes and began to return fire. Missiles streaked out against the walls of Zalathras and impacted in pale booms of mottled smoke. They left barely a scar. It took time before the ork gunners realised their mistake and began to aim higher, at the lip of the battlements themselves.

They lacerated the casemate slits and the merlons that sheltered the defending militia with autogun fire, beginning the business of suppressing Zalathras' defenders. The fire became intense beyond belief, the air in that deadly half-mile full of every kind of kinetic and energy projectile. The orks advanced stubbornly, but they were paying in hundreds for every yard gained. And at the end of it, the walls would still be looming over them.

'I don't understand,' Boros was saying. 'They're just throwing themselves at us. Even if they made it to the foot of the wall, they couldn't scale it – those ladders are too short.'

'They're keeping us in place and using up our ammunition, wearing us down.' Marneus Calgar told him. 'They can afford the casualties, and the ammunition expenditure. They are using us up, Boros. It is attrition, pure and simple. But it will not go on this way. They have other plans...' He scanned the battlefield beyond the current hecatomb before the walls.

'Lieutenant Janus,' he said over the vox.

'Janus here, my lord.'

'Enemy formation shifting west around the walls at some four miles. Strength, perhaps eight to ten thousand. They are heading for the perimeter at the Minon Districts. Reinforce the wall in that sector and keep me informed of events.'

'Yes, my lord.'

The noise was incredible, a concentrated assault on the hearing. And the blue sky above began to disappear as the smoke thickened under it, cutting off the sunlight.

But then something else cut off the sunlight. It came arrowing up from the south, at first a mere dot in the sky. But it grew larger, a contrail streaking out behind it.

'That's no fighter-bomber. That is a large craft,' Colonel Boros said in alarm.

'All anti-aircraft batteries are to concentrate on that aircraft,' Calgar said. 'Hit it with everything we have, Boros. It must be destroyed – it is imperative.'

'Yes, my lord.' Boros spoke into his vox mike. 'All guns, all guns...'

Calgar pulled up his own people on the vox. 'Brother Valerian, it is approaching. Proxis, get into position. Inform the vehicle crew to stand to and begin loading of the ordnance.'

'Acknowledged.'

'Here it comes,' he said, and watched as the aircraft drew closer.

It was a potbellied heavy lifter, of the kind used to transport massive ore skips and equipment pods cross-planet. Painted ork scarlet, it came on at high speed, an ugly craft even before the orks had got hold of it. The stubby wings were at least a hundred yards from tip to tip, and its engines were blaring and muttering as if badly maintained.

Skeins of anti-aircraft fire lanced up from the city to meet it. The surviving Hydra platforms on the walls sent up a thick curtain of tracer, and the aircraft was surrounded by black exploding clouds.

But now they could see, as it drew closer, that the lifter had been modified in another way. It was carrying something slung below its belly. Not an ore skip or pod, but something immense dangling from its hull, something that moved, an incredible bulk with a twitching tail.

'What in Throne is that?' Boros asked, wide-eyed.

'An ork weapon, one that lives and breathes,' Calgar told him grimly.

'Brother Valerian encountered it in the Ballansyr mines where it was being housed, waiting for this moment. The ork name for it is *squig-goth* – a great marauding beast of war, the largest I think I have ever seen.'

''They're going to drop it on us!' Boros cried out.

'Shoot it down, colonel. Do not let them drop it inside the walls.'

Calgar looked at the approaching behemoth in the sky. The orks had plastered the hull of the lifter with crude welded armour, and he saw the shimmer of a void shield as the Hydra rounds skittered across it and bounced back.

A single Fury could have brought it down. But all the Furies were gone, now. And he had to admit a grudging modicum of respect for the ork warlord. Whoever he was, he had played a long game, making sure that every defensive asset available to the city was used up before launching this last attack.

A squiggoth. They were seldom seen by those who lived to speak of it afterwards. Creatures of mindless ferocity, the largest of them had been known to contend with Titans.

The orks had indeed saved the best for last.

The huge aircraft was shuddering in the sky. Barely a mile away now, its shadow fell over the ork masses below, and they set up a great hoarse roaring, raising their weapons over their heads in exultation at the sight. The squiggoth suspended below the craft was tossing its head and adding a long, gargling roar to the din. Calgar could see the armour plating that had been implanted in its very hide, the gun platform on its back, the great gleaming spurs attached to its feet. It must have weighed eighty or a hundred tons, and its swaying bulk was dragging the battered lifter from side to side in the sky.

A lucky missile strike from a platform on the wall got through the darkening void shield, and struck the tailplane of the ork craft. It yawed in the air, the void shields flickered and died, and at once a thousand tracers speared into its scarlet hull. A ripple of bright explosions went down one side, and the aircraft dipped sharply, the nose aimed at the earth below.

Boros struck one fist into another at the sight. 'Yes!'

It was going down. The squiggoth struggled in its harness, bellowing, and fell half-free. Seconds later a final missile streaked into the belly of the aircraft and exploded. The harness was blown asunder. The aircraft fell like a stone, the beast it carried tumbling free of it onto the battlefield below.

'Take cover!' Calgar shouted, augmenting his voice so it carried like a klaxon along the walls.

The ork craft crashed to earth some four hundred yards short of the walls, striking the wet earth with an enormous staggering concussion that could be felt even through the plascrete foundations of the Vanaheim Gate. It buried itself in the muck, its nose crumpling, the rest of it smashed apart. Seconds later, there was a massive explosion as the engines went up, and a huge, towering fountain of earth and metal was blasted almost a hundred yards into the air. Shards of metal were sent bouncing off the city walls. Others were hurled clear over them to flatten entire habs in the districts beyond. Burning fuel sprayed out in a flaming lake. The ork formations there were torn asunder, body parts blown halfway across the battlefield, scores buried in the muck that rained down in the wake of the crash.

There was a stunned moment almost of silence on that part of the field, and then the orks came on again, bellowing with rage.

And something hauled itself out of the mire along with them. Something monstrous that towered over them and raised its red maw to howl defiance at the Vanaheim Gate.

The squiggoth rose up out of the muck like some primeval monster of nightmare, streaming water, tossing the orks about it aside like toys and trampling them underfoot. It pulled itself free of the crater its fall had created, and looked around, as though striving to find a focus for its rage.

'Brothers,' Calgar said over the Ultramarines' vox, 'meet me in the shadow of the Gate. We have work to do.'

He turned to Boros. 'Keep them at their posts, colonel – no matter what happens, your men must hold the wall.'

'What about–' Boros could only point at the immense monstrosity that was now powering towards them, slimed with mud.

'You leave that to me.'

HIS BROTHERS WERE waiting for him there, as calm and collected as though about to go on parade. In the shadow of the great barbican he stood with them, facing the piles of rubble and reinforced beams that had been piled up behind the damaged gate.

Back down the street leading up to the barbican, a huge shape sat in the roadway, covered with a cameleoline tarp. Before it was Lieutenant Lascelle and a company of militia. To its rear, half a regiment was hidden in the ruins and alleyways leading off the street.

Calgar turned to the militia. 'Men of Zalidar,' he said, and his suit speakers made his voice boom and echo to a great shout. 'Today we must stand in this place and hold it. This is the last defence of your world, the last chance you have to save it. There must be no retreat today. The fate of Zalidar will be decided in this place, no other. You must stand fast, or die. There will be no retreat.

'And I, Marneus Augustus Calgar, Lord Macragge, I stand with you here at this hour. Fight with me, and whether you live or die, what you do here today will never be forgotten.'

He raised his eyes to the sky, and in a quiet voice said, *'Suscipiat Imperator sacrificium nostrum.'*

Then there was a tremendous crash as the squiggoth hurled itself at the Vanaheim Gate.

FIFTY FEET HIGH, the great beast of the orks absorbed bolter rounds as though they were flea bites. It charged the gate again and again, lowering its armoured head and squealing in bestial rage as it attacked. It was under the lip of the barbican itself, and thus it was difficult to direct fire upon it. Men dropped grenades upon its steaming back from the summit of the Vanaheim, but the orks swept the battlements with a withering fire and drove the defenders there below, into the casemates.

The animal was streaming blood from a hundred wounds, but its vitality was undimmed. The broken platform atop its back was smashed and broken, full of the mangled corpses of orks and gretchin, but the armour that had been affixed to its immense bulk remained largely in place, and its ten-foot skull was protected by a great helm-like carapace adorned with horns.

It smashed this into the buckled adamantium plates of the gate and tore them loose, buckled the steel underneath as though it were tin, and finally got its horned snout under one gate to tear it free of its hinges. Then it climbed over the wreckage and began to work on the piled barricade behind, while the orks crowded around its feet, oblivious to those it trampled and killed in its berserk rage.

Calgar saw the enormous snout root through the girders and rubble and worry them aside. He opened up with the storm bolters on the underside of his power fists, the ancient weapons springing to bright, blazing life, following the targeting reticle in his helm display.

As the opening under the Vanaheim grew, so orks began to wriggle past the head of the beast, into the barbican itself, firing bolters and flamers as they came.

'Brother Antigonus, target the orks with your squad. Mathias, Proxis, mop up any who make it into the street. Brother Orhan, go to the vehicle and make sure it is ready to engage. Brother Valerian, I may need you soon. Stand ready.'

The Ultramarines went to work with the calm implacability of their kind. The infiltrating orks were shot to pieces, one blown up in a cloud of flaming promethium as the tank on his flamer was hit. The fire burned under the gateway, making the smoke-shrouded morning seem as dark as dusk.

The squiggoth seemed spurred to greater heights of effort by the flames. Its bellowing was magnified by the towering arch of the gate, a noise that could be felt in the flesh as much as heard. It powered bodily into the rubble, knocking aside the great bracing girders as though they were branches of green wood. Its forefeet appeared, scrabbling at the barrier and pulling it down. Lumps of rockcrete as big as Land Speeders tumbled down, rolling into the square before the gate.

The beast shouldered into the gateway, looming up to dwarf the Ultramarines who stood before it. Calgar aimed his fire at its head. The storm bolter rounds clinked and spat and bit into the animal, blasting free divots of smoking flesh. One eye was blasted out of its socket. But this seemed only to madden the squiggoth further. With a tremendous thrust it smashed clear through the remnants of the barricade, sending boulders and lumps of masonry flying fifty yards through the air. The barricade disintegrated, became a scattering of mounded rubble. And behind the huge beast the orks set up a triumphant roar.

For the first time, the way into the city was open to them.

'Brother Orhan,' Calgar said, 'It is time. On me, my brothers. Clear the way.'

The orks were streaming by the hundred around the feet of the huge squiggoth, clambering over the shattered gates and the debris that lay behind them. The beast seemed dazed by its achievement and the punishment it had taken. It stood with its blood making steaming puddles around its feet, gargling in its pain, shaking its mutilated head.

Calgar and the Ultramarines split into two lines that went down each side of the street. Still firing with deadly effect into the mob of orks that was pouting around the squiggoth, they went to ground in the ruins.

The tarp was pulled off the large angular shape in the roadway behind them by Lascelle and his men, who then quickly sprinted back down the street several hundred yards before taking up their own firing positions.

A Colossus siege tank stood there, squat and box-shaped, the black maw of its gun pointed directly into the gateway. It had been heavily restored and modified over the past few weeks. The bombard on its platform had been rebuilt for direct fire. Brother Orhan stood on the open deck of the vehicle.

His voice came over the vox. 'All clear. Firing in three, two, one–'

There was no sound. Just an enormous absence. The Ultramarines were rendered deaf by their auto senses to protect them, so they did not hear the gargantuan boom that rolled out of the weapon. But they felt the blast-wave. It staggered them, knocking several of them to their knees and blowing others into the sides of nearby buildings.

A great pall of smoke and dust mushroomed up, enveloping the entire Vanaheim gate and hundreds of yards of the walls. The concentric blast-waves travelled out in rippling circles. Even on the battlements high above, the militia were deafened and blinded and thrown around in a dark storm of debris.

As the initial detonation subsided, so the auto-senses of the Ultramarines came back online. Calgar engaged infrared to peer through the murk, and the outlines of the Vanaheim Gate appeared through it. He stood up. Runes were winking amber on his helm display and he was shrouded in dust, a tawny giant that strode forward alone into the gateway.

The squiggoth had been blown to pieces, and there was a line of death and gore reaching out of the gateway for fully five hundred yards. Hundreds of orks had died as the heavy round had ploughed onwards across the battlefield, a mass of shrapnel enlarging the blast radius. A vast smoking crater had been gouged out of the earth, and, all around it, thousands of the enemy were struggling to their feet out of the muck that half buried them, or squealing with the furious anger of their wounds.

Calgar strode alone through the barbican until he stood in the charnel house under the Vanaheim. The interior of the gateway had been heavily damaged, with chunks blown out of the construction, wiring and plasteel reinforcement laid bare. But the Vanaheim still stood.

Calgar looked out over the immense field before him, at the massed formations that were coming to their senses in the aftermath of the blast. He dialled up his suit speakers to maximum.

'*Guilliman!*' he shouted, and the roar of that cry carried for miles over the plain. He raised the Gauntlets of Ultramar above his head and let them crackle with the full surge of his ancient armour's power.

*Now,* he thought. *Come to me.*

# TWENTY-THREE

'THE GATE IS down,' Lieutenant Yeager said to Fennick, his face as pale as chalk. He looked again at the vox console as if he could not quite believe what he had just heard.

Fennick walked over to the balcony and looked out. Alphon Spire was over two and half miles from the Vanaheim, but the astonishing boom of the bombard cannon had rattled tables in the map room.

He had known of that strategy, had worked to make it happen, but he had never truly believed that it would prove necessary.

The knowledge that the way into the city was open at last shook him. He had to steady his breathing while he looked out at the plain far below. The orks moved across it in numbers that seemed undiminished, despite the six weeks of slaughter they had endured.

The Ultramarines Seventh Company might be out there, on their way, but how could the city hold out now? It was a matter of hours before they were overwhelmed. Even Marneus Calgar could not hold the Vanaheim against such numbers, not now.

'Seal the spires,' Fennick said to Yeager. He turned around, facing the young lieutenant and the other staff members and aides who filled the room. Their talk had stilled; they were all watching him now with something of the same despair in their eyes.

'I want every blast door closed, every entryway manned by what militia are already here. We will not take any off the walls, but we must secure ourselves inside these structures for as long as possible. It will not be long now, gentlemen. Help is on the way. We have only to hold out another day or two.'

'What of Lord Macragge?' one of his aides asked.

'He has made his choice, and Throne be with him in his fight. But we must look to ourselves now, and make our own choices. Send word to Kalgatt and Minon also – the spires must all be locked down. The orks may breach our walls, but we can still hold out in here, for a while at least.'

The room became busy again, the vox specialists bent over their consoles, other officers running out to gather up the militia who were scattered throughout the hive on policing duties. It would take time to close down such an immense structure with so many people in it.

Fennick closed his eyes. He hoped Marneus Calgar could buy them that time.

This is what Zalidar will become famous for – this is how we will be written into the histories, he thought.

The place where Marneus Calgar died.

He wanted to be down there, fighting with him. How better could a man lay down his life, than in that place, in such mighty company?

Roman Lascelle was down there, the rake and the dandy long burned out of him, and so was Boros, who was Fennick's closest friend. Even Admiral Glenck had requested a place on the walls today, to play his part in the great drama, to be there when the curtain closed on them all. Fennick had been astonished by the man's decision. They had shaken hands, their old animosities forgotten.

And I am here, cutting myself off from it, sealing myself in – perhaps to no avail. Is that cowardice?

It would be seen as such, by whoever recorded the events that had happened here. He was sure of that. But he was no coward – he was a man with responsibilities. He could not turn his back on the people he had been appointed to lead and look after. If that looked like cowardice, well then so be it. He would leave it to history to decide.

Boros, he thought. Fight well. Find a good death. And forgive me.

THE ORK HOSTS out on the plain had reached the foot of the walls and were now raging there like a tide baffled by sheer cliffs. They raised up their scaling ladders like scaffolding against Zalathras' defences, but even when slotted together to the maximum height the metal would bear, they were still short of the battlements.

They reared them up anyway, consumed by a feverish lust for killing that it seemed no amount of carnage could sate.

Noon came and went, but such was the volume of smog that hung over the city that it seemed the battle continued in a grey twilight, the sun obscured by the pillars of black billowing smoke that rose both within Zalathras and without.

To the men on the walls, firing their lasguns until the barrels glowed, dropping grenades, ducking for cover, hauling away their shattered dead comrades, it seemed that time itself had lost all meaning. Ten minutes was a long time, an hour became an eternity, and to try and look beyond the day itself was an absurd exercise.

There was only the second-to-second struggle to kill the enemy and stay alive, to hope for luck, for some stroke of fortune – a relief army, or a sudden loss of will in the ork attackers.

But the orks did not oblige. Now that the gates were finally down, and they were united under a single warlord, and the infectious fervour of the Waaagh! had swamped what little reasoning they possessed, they came on regardless of tactics and casualties, driven to assault the walls by a black impulse which mastered even that of self-preservation.

In the shadow of the Vanaheim fortress, in the arch of the broken gate, Marneus Calgar stood with twelve of his brethren, and fought the ork tide that tried to flood past into the defenceless city beyond.

The Ultramarines had divided themselves. Calgar, Proxis, Orhan and Mathias fought hand to hand in their superior armour and with their superlative close-combat weapons.

Brother Antigonus and the six remaining members of his squad hung back and blasted the enemy at range, while Brothers Parsifal and Valerian constituted a kind of reserve.

The Apothecary and the Librarian darted in where the need was greatest and then pulled back again, keeping the enemy off balance, saving their brethren from sudden surges and berserk lunges.

Twelve Ultramarines, the finest of their Chapter. And behind the gate, Lieutenant Roman Lascelle and his militia company, busy rearing up new defences, laying booby traps, and contributing a platoon every now and then when Valerian called for it.

But they could not stem that immense flood of hate forever, nor could they fight such an implacable foe without loss.

Even in such a close-packed mill of murder, the Ultramarines were able to work together. When one stumbled, or momentarily left his guard open, then another of his brethren would step in.

Calgar was always at the foremost spot of the defence, alternating between the storm bolters and the power fists of the Gauntlets of Ultramar. He would blast the foe back with a point-blank volley of the storm bolters, allowing Antigonus and his squad to toss some grenades into the throng, which would open them out further.

Momentarily thinned, the orks would then be cut down by withering, heavy bolter fire from Brother Kadare, expertly weaving his bursts between his battle-brothers as they fought. Then Brother Dextus would squeeze out a stream of promethium from his flamer, and the orks would topple, wriggling and burning and smearing the burning chemicals on their fellows.

There would be a lull of a few minutes before the enemy re-formed and came on again. The Ultramarines would change magazines, collect themselves, and once in a while Brother Parsifal would be able to make some swift treatments to the wounds they all now carried.

This went on for hours, until it became almost a kind of murderous routine.

But even the Adeptus Astartes were not immune to fatigue. Their power armour injected them with stimulants and coagulants and analgesics, but such exertions took a toll even on the strongest. And they began to make mistakes.

Marneus Calgar was the focus of the orks' rage. He stood out, his ancient artificer armour still splendid despite the battering it had received, and the Iron Halo that protected him flamed and flickered above his helm, drawing the strongest and most savage orks like moths to a candle.

Time and time again, Proxis or Orhan saved him from being beaten down and dragged into the maw of the ork mob, and once, when he was knocked off his feet by a great dark-skinned ork chieftain, Brother Mathias stepped over him and beat the creature back with great flaming swings of his crozius arcanum, smashing the ork's skull into a rag of shattered gore. As the great ork fell, those around him backed off for a few minutes, and Calgar regained his feet, shaking the blood from his fingers.

'Parsifal, report,' he said, breathing heavily, his helm display alight with flickering runes and sigils. He kept his eyes on the orks a hundred yards away. They had drawn off, and every time they did, the defenders in the Vanaheim casemates above poured a torrent of fire and a hail of grenades into them. They milled around, the large orks killing some of their lesser kind in their anger and frustration, and firing wildly up at those in the fortress above who were tormenting them.

'Brother Orhan and Brother Mathias have both received moderate wounds to their limbs, but are still functioning. Brother Jared is dead, but his gene-seed has been retrieved. Brother Herod will need some more treatment before he can rejoin the line.'

'Get to it. We need every pair of hands. Lieutenant Lascelle.'

'My lord.'

'Move your men up. How are the emplacements coming?'

Lascelle's voice crackled over the vox; the frequencies were all becoming degraded by the chaos of the day, the multiple users, and the endless explosions of heavy ordnance that were going off all around.

'I have two heavy stubbers, tripod-mounted.'

'That's all?'

'Everything else is already in action on the walls, my lord.'

'Very well.'

Proxis stepped up to Calgar's shoulder. The Ancient's once ornate armour was now scraped and battered down to its essentials, with a scrap of gold and blue on it here and there, and the ugly repair to the breastplate looking like nothing so much as a field dressing made out of ceramite. He checked his power axe. The orks dreaded and craved such weapons, and it had done good service in the past few hours.

'The day draws on,' he said. 'It is past noon.'

'Already?' Calgar said.

'The hours go by so quickly when one is enjoying oneself, I find,' Proxis said. He was grinning inside his helm, Calgar was sure.

'Let us hope Captain Ixion does not miss all the festivities,' the Ancient added.

'He would never forgive himself,' Calgar agreed. They looked at one another, two brutal masks splattered with blood and sundered flesh.

'It is an honour to fight at your side, my lord,' Proxis said quietly.

'I would not have it any other way, brother.'

Then the orks surged forward again, and the moment of stillness passed, and the mayhem engulfed them once more.

Proxis died an hour later at the hands of a stunted ork that crept between the legs of its taller kin and stabbed upwards with its short-handled chainsword.

The blow slashed through the knee joint of the Ancient's superlative armour, and was just enough to distract him as the great ork he was fighting stepped forward and lunged for his throat with a fizzing power sword.

The weapon took Proxis through the chest, slicing through the hastily repaired breastplate and entering his primary heart, splitting the organ in two within his chest. The Ancient went to his knees without a word, the axe falling from his nerveless fingers.

Calgar whirled round and tore the head from the great ork's shoulders with a sweep of one fist, stifling the cry of grief that wanted to howl out of his own chest. For a few moments after, he lost himself, let all discipline slide from his brain, and became as intent on mindless murder as the creatures who were trying to kill him.

He advanced into the pack of orks in a white silence of howling fury, lifted one from the ground and clubbed half a dozen others to death with the body until it fell apart. Then he opened up with the storm bolters, blasting back dozens of the foe, tearing them up into unrecognisable chunks of steaming meat.

It was Brother Mathias who stopped him from plunging deeper into the ork mob, who cleared a path back to the gateway along with Brother Orhan.

The three of them said no word to each other, but for a while they stood there alone and held the gate in a paroxysm of naked murder, laying about themselves with all the hatred and fury their grief had kindled, until even the orks could take no more and fell back again.

By that time, Brother Parsifal had done his work, and retrieved Proxis' gene-seed, and his body had been hauled back to the stubber emplacements where the militia cowered.

His body had not been defiled. His armour and weapon, both ancient treasures of the Chapter, were safe – for now at least. But Proxis was gone. He had joined with the Emperor's Peace at last.

Marneus Calgar stood and spoke no word while his brothers moved up around him and covered the approach to the gate once more, taking cover behind the mounded enemy dead. Mathias and Orhan came to stand with him, saying nothing. There were no words.

Autogun rounds sparked and ricocheted off Calgar's armour, but he paid them no heed. For a moment, he did not truly care.

'*We are the pilgrims, master*,' he murmured at last, his eye burning inside his helm. '*For us to go ever farther…*'

Farewell, my brother.

# TWENTY-FOUR

THE LONG DAY drew on, and the killing continued in a frenzy that the men on the walls could barely comprehend as possible. Over in the Minon Districts, Lieutenant Janus' firefighters helped repulse an attempt to scale the walls with rocket-fired grappling hooks.

No sooner had that been thrown back than they had to mount up in their vehicles and speed north to help foil another attack. The orks were probing the entire perimeter of the city now, but still their main effort was reserved for the Vanaheim Gate, and the Ultramarines who defended it.

And there, as evening approached, the Ultramarines fought on.

THERE WERE FEWER of them now. The orks had managed to flood past Calgar, Mathias and Orhan and barrelled into Antigonus' squad. In moments it had become one giant melee, and in that confused scrum Brothers Ardius, Tarsus and Herod had died.

Lieutenant Lascelle and his men had helped stem the irruption, firing the stubbers into friend and foe alike, knowing that the Space

Marine armour was more likely to shrug off the heavy slugs than the mainly unarmoured orks.

Slowly, the enemy had been killed and pushed back, and Calgar had strewn the gateway with yet more corpses using long rippling volleys from his storm bolters. The situation had stabilised.

That had been an age ago, it seemed. They felt the loss of their brethren, the surviving Ultramarines. The support of stubbers and lasguns was no substitute for Adeptus Astartes-aimed bolter fire.

The day darkened, and for a brief interval the attacks grew less intense. There was a lot of cheering and shouting out on the plain, and the orks were coursing in a river of bodies that seemed almost like some kind of triumphal parade, even while they still sent in attacks on the wall.

Calgar and his brothers stood in the gateway, the dead piled knee- and waist-high around them. Calgar was as weary as he had ever been in his life. He stood dripping ork blood while Brother Orhan replenished the storm bolter ammunition in his dorsal magazines. He flexed his fingers in his power fists, and checked his power levels. Even the magnificent ancient armour he wore had its limitations. Its power-pack was seriously drained by the continuous use of the fists and the Iron Halo. He had only a few hours left before he would have to recharge.

A few hours may just be enough – for all of us, Calgar thought grimly.

'What is going on out there?' he asked Brother Valerian. 'It sounds almost as though the xenos are celebrating.'

The Librarian advanced stiffly until a volley of autogun and bolter fire made him pull back into the cover of the corpse-piled gateway. His hood glowed.

'Their leader is here,' he said simply. 'The ork warlord has come up from the river and is now in the battleline. I can feel his mind, my lord. For an ork, it is surprisingly subtle. He is no fool.'

'I never thought he was,' Calgar said.

'Your dorsal magazine is refilled, my lord,' Orhan said.

'Thank you, brother. That should keep me standing a while longer.'

A rune was blinking in Calgar's helm display, a vox channel. He closed down all other frequencies and blinked it open.

'My lord, how do you fare?' a voice said.

'We are holding, Ixion, but barely. It is good to hear your voice, brother. How far out are you?'

'We are approaching the ork fleet from the far side of the planet, high orbit. We will be ready to engage in six hours. The landings will commence as soon as we have gained orbital superiority.'

'Excellent. Ixion, you will hold off on landings until you have direct word from me.'

'My lord, surely–'

'This Waaagh! must be broken here, before it has a chance to metastasise. The key to doing that is to kill the leader. He thinks he is close to final victory here – I must end him, one way or another. If you begin landings it will be a long, hard struggle to defeat the Waaagh! But if I can kill the leader before you even arrive, then all Seventh has to do is mop up a mass of leaderless tribes.'

'I see, my lord. It is a high-risk strategy.'

'All the good ones are.'

'If I may say so, lord, the risk to you personally is enormous.'

'Perhaps. But it will save the lives of our brethren in the long run. Even Seventh Company would have a hard time destroying this Waaagh! as it stands. This is one cancer which must be cut out with a scalpel, Ixion. Once that is done, we will move in with the hammer.'

'Yes, my lord. Throne watch over you.' A pause. 'The *Fidelis* survived. It is at Calth now, undergoing repairs.'

'I rejoice to hear it. Pass on my compliments to Shipmaster Tyson.'

'Tyson died, my lord. The ship suffered heavy damage.'

Calgar sighed. Tyson had been a good man.

'One other thing, Ixion. If I am incapacitated, then Brother Valerian will be your point of communication with this world, and Brother Mathias will be in command here until your own arrival. Clear?'

'Quite clear, my lord.'

'A lot can happen in six hours, Ixion. If disaster strikes, and you find Zalathras completely overrun by the time you are ready to start the landings, then you know what to do.'

There was a pause in the vox, a hissing silence.

'There is no Chaos taint on this world, my lord.'

'The ork infestation is intense. Zalathras is the last point of resistance on the planet. If it has gone, then the world is not worth trying to retake. You will destroy it from orbit. Is that clear?'

'Perfectly clear, my lord.'

'Calgar out.'

He closed off the channel, reopened that of his immediate brethren. Six hours was indeed a long time. He felt the weariness in his frame. The constant, intense hand-to-hand fighting was draining beyond any other form of warfare. He had not felt so physically used up since the Behemoth campaign, half a century before.

The armour he wore analysed his blood as he stood there and administered yet more stimulants, though its internal chemical supply was near exhausted.

Six hours. He was glad he had put in place a fall-back plan.

'Here they come again,' Brother Valerian said. And then, puzzled, he added. 'This is something different.'

The orks before the gate advanced in what were, for them, ordered ranks. While all across the wide battlefield before the walls their kin raged and assaulted in blind ferocity, these orks came on in a line, marching through the bloody muck with a great tattered scarlet banner hanging over them.

And in their midst, a great litter was carried upon which stood one of the largest orks Calgar had seen, fully armoured and carrying a great curved power sword in one hand while the telltale penumbra of a power field flickered on his other fist. A chant went up from the advancing line. They were repeating a name – not Calgar's this time. A barbarous ork word.

'Brug, Brug, Brug!'

'It appears my opposite number has decided to get a closer look at the fray,' Calgar said, and he felt a glow of relief. The stand in the gate had not been for nothing. They had drawn out the ork warlord at last.

'They think we're done,' Brother Mathias said, joining him, his white skull helm glinting through its grime, catching the last light of the sun. 'He is here to gloat, to watch us go down.'

'Indeed,' Calgar agreed. 'Note the orks around him – well-armoured, large killer-types. They must be his bodyguard. They will come at us next, while he watches. Brothers, be ready. The next attack will be the worst. They will fight like fiends while his eye is upon them.'

'We fight with your eye on us, lord,' Valerian said. 'Let them come. We will show them what killing is.'

The surviving Ultramarines gathered around Calgar as he stood there. There were seven of them left alive.

The ork warlord held up his power sword. It shone and glittered in the light of the setting sun. Night was almost upon them.

Then he thrust the blade forward with a high, gargling shout in his own barbarous tongue.

The line of orks around him charged forward, roaring.

And it began again.

Night passed over Zalathras – for untold thousands, the last night they would ever know. The ork hosts swarmed around the walls like a mass of maggots intent on consuming an injured animal.

They reared up the siege ladders upon mounds of their own dead, coming ever closer to the lip of the battlements. In places, some of the more agile of their kind were able to leap up from the topmost rung and land on the catwalks above, to spread mayhem there until they were brought down.

The defence of the city had been stretched to breaking point. In the north, the firefighters were all but destroyed by a surprise assault that came close to scaling the walls. Lieutenant Janus died there in the thick of it, a long way from his home on Macragge, and into the dark with him went thousands more of the militia, dying where they stood, knowing that there was nowhere to run to if the walls were breached.

And all of them, every man, knew that Marneus Calgar was still fighting in the Vanaheim Gate. That knowledge inspired in them a desperate valour. They fought as stubbornly as the most seasoned veterans of the Astra Militarum, like men who have only one hope left. Deliverance might yet appear with the rising of the sun.

BROTHER ORHAN WAS killed close to midnight, the big orks nudging him away from his fellows with a cascade of blows and then swamping him as he staggered in their midst swinging his axe and cleaving half a dozen to pieces before he went down. Brother Parsifal tried to retrieve his body, helped by Valerian and Calgar himself, but the press of the enemy was too great. The Ultramarines were shunted back into the barbican, retreating step by step while Brother Kadare fired bursts of heavy bolter rounds to cover their retreat and Brother Antigonus moved up to flood the enemy line with blast after blast of flamer fire, the promethium rising up in a blazing wall that lit up the interior of the gateway.

He got too close, and received a fusillade of autogun bullets that smashed him backwards. Calgar beat the enemy back from his body, and Antigonus crawled out of the barbican, firing his bolt pistol as he went.

The big orks they fought now were well armoured and in strength were more than a match for even the augmented strength of the

Adeptus Astartes. They snatched Parsifal off his feet and piled onto him with suicidal abandon. When Calgar cleared them off the Apothecary with gouts of storm-bolter fire, Parsifal was lying with his limbs rent from his body. His head had disappeared.

Antigonus died soon after, still firing his bolt pistol and cursing the enemy aloud over the vox. He had bled to death inside his punctured armour, the wounds he carried too much even for the self-healing systems of his kind.

And so the night went on.

GHENT MORCAULT SAT in the pilot's chair of the *Mayfly*, staring out at nothing. Calgar had given him the vox frequency of the Ultramarines and he sat there clutching his pitchthorn stick and listening as the Adeptus Astartes died one after another. Tears streamed down the old man's face – grief for the Ultramarines, for his city, for the world he loved and the crew he had abandoned.

He flipped the ignition switches, warming up the atmospheric engines. The main drives were inoperable, and the ship was a holed hulk, but Fennick's engineers had worked with Jon Gortyn to make her airworthy, for a short while at least.

A short while was all that was needed.

Over the vox came the voice of Marneus Calgar himself. The Lord of Macragge was breathing heavily, and there was a catch to his voice that spoke of some damage to his lungs. It shocked Morcault to hear the bone weariness in Calgar's voice. The Chapter Master of the Ultramarines was more than a man; it did not seem possible that he should sound so like a harried, exhausted human being.

'Morcault, the time is close. We are nearly at our end here. I am patching through the coordinates. Just outside the Vanaheim. He stands on a litter amid a group of great orks.' A panting grunt, as though the Lord of Macragge had been struck a blow.

'Do not fail me. You know the consequences.'

'I do,' Morcault said.

If he or Calgar failed in their aim, then the likelihood was that Zalidar would be destroyed from orbit by the *Andronicus* battlefleet of the Ultramarines.

Morcault could not bear that thought. His beautiful world, whose mountains and jungles he had explored for almost forty years, reduced to a dead cinder in space. It could not be allowed.

'Wait for my word,' Calgar said. 'I must be sure of his position. This last gambit cannot fail.'

The vox cut off. Morcault sat tapping his stick on the deck plates of the bridge, while around him the *Mayfly* hummed with power, the retros warming up in preparation for take-off. The old man flexed his right hand, staring at the swollen knuckles, the blue veins that ran across it.

I am not the pilot I once was, but I am still good enough. I will not let you down.

# TWENTY-FIVE

IT WAS NOT long before the dawn, now, and in that black hour the unrelenting violence seemed to ease a little, as though to take a breath before the final act.

All along the walls of Zalathras, the ork armies brought up fresh formations from their inexhaustible reserves to fill the gaps in the line and prepare for more assaults, while on the walls themselves the militiamen gulped warm water from their canteens, reloaded their weapons, changed power-packs, and closed their eyes for a moment of rest or prayer.

And in the deep shadow under the Vanaheim fortress, Marneus Calgar stood alone.

BROTHER MATHIAS WAS lying, gravely wounded, at the rear of the barbican, watched over by Roman Lascelle and the remnants of his militia company. The Ultramarine Chaplain had lost an arm to an ork power sword, and half his helm had been cleaved from his head a moment later. His right fist held onto his crozius in a grip that only death would loosen.

Brother Kadare was dead amid a gleaming pile of spent casings, shot through and through, face to the enemy, still kneeling upright as though he might at any moment rise to his feet and continue fighting. But his soul was gone to the Emperor's Peace.

And Brother Valerian was slumped at Calgar's feet, still conscious, but with his psychic hood ripped clear off his armour and his helm gone. His eyes were clear, but an ork had carved out his bowels. They rested in his lap, a steaming mass he cradled in his fists.

As he stood there, Calgar stooped and set one powered-off gauntlet on the Librarian's head, as gently as a father might caress his son.

'You have done good service, brother. You must hang onto life for me. I have lost too many friends, these last days.'

The Librarian smiled faintly. 'I shall do my utmost, my lord.' His face grew grave. 'Do not die here. We cannot lose you too. The price has been too high.'

'We pay it, whatever it may be,' Calgar said, straightening.

The Lord of Macragge's superlative artificer armour was broken and holed in a dozen places. One of his power gauntlets was as dead as a lump of scrap metal; the power field on the other flickered like the last light from a candle burnt down to the wick. His helm display was full of flashing red runes.

It was almost done.

Father, into your hands I commend my spirit.

He blinked on Morcault's sigil.

'Now. Go now, and may the Emperor guide you.'

The old man replied at once. 'It shall be done, my lord. I shall be there in a few minutes.'

Calgar sagged. The orks were moving in on him, as wary as wolves of old Terra circling a wounded lion. And a hundred yards beyond them, the ork warlord Brug stood on his shoulder-borne litter, watching.

Calgar had hoped to draw him in face to face, to break apart that snarling skull in his hands, and feel the ork's life give out within his grasp. It was not to be. The warlord was too intelligent to risk all, now that he was on the brink of seizing all. It was up to Morcault now.

His bodyguard moved in, weapons raised. Marneus Calgar strode forward to meet them.

And out of the north, the *Mayfly* came careering through the sky with a hoarse roar.

All across the city, men and orks looked up at that sound, which carried even over the endless gunfire and the artillery. Ork anti-aircraft guns, caught out by the appearance of the little freighter, were slow to aim and fire. A trail of clouds exploded in the *Mayfly*'s wake as they frantically tried to draw a bead on the craft, but they were just a little too slow.

The *Mayfly* came arcing over the southern walls of Zalathras. High up in the Alphon Spire, Lord Fennick watched it streak across the dawn light in the sky, afterburners flaring.

'You old bastard,' he whispered.

From halfway up the Kalgatt Spire, Hester saw it, too. She and Jodi Arnhal and Jon Gortyn watched, while little Scurrios wept like a child behind them. Gortyn set a hand upon her shoulder, and she grasped it in her own.

On the walls below, in the midst of the unending carnage, Colonel Boros looked up gasping, frowning, wondering what it signified.

Roman Lascelle could not see it, because the blood from the head wound that he had taken had sealed shut his eyes. He was lying beside Brother Valerian. The Librarian was smiling.

And Marneus Calgar smashed the orks back from him with new energy, beating them down, firing with the one storm bolter he had left that worked. He was still fighting in the gate when the *Mayfly* dived down from the near vertical towards the ground beyond.

He caught a glimpse of the ork warlord looking up, jaws agape in shock, and he saw the bright white bloom of the explosion as the ship hit the ground, a massive explosion that blasted Brug and his bodyguard to atoms and sent them flying, tore apart hundreds of the foremost orks, and sent up a massive wall of mud and earth and hurtled corpses and wreckage.

Calgar was blown backwards by the blast, tumbled end over end as though he were a leaf caught in a gale. His armour died, went dark, struggled to come back online. He ripped off his broken helm and keyed the vox, croaking with effort.

Morcault had fulfilled his trust in him.

'*Andronicus*, this is Calgar. Do you read?'

He struggled to his knees. A curtain of fire burned out beyond the Vanaheim Gate, and the ork host there had been smashed asunder. He was no psyker, but even he could feel in the air the mass dismay of the xenos armies. They had lost their leader, the focus that had brought them here and welded them together. The Waaagh! was collapsing.

'*Andronicus* – Ixion, can you hear me?'

His ears rang. There was blood streaming down his face.

'Captain Ixion here, my lord.'

Calgar knelt there as though praying. The sun was coming up over the hills beyond Zalathras, the dark night finally ending. The light cast a long shadow behind him.

'Captain Ixion, the ork host is fracturing. You may commence the landings. Send down my brethren, and let us cleanse this place once and for all.

'Calgar out.'

# EPILOGUE

Men's memories are fickle things. They take the events of the past and make of them a story, and oftentimes they change that story to fit their own preconceptions of how things should be. In the gap between what has happened and what men make of it lies the truth, and often it is lost, or changed almost beyond recognition.

That is what happened with the story of Zalathras.

Years have gone by. There are fresh faces in the Chapter now. Ultramar is stable and protected, and in this part of the Imperium the Ultramarines watch over mankind as they always have. The wars of the past are commemorated in the side-chapels of the Fortress of Hera, and the names of the dead are carved upon the walls, while great Guilliman himself sits in state amid them.

In time every one of us, the lowliest and the mightiest of our brethren, becomes a mere name carved into that wall.

But our deeds live on in the heart of men. We become figures of story and legend, and the things we did in life are perpetuated in memory, and those memories blur over the years.

They say that I saved Zalidar. That is true. They say that I stood alone for a day and a night in the shadow of the Vanaheim Gate, and held back the ork hordes single-handed. They say that I slew the ork warlord in combat, face to face, before Seventh Company landed to purge the planet of the xenos and save the world for the Imperium. They say that Lord Fennick, the governor, was a coward and a traitor who sealed himself up in the safest place he could find while heroes like Boros and Lascelle and Glenck fought and died on the wall.

None of those things are true. I know that, but it no longer matters, because it is what men believe.

I know that an old man saved Zalathras, by giving up his life for the world he loved. His name is forgotten by nearly everyone now, but not by me.

I know that I did stand in the shadow of the gate for a day and a night, and I held the orks back and preserved Zalathras until that old man could redeem it with his sacrifice.

But I did not stand alone.

I was never alone; my brothers were always there with me.

## ABOUT THE AUTHOR

**Paul Kearney's** Warhammer 40,000 work comprises the short story 'The Last Detail' from Legends of the Space Marines and the Space Marine Battles novel *Calgar's Siege*. He studied at Lincoln College, Oxford, and has been widely published, as well as being longlisted for the British Fantasy Award. He lives and works in Port Glenone, Northern Ireland.

# BLADES OF DAMOCLES

PHIL KELLY

An extract from

# BLADES OF DAMOCLES

by Phil Kelly

CONTRAILS SCARRED THE skies ahead as the T-shaped aircraft of the tau duelled with box-nosed Thunderhawk and Stormraven gunships. Plummeting drop pods cut through their winding vapour trails, forming a lateral grid that cut the sky and gave shape to the squad's otherwise abstract fall.

Here and there airbursts blossomed, fire-lit smoke spreading in the cold air wherever a missile or interceptor shot hit home. Even those distant signs of conflict made Numitor's chest feel tight. Not long now, the sergeant told himself, as if comforting the beast rousing to wakefulness in his soul.

Not long.

SQUAD NUMITOR BURST from the cloudbanks to witness the birth of a planetary war. Tessellating hex-zones each large enough to accommodate a hive city trammelled the indigo wilderness. Smoothly contoured buildings jutted from each junction point, lights glittering in their thousands wherever the ivory edifices reached up from the wider superstructures. The landscape of the tau sept world had been almost perverse in its order, but that was changing fast – the Imperium's pre-invasion firestorm had torn ragged wounds across its surface. Megatonnes of ordnance were hurled from low orbit to break open the drop zones in the distance. Even those warheads detonated by tau flak were raining fire upon the cities below.

Numitor did not replace his helm. The chances of getting decapitated by sky-shrapnel were slim, and that was a gamble he was willing to take. It was worth it to drink in the spectacle of explosions blossoming below, to feel the blood-pounding rush of air hinting at the storm of violence to come. The tempestuous forces of the drop pulled at his skin, shook his bones and made his eyes and nose sting with sensation. He plunged through a high cloud and out again, needles of cold stinging his skin. It felt like a baptism.

The Ultramarines drop pod assault followed close behind the falling ordnance intended to clear a path for Operation Pluto. Livid fires billowed from shattered hexodomes and parallel plumes of dark smoke slanted into the skies from the black-rimmed craters that scarred the city's alien symmetry. In his peripheral vision, Numitor could see dozens of gunships diving in near-vertical vectors, the throaty roars of their engines audible even over the thunder of freefall and the bass crump of ordnance.

The Imperial craft slammed through a thinly spread drone blockade to scatter enemy fighter craft like raptors slicing through a prey-flock. Coming out of their dives as they reached their drop coordinates, each gunship opened its doors and disgorged the Assault Marines inside. Numitor's squad had been the first to make the drop, launching a good few seconds before Squad Sicarius, and even with the long freefall they would reach the planet first. He knew it was wrong to find joy in that, for it mattered little in truth. He smiled nonetheless.

'Beachhead established in quadrant Zeta Tert, Gel'bryn City,' said Aordus. 'Good place to start.'

'We'll be fighting long before we get there,' shouted Numitor. 'Look sharp, brothers. Hunter-killers incoming. On my mark.'

A cluster of four wide, flat-bodied missiles blazed upwards from an intact hexodome.

'Scatter!' ordered Numitor. His men reacted a second before the seeker missiles reached their position. They triggered their jump packs simultaneously, blazing out in a ten-pointed star that saw the tau missiles sail harmlessly through the middle of their formation.

Three more of the xenotech warheads hurtled upwards. Numitor flipped and boosted straight down, swiping the fingertips of his power fist into the leading missile moments before it could strike Brother Duolor. It detonated with mind-numbing force as the other two shot past, missing their mark. The sergeant was flung outward, flailing and burning, but the flames found no purchase on his ceramite. He tucked into a somersault before righting his vector with a blast of his jump pack.

Trailing smoke, Numitor heaved in a great draught of air – not the stale, recycled air of a spaceship hold, but the cold, pure blast of freefall. He roared with the sheer catharsis of it. Elation flooded his body, despite the burning pain in the side of his face, despite the chemical tang of incendiaries in his multi-lung. His vox buzzed like a trapped insect, abruptly pulling him back to his senses.

'Sergeant,' said Aordus, 'do we proceed to Zeta Tert?'

'Hold course,' called out Numitor, craning his head to look upward. 'Zeta Tert, squad! Adjust vectors accordingly.'

High above, three remaining missiles looped around, doubling back in tight parabolas to close on the sergeant's squad.

'Ha!' shouted Numitor triumphantly. 'I thought as much. Ready pistols!'

The sergeant turned in mid-fall to face the night sky and the blunt-nosed missiles rocketing towards them. He unclamped his bolt pistol and snapped off three shots in close succession, his back to the ground even though his freefall was at terminal velocity. Numitor's squad followed his lead. Mass-reactive bolts hurtled upwards, the last volley catching the incoming missiles a spear's throw from their position. A canopy of fire bloomed above them, red and yellow against the darkening purple sky.

Nodding in satisfaction, Numitor turned back to his headlong descent.

From the hexodomes below tracer fire spat high, each stream stuttering phosphor-white. Black clouds of flak boomed as tau gunners intercepted the storm of Space Marine insertion craft hammering towards the xenos landscape. To their east flank, a cluster of hunter-missiles slammed into a plummeting drop pod. Numitor felt the blast wave of the explosion as it sent cherry-red metal scything in all directions.

Flailing Space Marines fell burning from the wreckage towards the planet's surface.

They had fifteen seconds, if that.

'Intercept that stricken squad!' ordered Numitor, leaning into a diagonal vector and waving his squad to follow. He boosted hard, drawing his arms in close to streamline his body and angling his hands to fine-tune his path. His unit, close behind him, did likewise.

Nine seconds left.

A trio of falling Tactical Marines had righted themselves as best they could and were aiming their bolters downward, determined to take some kind of toll on the tau world before their deaths. The Tactical squad's sergeant stretched out to catch one of his brothers by the arm as he pinwheeled past, yanking him in close. Numitor and his squad dived into their midst, each clamping an outstretched hand onto a falling battle-brother. There was no way Numitor and his squad could stop them entirely, pull them out of harm's way, but they were still Assault Marines of the Eighth, the masters of the jump drop. This was their sky to rule.

'Hard diagonal, due west!' shouted Numitor.

With a burst of his jump pack engines at full yield, Numitor yanked the Tactical Marine's descent into a sharp westward course. His squad did the same, their power armour preventing their arms from being ripped out of their sockets by the sudden weight. Slowly, agonisingly, their efforts bore fruit.

Three seconds.

'Breakfall!' shouted Numitor. 'Ready!'

A bulbous white tower loomed suddenly upwards, its giant mushroom canopy studded with strange antennae. Numitor heaved hard, twisting his body so his jump pack bolstered the motion as he and his squad flung their battle-brothers sidelong towards the tau building's upper slope.

The Tactical Marines struck it hard, but their armour took much of the impact. As they slid downward, they each drew their combat knives and drove them deep into the building's curving roof, turning their skidding descent into a series of sharp halts.

By the time the Space Marines had mag-locked their boots onto the alloy of the building's roof, Numitor had landed in their midst, and was already boosting back upwards. He caught a fifth falling battle-brother by the backpack and slowed his descent enough for him to hit the cream-coloured roof crumpled, but alive. The rest of Squad Numitor had touched down nearby, wispy circles of exhaust expanding around each of their landing sites. Pulse rounds shot from the balcony of a taller tau building to punch into their midst. The Tactical Marines turned their shoulders into the incoming fire, bolters aimed to launch a devastating counter-attack.

'That was non-Codex drop procedure,' said one of the rescued Space Marines.

The Tactical Marine sergeant snapped off a shot with his bolter, and a distant explosion mingled with xenos screams. 'We're alive, ingrate,' he growled to his squadmate, 'so make it count.' He turned